Louie and Bear

BITE BACK

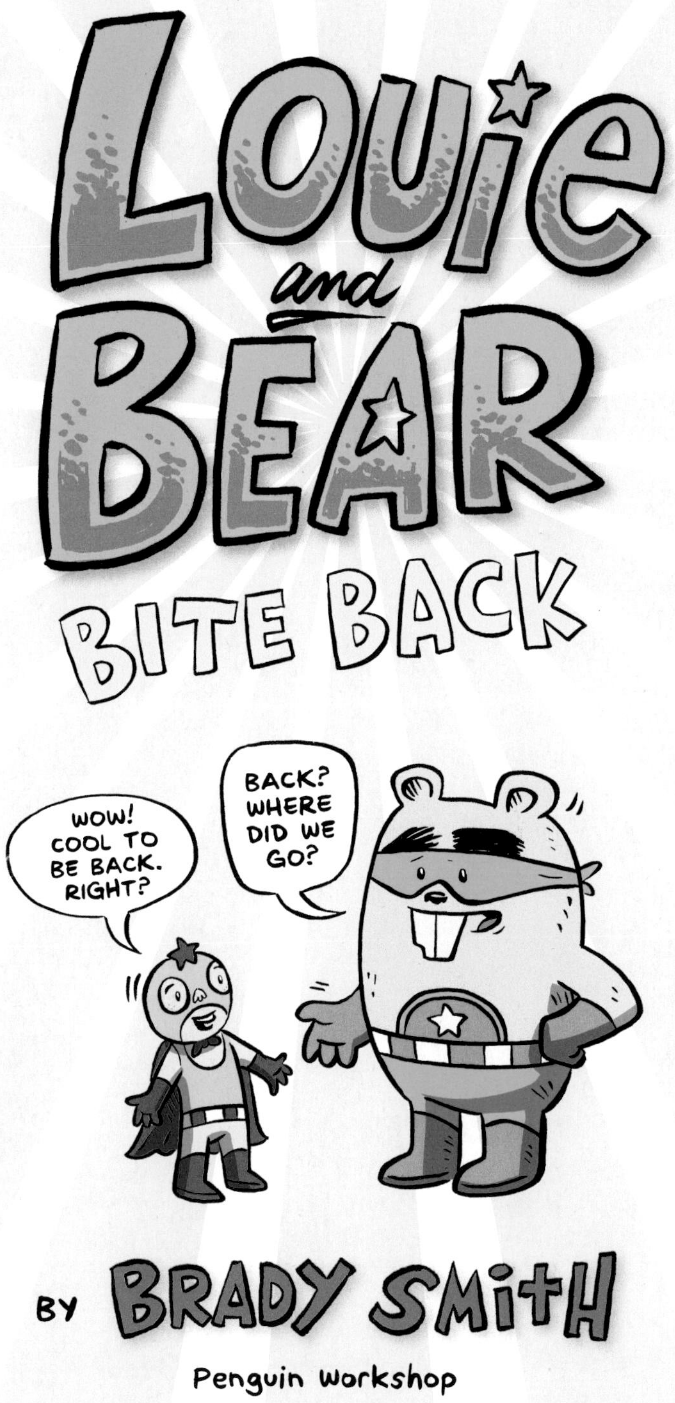
WOW! COOL TO BE BACK. RIGHT?
BACK? WHERE DID WE GO?

BY BRADY SMITH

Penguin Workshop

AUTHOR'S NOTE

This book is dedicated to my parents, Pat and JoAnn Smith.

Thank you for everything. And by "everything" I mean, feeding me, teaching me right from wrong, protecting me from wild animals (I'm sure there were some around at some point) and even wiping my butt.

Mostly, though, thanks for always being so loving, supportive, encouraging and just a blast to be around. As parents go, Jill and I hit the jackpot.

I love you Mom and Dad.

ABOUT THE CREATOR

Brady Smith is an actor, artist, and author. He lives in Los Angeles with his wife, actress Tiffani Thiessen, their two kids, four dogs, six chickens, and one super-chatty parakeet.

You can see more of his art at www.bradysmith.com and lots of silliness on his Instagram account, @bradysmithhere.

PENGUIN WORKSHOP
An imprint of Penguin Random House LLC, New York

First published in the United States of America by Penguin Workshop,
an imprint of Penguin Random House LLC, New York, 2022

Copyright © 2022 by Brady Smith

Visit us online at penguinrandomhouse.com.

Library of Congress Cataloging-in-Publication Data is available.

Manufactured in China

ISBN 9780593224175   10 9 8 7 6 5 4 3 2 1 WKT

Colors by Meaghan E. Casey
Design and lettering by Jamie Alloy

CHAPTER 1

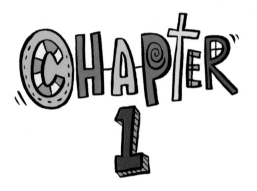

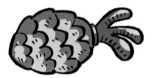

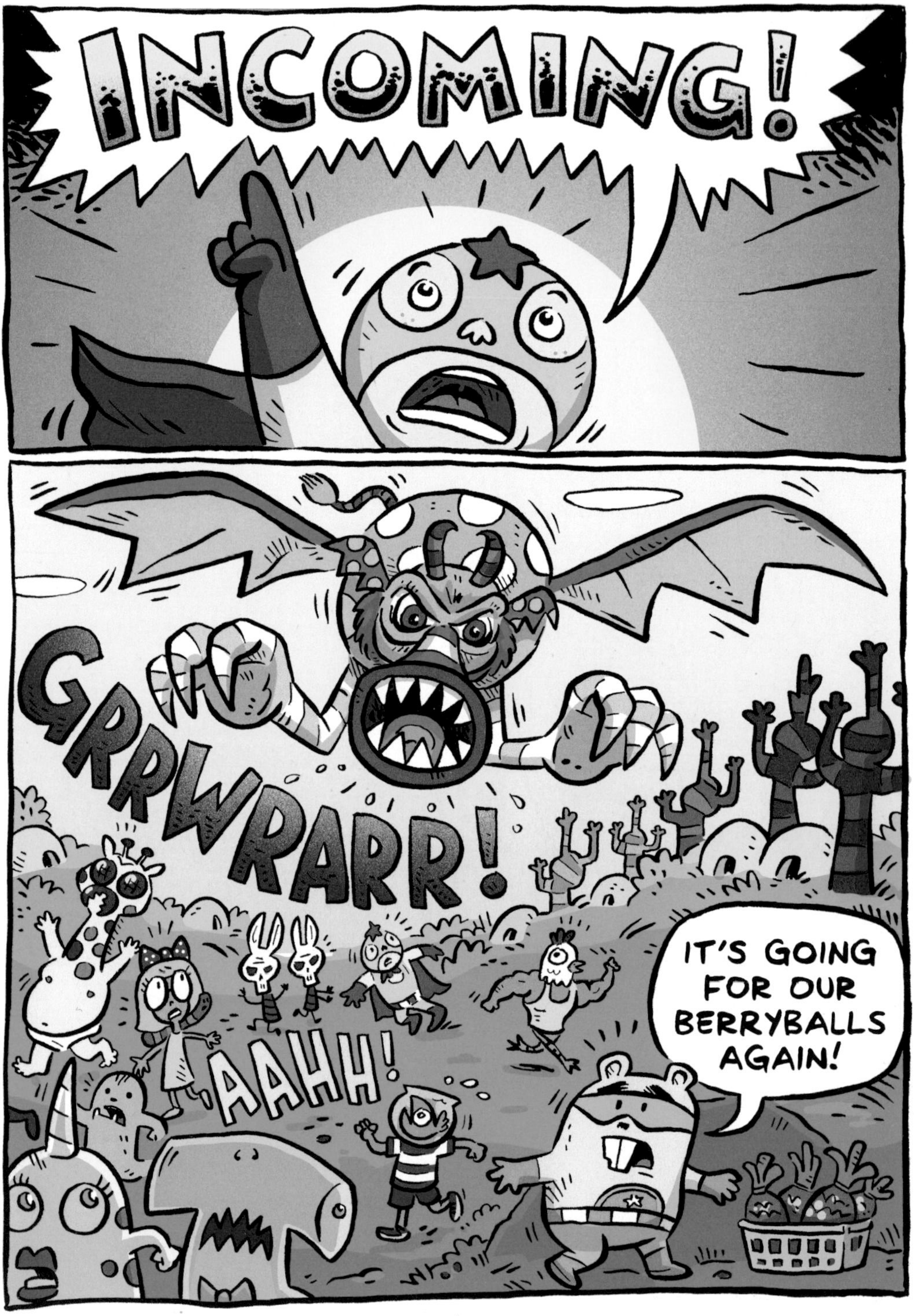
INCOMING!
GRRWRARR!
AAHH!
IT'S GOING FOR OUR BERRYBALLS AGAIN!

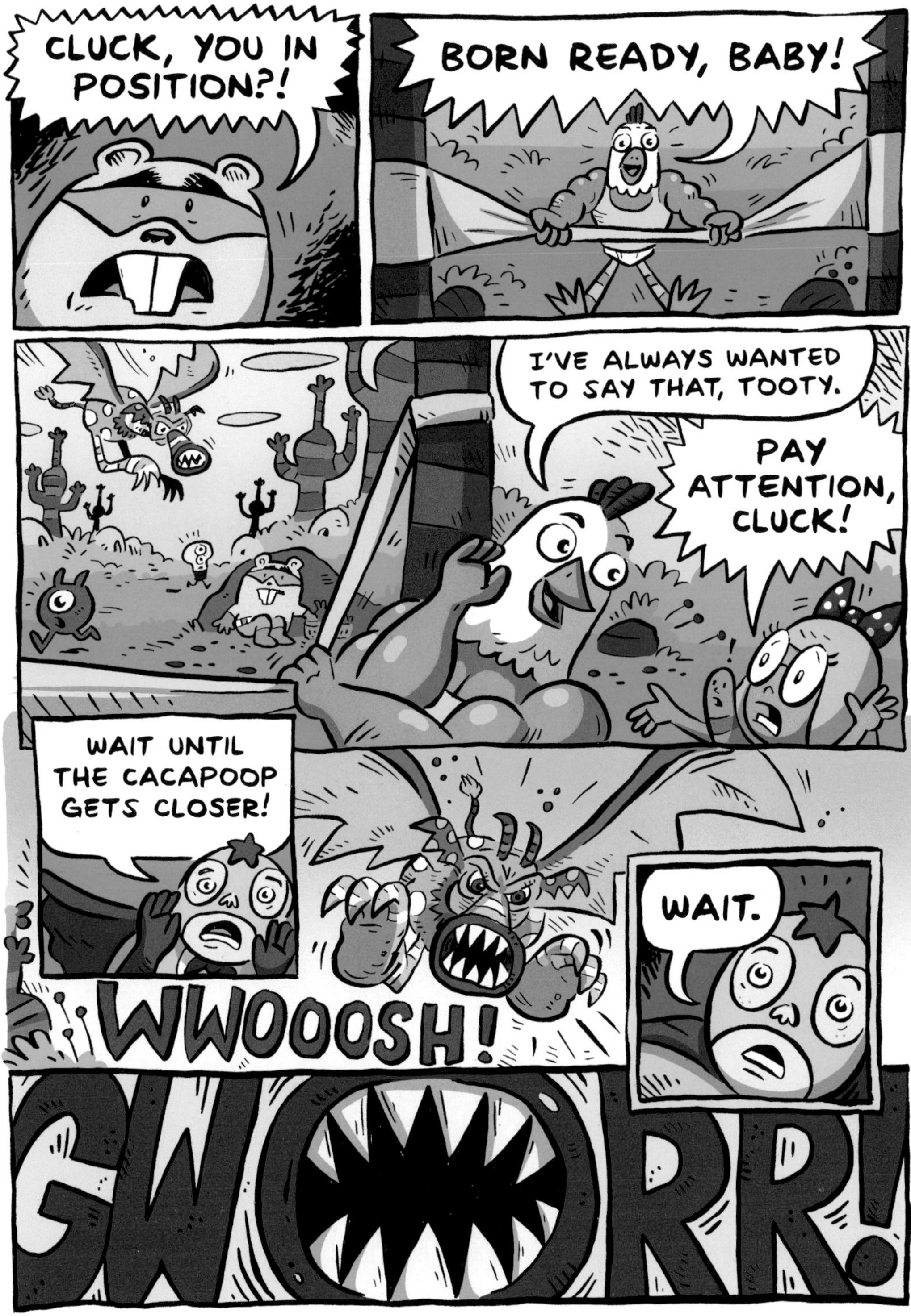
CLUCK, YOU IN POSITION?!
BORN READY, BABY!
I'VE ALWAYS WANTED TO SAY THAT, TOOTY.
PAY ATTENTION, CLUCK!
WAIT UNTIL THE CACAPOOP GETS CLOSER!
WWOOOSH!
WAIT.
GWORR!

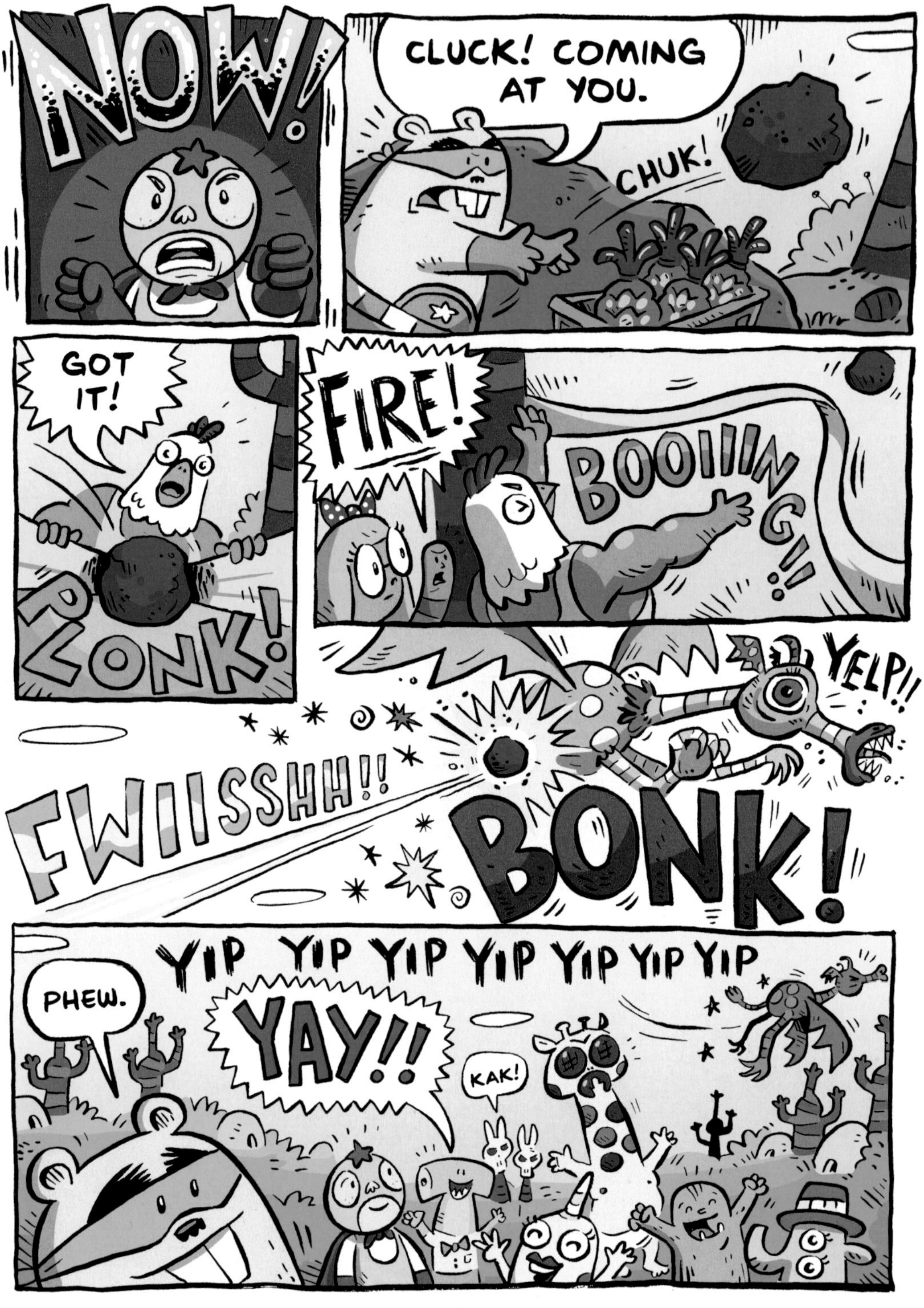
NOW!
CLUCK! COMING AT YOU.
CHUK!
GOT IT!
PLONK!
FIRE!
BOOIIING!!
FWIISSHH!!
BONK!
YELP!!
YIP YIP YIP YIP YIP YIP YIP
PHEW.
YAY!!
KAK!

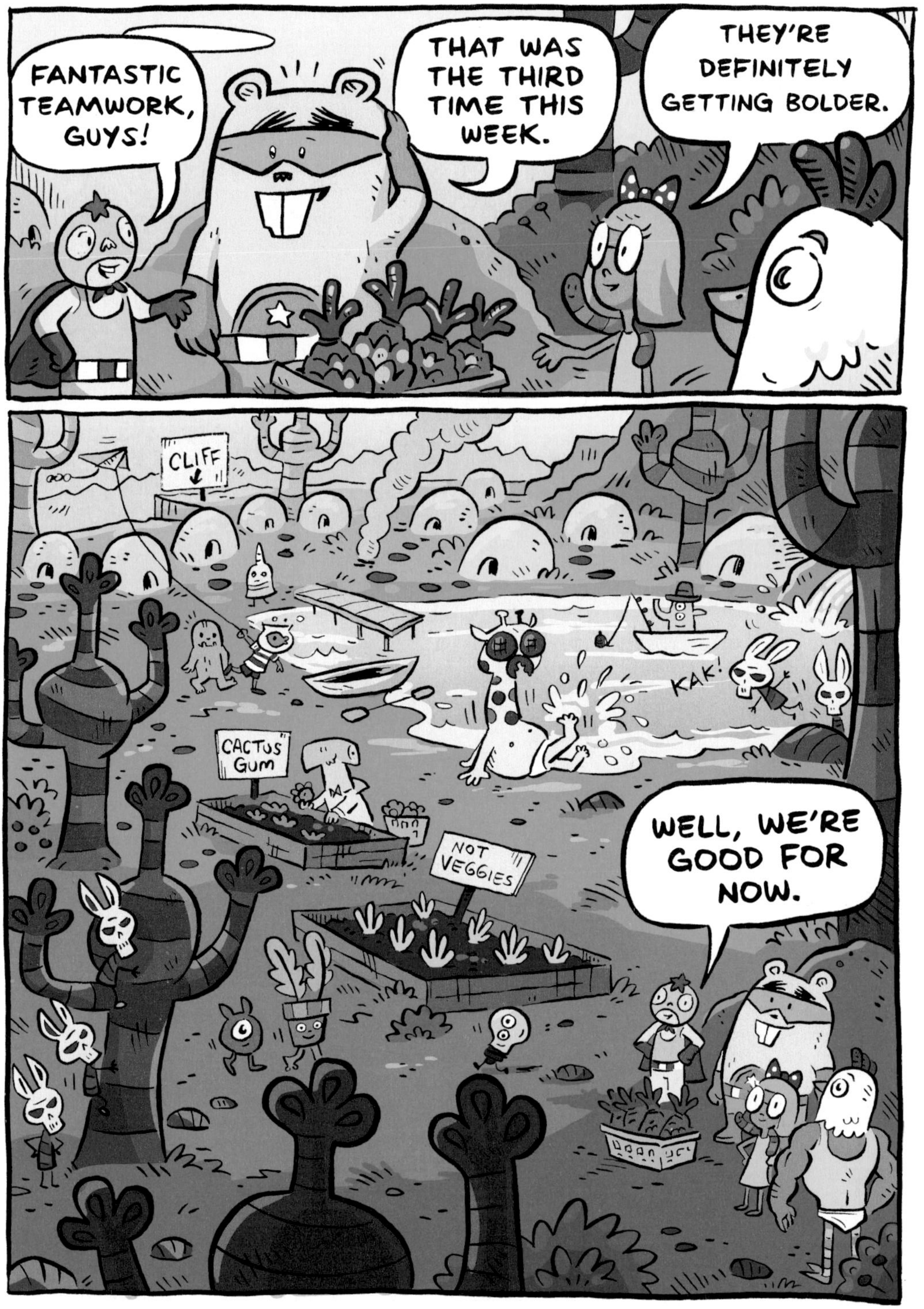
FANTASTIC TEAMWORK, GUYS!
THAT WAS THE THIRD TIME THIS WEEK.
THEY'RE DEFINITELY GETTING BOLDER.
CLIFF
CACTUS GUM
KAK!
NOT VEGGIES
WELL, WE'RE GOOD FOR NOW.

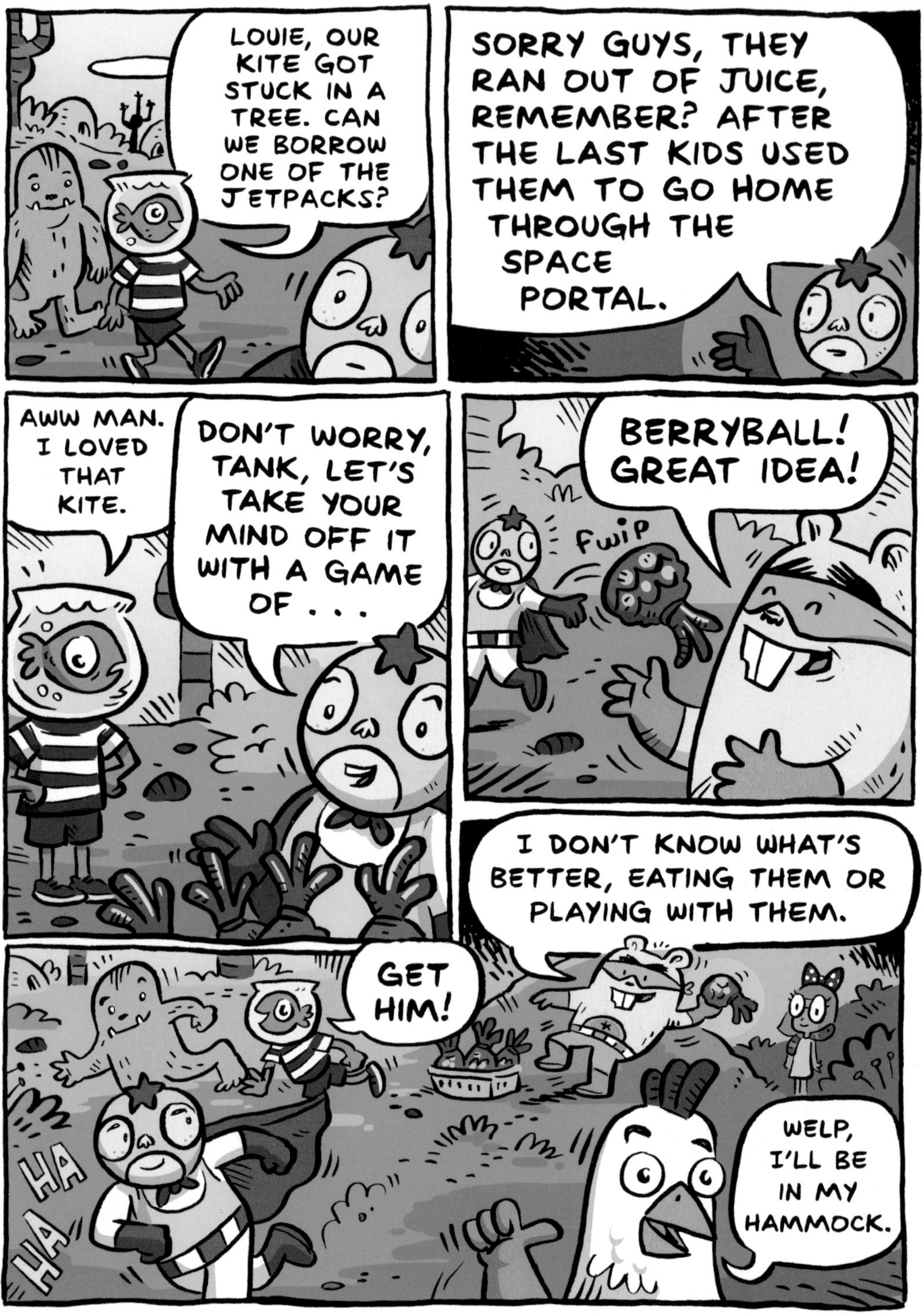
LOUIE, OUR KITE GOT STUCK IN A TREE. CAN WE BORROW ONE OF THE JETPACKS?
SORRY GUYS, THEY RAN OUT OF JUICE, REMEMBER? AFTER THE LAST KIDS USED THEM TO GO HOME THROUGH THE SPACE PORTAL.
AWW MAN. I LOVED THAT KITE.
DON'T WORRY, TANK, LET'S TAKE YOUR MIND OFF IT WITH A GAME OF . . .
BERRYBALL! GREAT IDEA!
FWIP
I DON'T KNOW WHAT'S BETTER, EATING THEM OR PLAYING WITH THEM.
GET HIM!
HA HA
WELP, I'LL BE IN MY HAMMOCK.

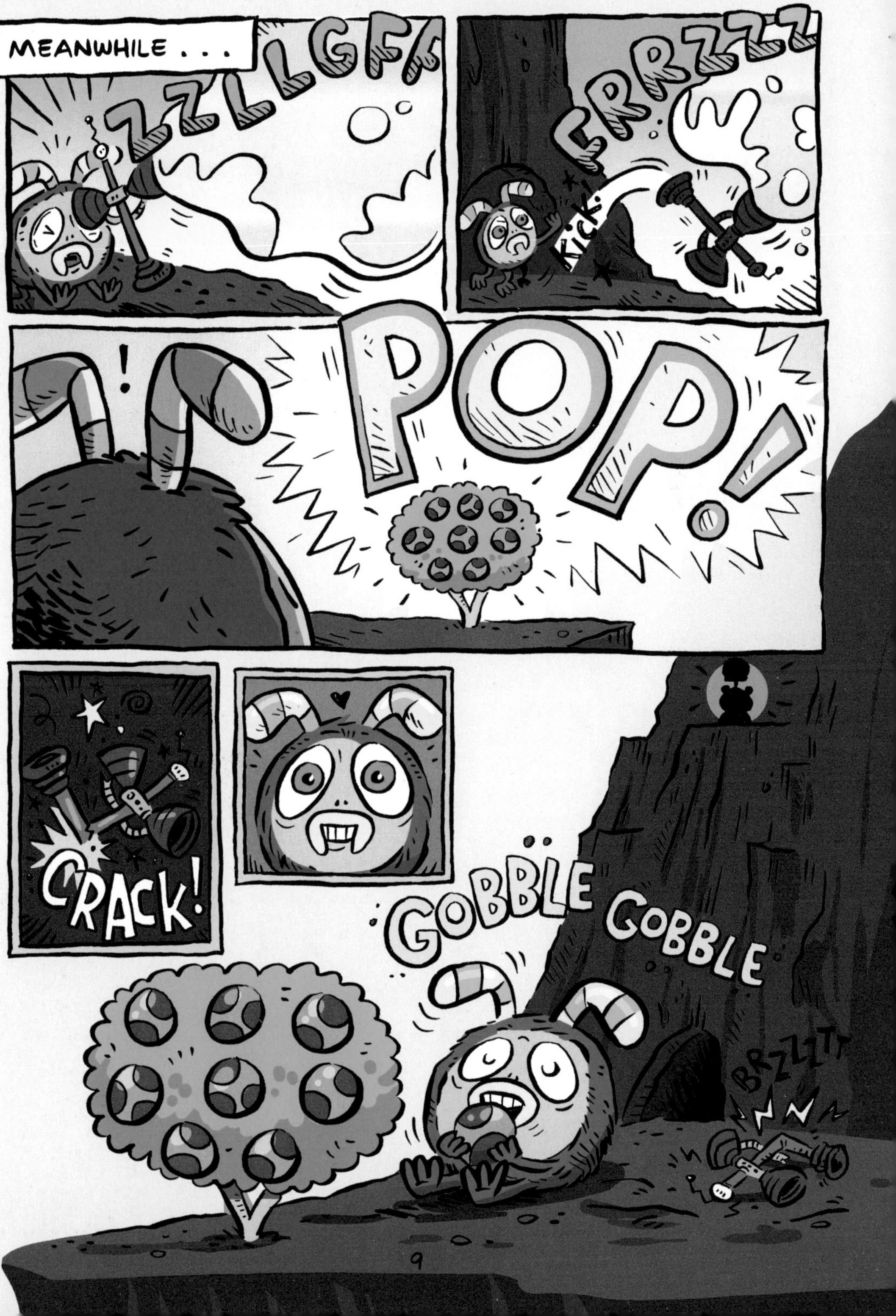
MEANWHILE . . .
ZZLLGFA
FRRZZZZ
KICK
!
POP!
CRACK!
GOBBLE GOBBLE
BRZZZTT

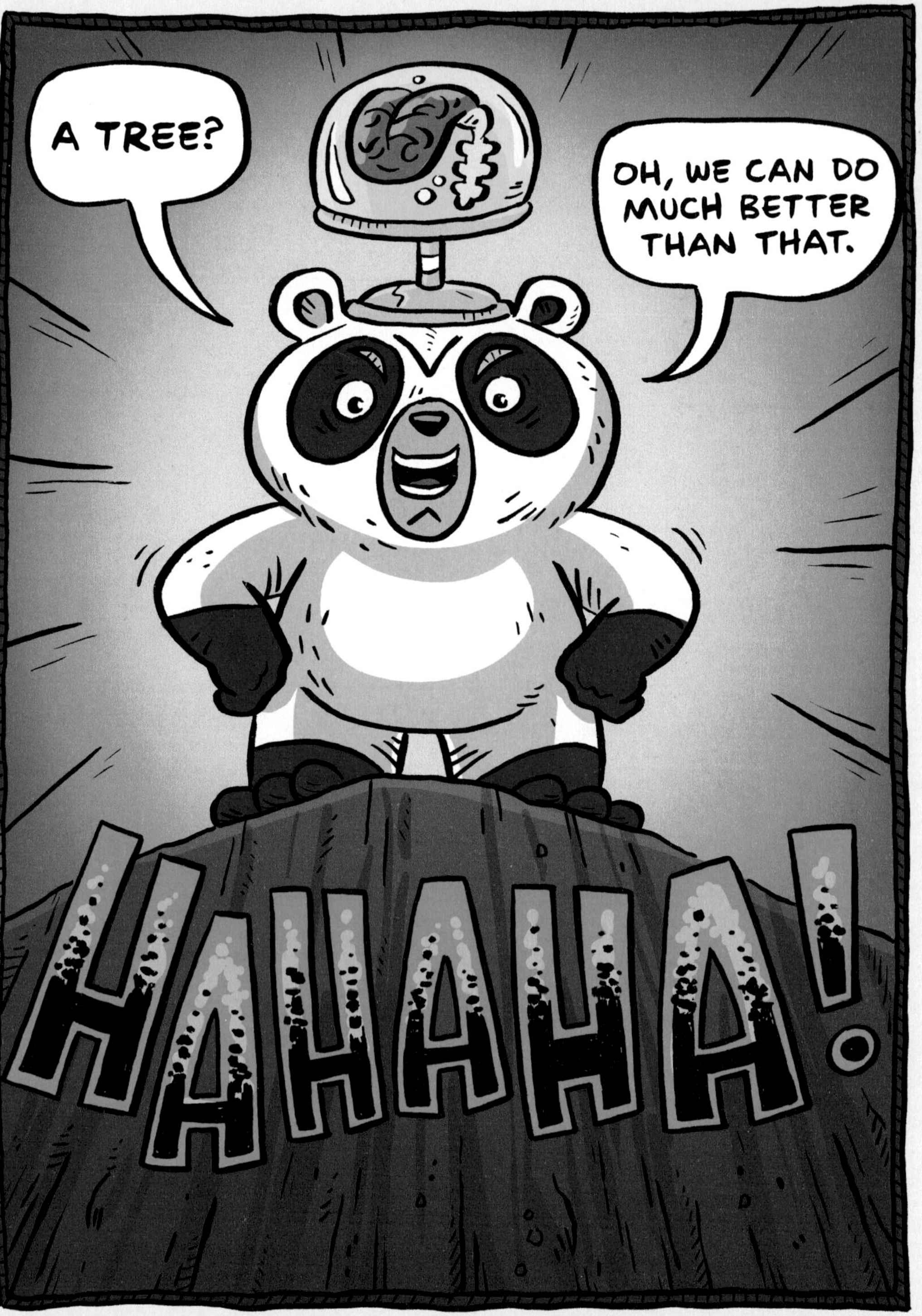
A TREE?
OH, WE CAN DO MUCH BETTER THAN THAT.
HAHAHA!

CHAPTER 2

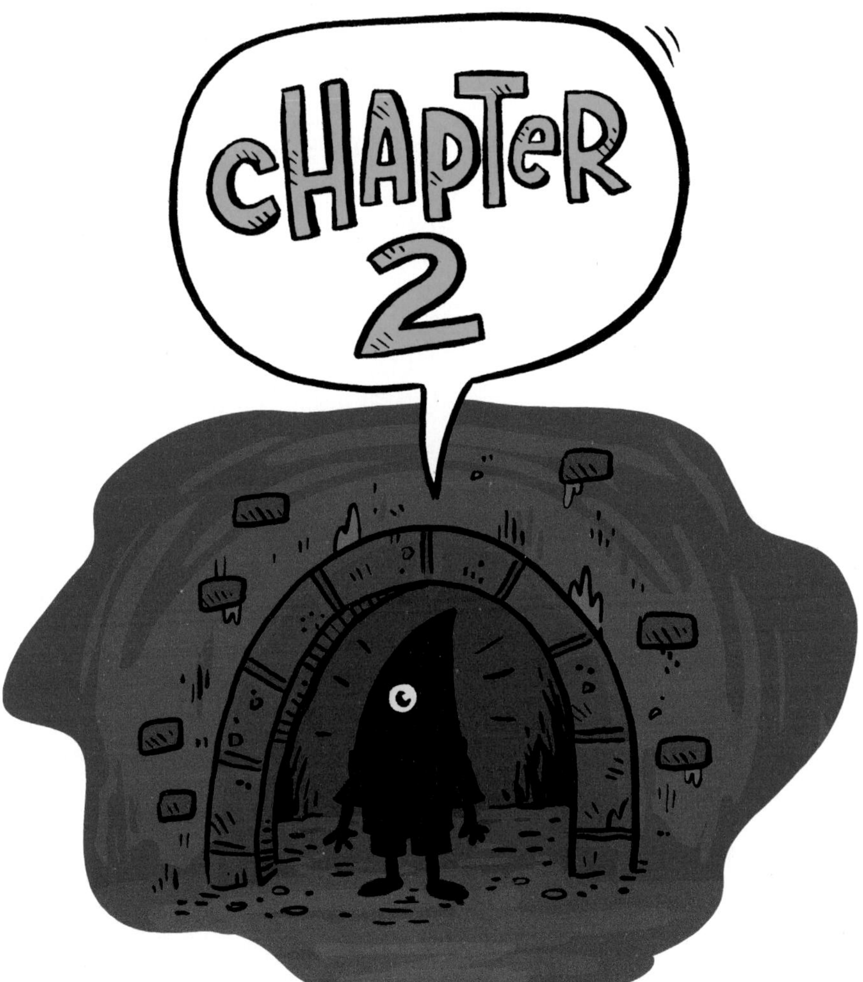

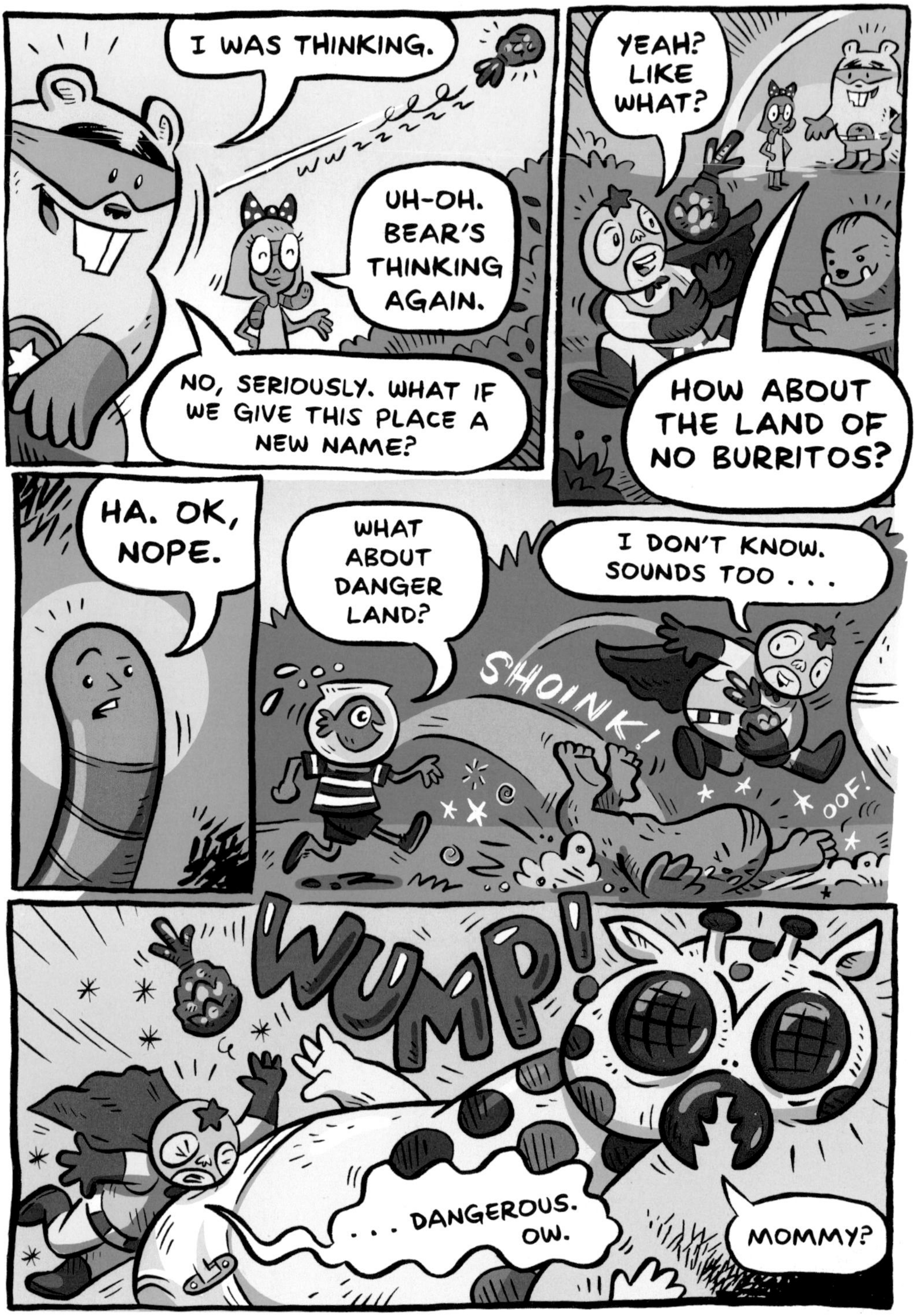
I WAS THINKING.
WWZZZZZ
UH-OH. BEAR'S THINKING AGAIN.
NO, SERIOUSLY. WHAT IF WE GIVE THIS PLACE A NEW NAME?
YEAH? LIKE WHAT?
HOW ABOUT THE LAND OF NO BURRITOS?
HA. OK, NOPE.
WHAT ABOUT DANGER LAND?
I DON'T KNOW. SOUNDS TOO . . .
SHOINK!
OOF!
WUMP!
. . . DANGEROUS. OW.
MOMMY?

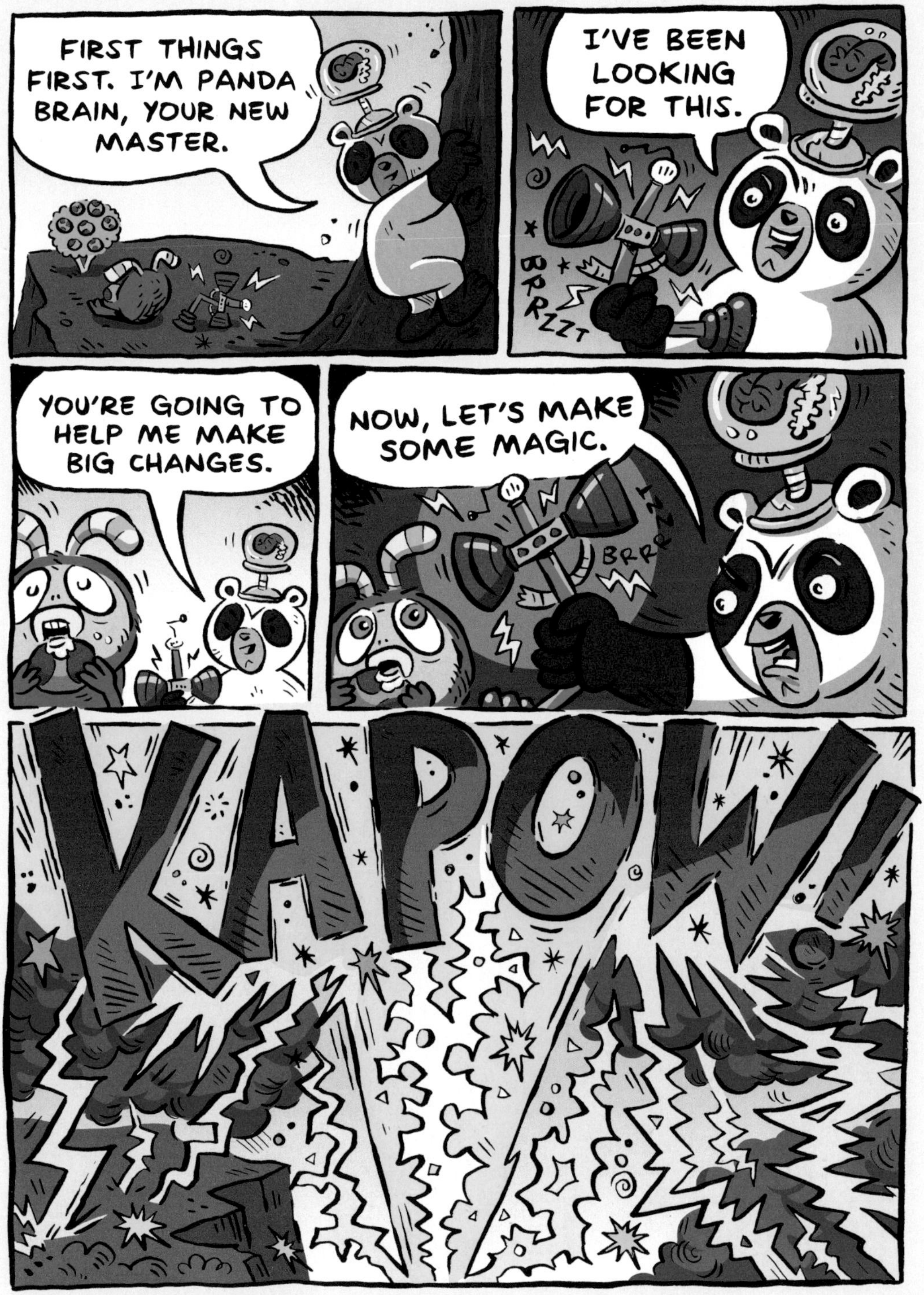
FIRST THINGS FIRST. I'M PANDA BRAIN, YOUR NEW MASTER.
I'VE BEEN LOOKING FOR THIS.
BRRRZZZT
YOU'RE GOING TO HELP ME MAKE BIG CHANGES.
NOW, LET'S MAKE SOME MAGIC.
BRRR
XAPOW!

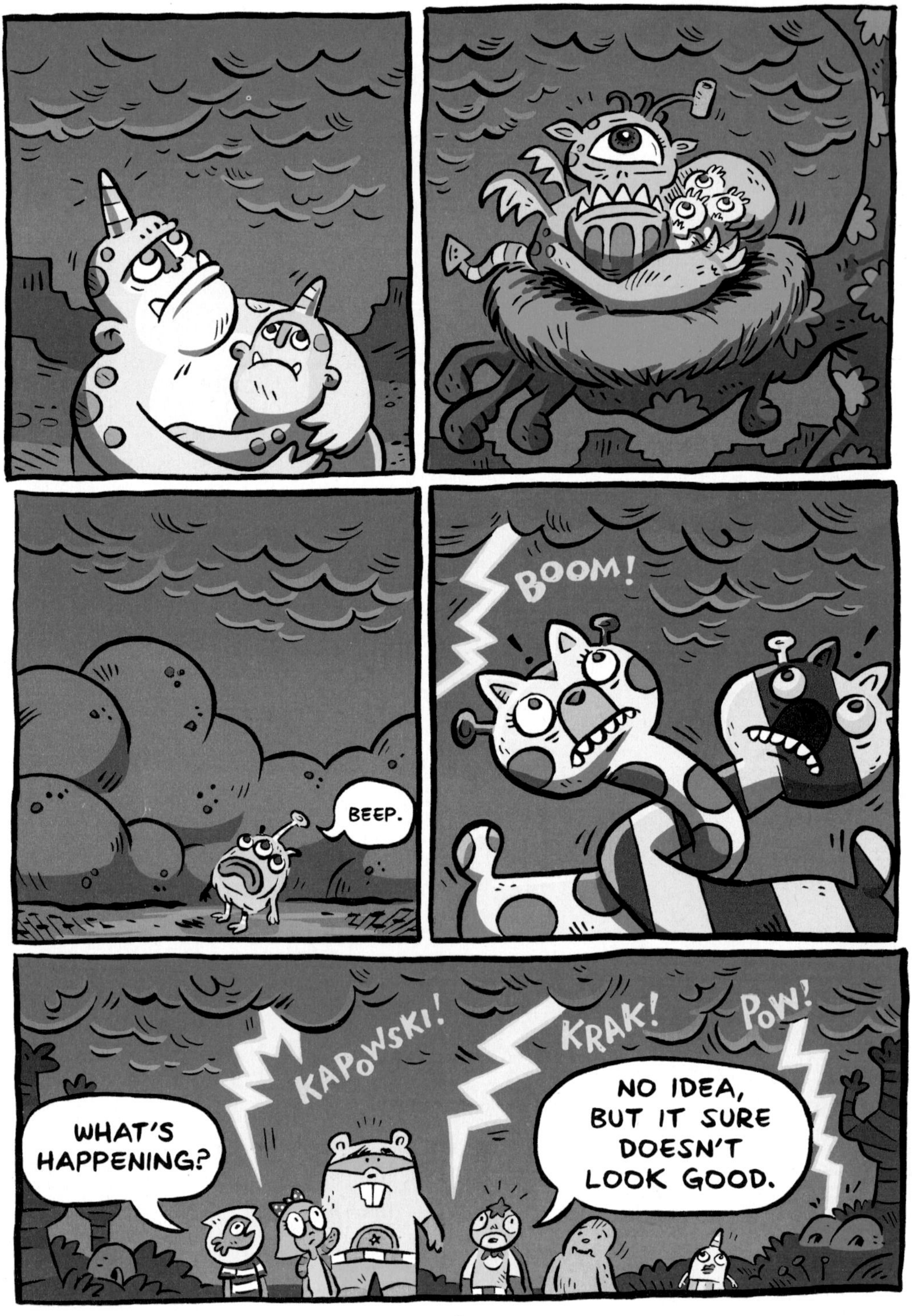
BEEP.
BOOM!
KAPOWSKI!
KRAK!
POW!
WHAT'S HAPPENING?
NO IDEA, BUT IT SURE DOESN'T LOOK GOOD.

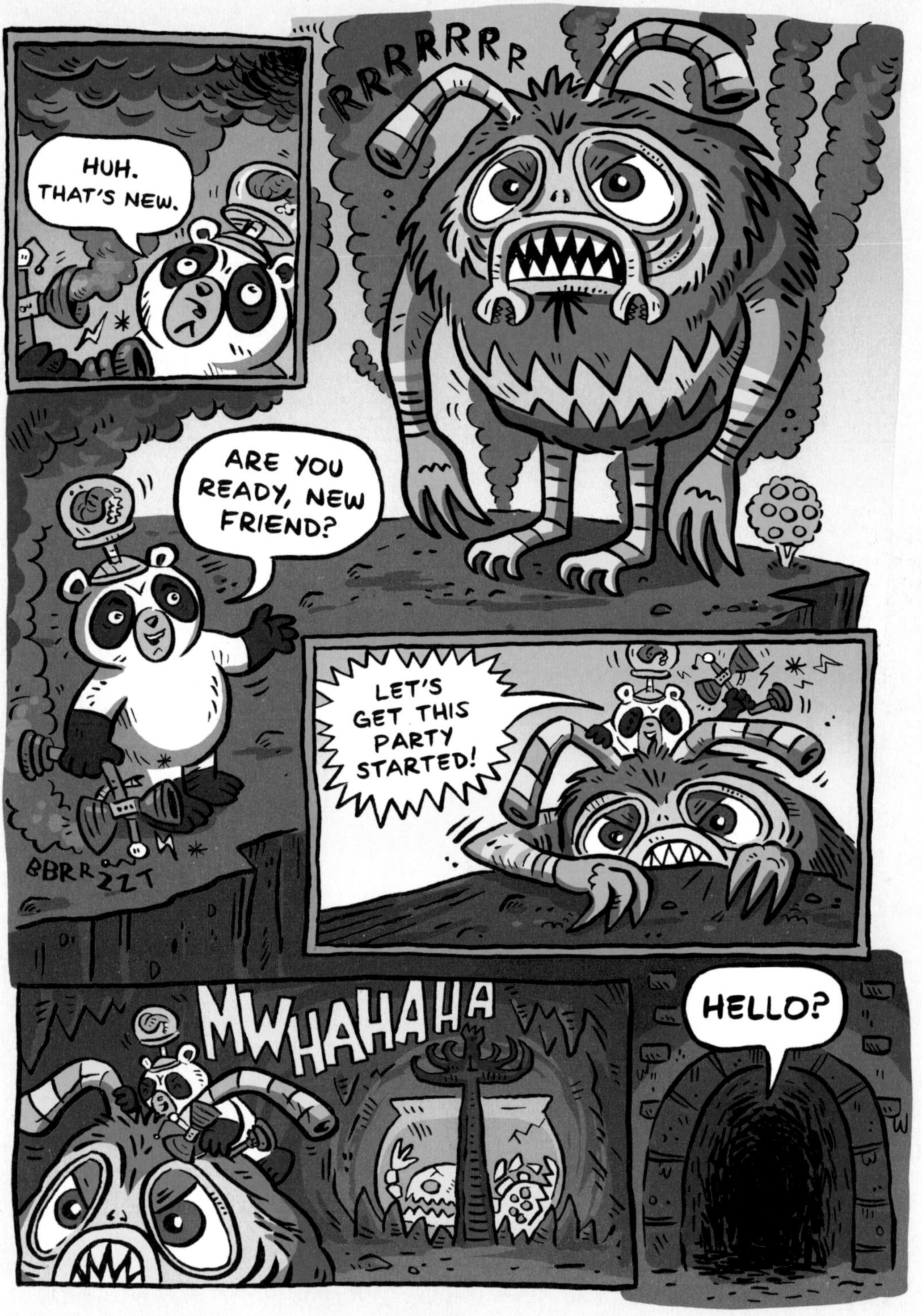
HUH. THAT'S NEW.
RRRRRRRR
ARE YOU READY, NEW FRIEND?
BBRRRZZT
LET'S GET THIS PARTY STARTED!
MWHAHAHAHA
HELLO?

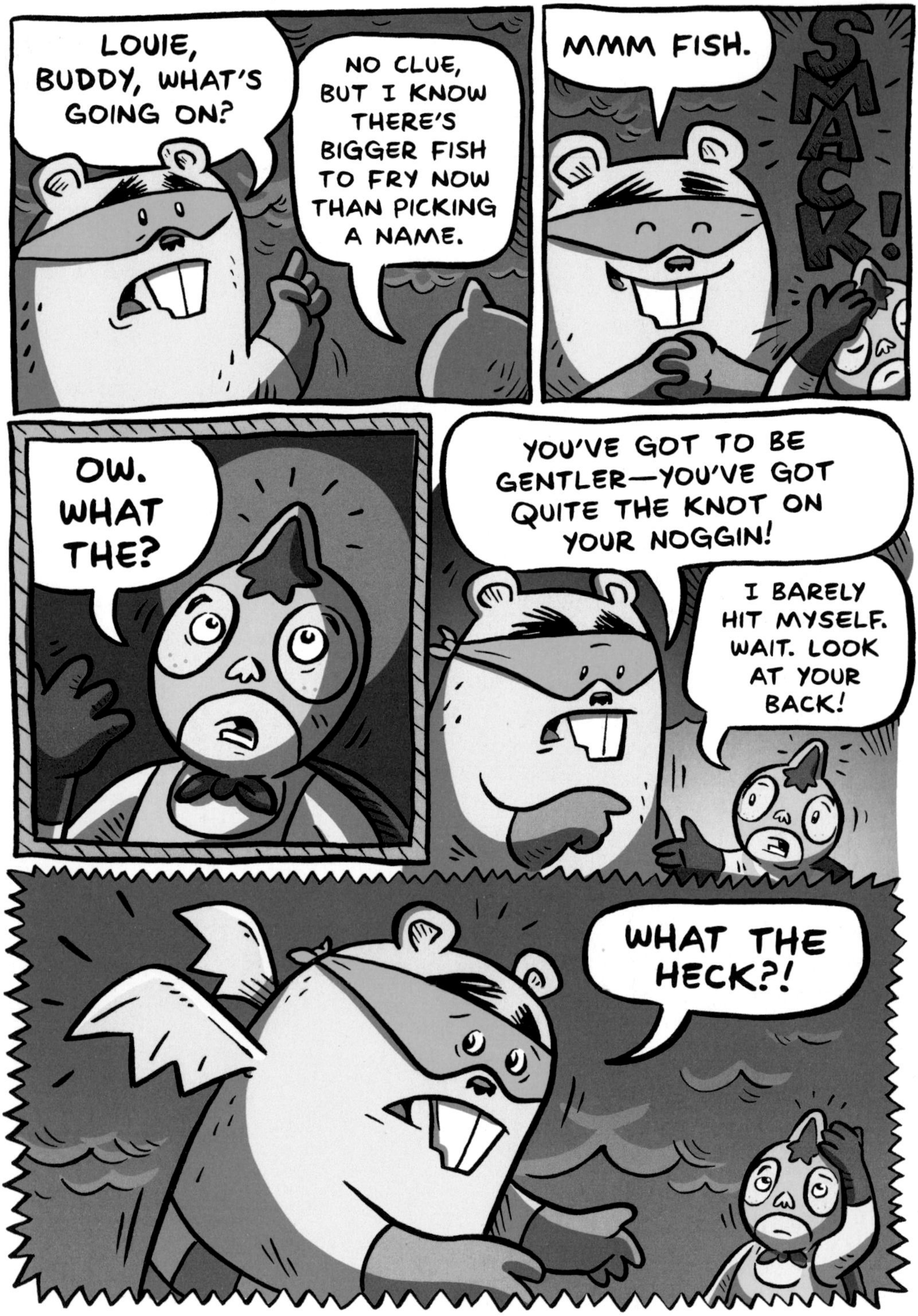
LOUIE, BUDDY, WHAT'S GOING ON?
NO CLUE, BUT I KNOW THERE'S BIGGER FISH TO FRY NOW THAN PICKING A NAME.
MMM FISH.
SMACK!
OW. WHAT THE?
YOU'VE GOT TO BE GENTLER—YOU'VE GOT QUITE THE KNOT ON YOUR NOGGIN!
I BARELY HIT MYSELF. WAIT. LOOK AT YOUR BACK!
WHAT THE HECK?!

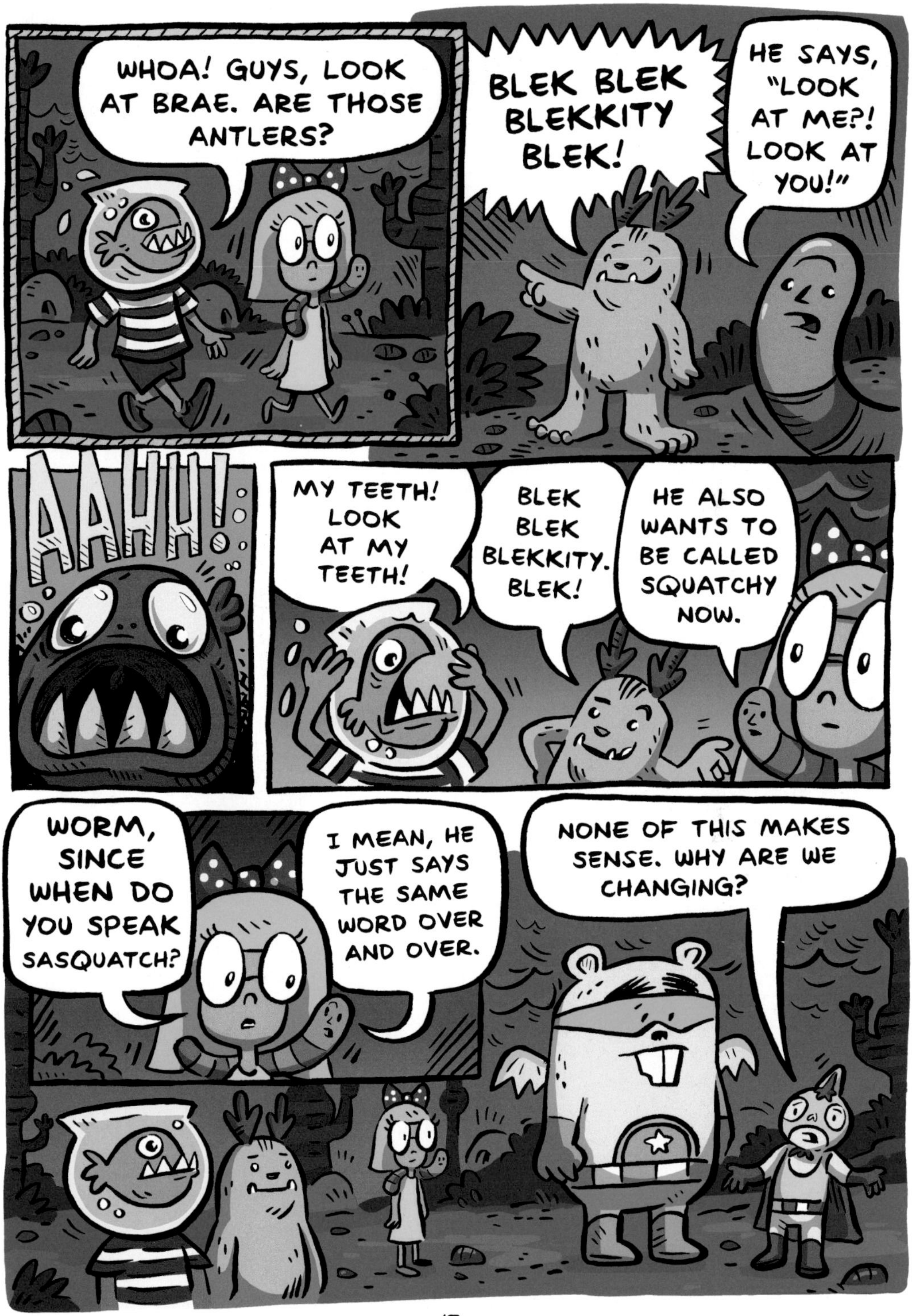
WHOA! GUYS, LOOK AT BRAE. ARE THOSE ANTLERS?
BLEK BLEK BLEKKITY BLEK!
HE SAYS, "LOOK AT ME?! LOOK AT YOU!"
AAHH!
MY TEETH! LOOK AT MY TEETH!
BLEK BLEK BLEKKITY. BLEK!
HE ALSO WANTS TO BE CALLED SQUATCHY NOW.
WORM, SINCE WHEN DO YOU SPEAK SASQUATCH?
I MEAN, HE JUST SAYS THE SAME WORD OVER AND OVER.
NONE OF THIS MAKES SENSE. WHY ARE WE CHANGING?

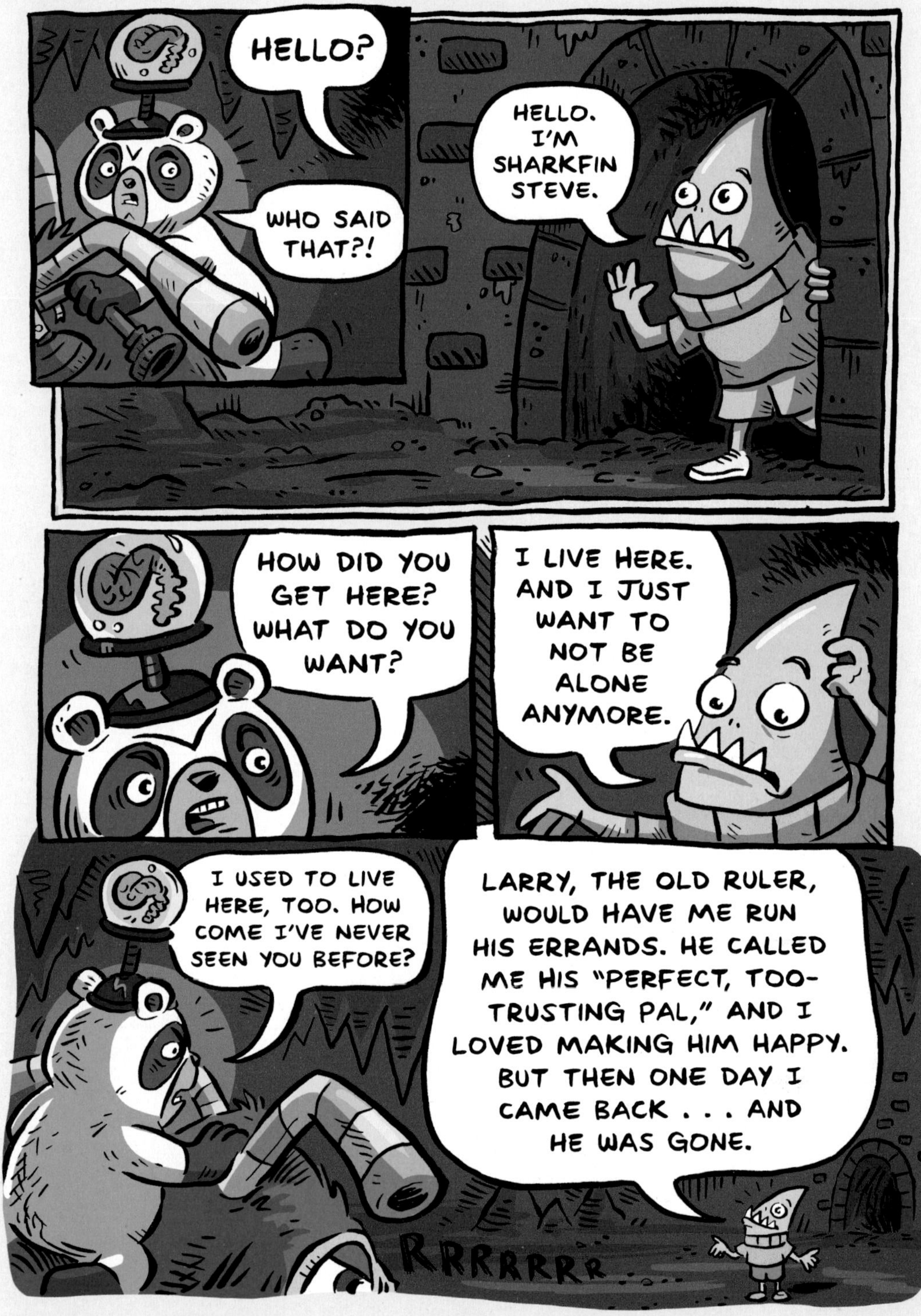
HELLO?
WHO SAID THAT?!
HELLO. I'M SHARKFIN STEVE.
HOW DID YOU GET HERE? WHAT DO YOU WANT?
I LIVE HERE. AND I JUST WANT TO NOT BE ALONE ANYMORE.
I USED TO LIVE HERE, TOO. HOW COME I'VE NEVER SEEN YOU BEFORE?
LARRY, THE OLD RULER, WOULD HAVE ME RUN HIS ERRANDS. HE CALLED ME HIS "PERFECT, TOO-TRUSTING PAL," AND I LOVED MAKING HIM HAPPY. BUT THEN ONE DAY I CAME BACK . . . AND HE WAS GONE.
RRRRRRRR

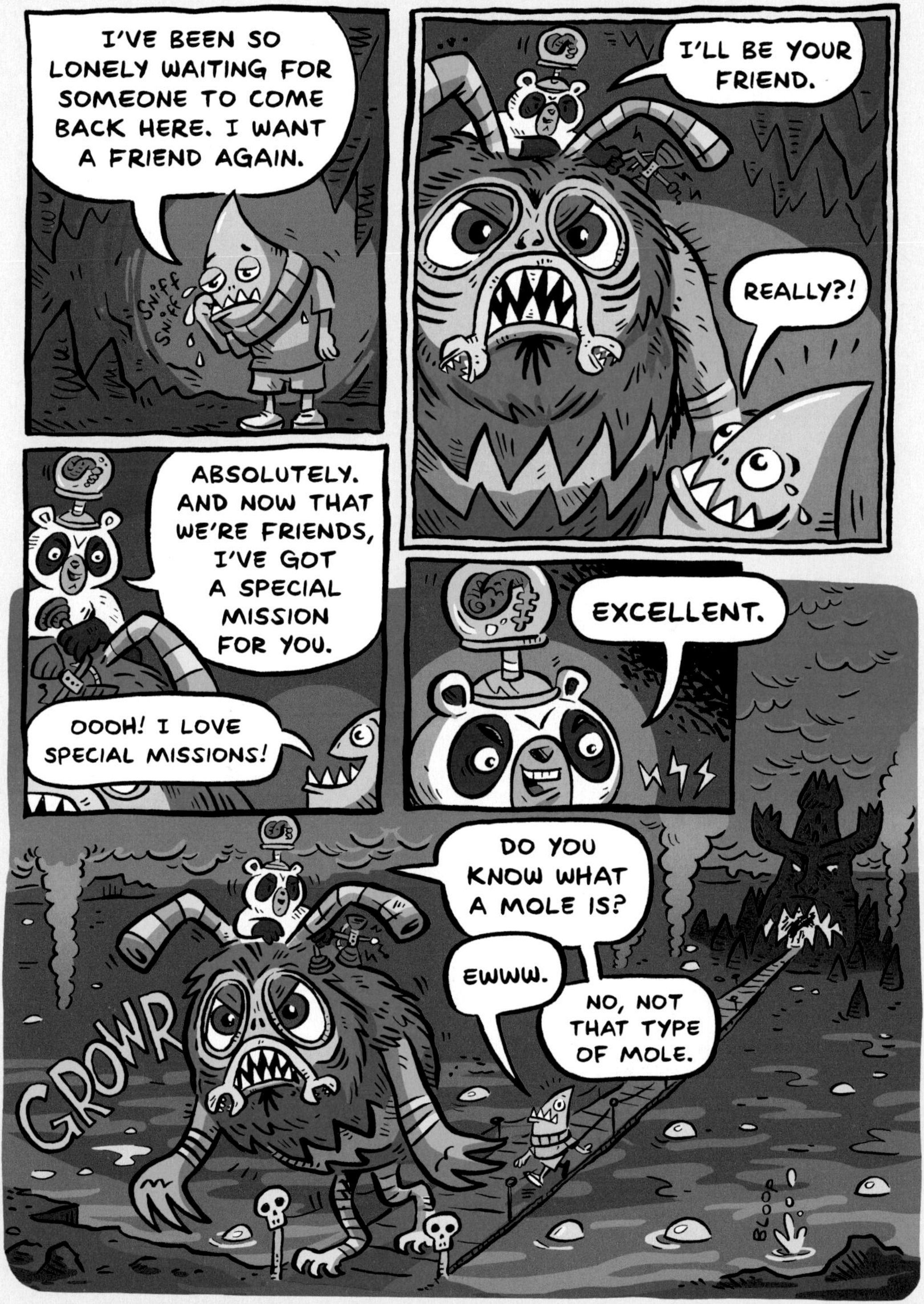
I'VE BEEN SO LONELY WAITING FOR SOMEONE TO COME BACK HERE. I WANT A FRIEND AGAIN.
SNIFF SNIFF
I'LL BE YOUR FRIEND.
REALLY?!
ABSOLUTELY. AND NOW THAT WE'RE FRIENDS, I'VE GOT A SPECIAL MISSION FOR YOU.
OOOH! I LOVE SPECIAL MISSIONS!
EXCELLENT.
DO YOU KNOW WHAT A MOLE IS?
EWWW.
NO, NOT THAT TYPE OF MOLE.
GROWR
BLOOP

Chapter 3

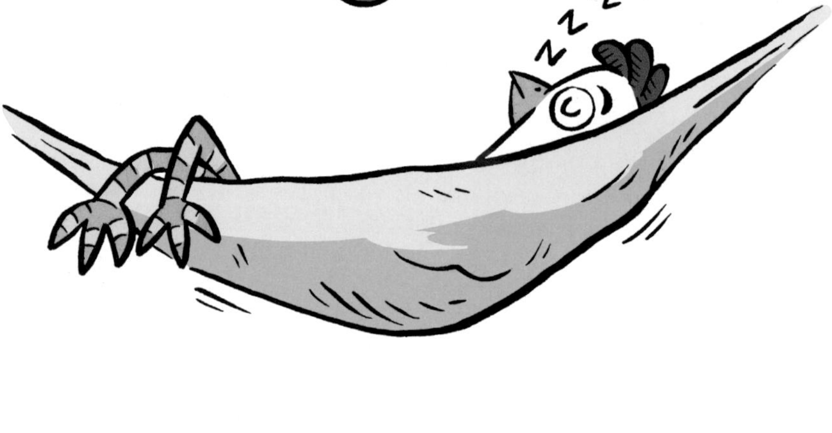
ZZZZZZZZZ

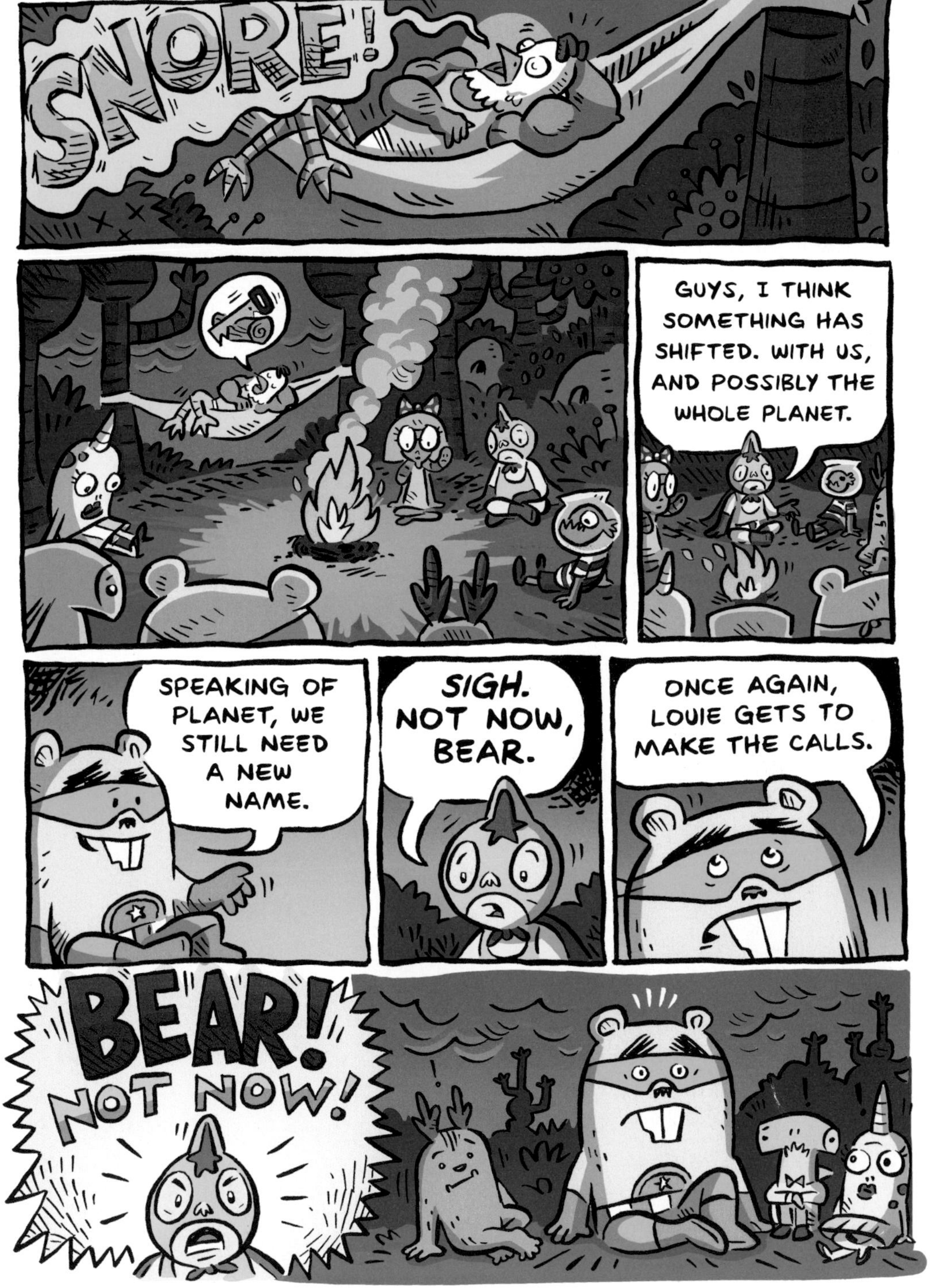
SNORE!
GUYS, I THINK SOMETHING HAS SHIFTED. WITH US, AND POSSIBLY THE WHOLE PLANET.
SPEAKING OF PLANET, WE STILL NEED A NEW NAME.
SIGH. NOT NOW, BEAR.
ONCE AGAIN, LOUIE GETS TO MAKE THE CALLS.
BEAR! NOT NOW!

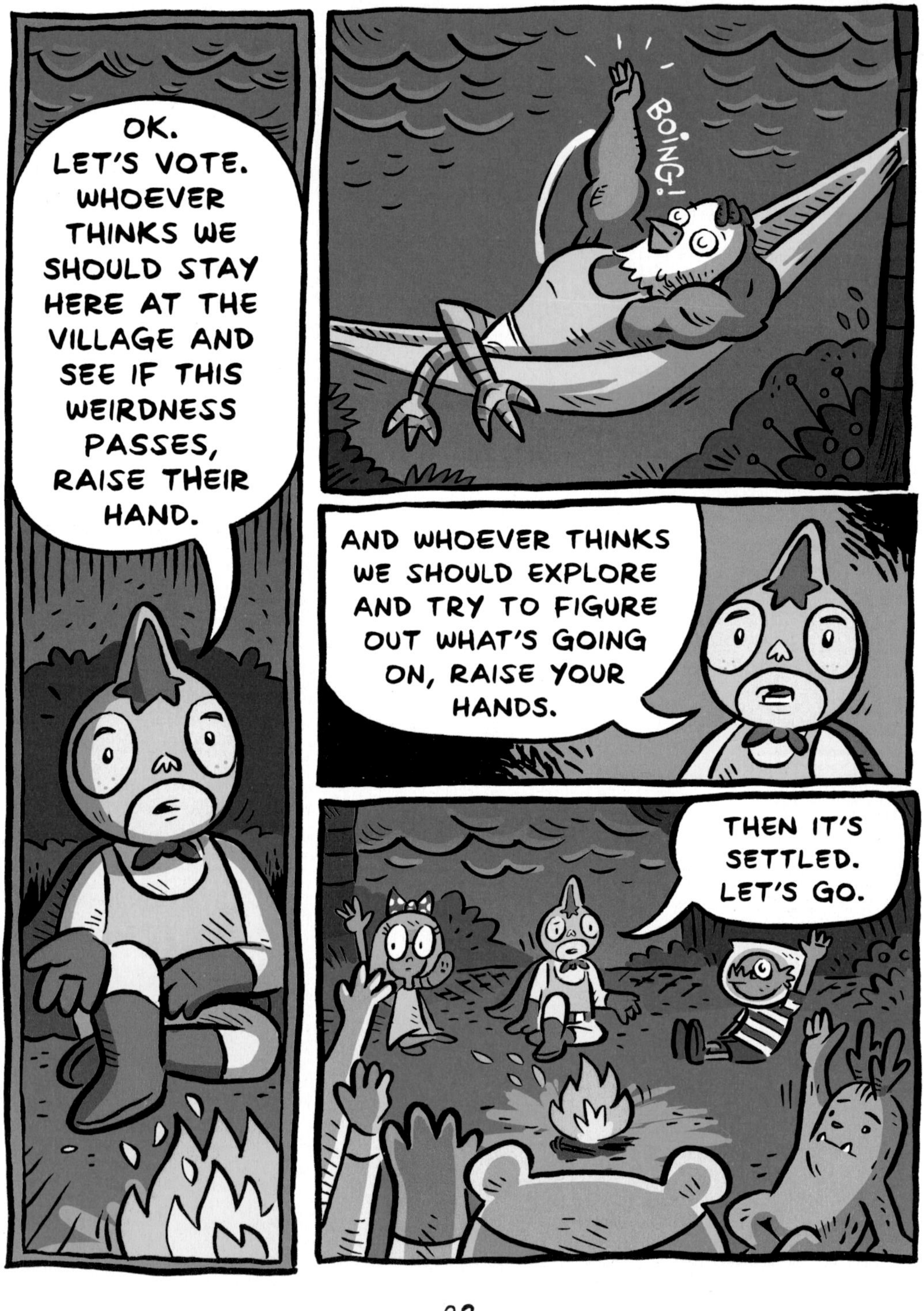
OK. LET'S VOTE. WHOEVER THINKS WE SHOULD STAY HERE AT THE VILLAGE AND SEE IF THIS WEIRDNESS PASSES, RAISE THEIR HAND.
BOING!
AND WHOEVER THINKS WE SHOULD EXPLORE AND TRY TO FIGURE OUT WHAT'S GOING ON, RAISE YOUR HANDS.
THEN IT'S SETTLED. LET'S GO.

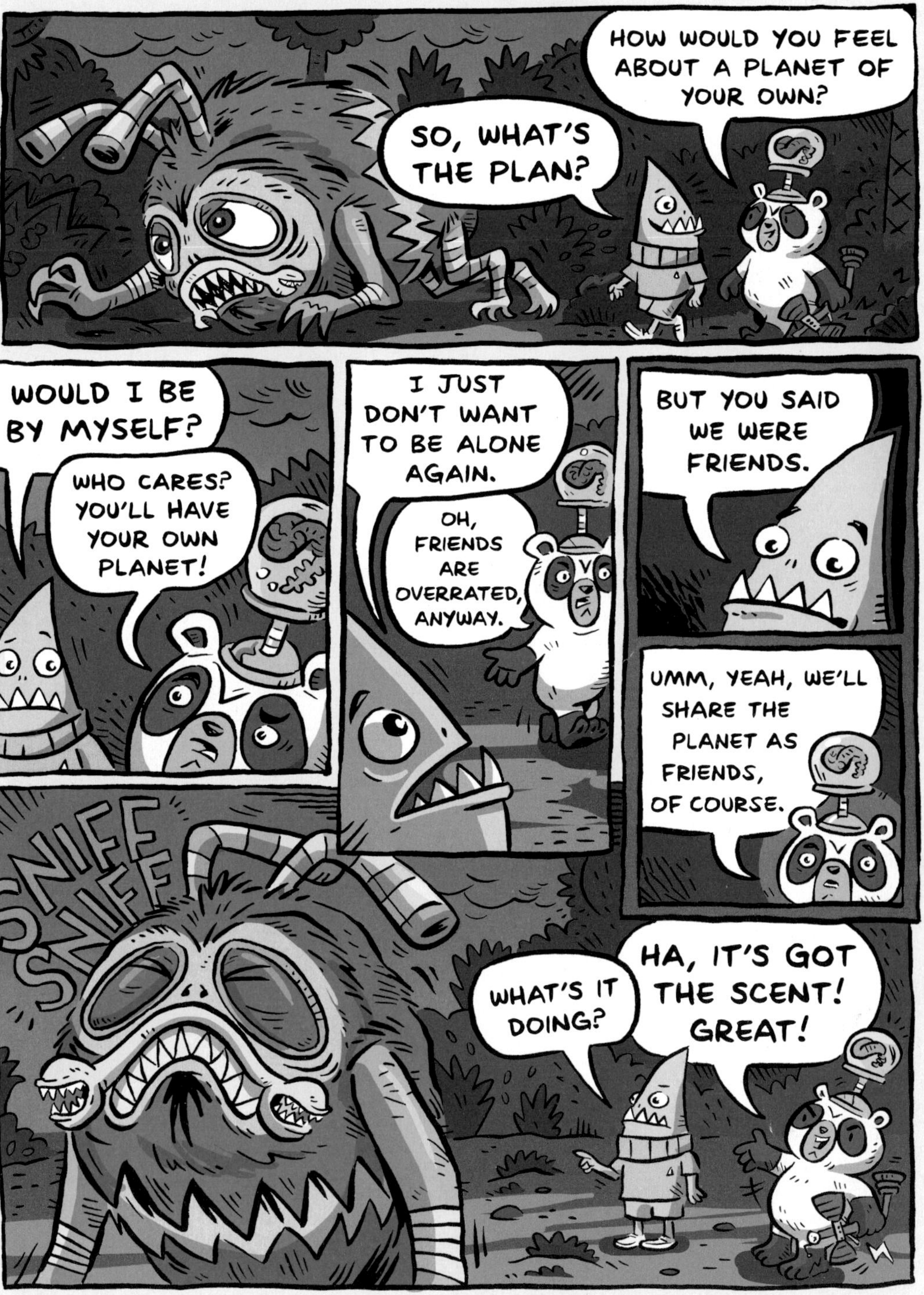
SO, WHAT'S THE PLAN?
HOW WOULD YOU FEEL ABOUT A PLANET OF YOUR OWN?
WOULD I BE BY MYSELF?
WHO CARES? YOU'LL HAVE YOUR OWN PLANET!
I JUST DON'T WANT TO BE ALONE AGAIN.
OH, FRIENDS ARE OVERRATED, ANYWAY.
BUT YOU SAID WE WERE FRIENDS.
UMM, YEAH, WE'LL SHARE THE PLANET AS FRIENDS, OF COURSE.
SNIFF SNIFF
WHAT'S IT DOING?
HA, IT'S GOT THE SCENT! GREAT!

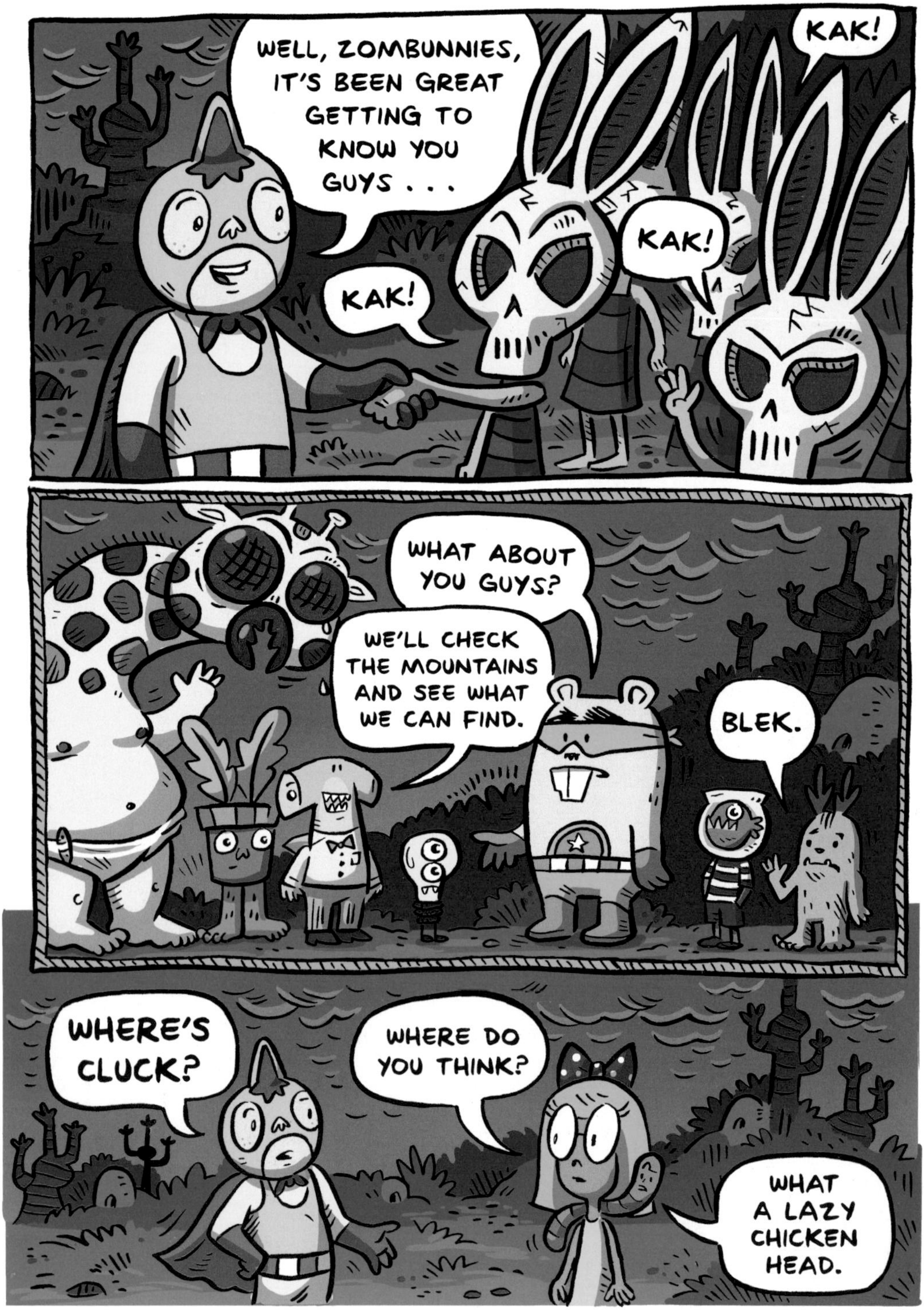
WELL, ZOMBUNNIES, IT'S BEEN GREAT GETTING TO KNOW YOU GUYS . . .
KAK!
KAK!
KAK!
WHAT ABOUT YOU GUYS?
WE'LL CHECK THE MOUNTAINS AND SEE WHAT WE CAN FIND.
BLEK.
WHERE'S CLUCK?
WHERE DO YOU THINK?
WHAT A LAZY CHICKEN HEAD.

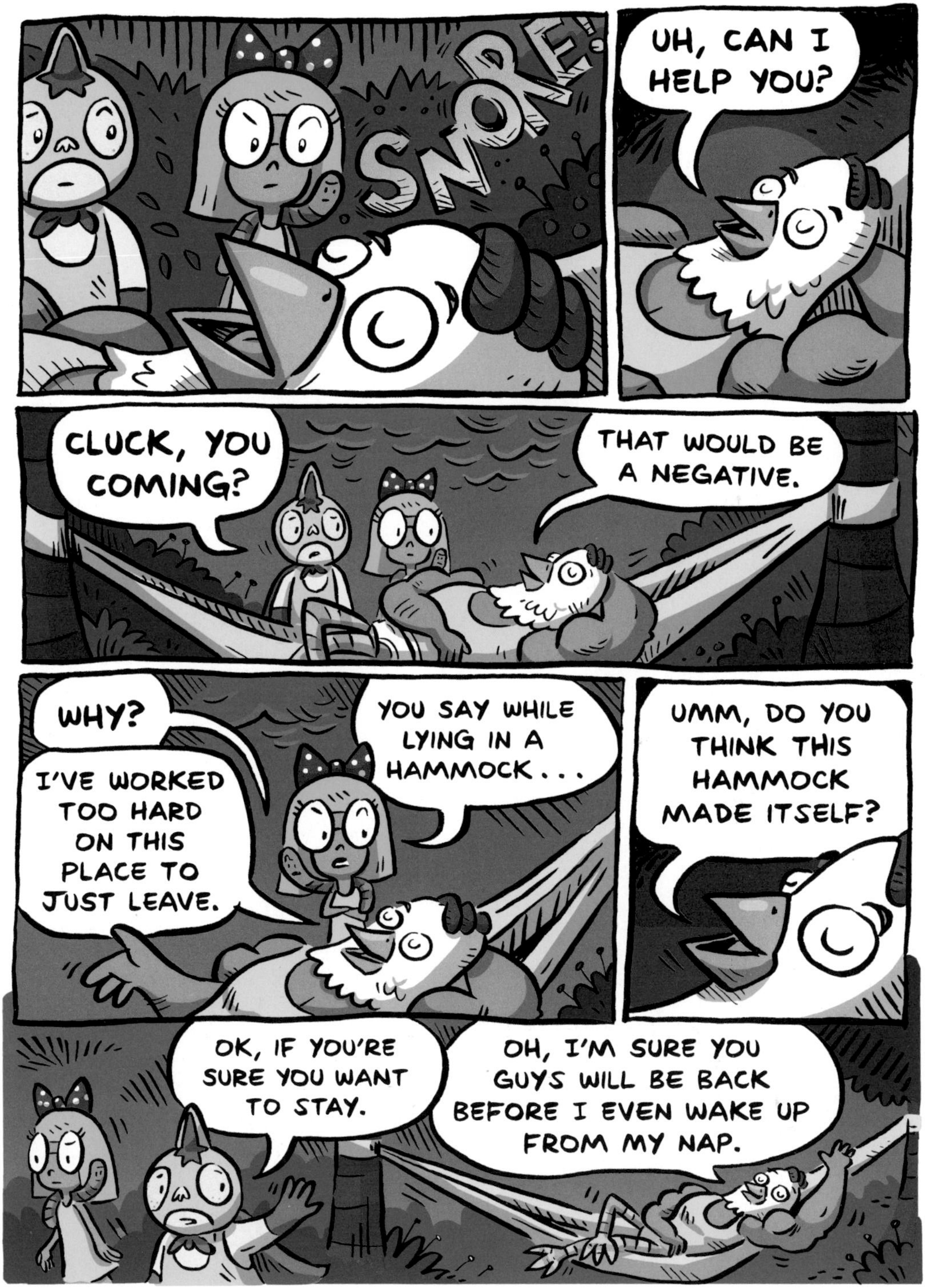
SNORE!
UH, CAN I HELP YOU?
CLUCK, YOU COMING?
THAT WOULD BE A NEGATIVE.
WHY?
I'VE WORKED TOO HARD ON THIS PLACE TO JUST LEAVE.
YOU SAY WHILE LYING IN A HAMMOCK . . .
UMM, DO YOU THINK THIS HAMMOCK MADE ITSELF?
OK, IF YOU'RE SURE YOU WANT TO STAY.
OH, I'M SURE YOU GUYS WILL BE BACK BEFORE I EVEN WAKE UP FROM MY NAP.

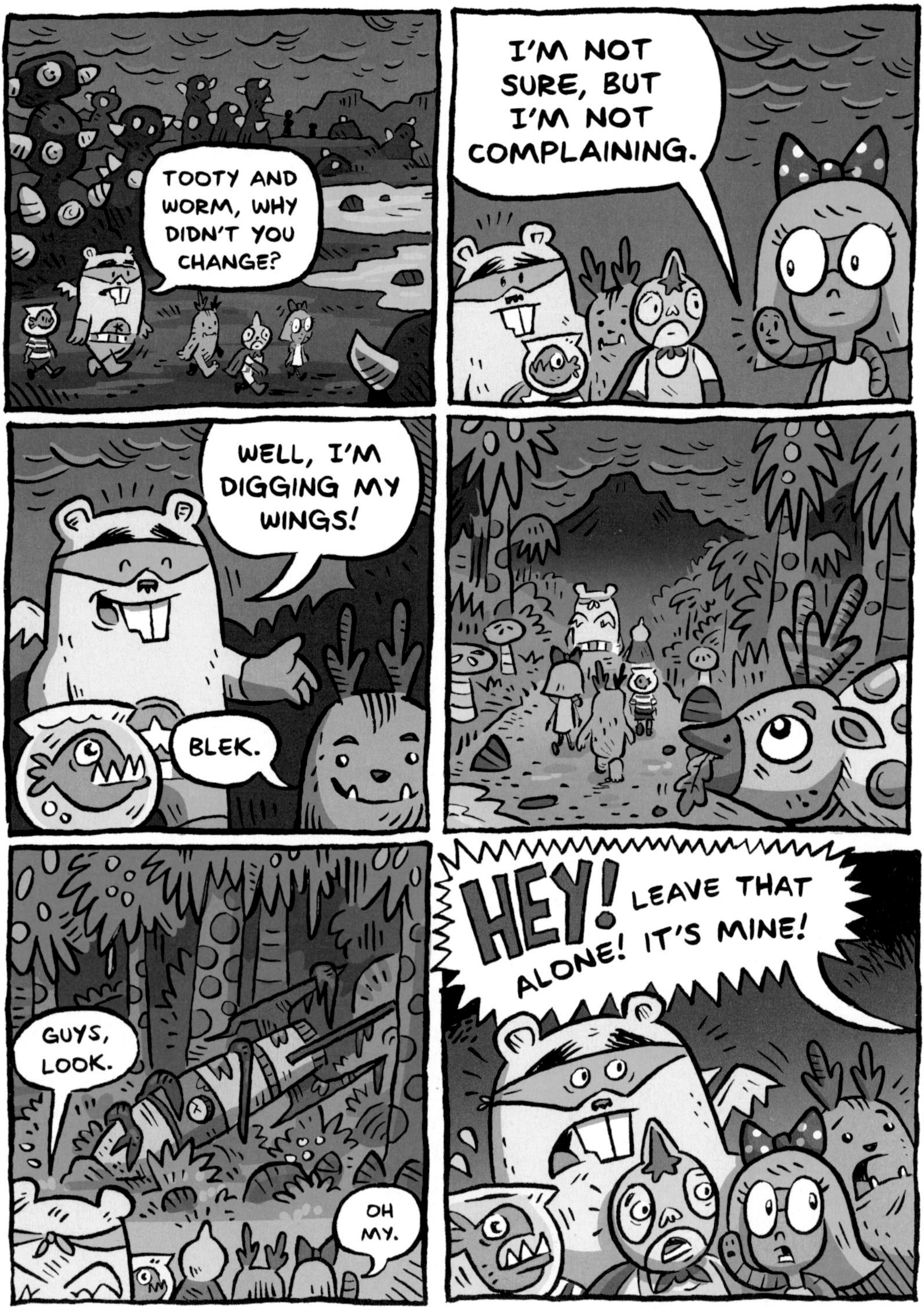
TOOTY AND WORM, WHY DIDN'T YOU CHANGE?
I'M NOT SURE, BUT I'M NOT COMPLAINING.
WELL, I'M DIGGING MY WINGS!
BLEK.
GUYS, LOOK.
OH MY.
HEY! LEAVE THAT ALONE! IT'S MINE!

chapter 4

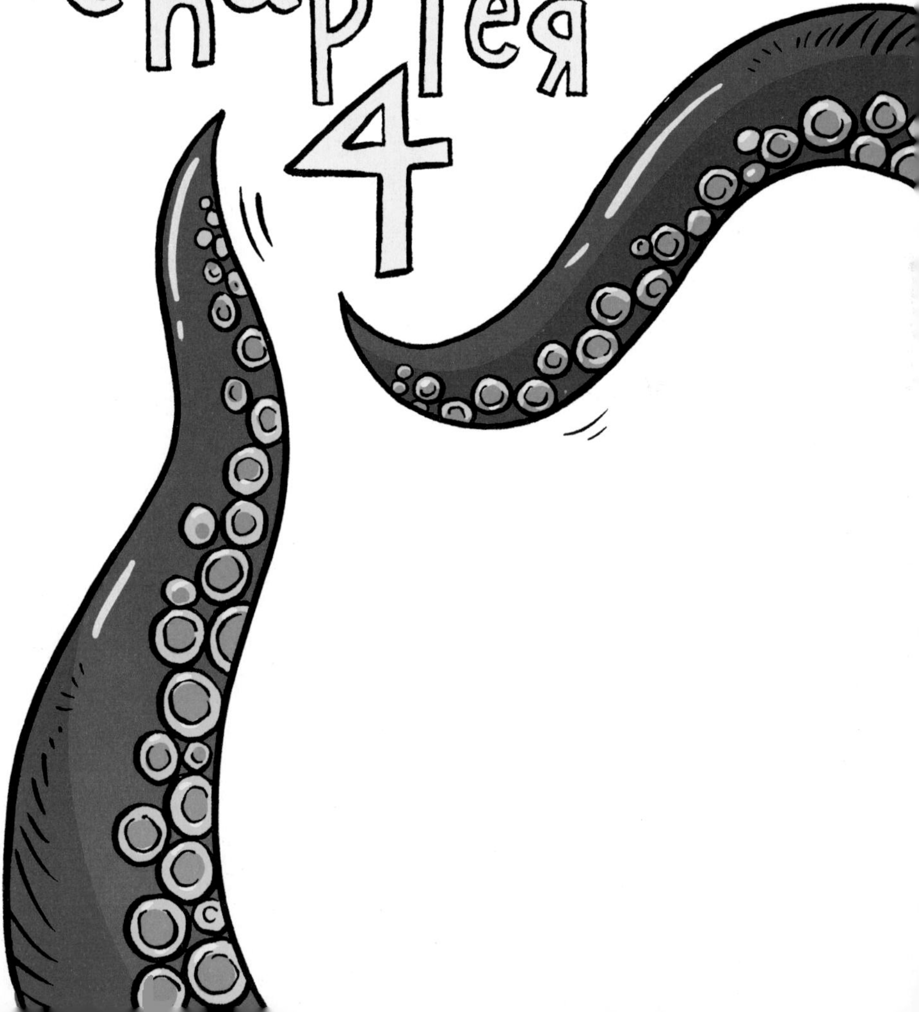

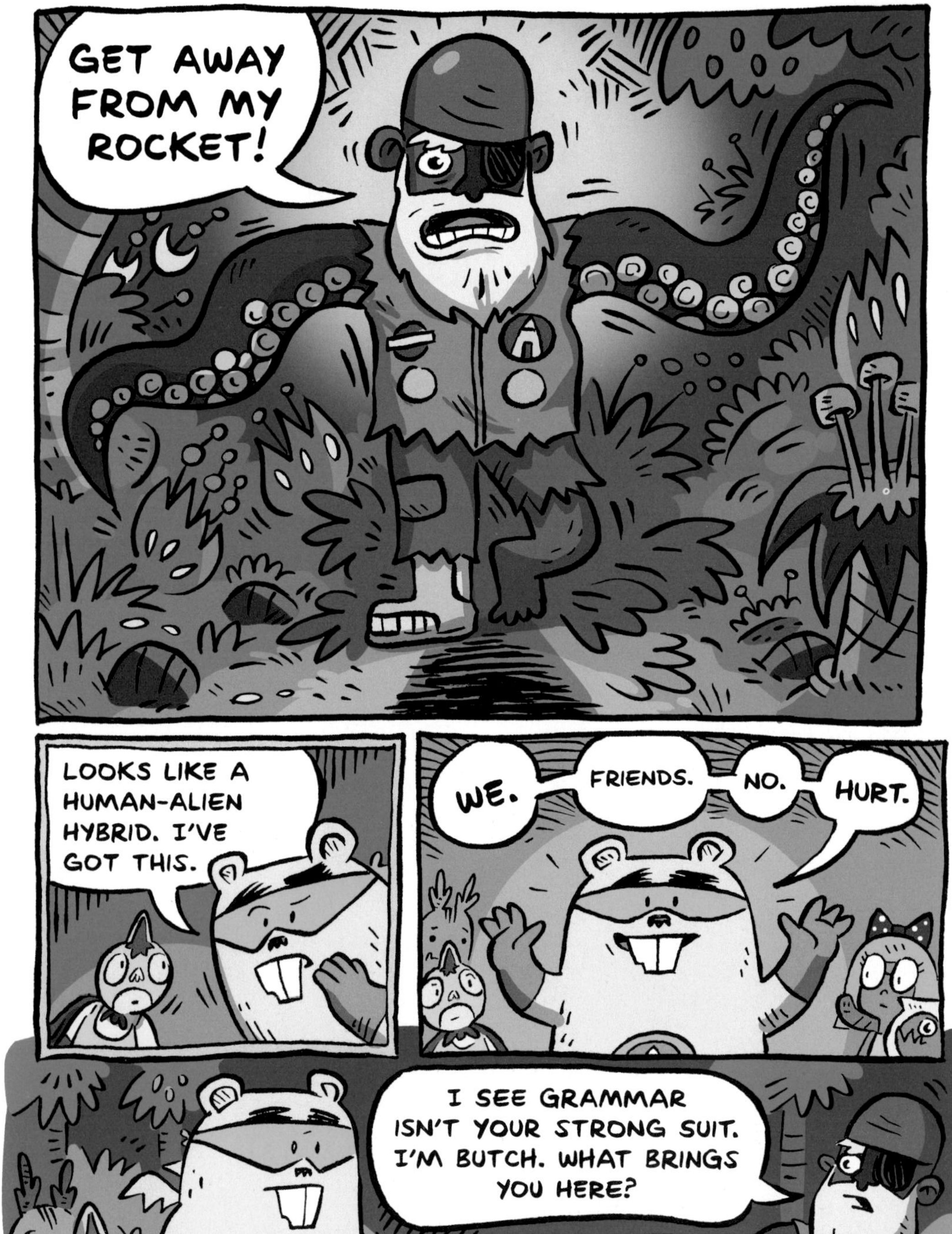
GET AWAY FROM MY ROCKET!
LOOKS LIKE A HUMAN-ALIEN HYBRID. I'VE GOT THIS.
WE.
FRIENDS.
NO.
HURT.
I SEE GRAMMAR ISN'T YOUR STRONG SUIT. I'M BUTCH. WHAT BRINGS YOU HERE?

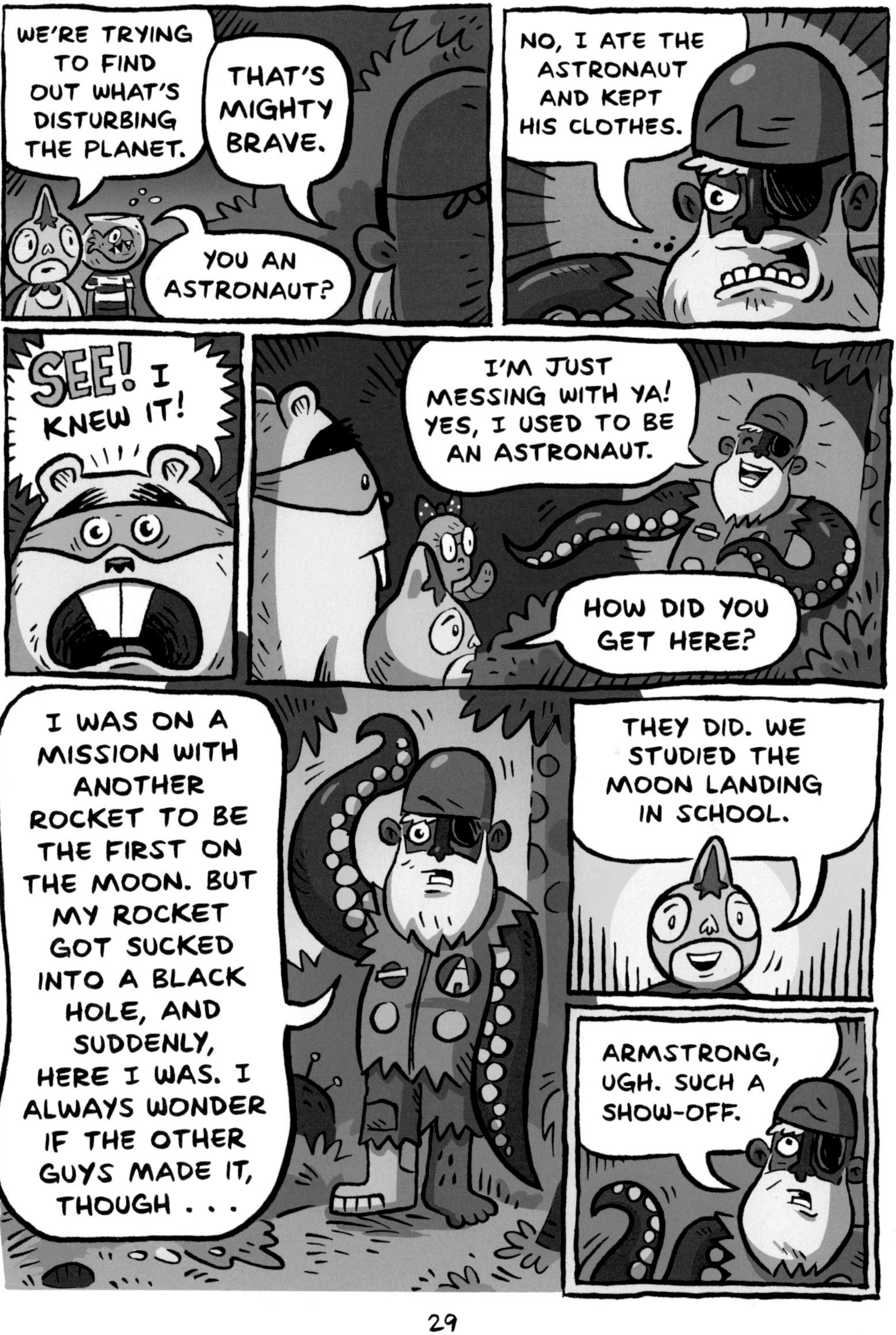
WE'RE TRYING TO FIND OUT WHAT'S DISTURBING THE PLANET.
THAT'S MIGHTY BRAVE.
YOU AN ASTRONAUT?
NO, I ATE THE ASTRONAUT AND KEPT HIS CLOTHES.
SEE! I KNEW IT!
I'M JUST MESSING WITH YA! YES, I USED TO BE AN ASTRONAUT.
HOW DID YOU GET HERE?
I WAS ON A MISSION WITH ANOTHER ROCKET TO BE THE FIRST ON THE MOON. BUT MY ROCKET GOT SUCKED INTO A BLACK HOLE, AND SUDDENLY, HERE I WAS. I ALWAYS WONDER IF THE OTHER GUYS MADE IT, THOUGH . . .
THEY DID. WE STUDIED THE MOON LANDING IN SCHOOL.
ARMSTRONG, UGH. SUCH A SHOW-OFF.

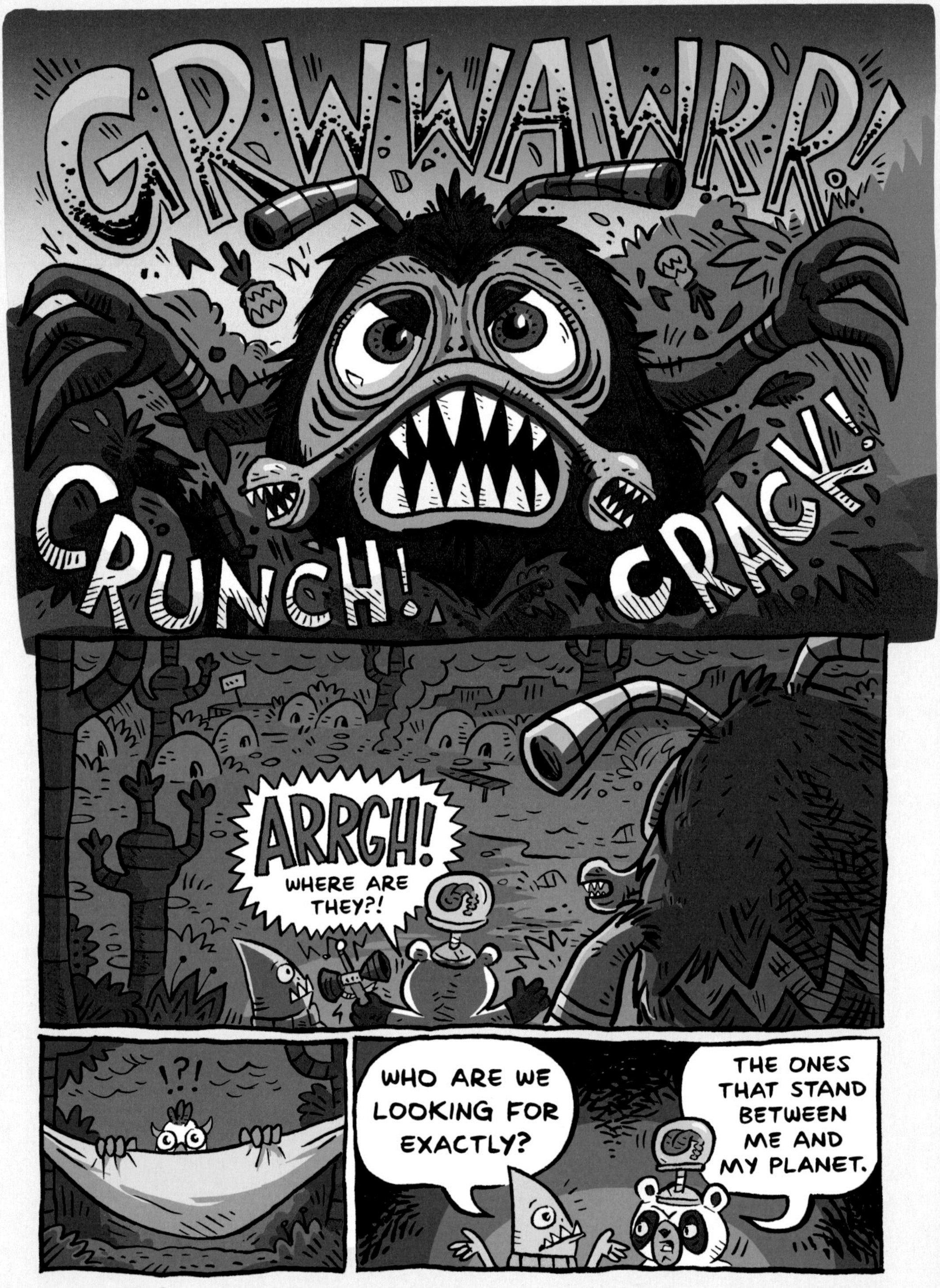
GRWAWRR!
CRUNCH!
CRACK!
ARRGH! WHERE ARE THEY?!
!?!
WHO ARE WE LOOKING FOR EXACTLY?
THE ONES THAT STAND BETWEEN ME AND MY PLANET.

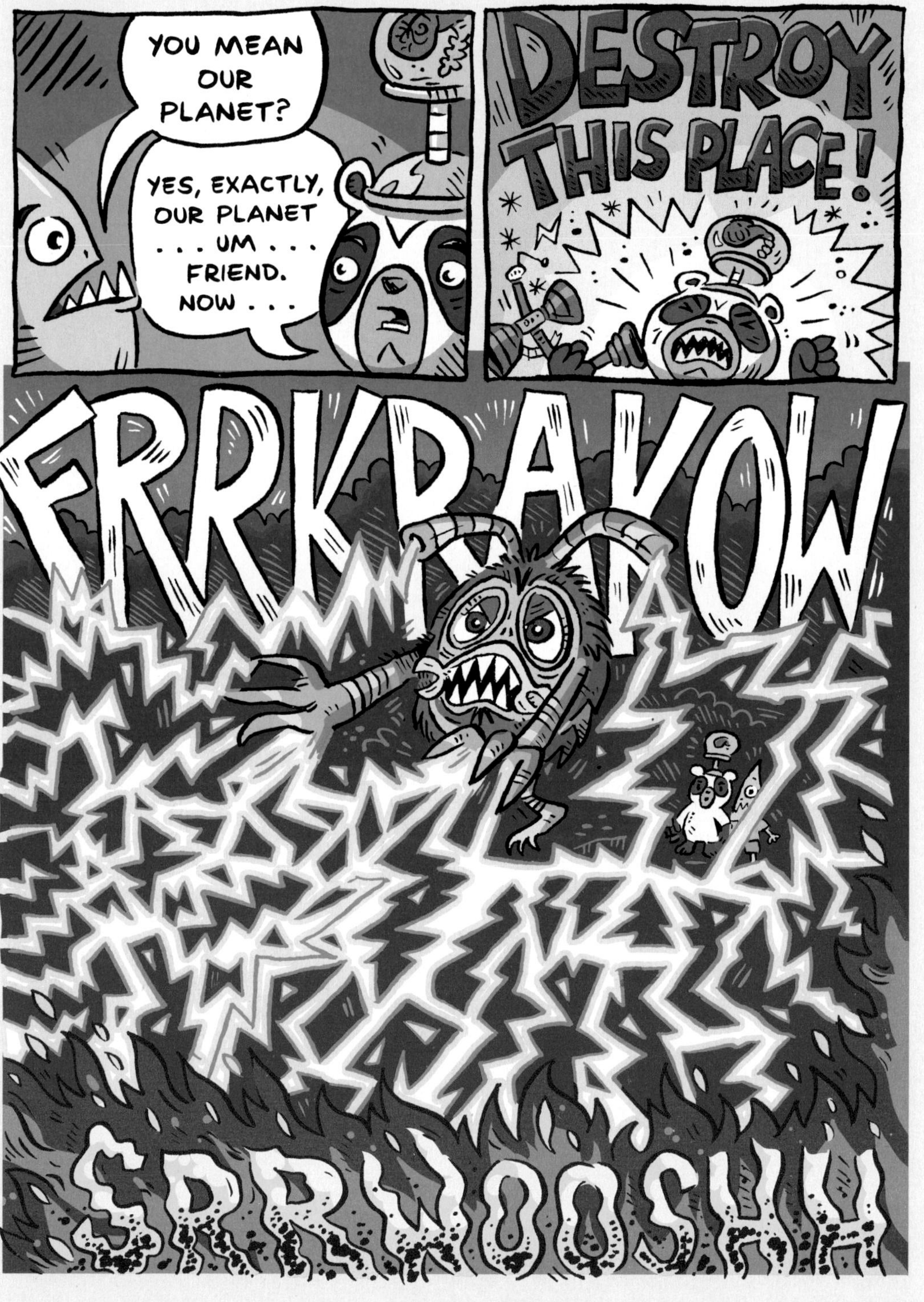
YOU MEAN OUR PLANET?
YES, EXACTLY, OUR PLANET . . . UM . . . FRIEND. NOW . . .
DESTROY THIS PLACE!
FRRKRAKOW
SPRWOOSHH

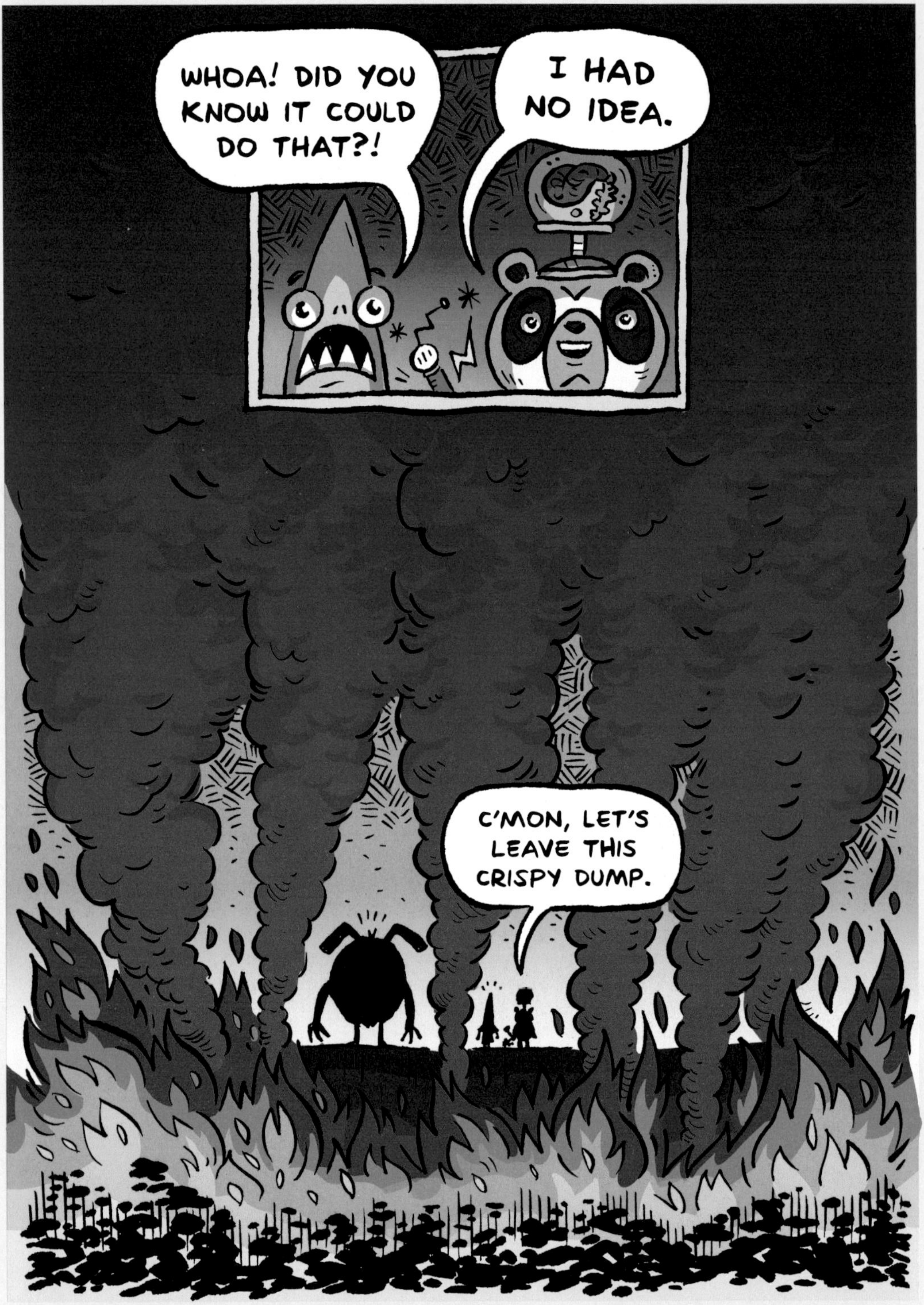
WHOA! DID YOU KNOW IT COULD DO THAT?!
I HAD NO IDEA.
C'MON, LET'S LEAVE THIS CRISPY DUMP.

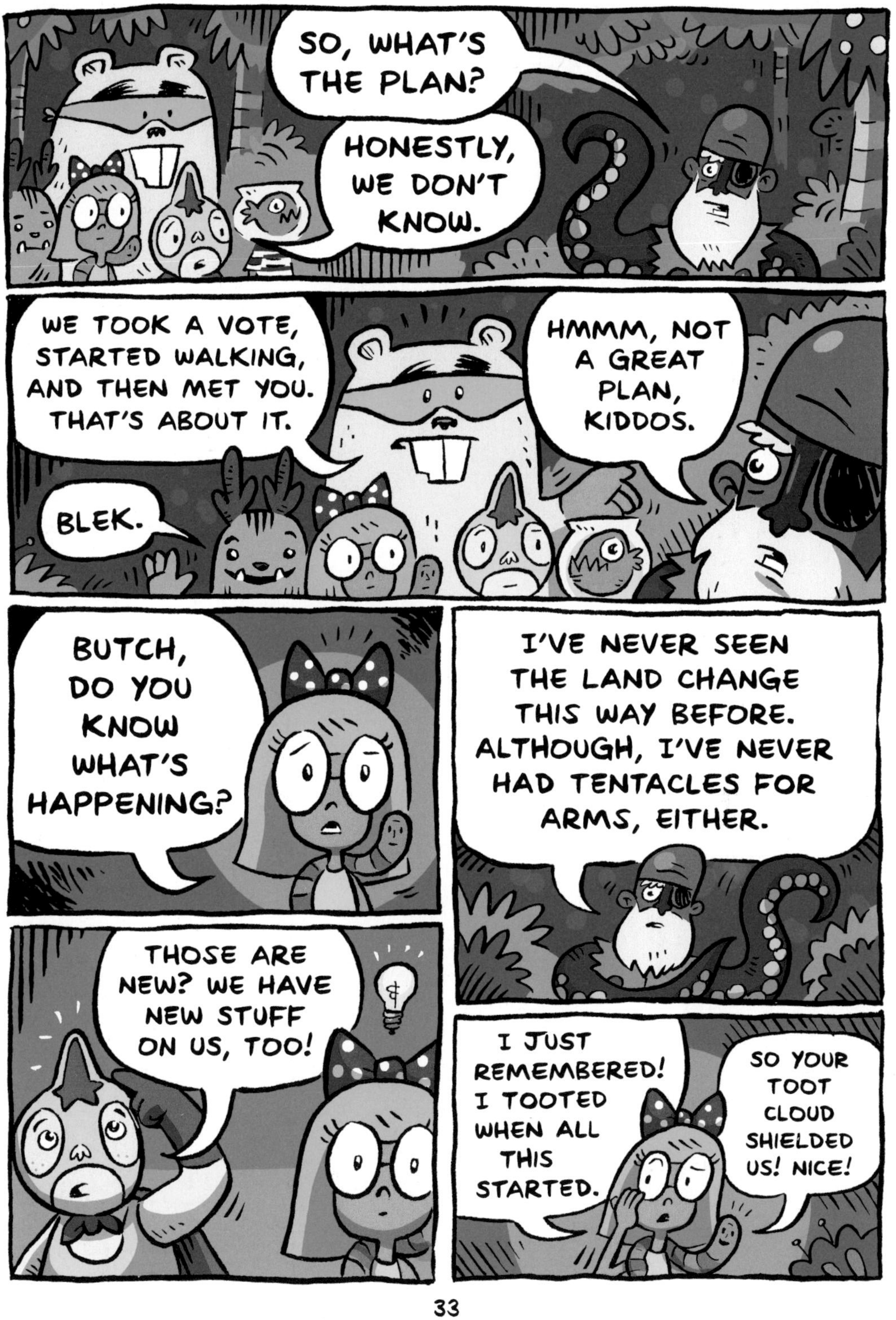

SO, WHAT'S THE PLAN?
HONESTLY, WE DON'T KNOW.
WE TOOK A VOTE, STARTED WALKING, AND THEN MET YOU. THAT'S ABOUT IT.
HMMM, NOT A GREAT PLAN, KIDDOS.
BLEK.
BUTCH, DO YOU KNOW WHAT'S HAPPENING?
I'VE NEVER SEEN THE LAND CHANGE THIS WAY BEFORE. ALTHOUGH, I'VE NEVER HAD TENTACLES FOR ARMS, EITHER.
THOSE ARE NEW? WE HAVE NEW STUFF ON US, TOO!
I JUST REMEMBERED! I TOOTED WHEN ALL THIS STARTED.
SO YOUR TOOT CLOUD SHIELDED US! NICE!

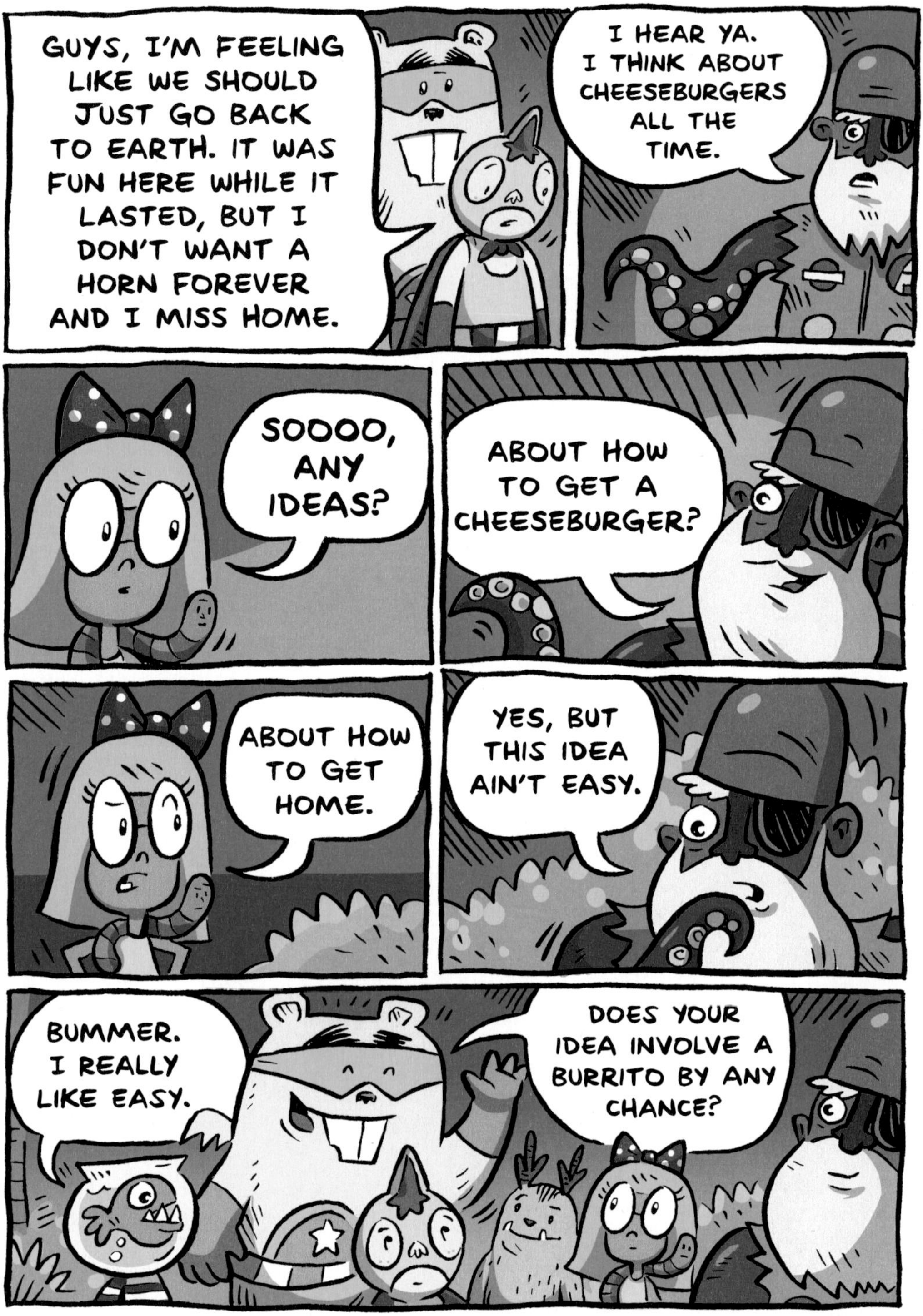
GUYS, I'M FEELING LIKE WE SHOULD JUST GO BACK TO EARTH. IT WAS FUN HERE WHILE IT LASTED, BUT I DON'T WANT A HORN FOREVER AND I MISS HOME.
I HEAR YA. I THINK ABOUT CHEESEBURGERS ALL THE TIME.
SOOOO, ANY IDEAS?
ABOUT HOW TO GET A CHEESEBURGER?
ABOUT HOW TO GET HOME.
YES, BUT THIS IDEA AIN'T EASY.
BUMMER. I REALLY LIKE EASY.
DOES YOUR IDEA INVOLVE A BURRITO BY ANY CHANCE?

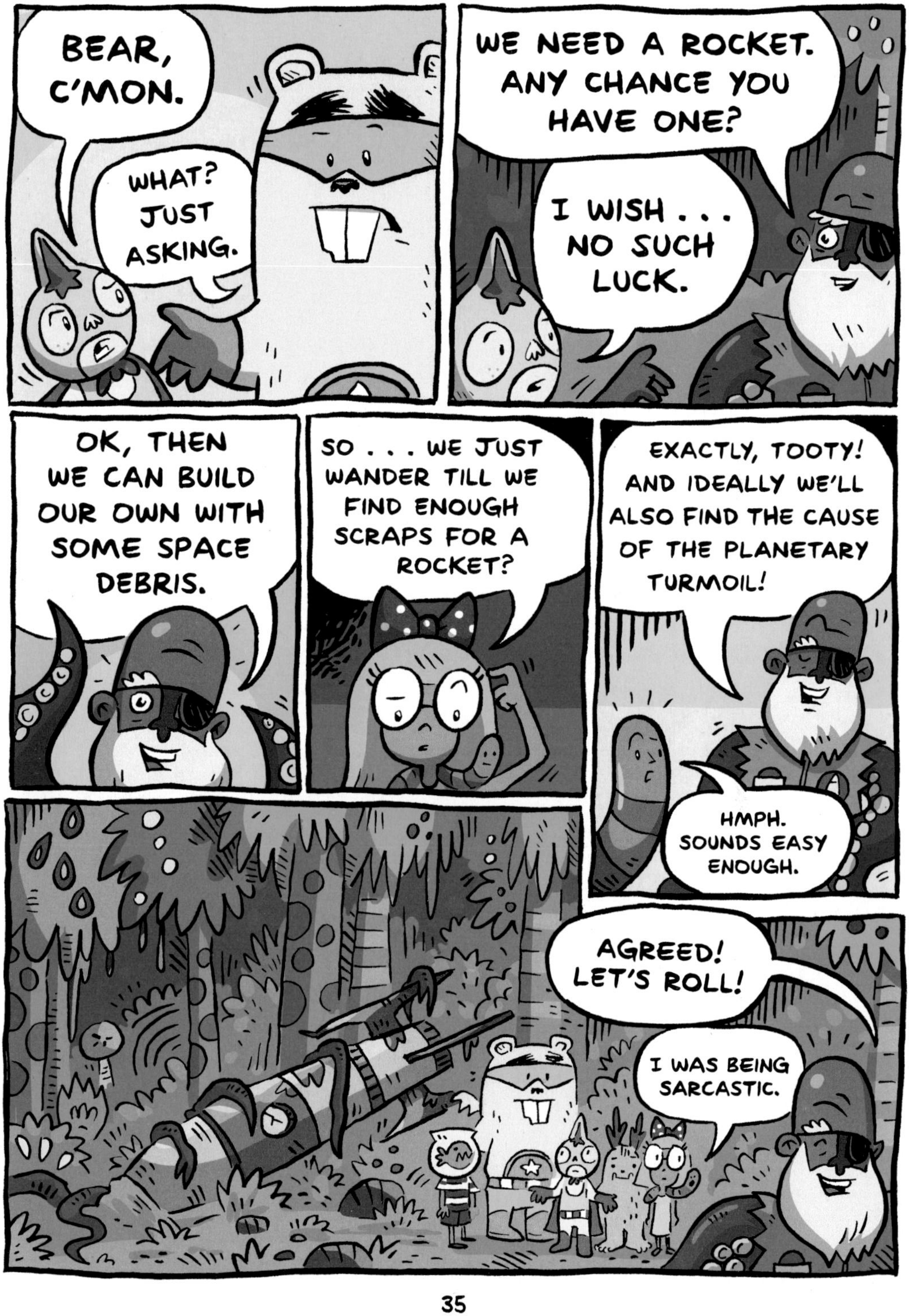
BEAR, C'MON.
WHAT? JUST ASKING.
WE NEED A ROCKET. ANY CHANCE YOU HAVE ONE?
I WISH . . . NO SUCH LUCK.
OK, THEN WE CAN BUILD OUR OWN WITH SOME SPACE DEBRIS.
SO . . . WE JUST WANDER TILL WE FIND ENOUGH SCRAPS FOR A ROCKET?
EXACTLY, TOOTY! AND IDEALLY WE'LL ALSO FIND THE CAUSE OF THE PLANETARY TURMOIL!
HMPH. SOUNDS EASY ENOUGH.
AGREED! LET'S ROLL!
I WAS BEING SARCASTIC.

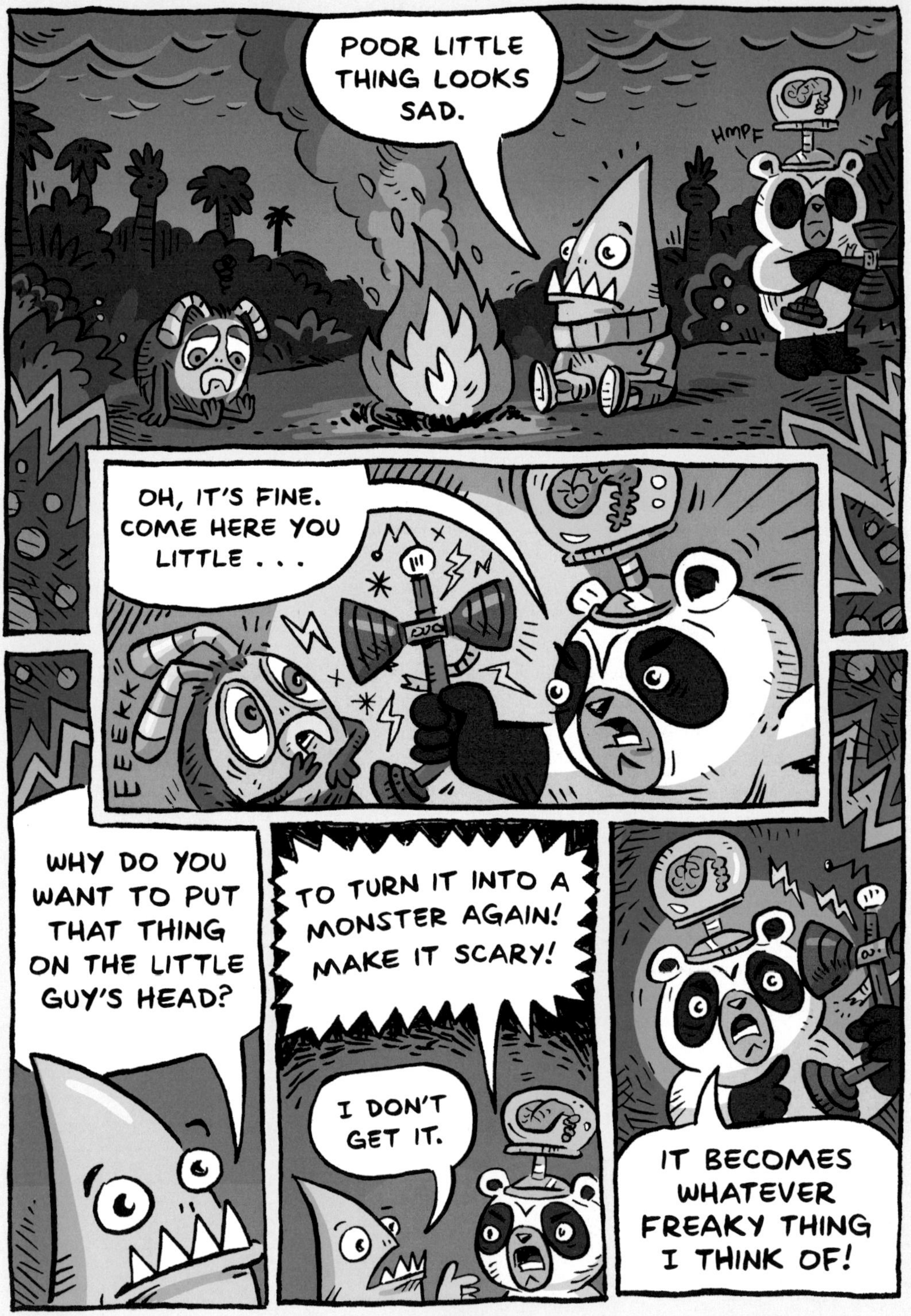
POOR LITTLE THING LOOKS SAD.
HMPF
OH, IT'S FINE. COME HERE YOU LITTLE . . .
EEEKK
WHY DO YOU WANT TO PUT THAT THING ON THE LITTLE GUY'S HEAD?
TO TURN IT INTO A MONSTER AGAIN! MAKE IT SCARY!
I DON'T GET IT.
IT BECOMES WHATEVER FREAKY THING I THINK OF!

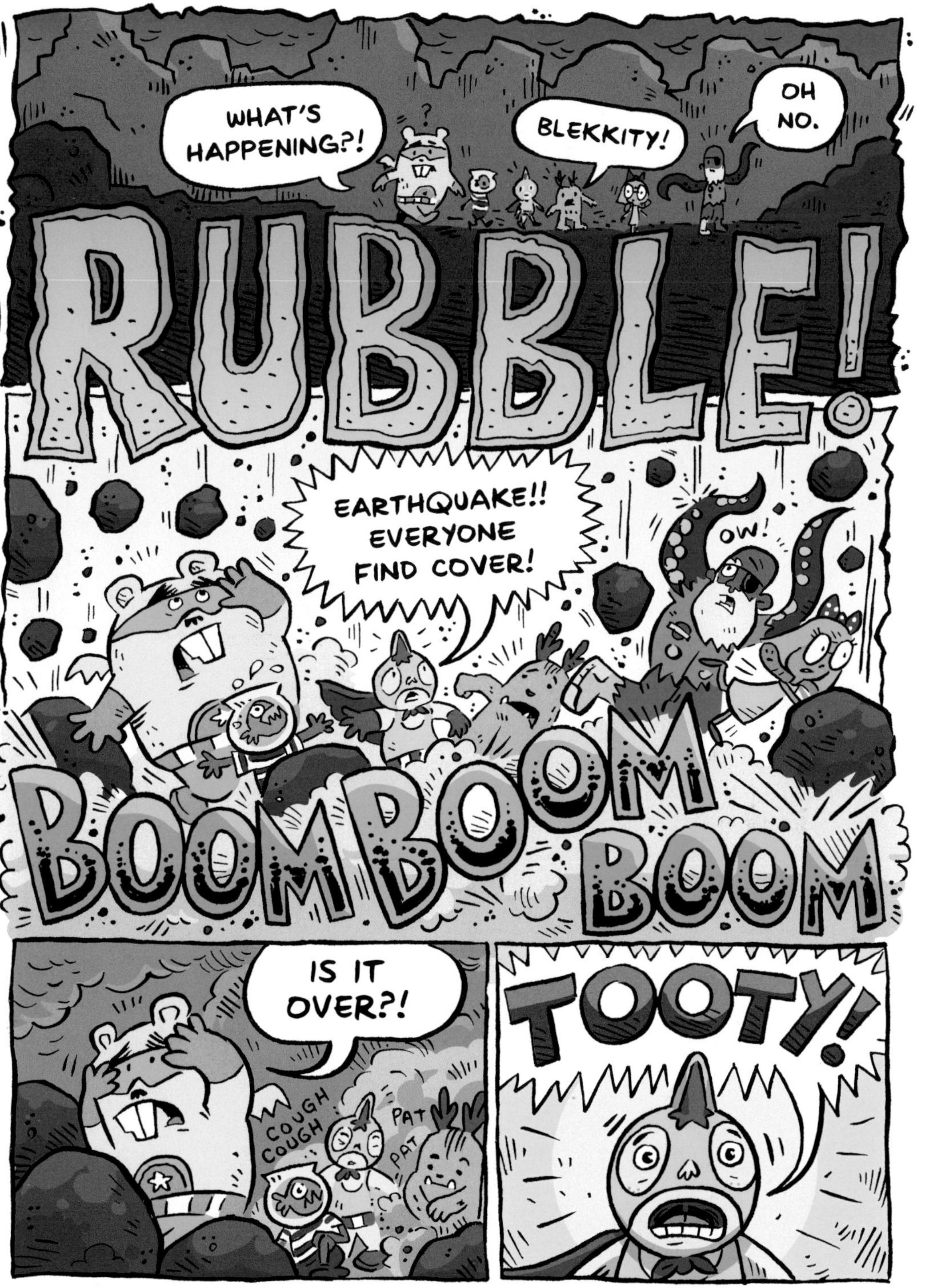
WHAT'S HAPPENING?!
BLEKKITY!
OH NO.
RUBBLE!
EARTHQUAKE!! EVERYONE FIND COVER!
OW!
BOOM BOOM BOOM
IS IT OVER?!
COUGH COUGH
PAT PAT
TOOTY!

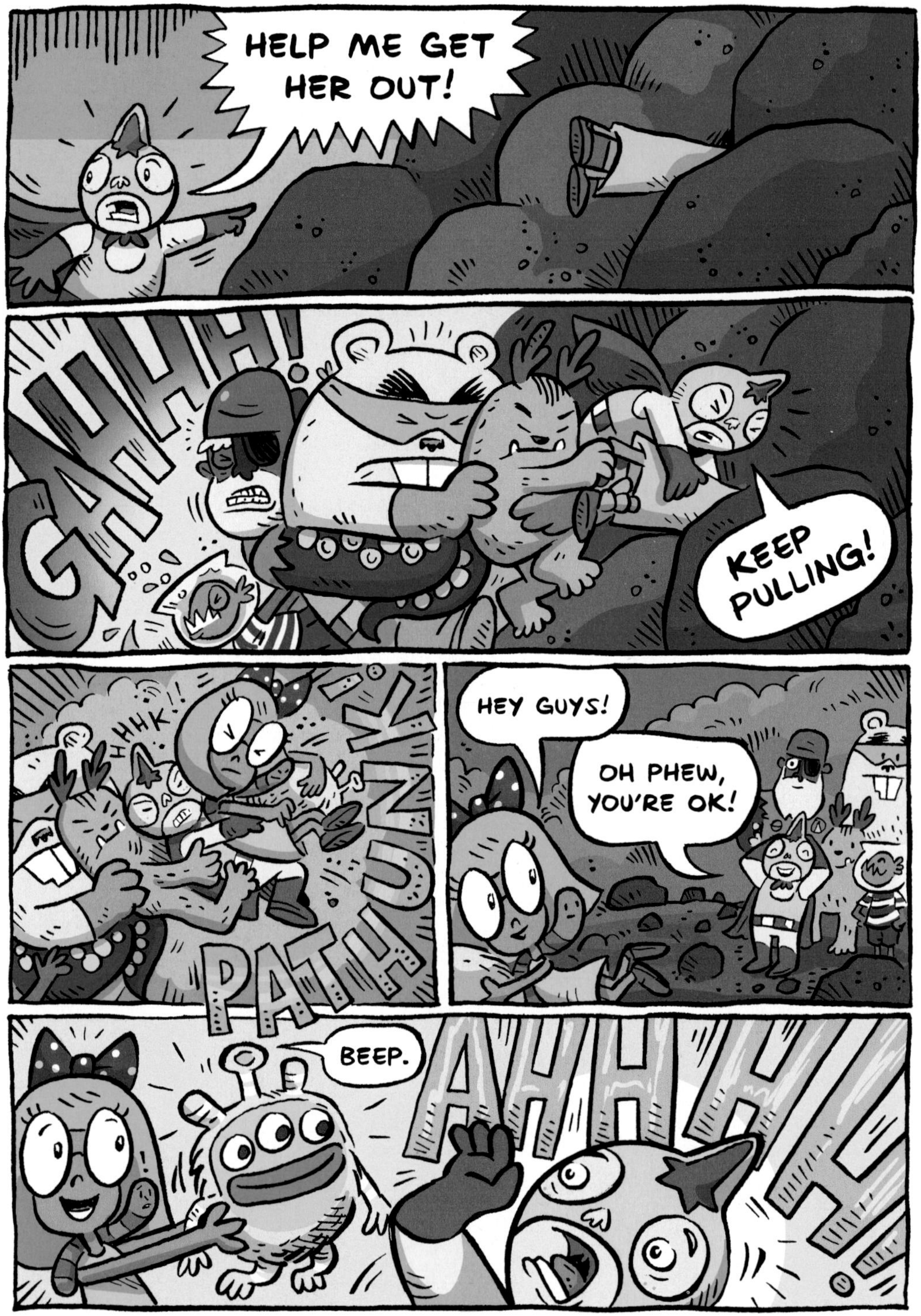

HELP ME GET HER OUT!
GAHHH!
KEEP PULLING!
HHHK!!
PATHUNK!
HEY GUYS!
OH PHEW, YOU'RE OK!
BEEP.
AHHHH!

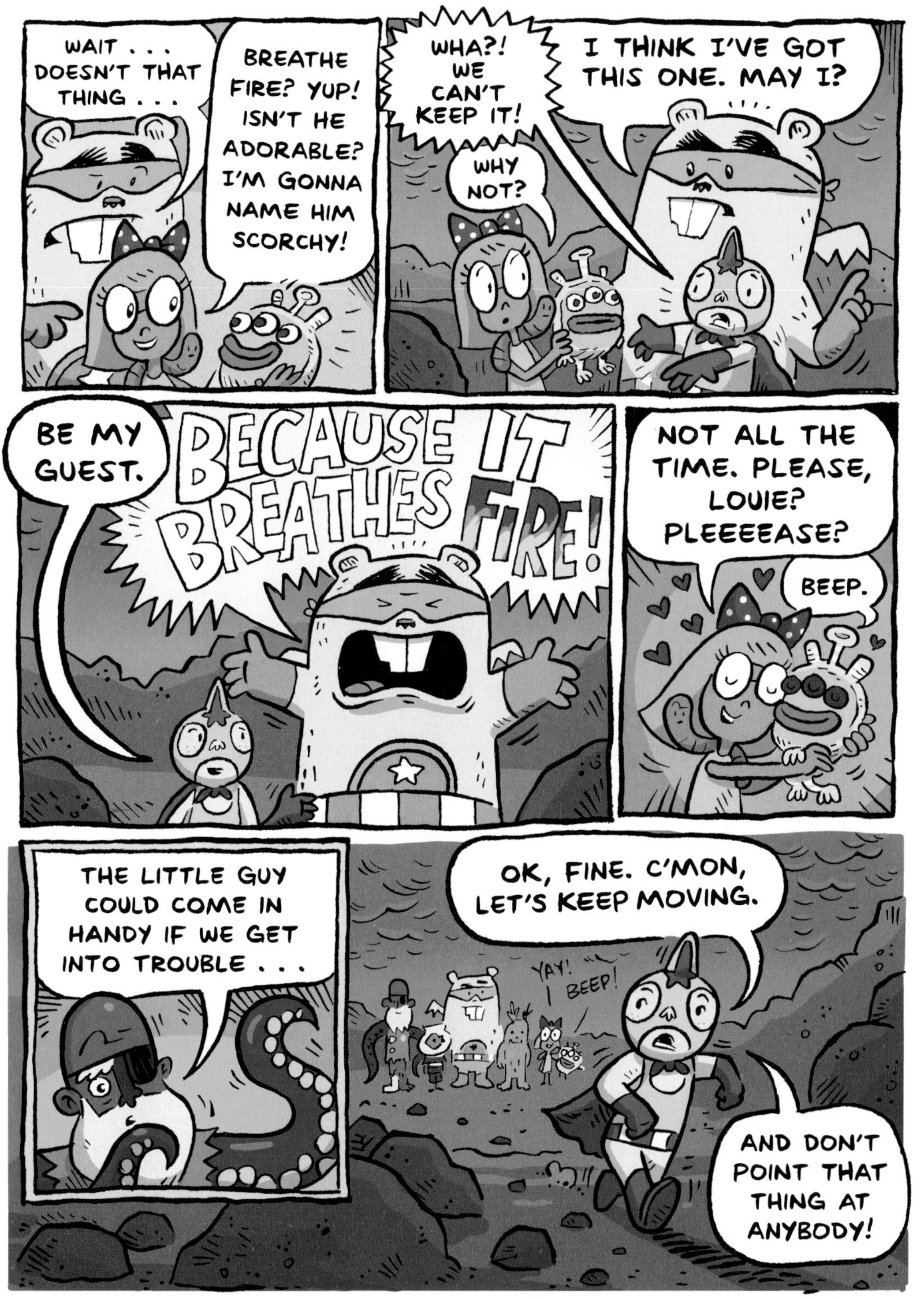
WAIT . . . DOESN'T THAT THING . . .
BREATHE FIRE? YUP! ISN'T HE ADORABLE? I'M GONNA NAME HIM SCORCHY!
WHA?! WE CAN'T KEEP IT!
WHY NOT?
I THINK I'VE GOT THIS ONE. MAY I?
BE MY GUEST.
BECAUSE IT BREATHES FIRE!
NOT ALL THE TIME. PLEASE, LOUIE? PLEEEEASE?
BEEP.
THE LITTLE GUY COULD COME IN HANDY IF WE GET INTO TROUBLE . . .
OK, FINE. C'MON, LET'S KEEP MOVING.
YAY!
BEEP!
AND DON'T POINT THAT THING AT ANYBODY!

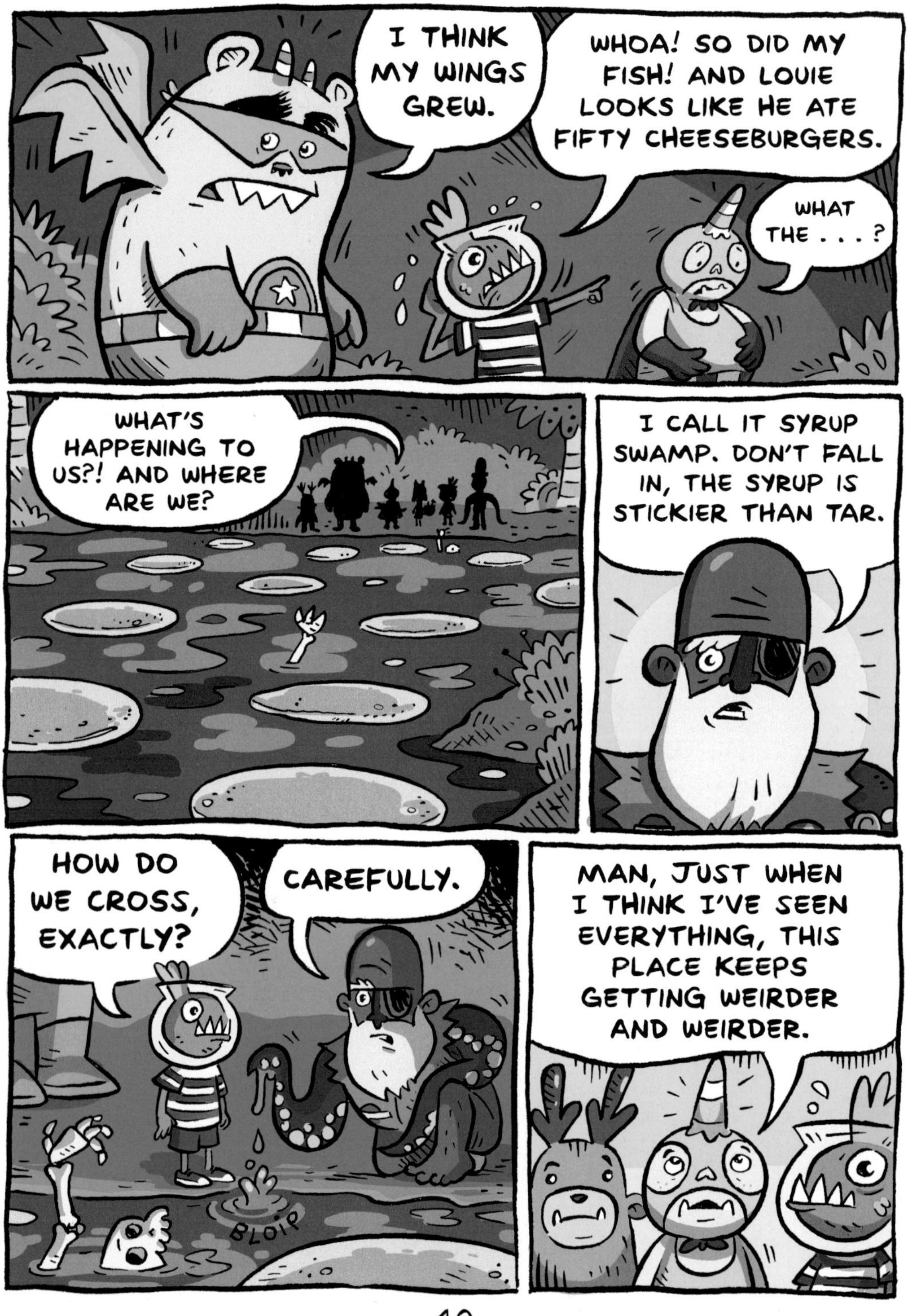
I THINK MY WINGS GREW.
WHOA! SO DID MY FISH! AND LOUIE LOOKS LIKE HE ATE FIFTY CHEESEBURGERS.
WHAT THE . . . ?
WHAT'S HAPPENING TO US?! AND WHERE ARE WE?
I CALL IT SYRUP SWAMP. DON'T FALL IN, THE SYRUP IS STICKIER THAN TAR.
HOW DO WE CROSS, EXACTLY?
CAREFULLY.
BLOIP
MAN, JUST WHEN I THINK I'VE SEEN EVERYTHING, THIS PLACE KEEPS GETTING WEIRDER AND WEIRDER.

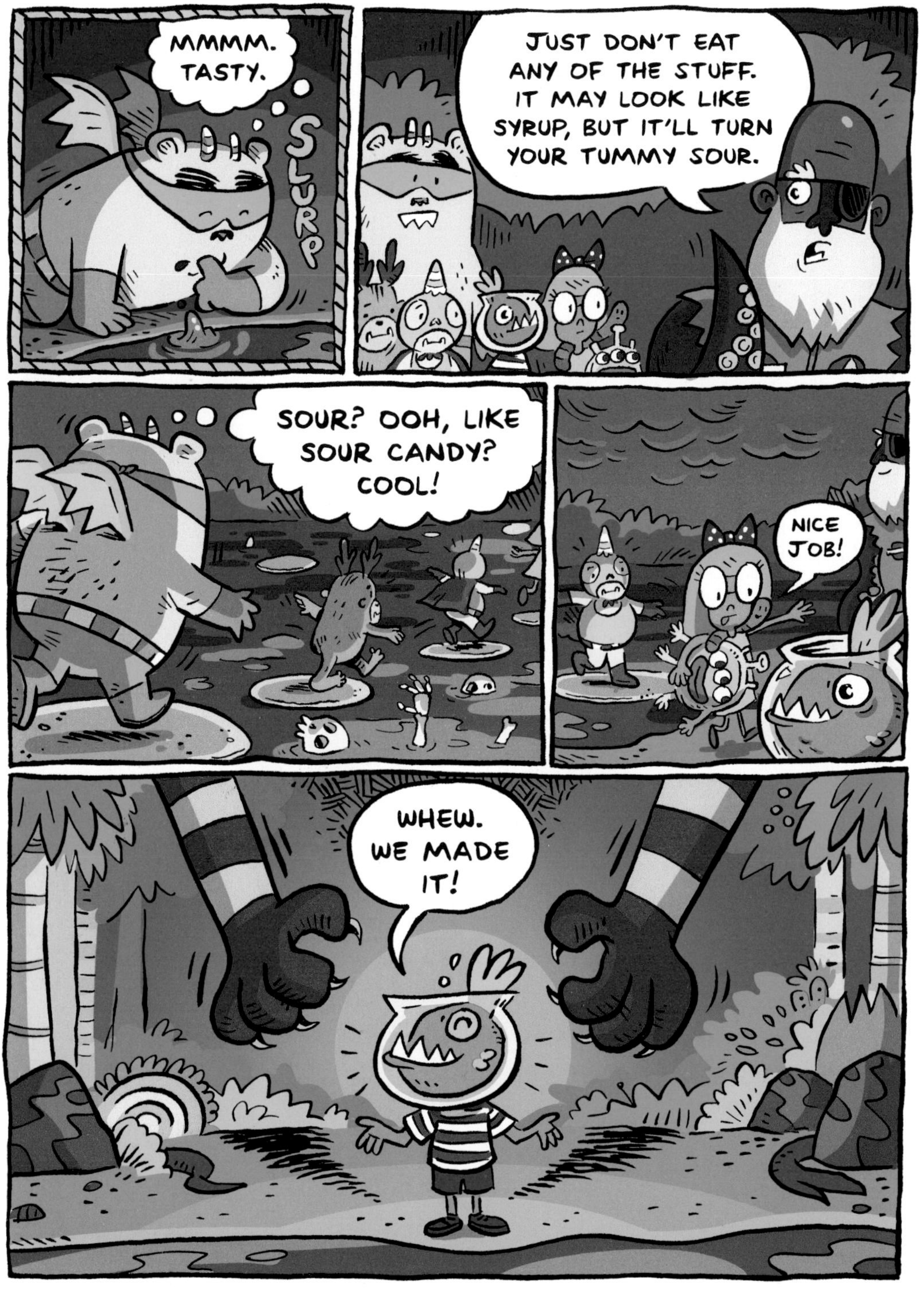
MMMM. TASTY.
SLURP
JUST DON'T EAT ANY OF THE STUFF. IT MAY LOOK LIKE SYRUP, BUT IT'LL TURN YOUR TUMMY SOUR.
SOUR? OOH, LIKE SOUR CANDY? COOL!
NICE JOB!
WHEW. WE MADE IT!

Chapter

5

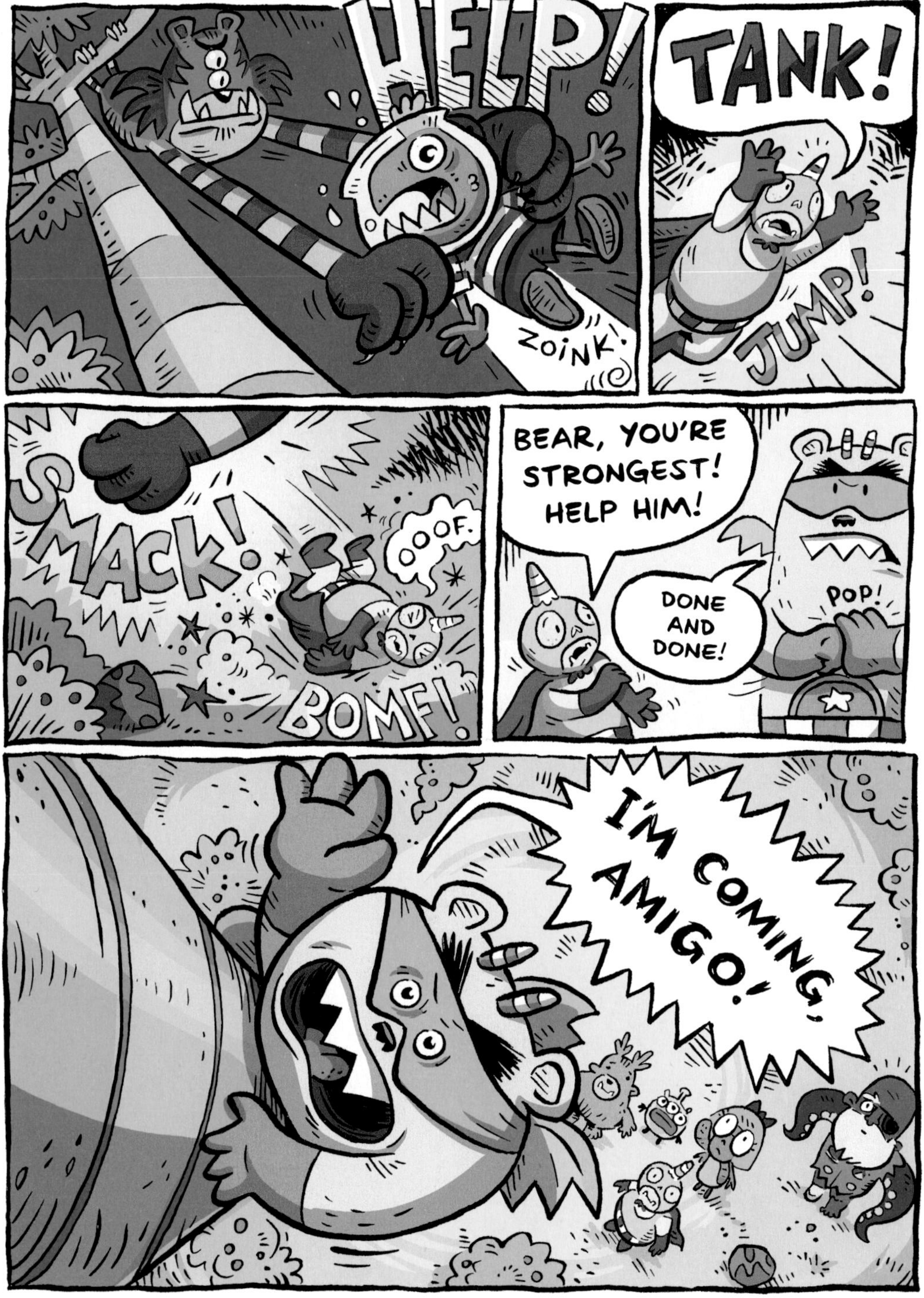
HELP!
ZOINK
TANK!
JUMP!
SMACK!
OOOF.
BOMF!
BEAR, YOU'RE STRONGEST! HELP HIM!
DONE AND DONE!
POP!
I'M COMING, AMIGO!

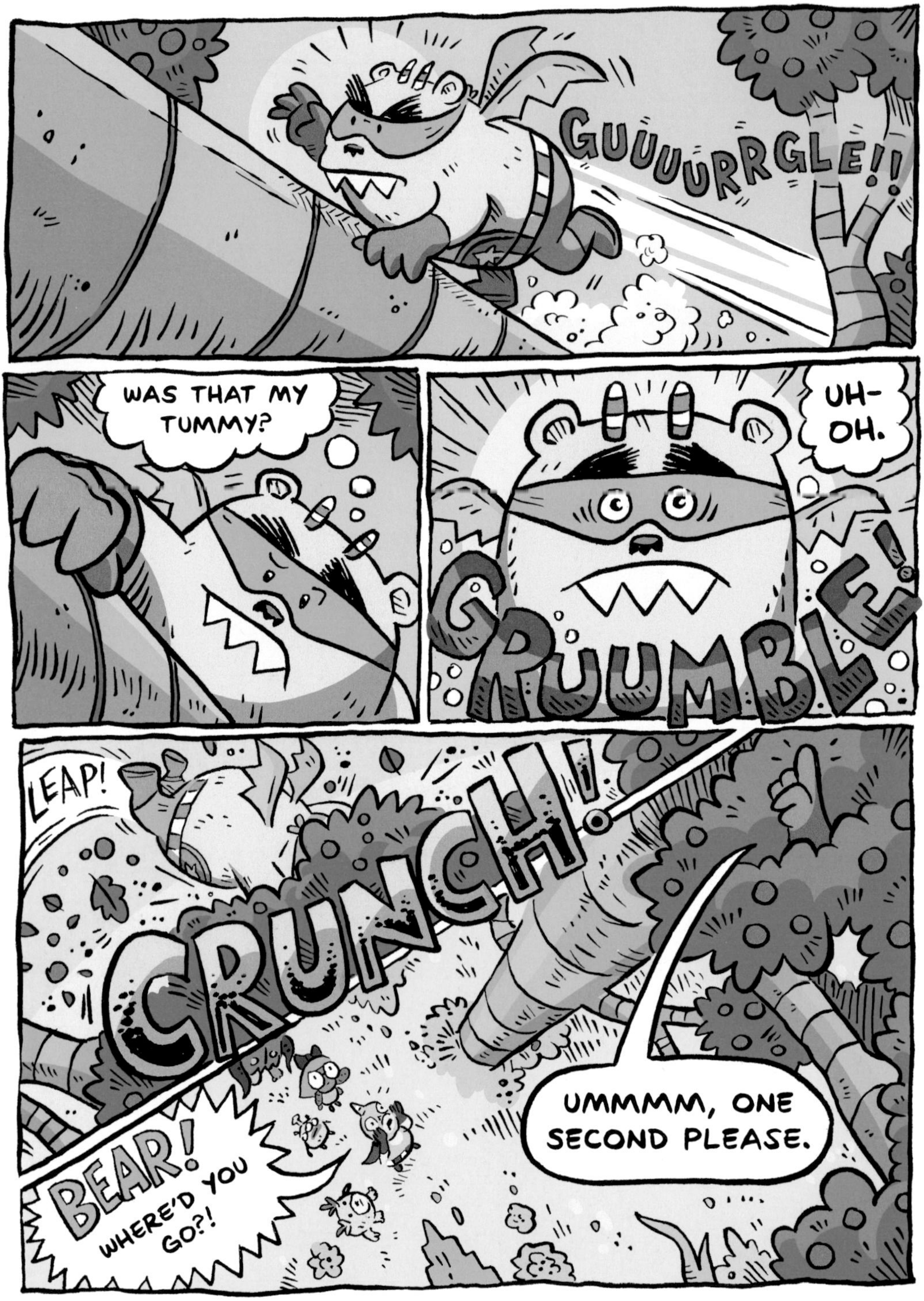
GUUUURRGLE!!
WAS THAT MY TUMMY?
UH-OH.
GRUUMBLE!
LEAP!
CRUNCH!
BEAR! WHERE'D YOU GO?!
UMMMM, ONE SECOND PLEASE.

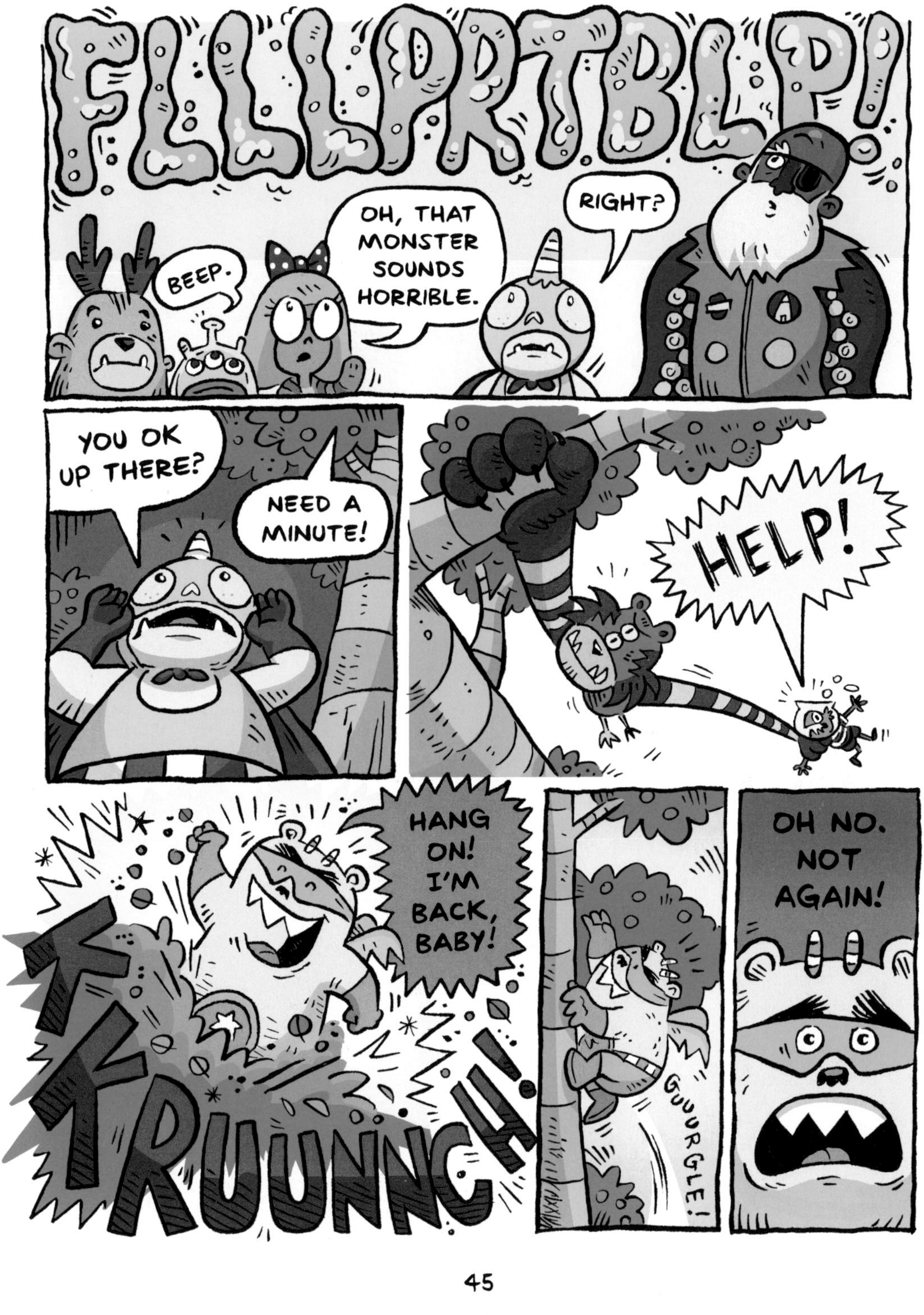
FLLLPRTBLP!
BEEP.
OH, THAT MONSTER SOUNDS HORRIBLE.
RIGHT?
YOU OK UP THERE?
NEED A MINUTE!
HELP!
HANG ON! I'M BACK, BABY!
KRUUNCH!!
GUUURGLE!
OH NO. NOT AGAIN!

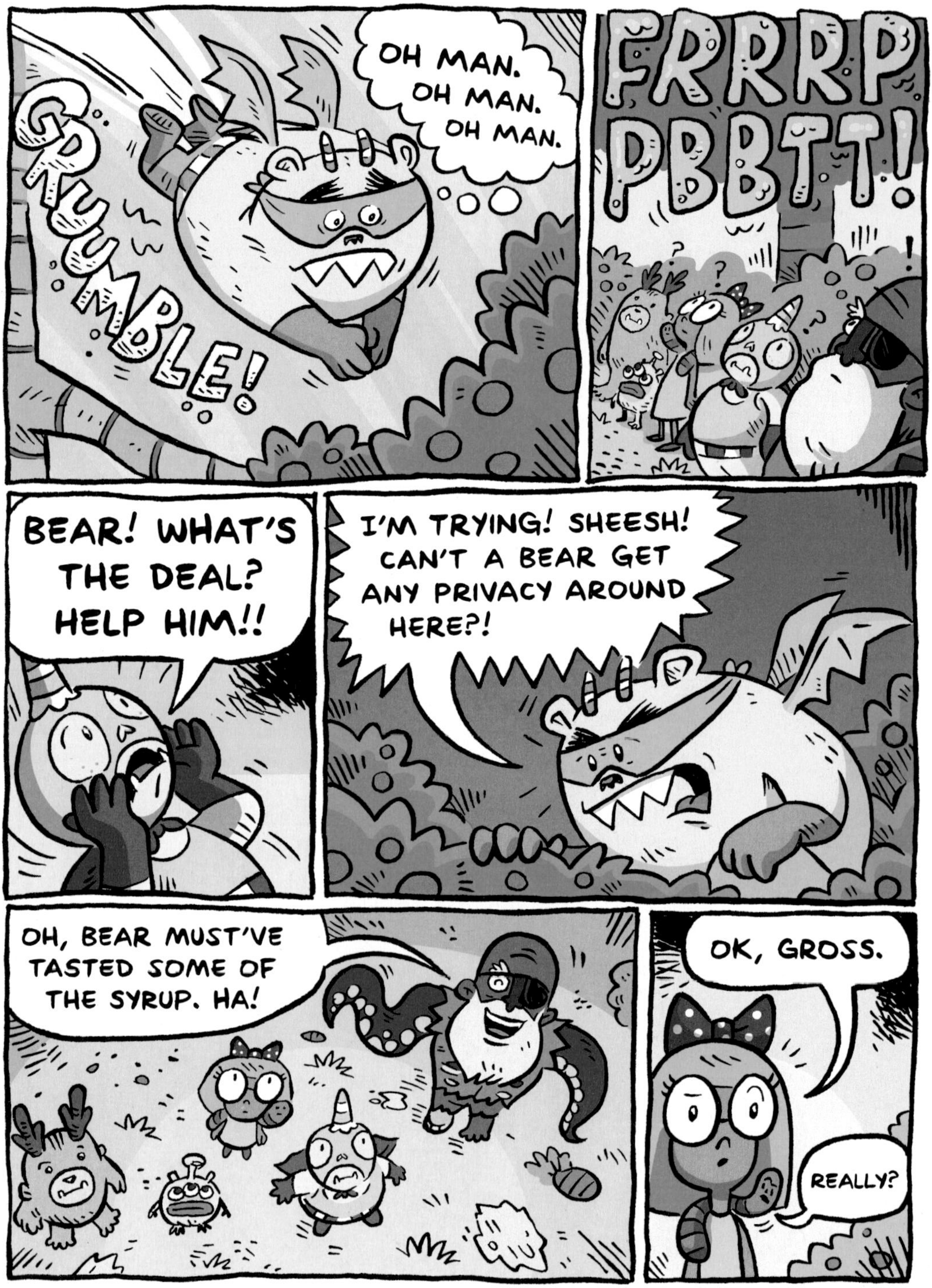

GRUMBLE!
OH MAN. OH MAN. OH MAN.
FRRRP PBBTT!
BEAR! WHAT'S THE DEAL? HELP HIM!!
I'M TRYING! SHEESH! CAN'T A BEAR GET ANY PRIVACY AROUND HERE?!
OH, BEAR MUST'VE TASTED SOME OF THE SYRUP. HA!
OK, GROSS.
REALLY?

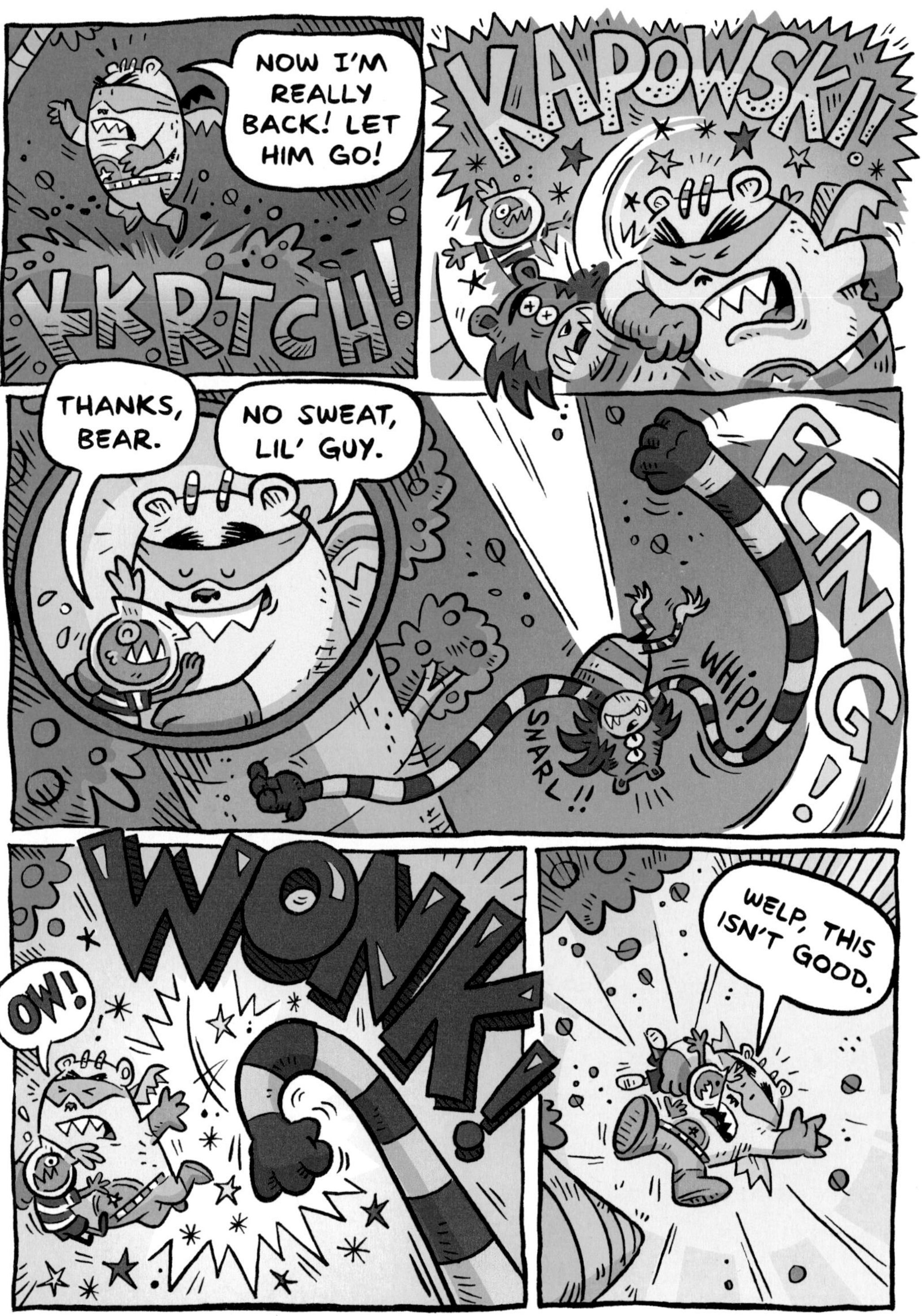
NOW I'M REALLY BACK! LET HIM GO!
KKRTCH!
KAPOWSKI!
THANKS, BEAR.
NO SWEAT, LIL' GUY.
FLING!
WHIP!
SNARL!!
WONK!
OW!
WELP, THIS ISN'T GOOD.

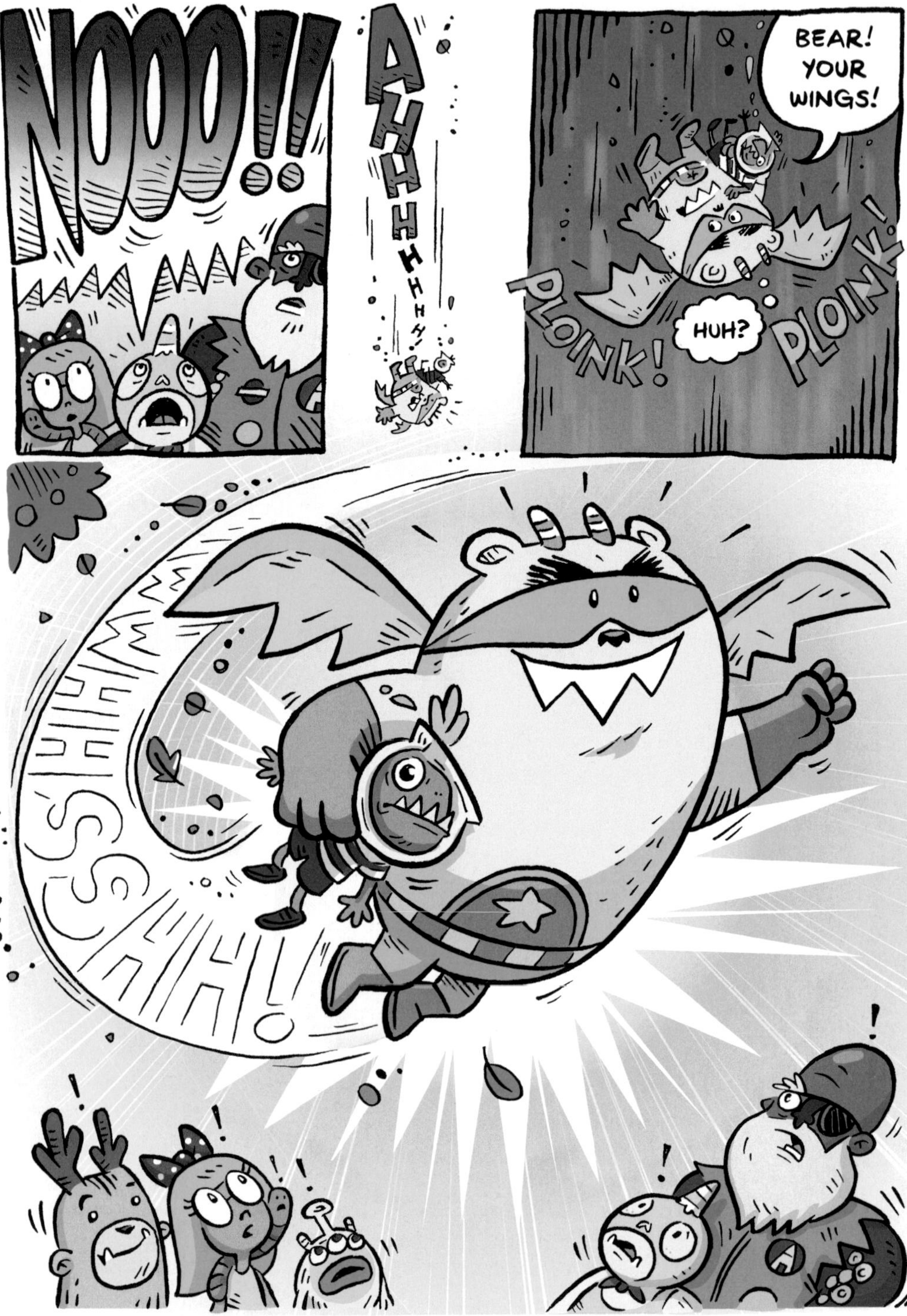
NOOO!!
AHHHHHHHH!
BEAR! YOUR WINGS!
PLOINK!
HUH?
PLOINK!
SHHHWWWSHHH!

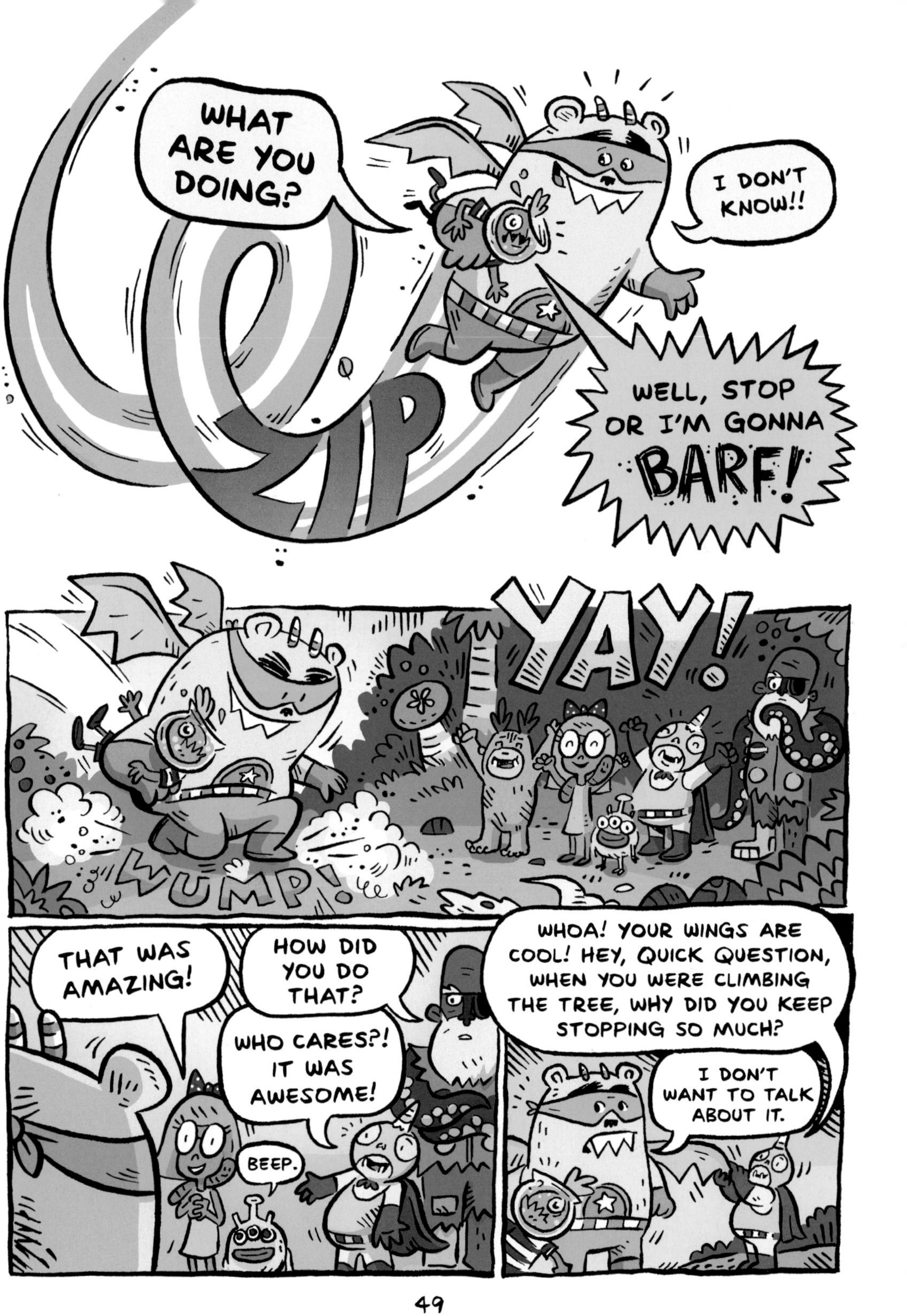
WHAT ARE YOU DOING?
ZIP
I DON'T KNOW!!
WELL, STOP OR I'M GONNA BARF!
YAY!
WUMP!
THAT WAS AMAZING!
HOW DID YOU DO THAT?
WHO CARES?! IT WAS AWESOME!
BEEP.
WHOA! YOUR WINGS ARE COOL! HEY, QUICK QUESTION, WHEN YOU WERE CLIMBING THE TREE, WHY DID YOU KEEP STOPPING SO MUCH?
I DON'T WANT TO TALK ABOUT IT.

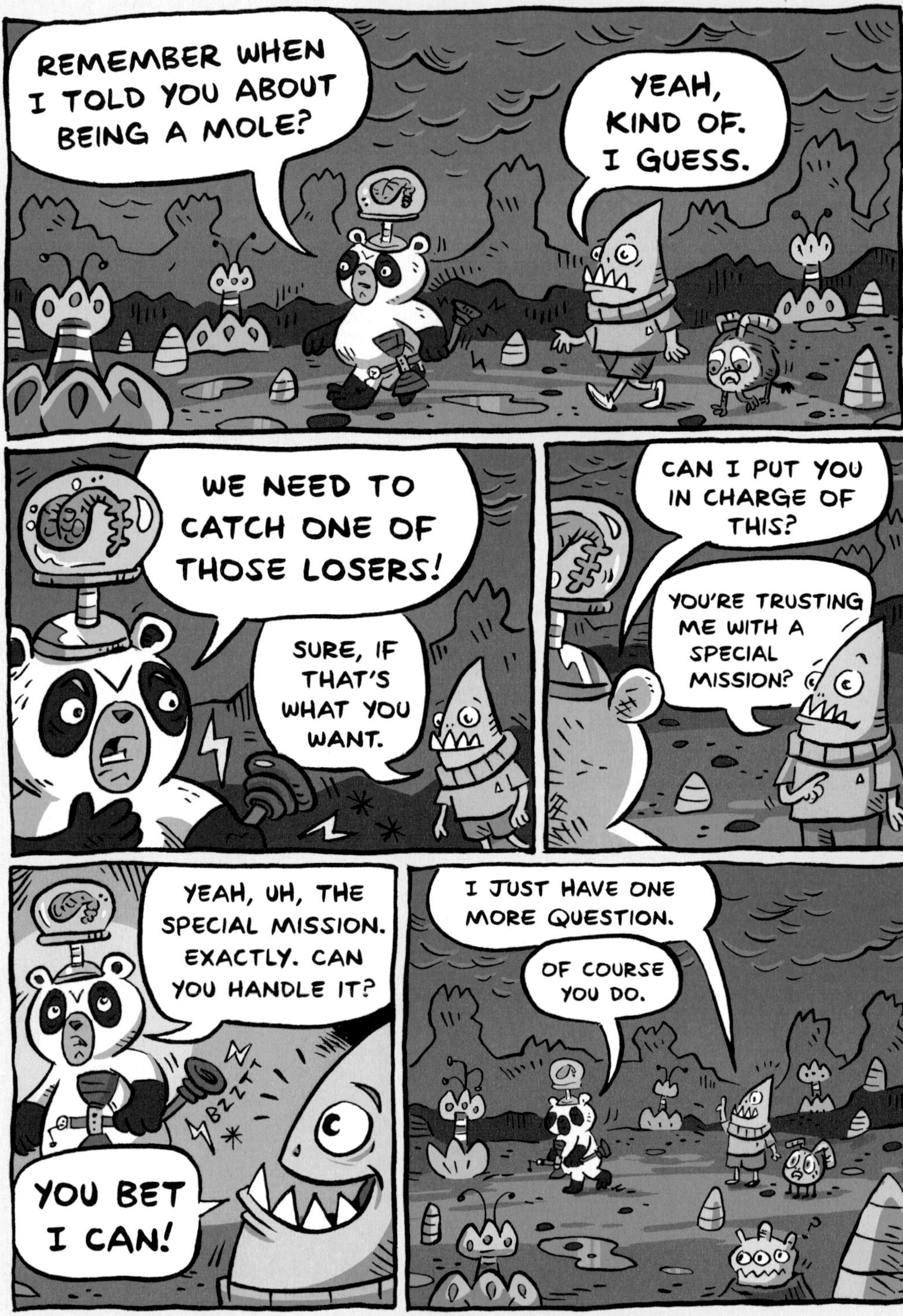
REMEMBER WHEN I TOLD YOU ABOUT BEING A MOLE?
YEAH, KIND OF. I GUESS.
WE NEED TO CATCH ONE OF THOSE LOSERS!
SURE, IF THAT'S WHAT YOU WANT.
CAN I PUT YOU IN CHARGE OF THIS?
YOU'RE TRUSTING ME WITH A SPECIAL MISSION?
YEAH, UH, THE SPECIAL MISSION. EXACTLY. CAN YOU HANDLE IT?
BZZZT
YOU BET I CAN!
I JUST HAVE ONE MORE QUESTION.
OF COURSE YOU DO.

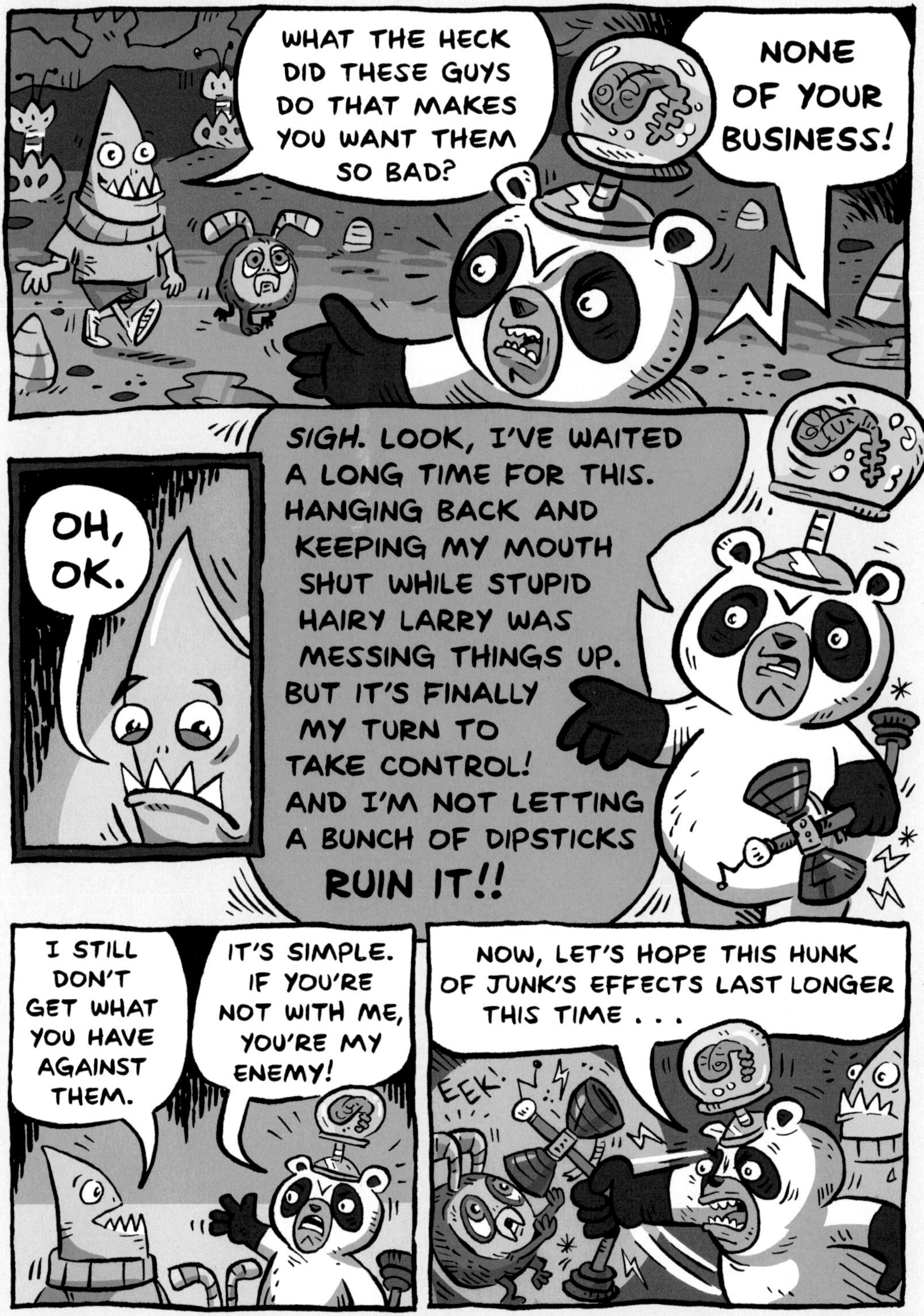

WHAT THE HECK DID THESE GUYS DO THAT MAKES YOU WANT THEM SO BAD?
NONE OF YOUR BUSINESS!
OH, OK.
SIGH. LOOK, I'VE WAITED A LONG TIME FOR THIS. HANGING BACK AND KEEPING MY MOUTH SHUT WHILE STUPID HAIRY LARRY WAS MESSING THINGS UP. BUT IT'S FINALLY MY TURN TO TAKE CONTROL! AND I'M NOT LETTING A BUNCH OF DIPSTICKS RUIN IT!!
I STILL DON'T GET WHAT YOU HAVE AGAINST THEM.
IT'S SIMPLE. IF YOU'RE NOT WITH ME, YOU'RE MY ENEMY!
NOW, LET'S HOPE THIS HUNK OF JUNK'S EFFECTS LAST LONGER THIS TIME . . .
EEK!

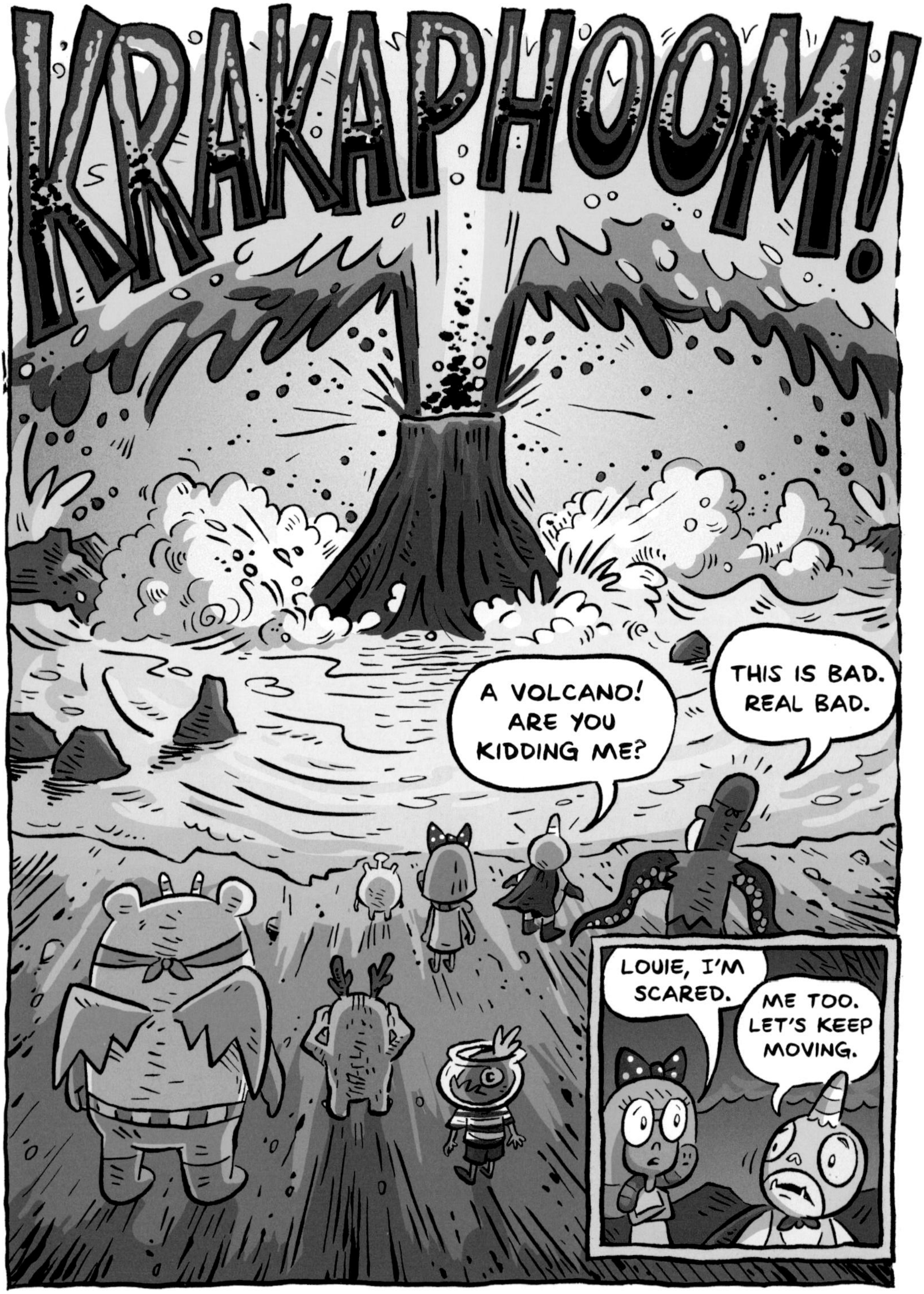
KRAKAPHOOM!
A VOLCANO! ARE YOU KIDDING ME?
THIS IS BAD. REAL BAD.
LOUIE, I'M SCARED.
ME TOO. LET'S KEEP MOVING.

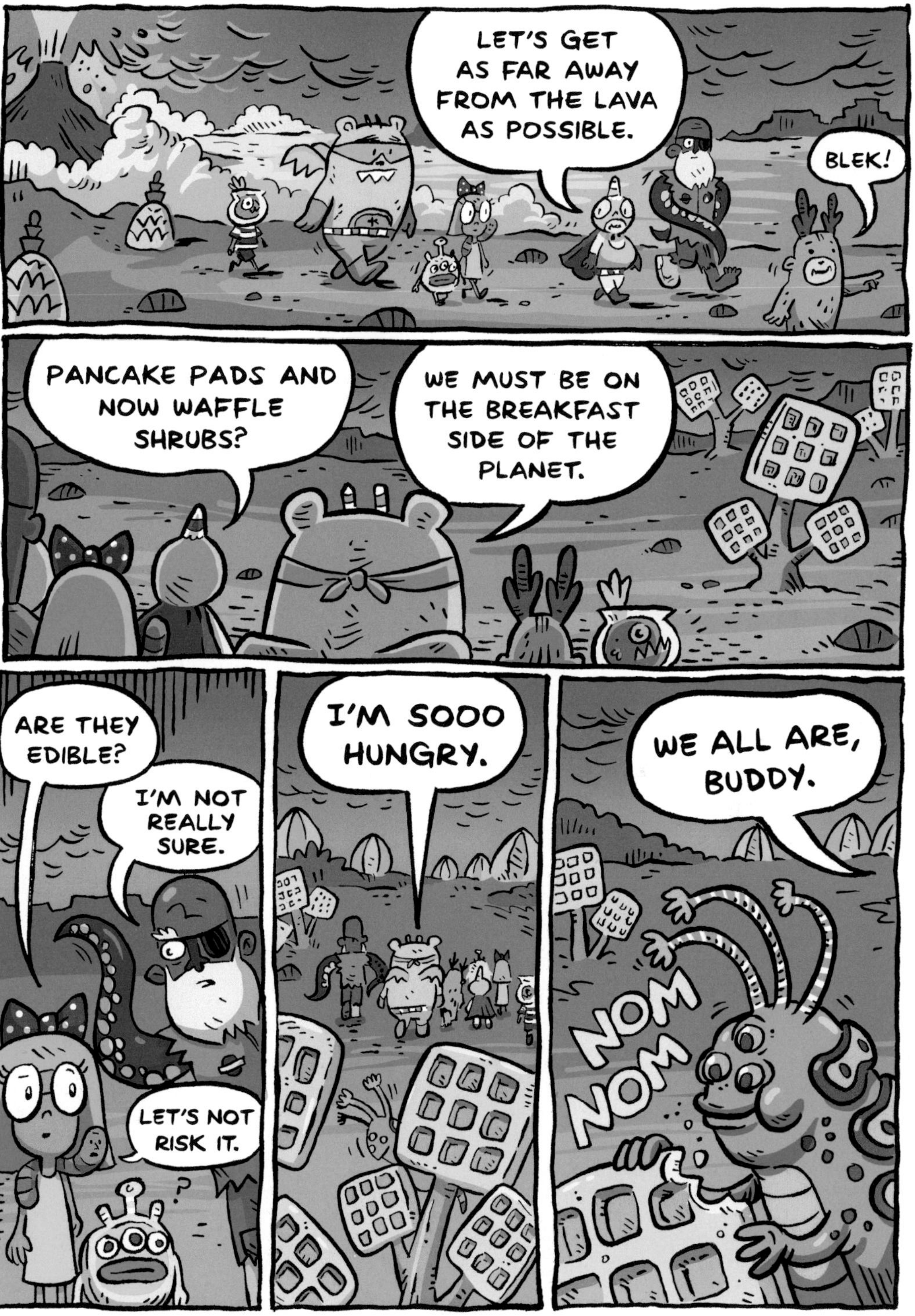
LET'S GET AS FAR AWAY FROM THE LAVA AS POSSIBLE.
BLEK!
PANCAKE PADS AND NOW WAFFLE SHRUBS?
WE MUST BE ON THE BREAKFAST SIDE OF THE PLANET.
ARE THEY EDIBLE?
I'M NOT REALLY SURE.
LET'S NOT RISK IT.
?
I'M SOOO HUNGRY.
WE ALL ARE, BUDDY.
NOM NOM

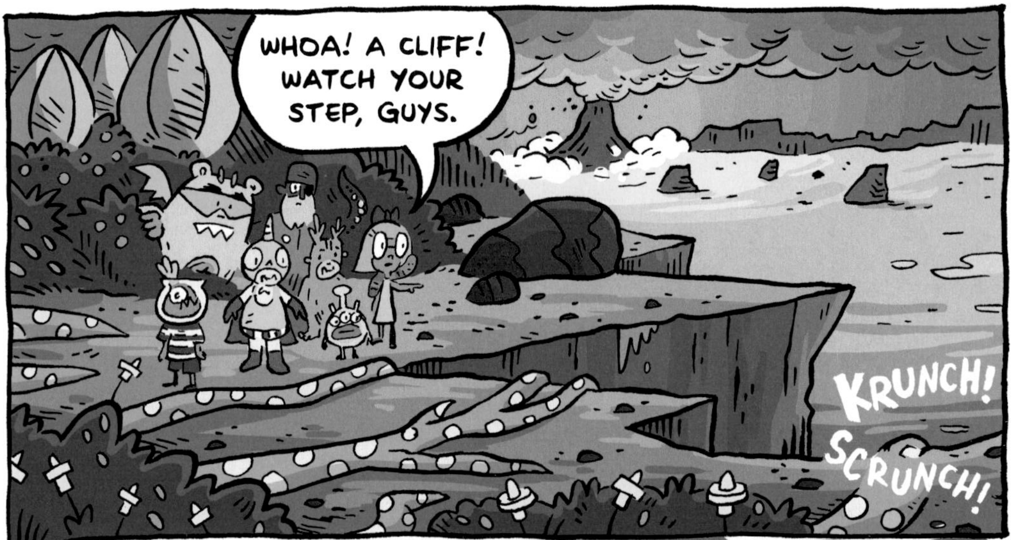
WHOA! A CLIFF! WATCH YOUR STEP, GUYS.
KRUNCH!
SCRUNCH!

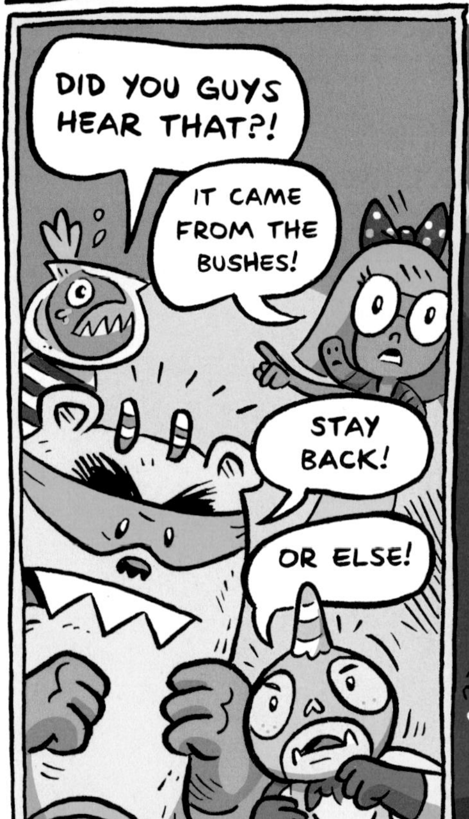
DID YOU GUYS HEAR THAT?!
IT CAME FROM THE BUSHES!
STAY BACK!
OR ELSE!

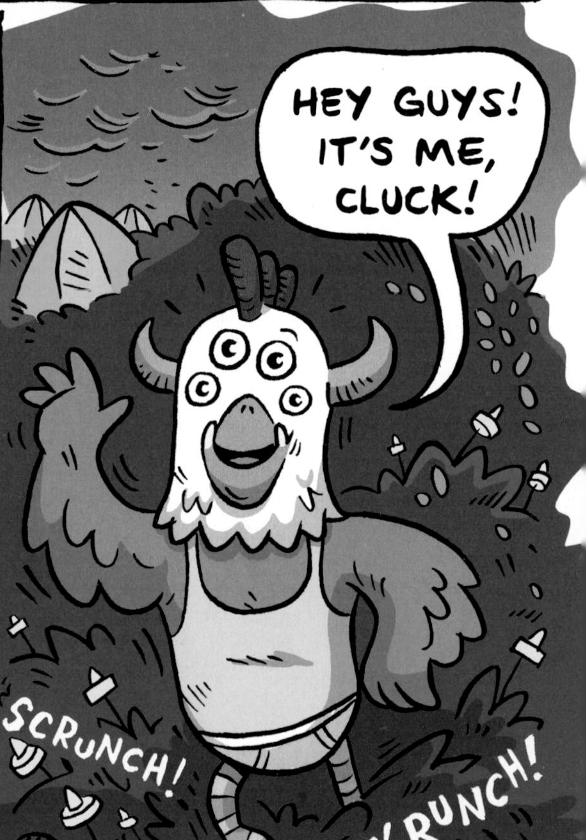
HEY GUYS! IT'S ME, CLUCK!
SCRUNCH!
KRUNCH!

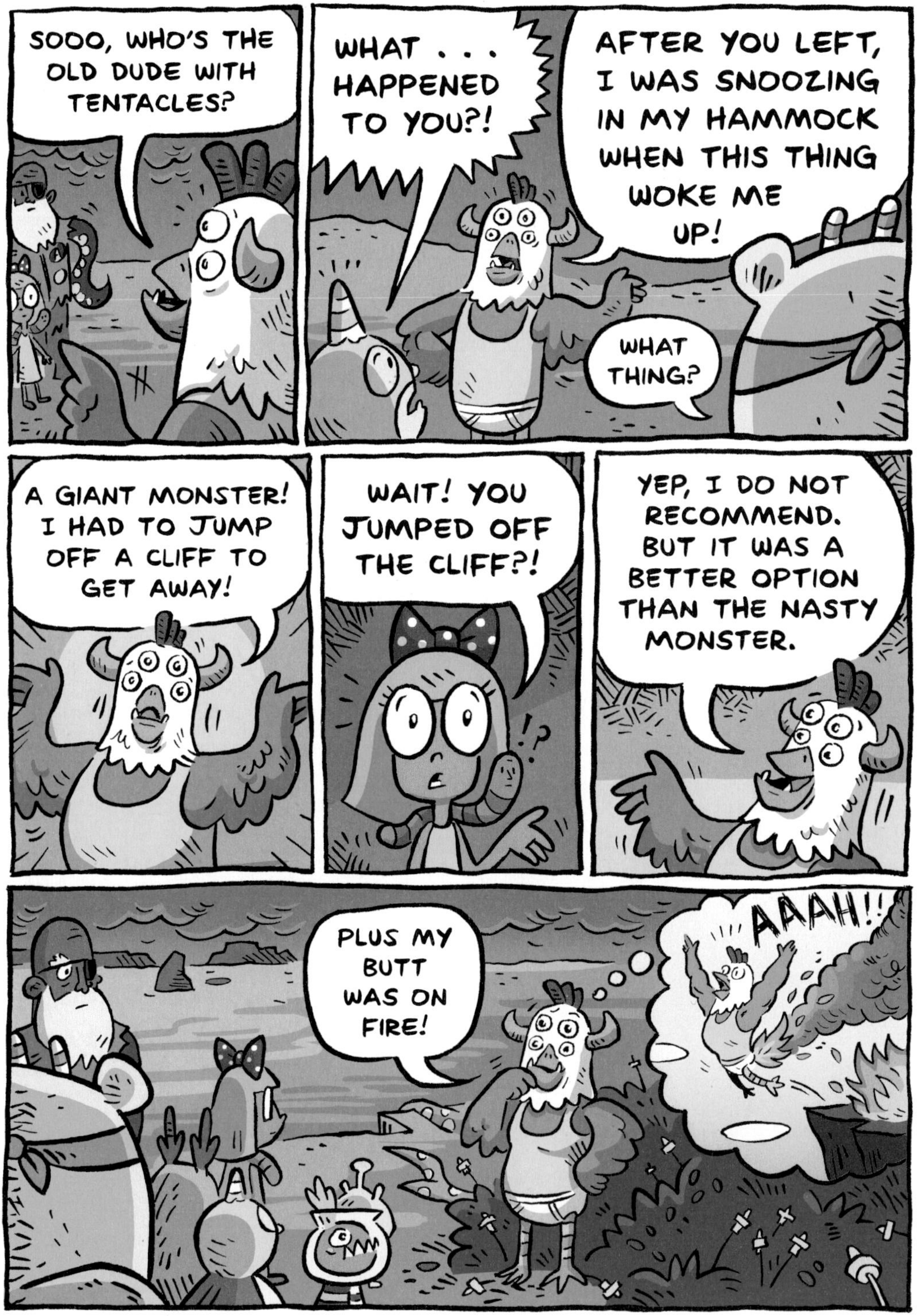
SOOO, WHO'S THE OLD DUDE WITH TENTACLES?
WHAT . . . HAPPENED TO YOU?!
AFTER YOU LEFT, I WAS SNOOZING IN MY HAMMOCK WHEN THIS THING WOKE ME UP!
WHAT THING?
A GIANT MONSTER! I HAD TO JUMP OFF A CLIFF TO GET AWAY!
WAIT! YOU JUMPED OFF THE CLIFF?!
!?
YEP, I DO NOT RECOMMEND. BUT IT WAS A BETTER OPTION THAN THE NASTY MONSTER.
PLUS MY BUTT WAS ON FIRE!
AAAH!!

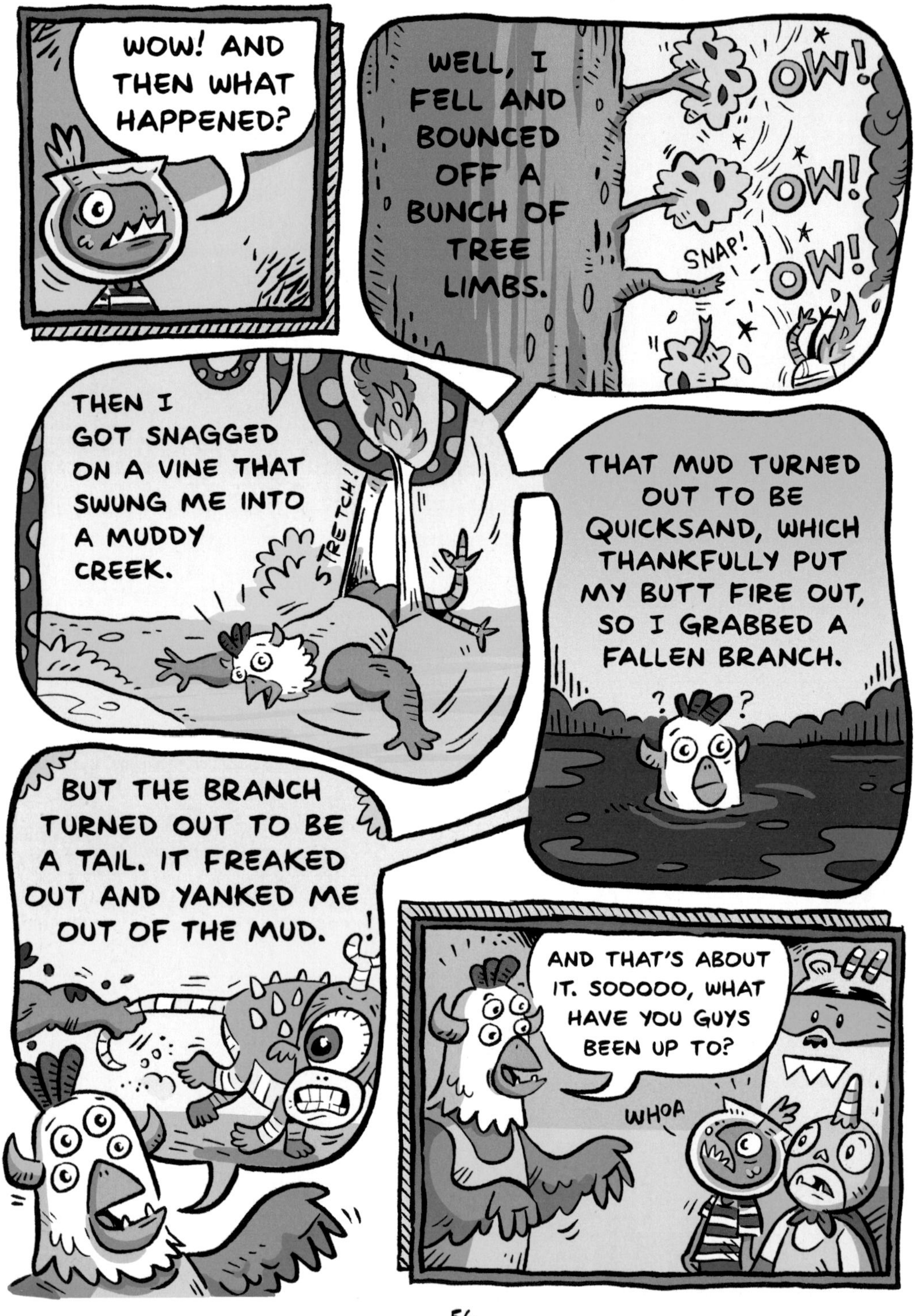
WOW! AND THEN WHAT HAPPENED?
WELL, I FELL AND BOUNCED OFF A BUNCH OF TREE LIMBS.
OW!
OW!
SNAP!
OW!
THEN I GOT SNAGGED ON A VINE THAT SWUNG ME INTO A MUDDY CREEK.
STRETCH!
THAT MUD TURNED OUT TO BE QUICKSAND, WHICH THANKFULLY PUT MY BUTT FIRE OUT, SO I GRABBED A FALLEN BRANCH.
? ?
BUT THE BRANCH TURNED OUT TO BE A TAIL. IT FREAKED OUT AND YANKED ME OUT OF THE MUD.
!
AND THAT'S ABOUT IT. SOOOOO, WHAT HAVE YOU GUYS BEEN UP TO?
WHOA

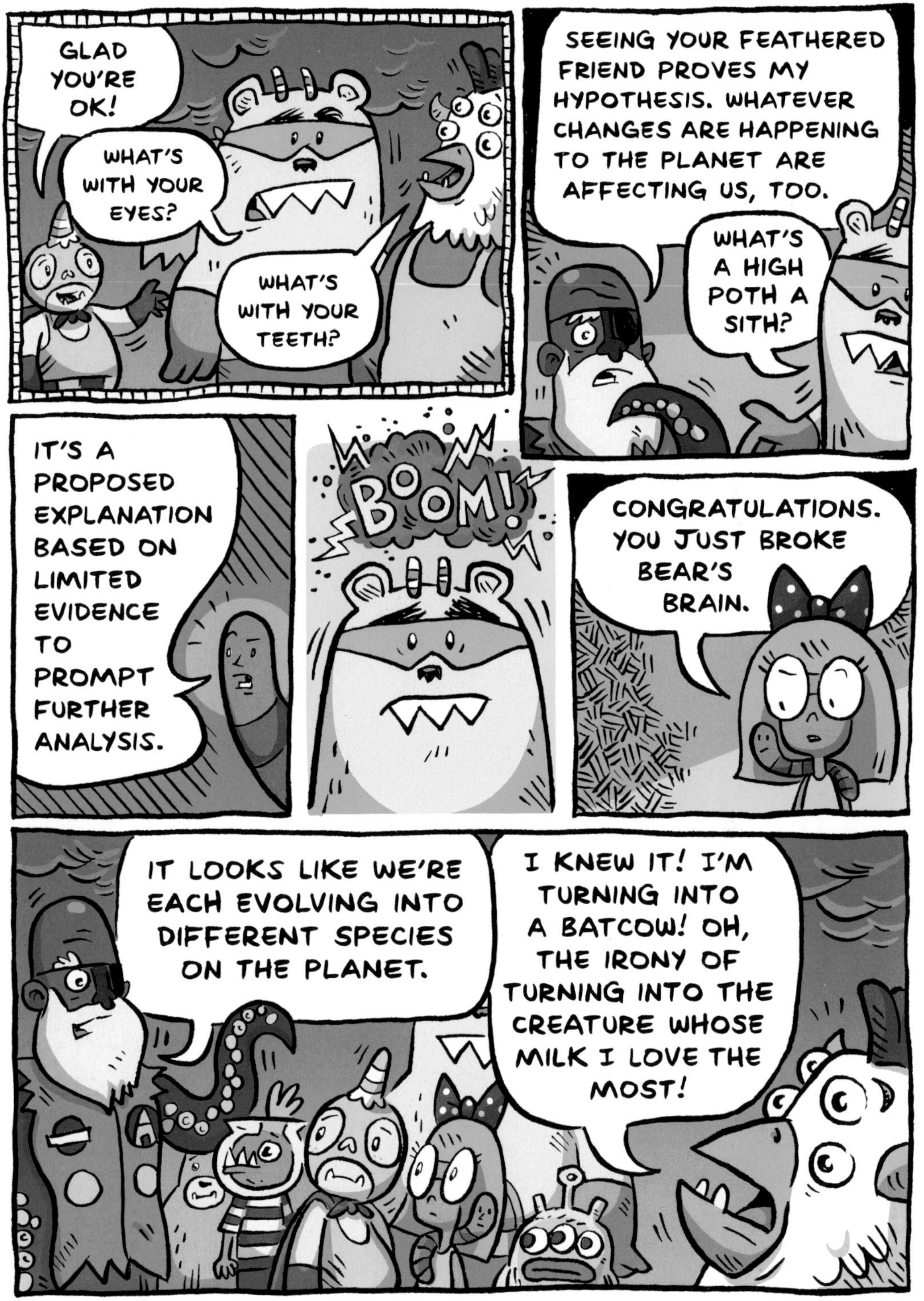
GLAD YOU'RE OK!
WHAT'S WITH YOUR EYES?
WHAT'S WITH YOUR TEETH?
SEEING YOUR FEATHERED FRIEND PROVES MY HYPOTHESIS. WHATEVER CHANGES ARE HAPPENING TO THE PLANET ARE AFFECTING US, TOO.
WHAT'S A HIGH POTH A SITH?
IT'S A PROPOSED EXPLANATION BASED ON LIMITED EVIDENCE TO PROMPT FURTHER ANALYSIS.
BOOM!
CONGRATULATIONS. YOU JUST BROKE BEAR'S BRAIN.
IT LOOKS LIKE WE'RE EACH EVOLVING INTO DIFFERENT SPECIES ON THE PLANET.
I KNEW IT! I'M TURNING INTO A BATCOW! OH, THE IRONY OF TURNING INTO THE CREATURE WHOSE MILK I LOVE THE MOST!

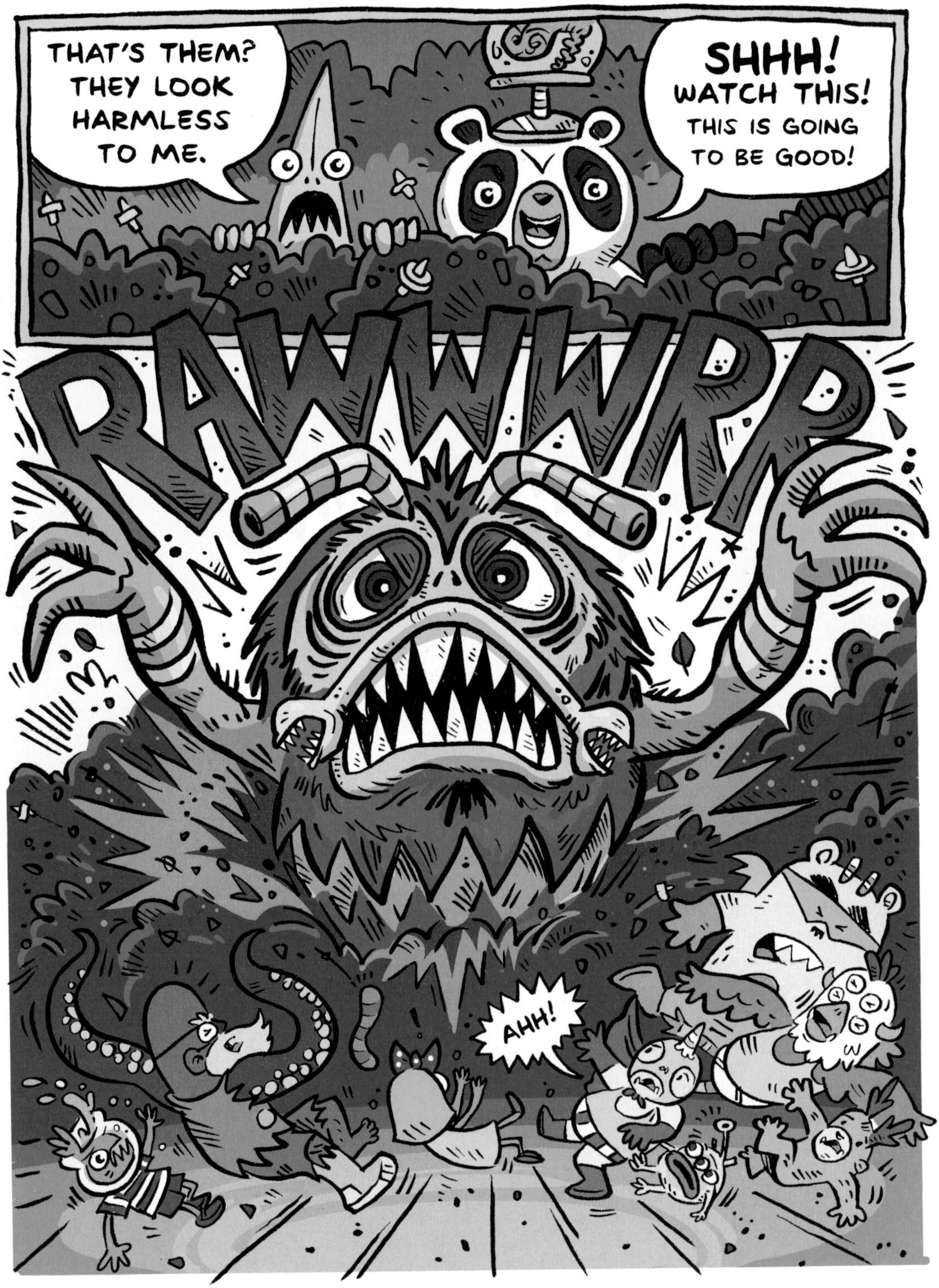
THAT'S THEM? THEY LOOK HARMLESS TO ME.
SHHH! WATCH THIS! THIS IS GOING TO BE GOOD!
RAWWWRR
AHH!

Chapter 6

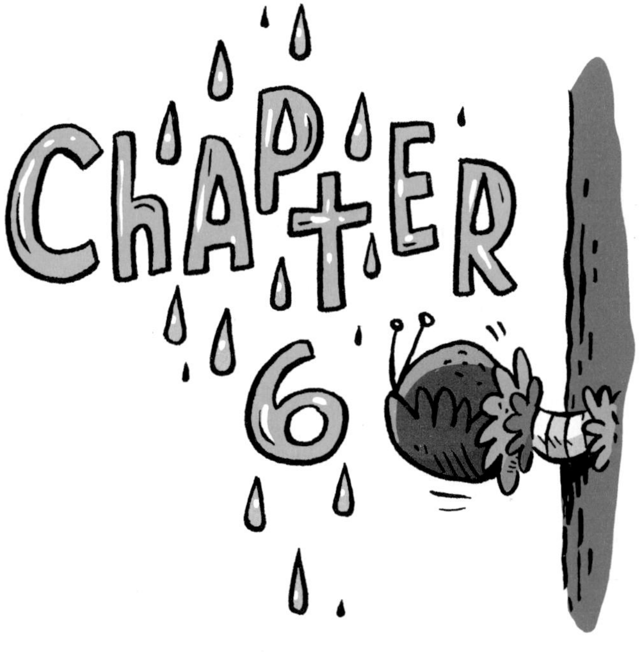
ChAPtER
6

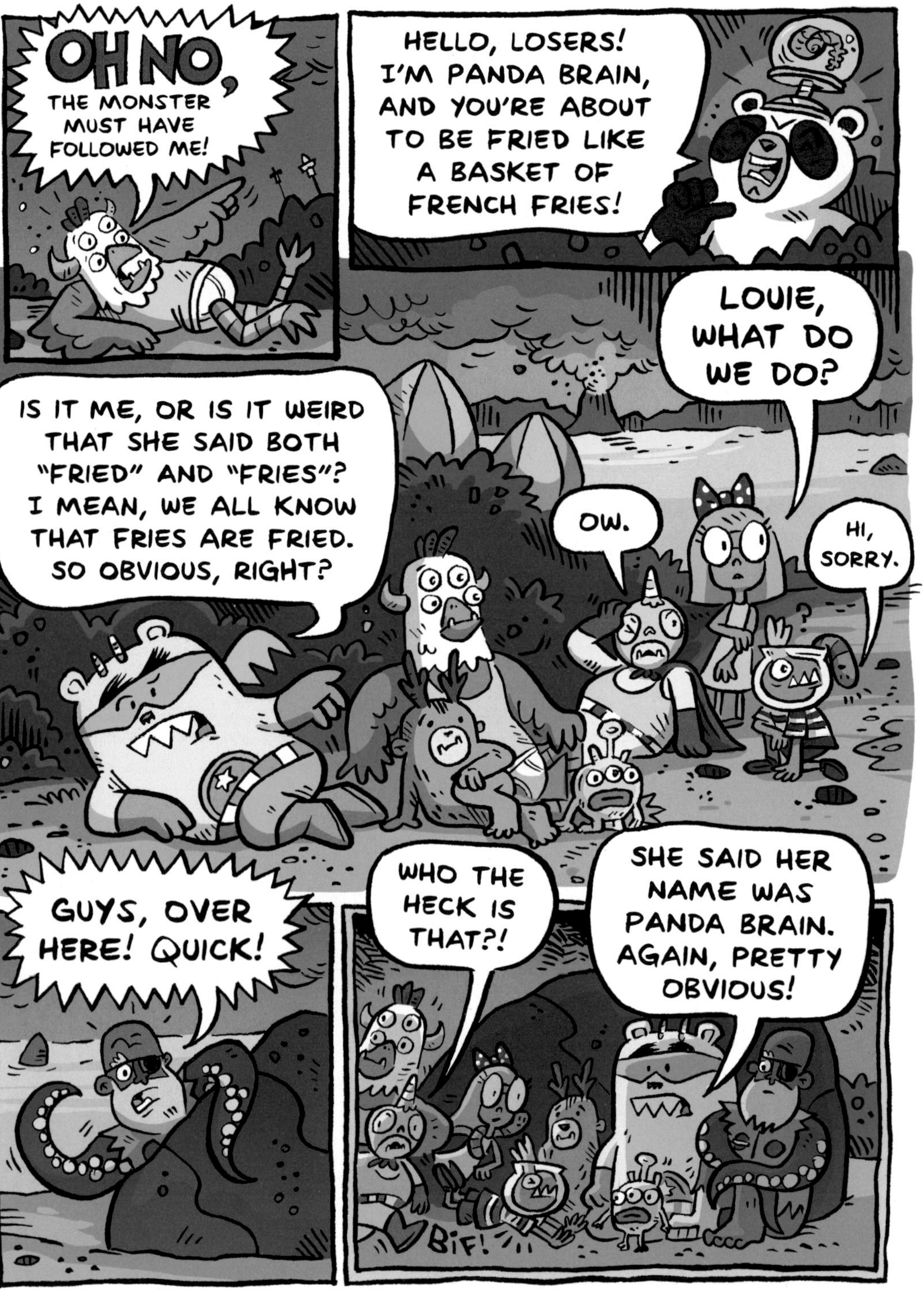
OH NO, THE MONSTER MUST HAVE FOLLOWED ME!
HELLO, LOSERS! I'M PANDA BRAIN, AND YOU'RE ABOUT TO BE FRIED LIKE A BASKET OF FRENCH FRIES!
LOUIE, WHAT DO WE DO?
IS IT ME, OR IS IT WEIRD THAT SHE SAID BOTH "FRIED" AND "FRIES"? I MEAN, WE ALL KNOW THAT FRIES ARE FRIED. SO OBVIOUS, RIGHT?
OW.
HI, SORRY.
GUYS, OVER HERE! QUICK!
WHO THE HECK IS THAT?!
SHE SAID HER NAME WAS PANDA BRAIN. AGAIN, PRETTY OBVIOUS!
BIF!

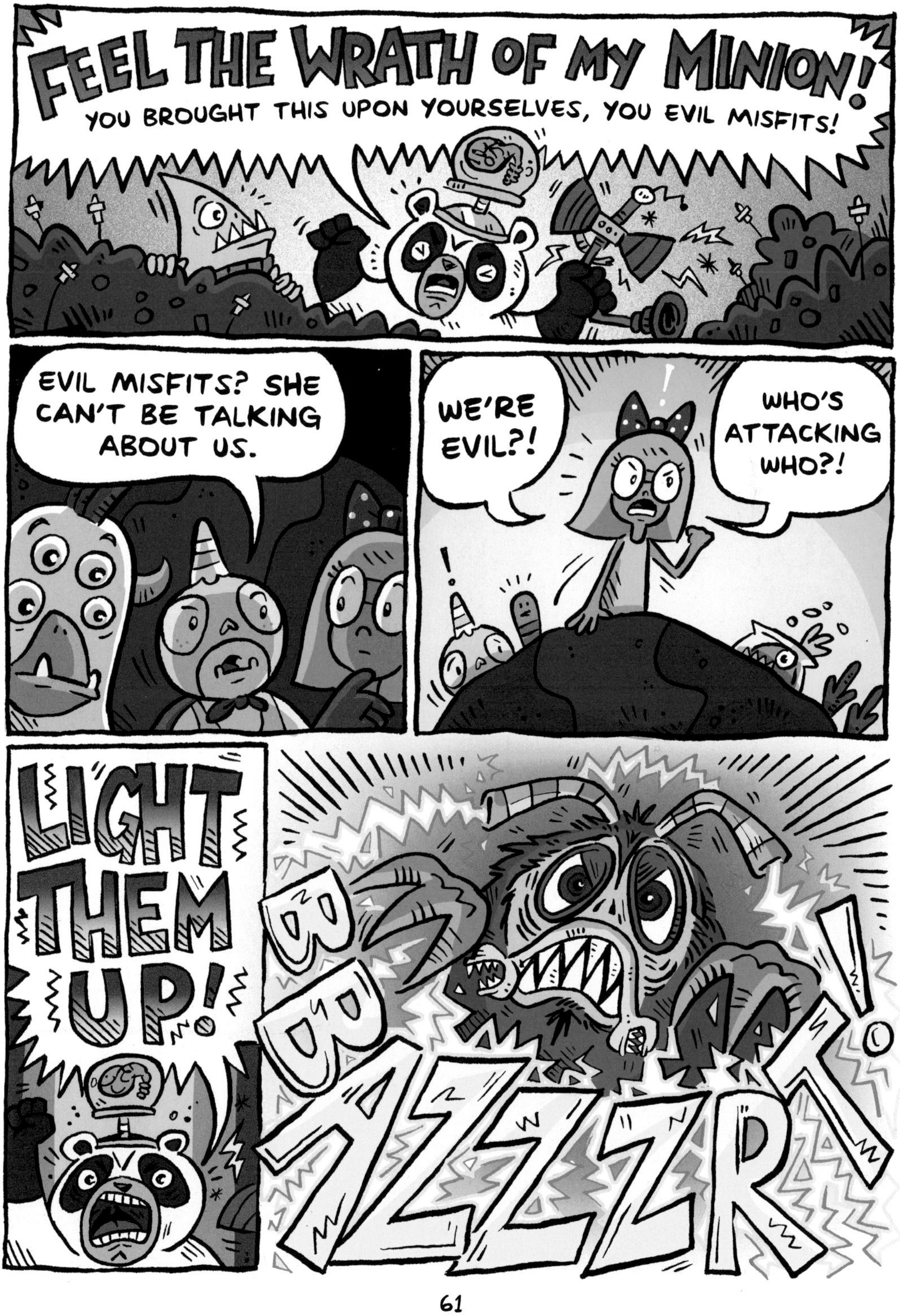
FEEL THE WRATH OF MY MINION!
YOU BROUGHT THIS UPON YOURSELVES, YOU EVIL MISFITS!
EVIL MISFITS? SHE CAN'T BE TALKING ABOUT US.
WE'RE EVIL?!
WHO'S ATTACKING WHO?!
LIGHT THEM UP!
BBBZZZZRT!

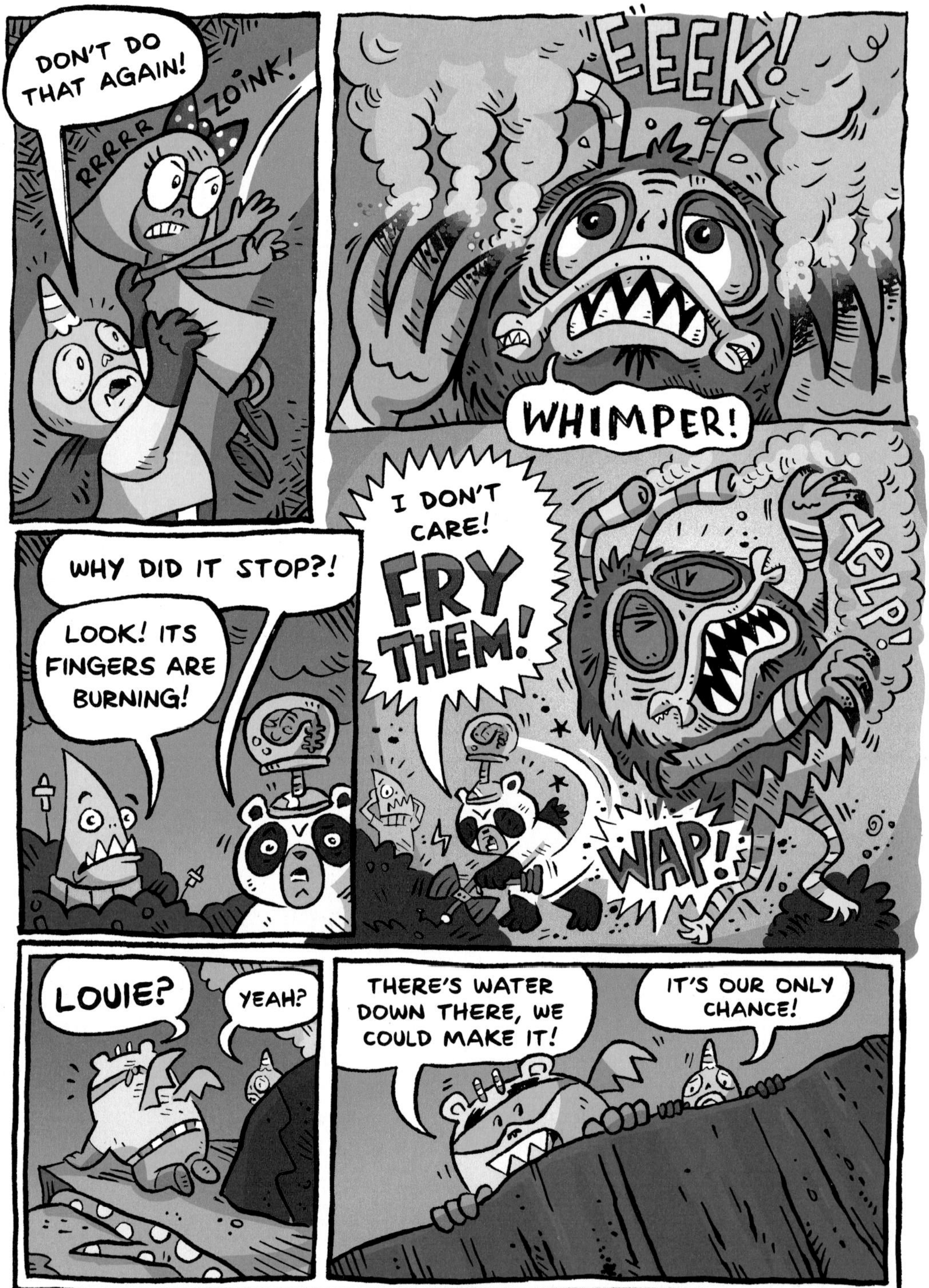
DON'T DO THAT AGAIN!
ZOINK!
RRRRR
EEEK!
WHIMPER!
WHY DID IT STOP?!
LOOK! ITS FINGERS ARE BURNING!
I DON'T CARE! FRY THEM!
YELP!
WAP!
LOUIE?
YEAH?
THERE'S WATER DOWN THERE, WE COULD MAKE IT!
IT'S OUR ONLY CHANCE!

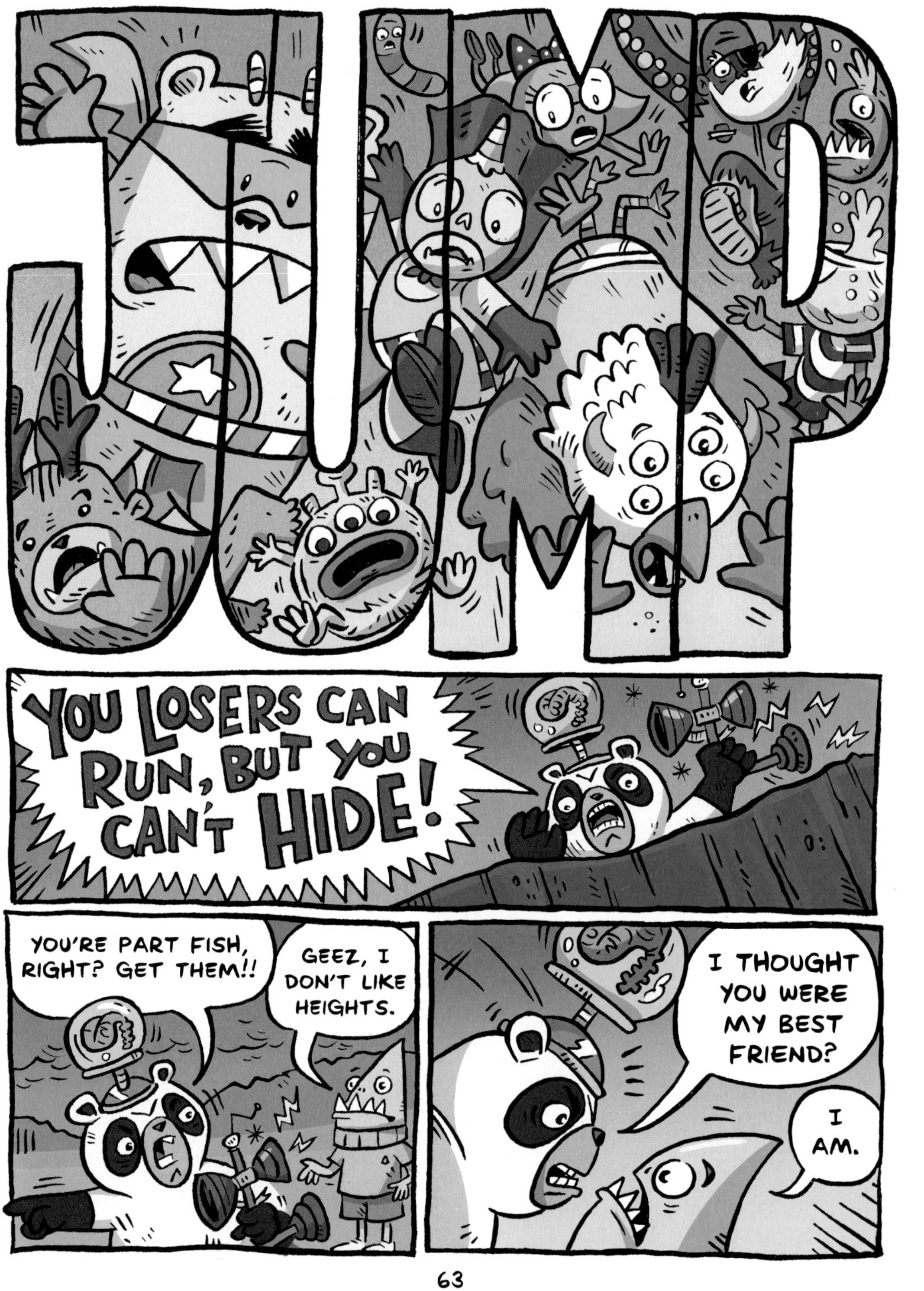
JUMP
YOU LOSERS CAN RUN, BUT YOU CAN'T HIDE!
YOU'RE PART FISH, RIGHT? GET THEM!!
GEEZ, I DON'T LIKE HEIGHTS.
I THOUGHT YOU WERE MY BEST FRIEND?
I AM.

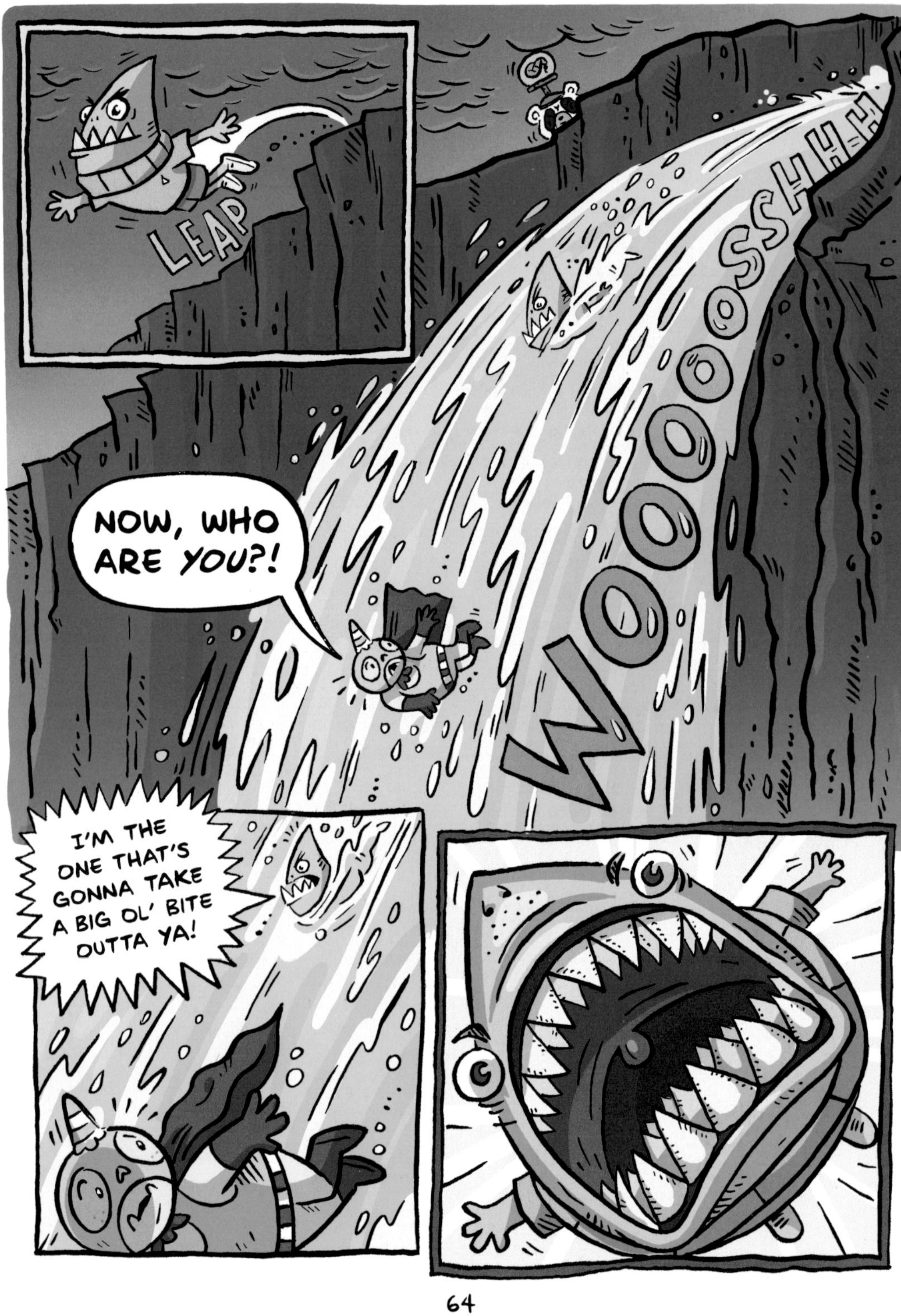
LEAP
WOOOOOOOSSHHH
NOW, WHO ARE YOU?!
I'M THE ONE THAT'S GONNA TAKE A BIG OL' BITE OUTTA YA!

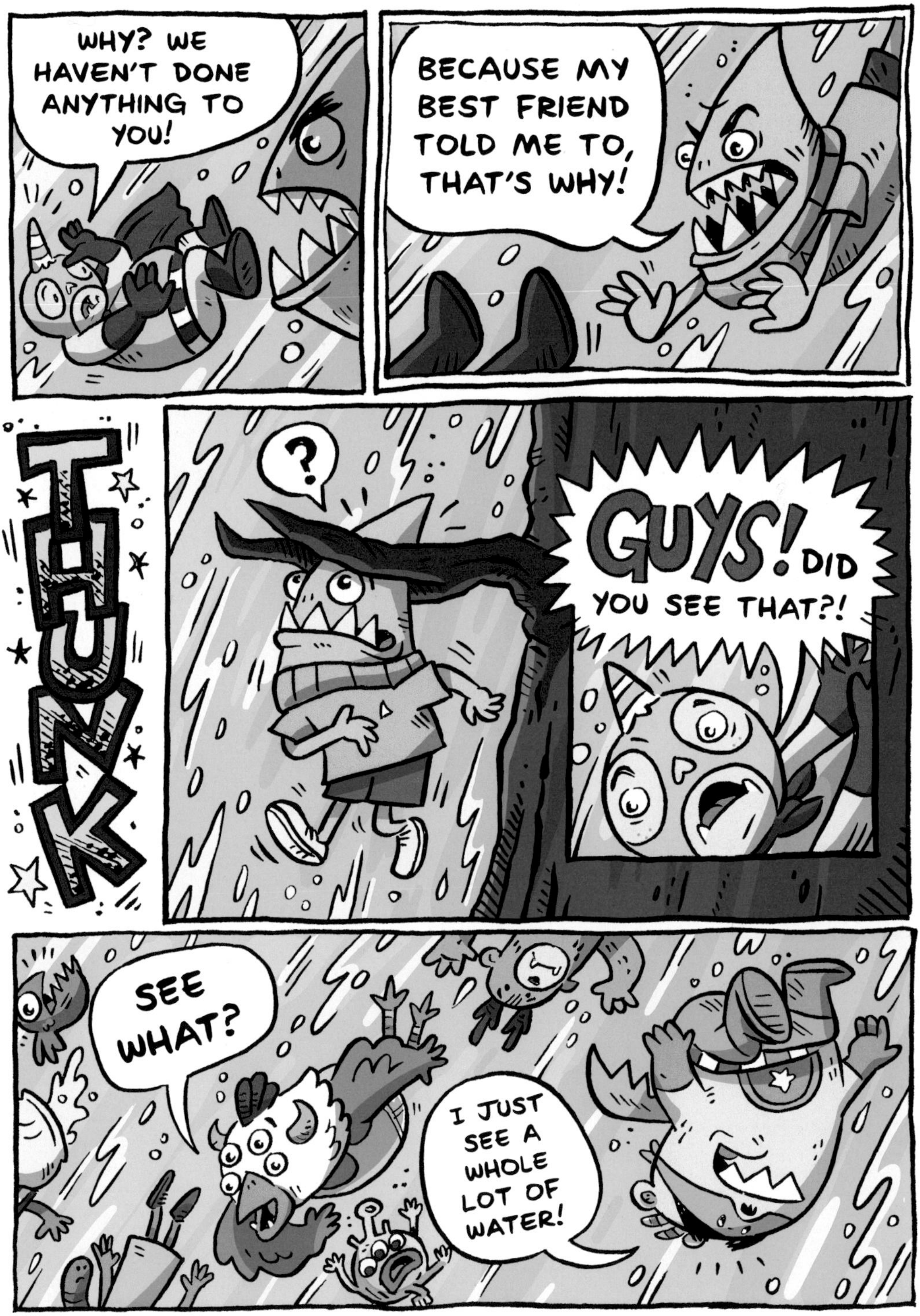

WHY? WE HAVEN'T DONE ANYTHING TO YOU!
BECAUSE MY BEST FRIEND TOLD ME TO, THAT'S WHY!
THUNK
?
GUYS! DID YOU SEE THAT?!
SEE WHAT?
I JUST SEE A WHOLE LOT OF WATER!

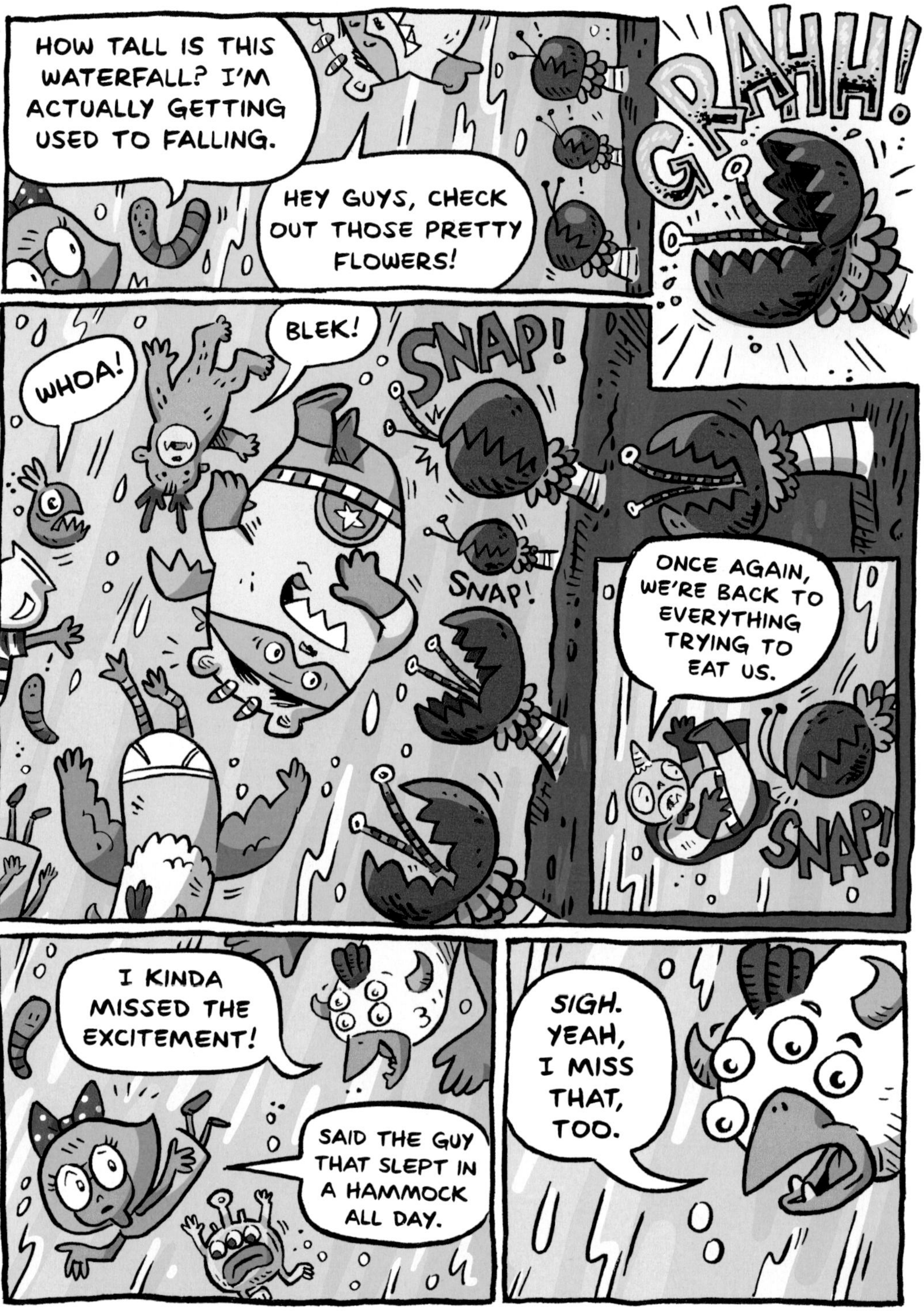

HOW TALL IS THIS WATERFALL? I'M ACTUALLY GETTING USED TO FALLING.
HEY GUYS, CHECK OUT THOSE PRETTY FLOWERS!
GRAHH!
WHOA!
BLEK!
SNAP!
SNAP!
ONCE AGAIN, WE'RE BACK TO EVERYTHING TRYING TO EAT US.
SNAP!
I KINDA MISSED THE EXCITEMENT!
SAID THE GUY THAT SLEPT IN A HAMMOCK ALL DAY.
SIGH. YEAH, I MISS THAT, TOO.

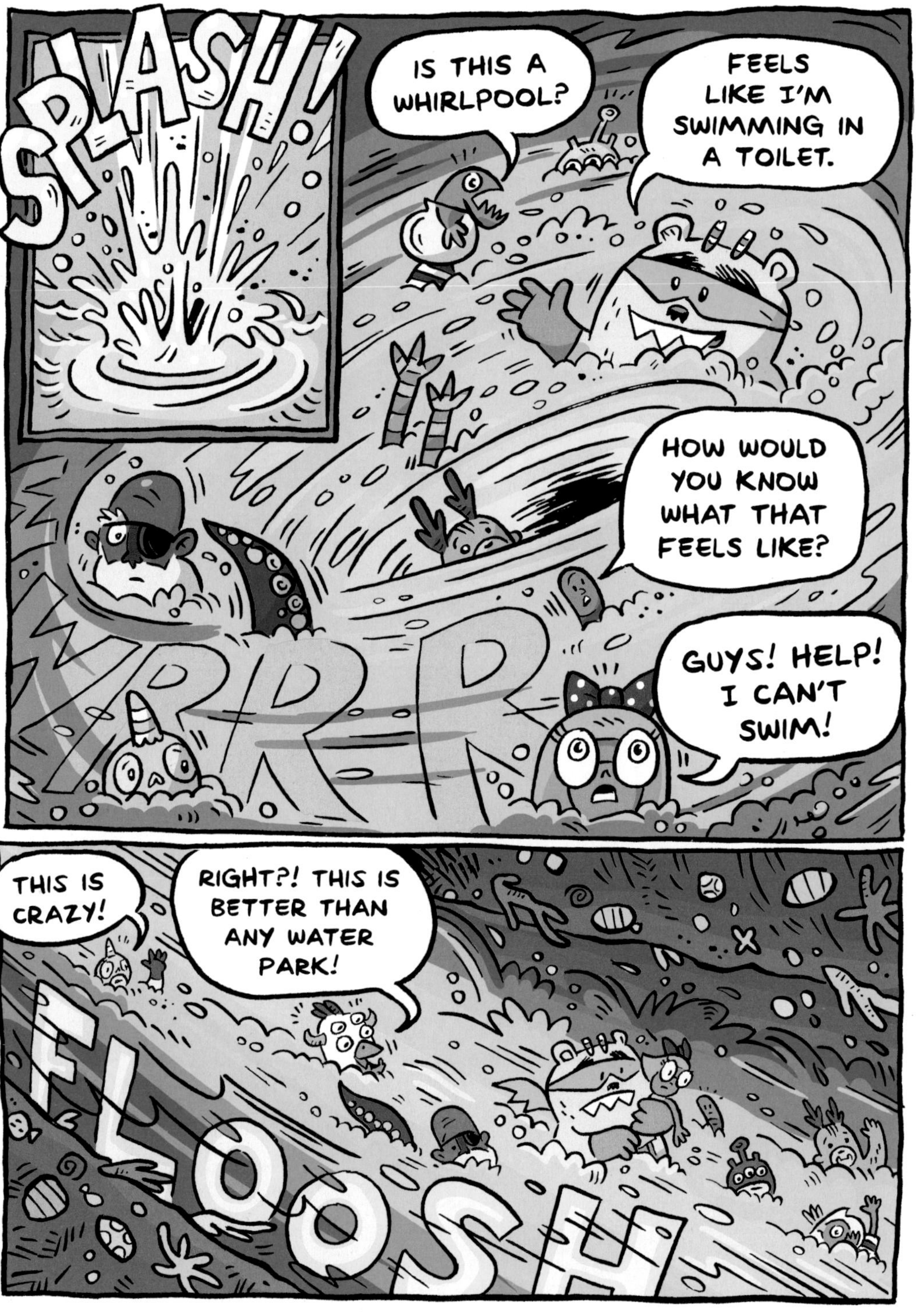
SPLASH!
IS THIS A WHIRLPOOL?
FEELS LIKE I'M SWIMMING IN A TOILET.
HOW WOULD YOU KNOW WHAT THAT FEELS LIKE?
WRRRR
GUYS! HELP! I CAN'T SWIM!
THIS IS CRAZY!
RIGHT?! THIS IS BETTER THAN ANY WATER PARK!
FLOOOSH

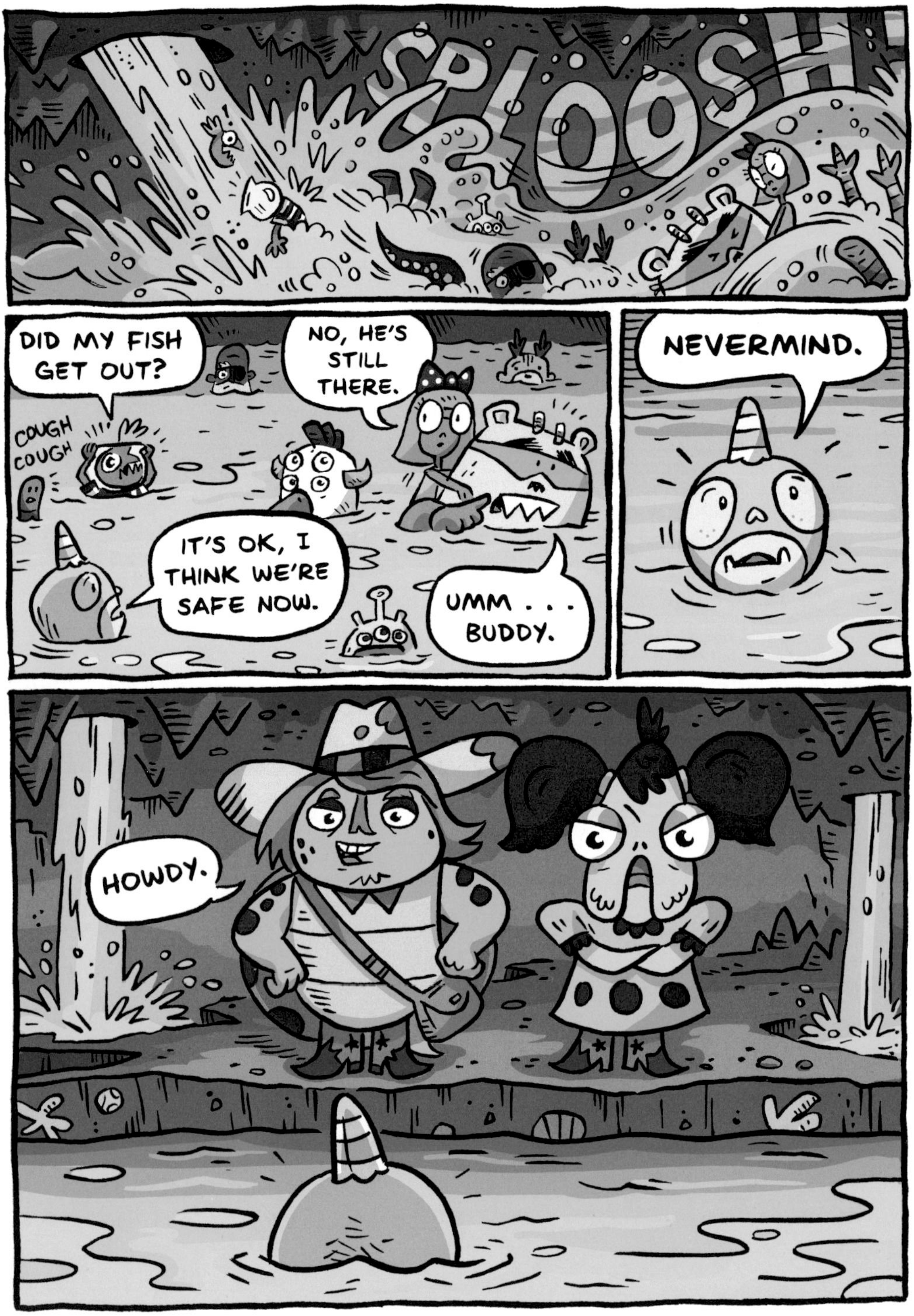
SPLOOSH!
DID MY FISH GET OUT?
COUGH COUGH
NO, HE'S STILL THERE.
IT'S OK, I THINK WE'RE SAFE NOW.
UMM . . . BUDDY.
NEVERMIND.
HOWDY.

CHAPTER 7

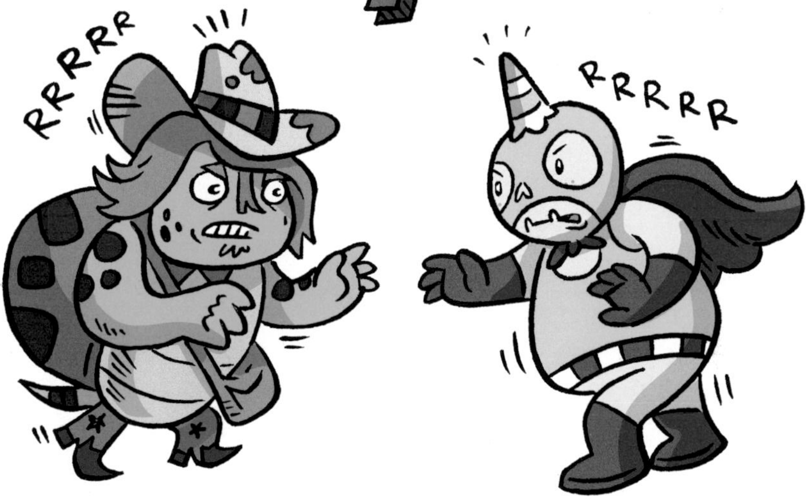
RRRRR
RRRRRR

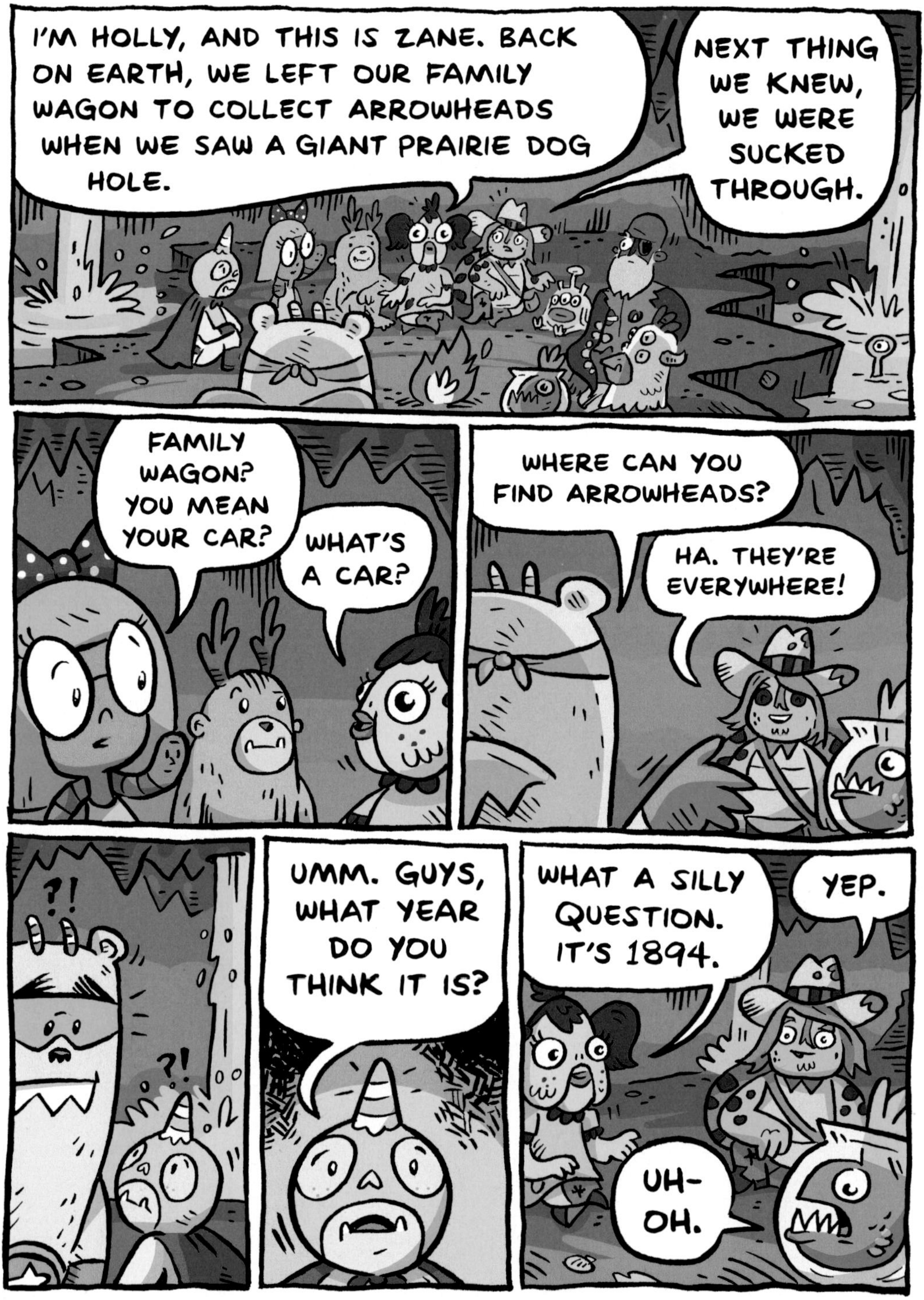
I'M HOLLY, AND THIS IS ZANE. BACK ON EARTH, WE LEFT OUR FAMILY WAGON TO COLLECT ARROWHEADS WHEN WE SAW A GIANT PRAIRIE DOG HOLE.
NEXT THING WE KNEW, WE WERE SUCKED THROUGH.
FAMILY WAGON? YOU MEAN YOUR CAR?
WHAT'S A CAR?
WHERE CAN YOU FIND ARROWHEADS?
HA. THEY'RE EVERYWHERE!
?!
?!
UMM. GUYS, WHAT YEAR DO YOU THINK IT IS?
WHAT A SILLY QUESTION. IT'S 1894.
YEP.
UH-OH.

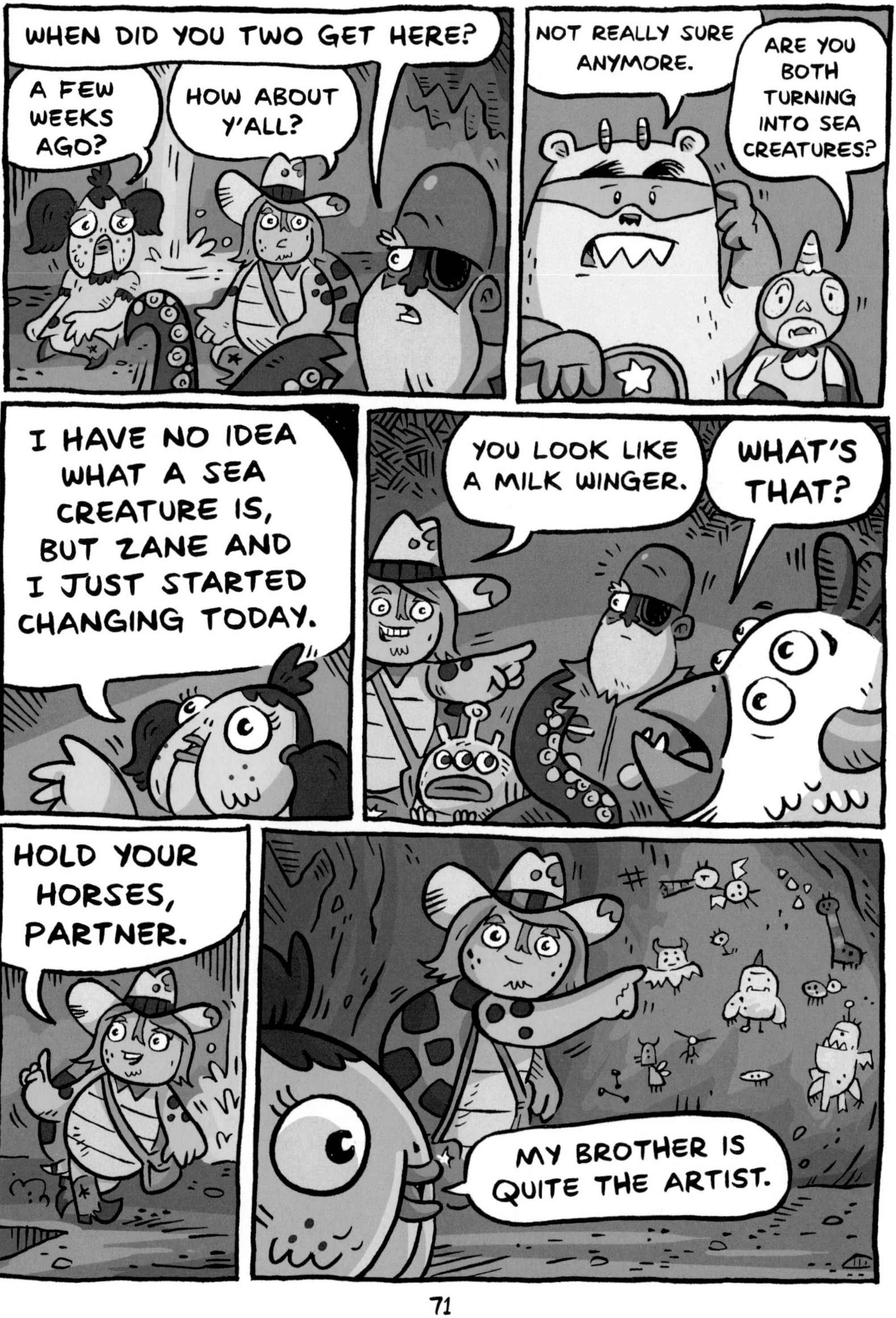
WHEN DID YOU TWO GET HERE?
A FEW WEEKS AGO?
HOW ABOUT Y'ALL?
NOT REALLY SURE ANYMORE.
ARE YOU BOTH TURNING INTO SEA CREATURES?
I HAVE NO IDEA WHAT A SEA CREATURE IS, BUT ZANE AND I JUST STARTED CHANGING TODAY.
YOU LOOK LIKE A MILK WINGER.
WHAT'S THAT?
HOLD YOUR HORSES, PARTNER.
MY BROTHER IS QUITE THE ARTIST.

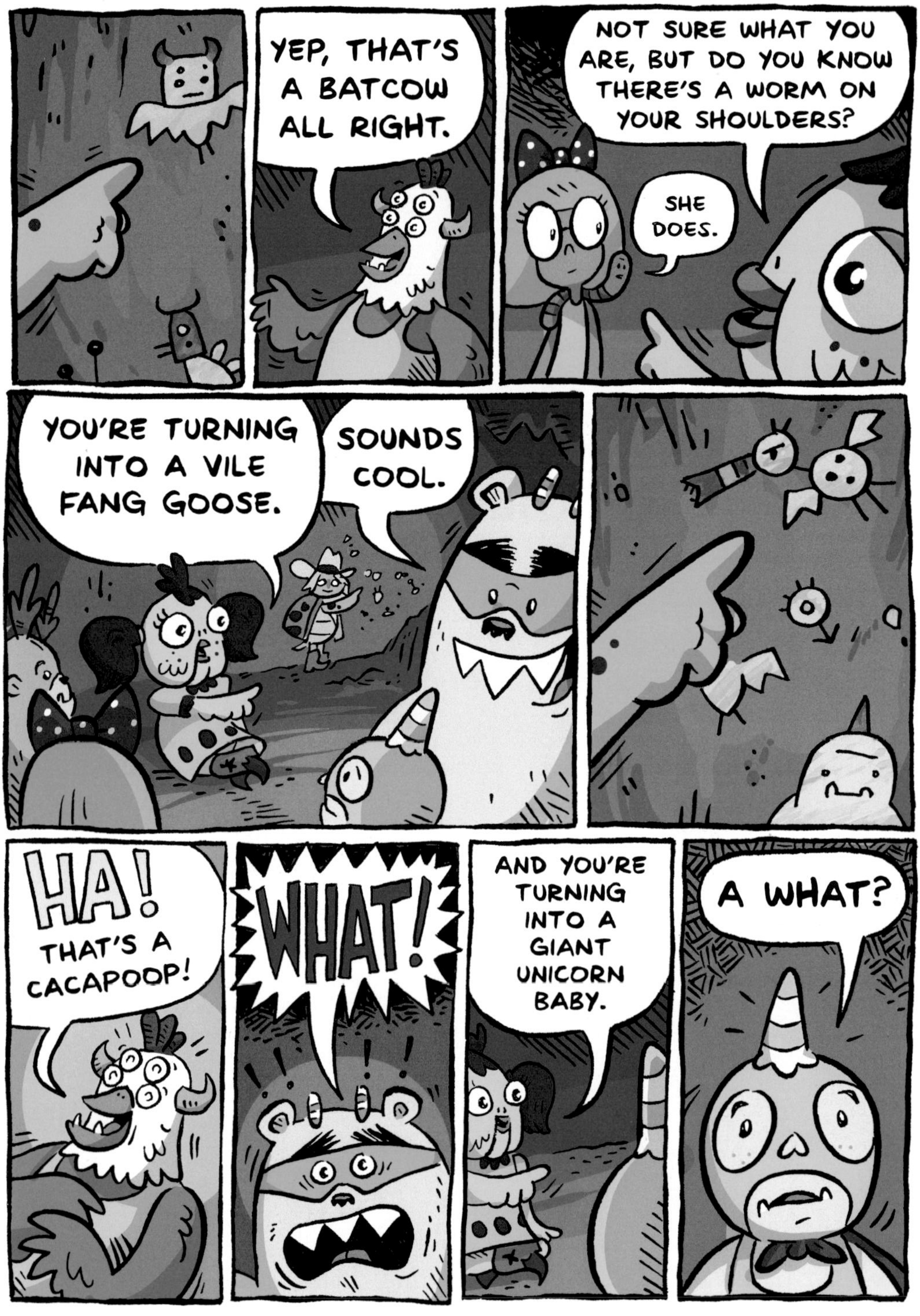
YEP, THAT'S A BATCOW ALL RIGHT.
NOT SURE WHAT YOU ARE, BUT DO YOU KNOW THERE'S A WORM ON YOUR SHOULDERS?
SHE DOES.
YOU'RE TURNING INTO A VILE FANG GOOSE.
SOUNDS COOL.
HA! THAT'S A CACAPOOP!
WHAT!
AND YOU'RE TURNING INTO A GIANT UNICORN BABY.
A WHAT?

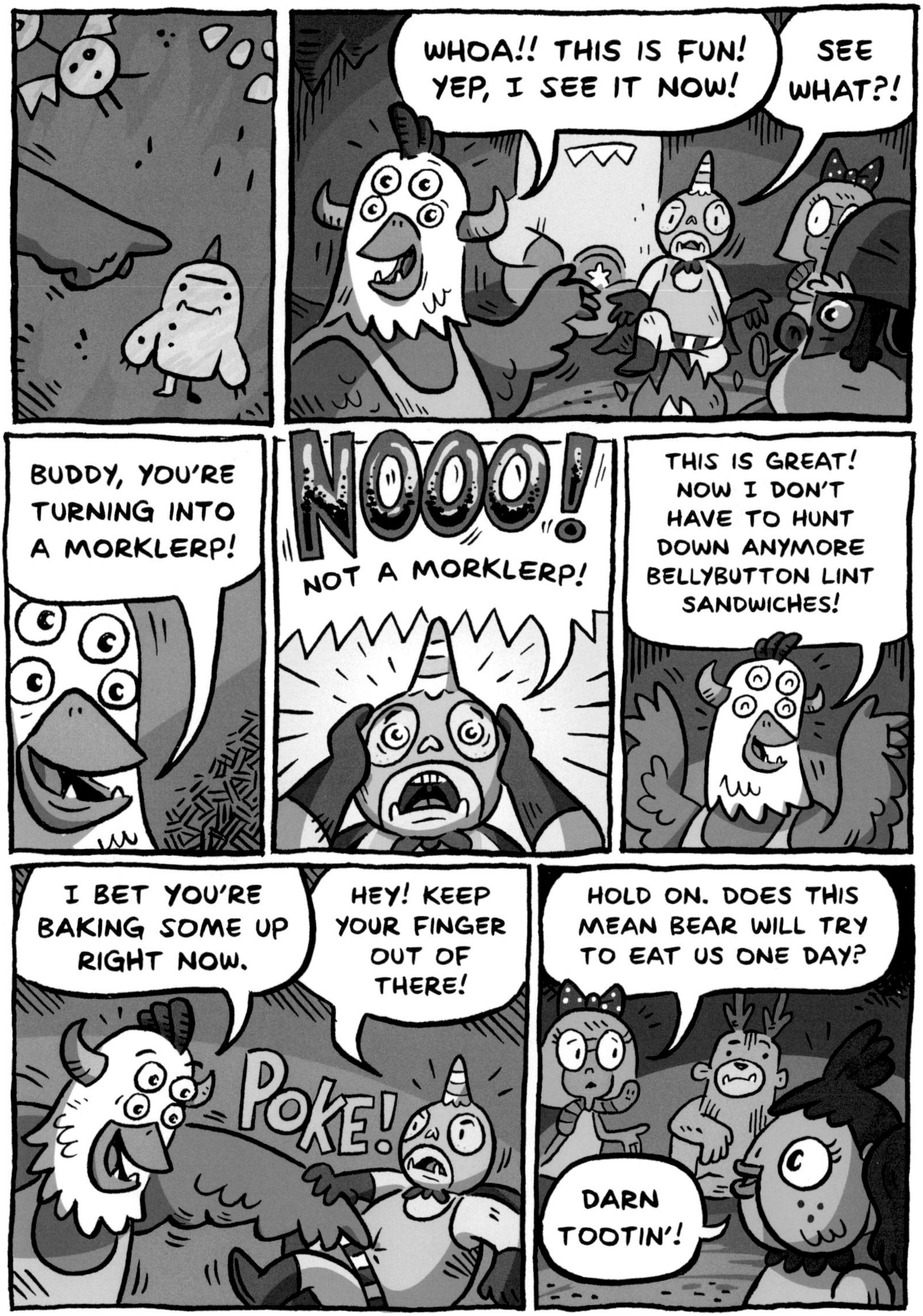
WHOA!! THIS IS FUN! YEP, I SEE IT NOW!
SEE WHAT?!
BUDDY, YOU'RE TURNING INTO A MORKLERP!
NOOO!
NOT A MORKLERP!
THIS IS GREAT! NOW I DON'T HAVE TO HUNT DOWN ANYMORE BELLYBUTTON LINT SANDWICHES!
I BET YOU'RE BAKING SOME UP RIGHT NOW.
HEY! KEEP YOUR FINGER OUT OF THERE!
POKE!
HOLD ON. DOES THIS MEAN BEAR WILL TRY TO EAT US ONE DAY?
DARN TOOTIN'!

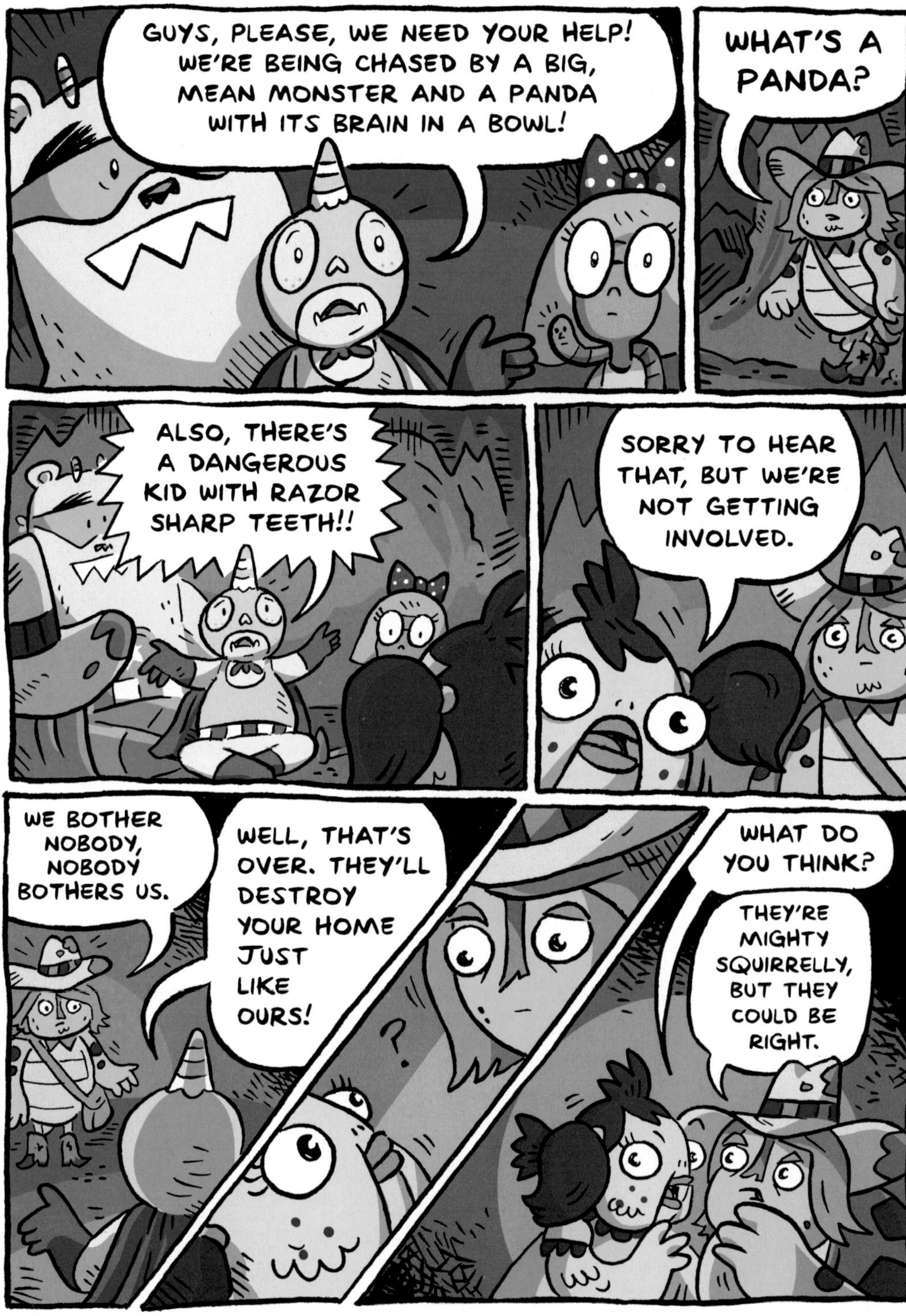
GUYS, PLEASE, WE NEED YOUR HELP! WE'RE BEING CHASED BY A BIG, MEAN MONSTER AND A PANDA WITH ITS BRAIN IN A BOWL!
WHAT'S A PANDA?
ALSO, THERE'S A DANGEROUS KID WITH RAZOR SHARP TEETH!!
SORRY TO HEAR THAT, BUT WE'RE NOT GETTING INVOLVED.
WE BOTHER NOBODY, NOBODY BOTHERS US.
WELL, THAT'S OVER. THEY'LL DESTROY YOUR HOME JUST LIKE OURS!
?
WHAT DO YOU THINK?
THEY'RE MIGHTY SQUIRRELLY, BUT THEY COULD BE RIGHT.

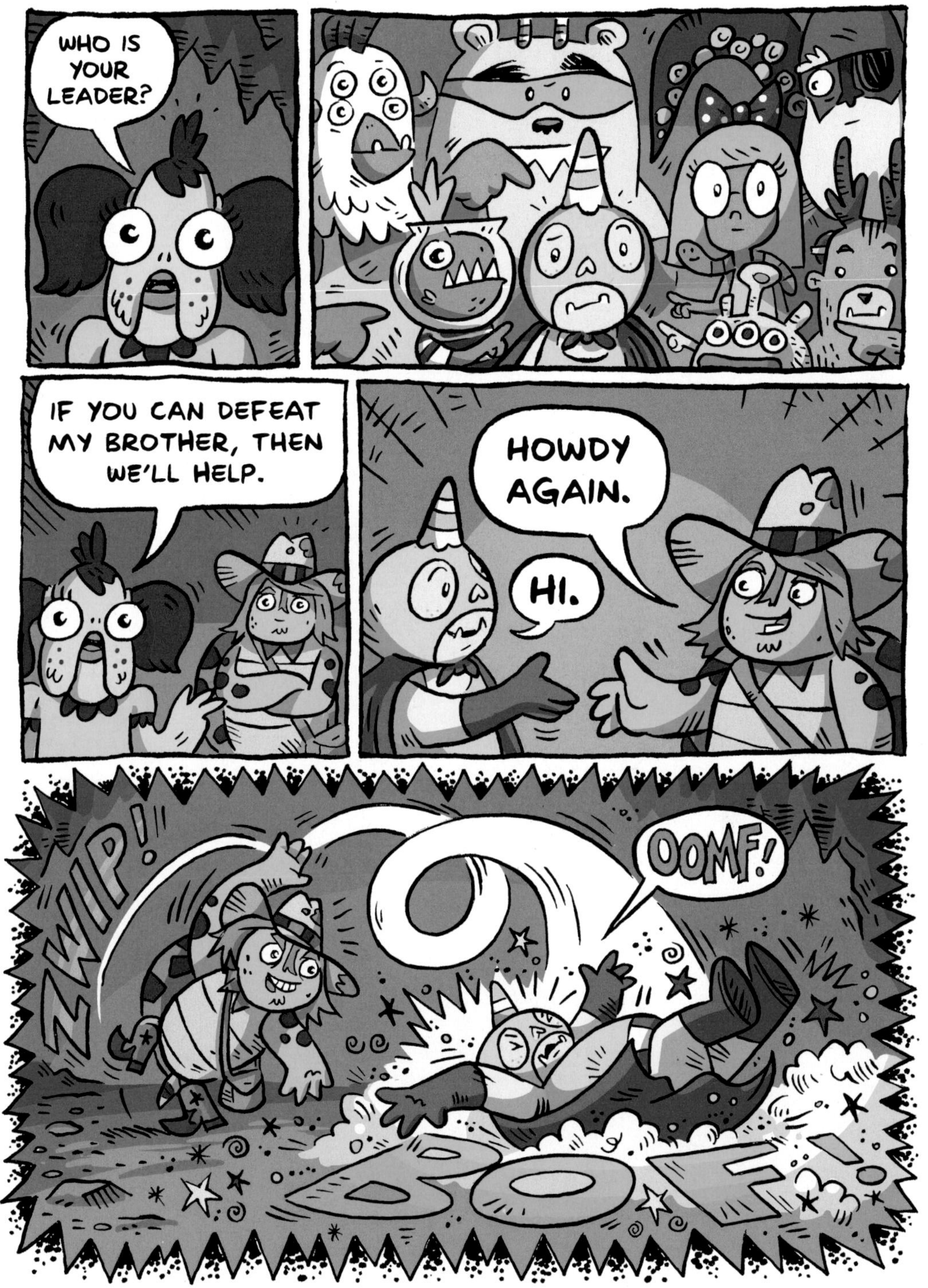
WHO IS YOUR LEADER?
IF YOU CAN DEFEAT MY BROTHER, THEN WE'LL HELP.
HOWDY AGAIN.
HI.
ZWIIP!
OOMF!
DOOF!!

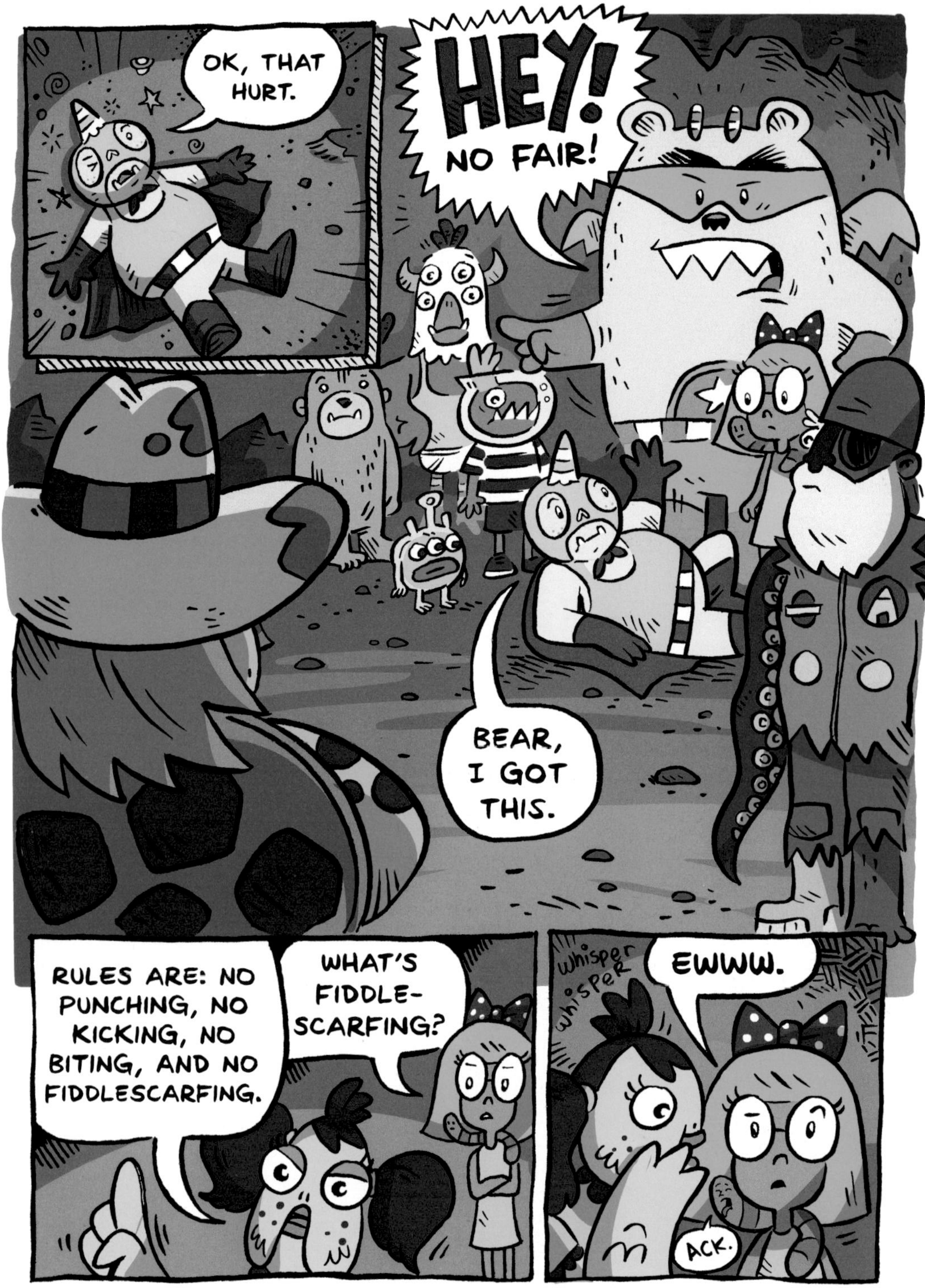

OK, THAT HURT.
HEY! NO FAIR!
BEAR, I GOT THIS.
RULES ARE: NO PUNCHING, NO KICKING, NO BITING, AND NO FIDDLESCARFING.
WHAT'S FIDDLE-SCARFING?
whisper whisper
EWWW.
ACK.

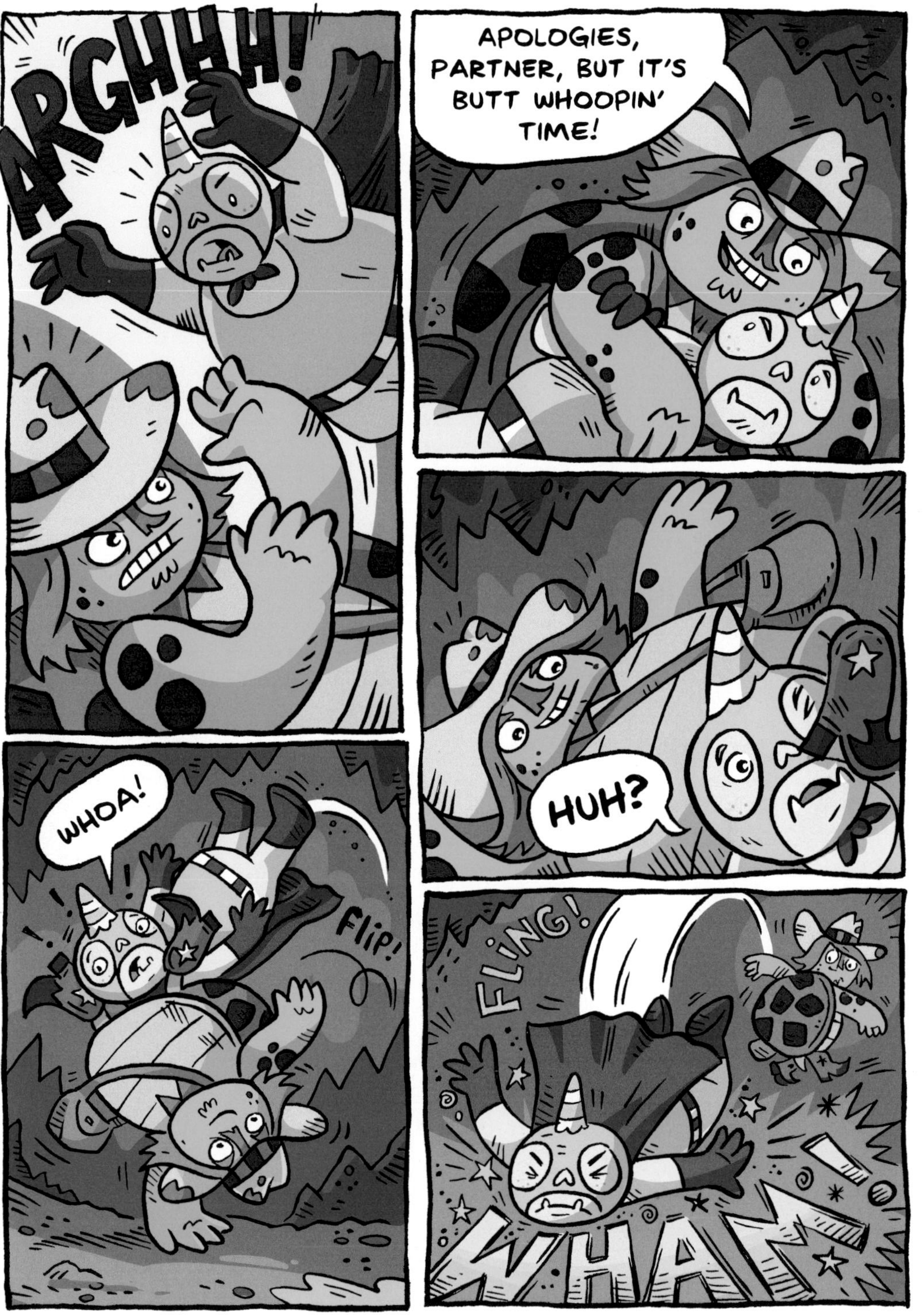
ARGHHH!
APOLOGIES, PARTNER, BUT IT'S BUTT WHOOPIN' TIME!
HUH?
WHOA!
FLIP!
FLING!
WHAM!

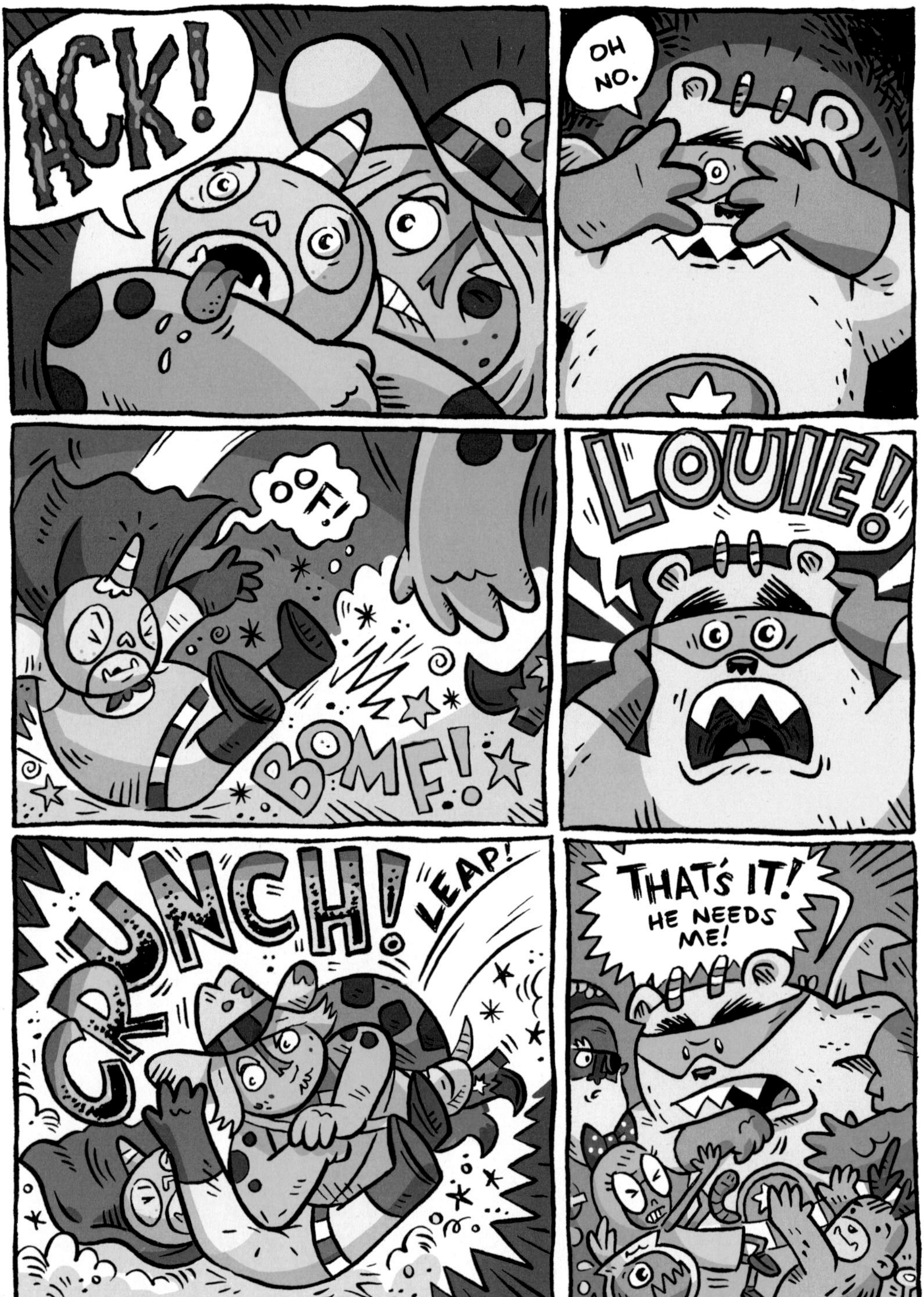
ACK!
OH NO.
OOF!
BOMF!
LOUIE!
CRUNCH!
LEAP!
THAT'S IT! HE NEEDS ME!

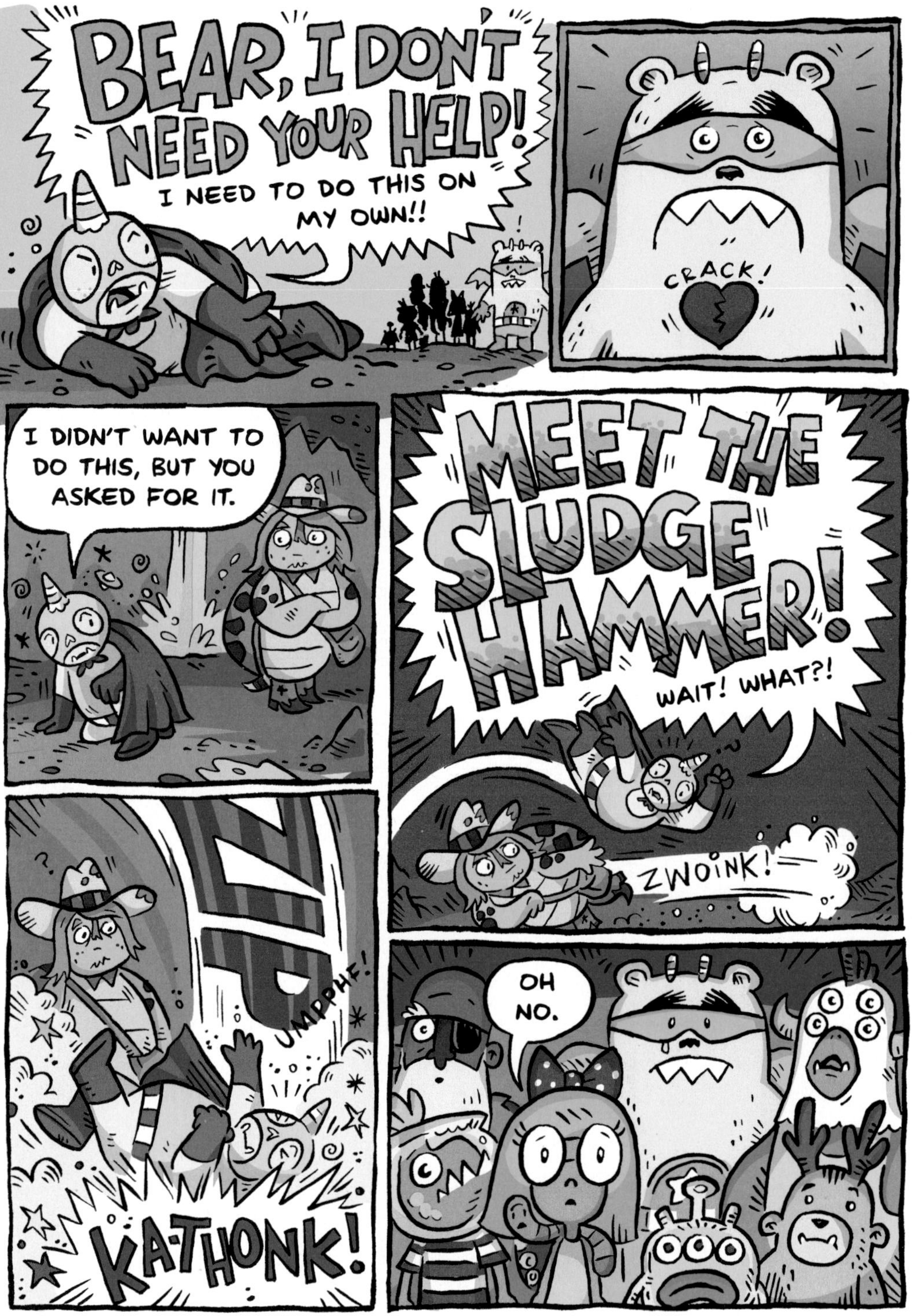
BEAR, I DON'T NEED YOUR HELP!
I NEED TO DO THIS ON MY OWN!!
CRACK!
I DIDN'T WANT TO DO THIS, BUT YOU ASKED FOR IT.
MEET THE SLUDGE HAMMER!
WAIT! WHAT?!
ZWOINK!
UMPPHF!
KA-THONK!
OH NO.

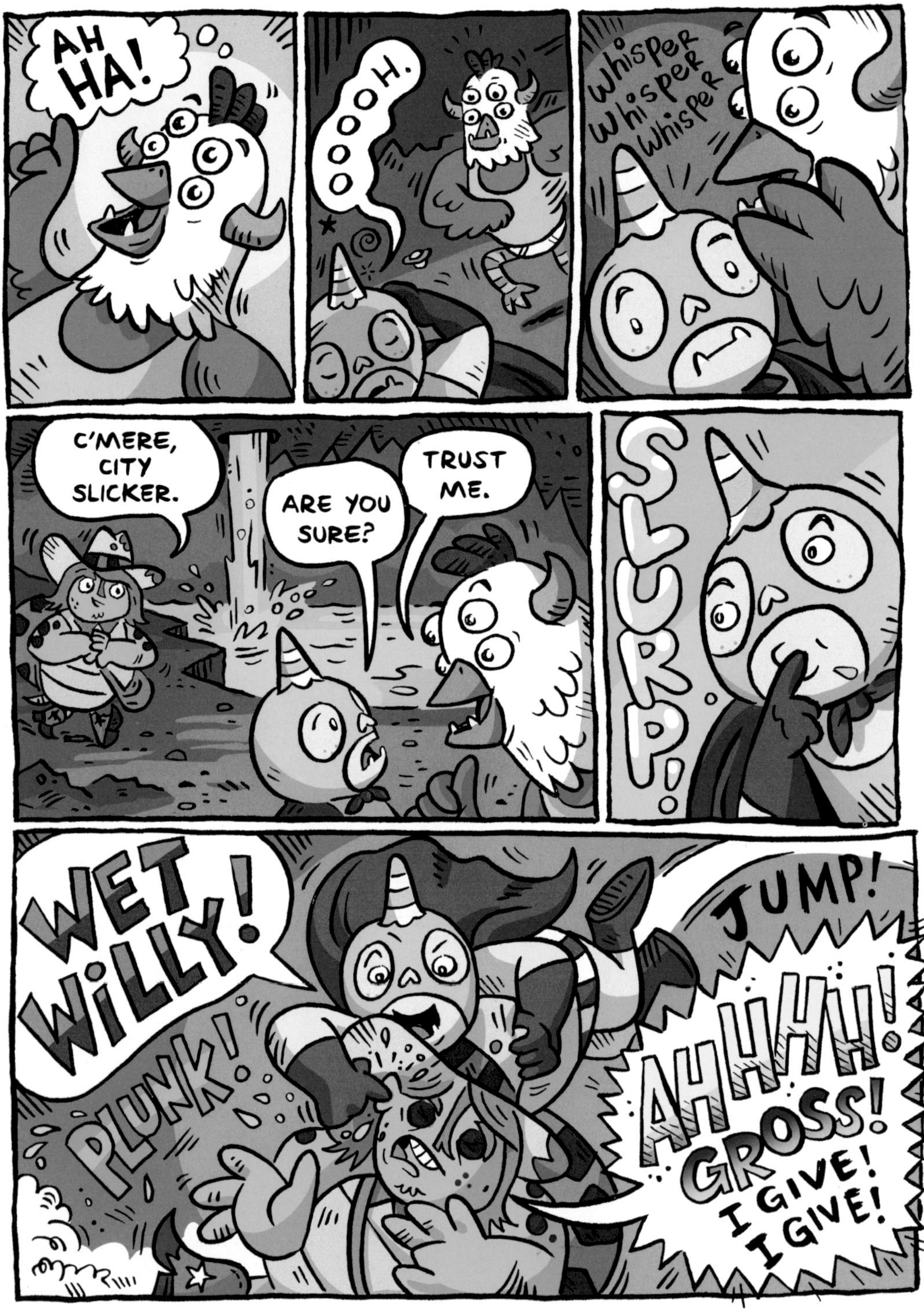
AH HA!
OOOOH.
whisper whisper whisper
C'MERE, CITY SLICKER.
ARE YOU SURE?
TRUST ME.
SLURP!
WET WILLY!
JUMP!
PLUNK!
AHHHH! GROSS! I GIVE! I GIVE!

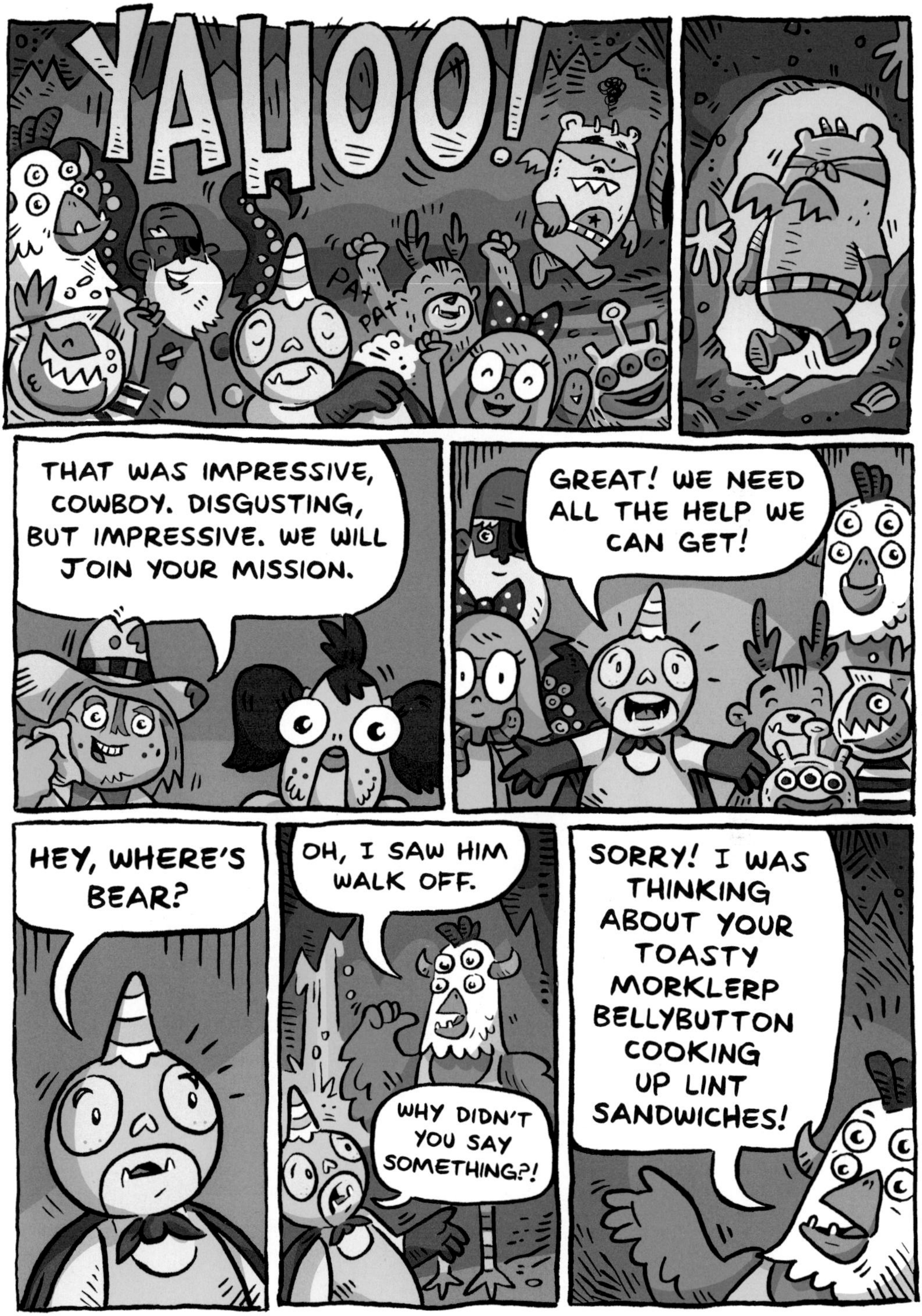
YAHOO!
PAT PAT
THAT WAS IMPRESSIVE, COWBOY. DISGUSTING, BUT IMPRESSIVE. WE WILL JOIN YOUR MISSION.
GREAT! WE NEED ALL THE HELP WE CAN GET!
HEY, WHERE'S BEAR?
OH, I SAW HIM WALK OFF.
WHY DIDN'T YOU SAY SOMETHING?!
SORRY! I WAS THINKING ABOUT YOUR TOASTY MORKLERP BELLYBUTTON COOKING UP LINT SANDWICHES!

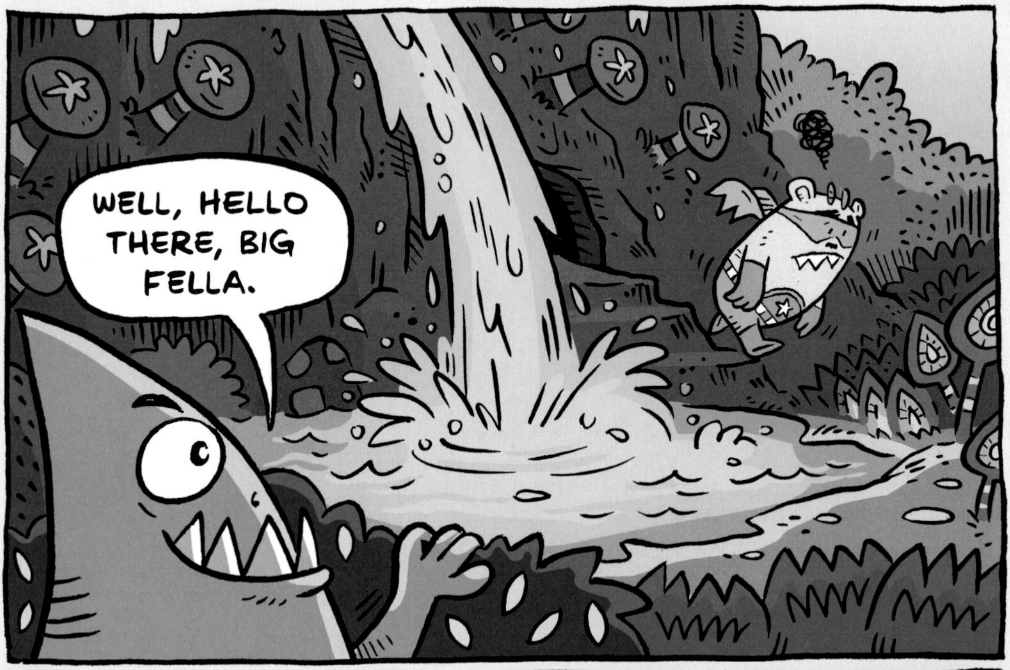
WELL, HELLO THERE, BIG FELLA.

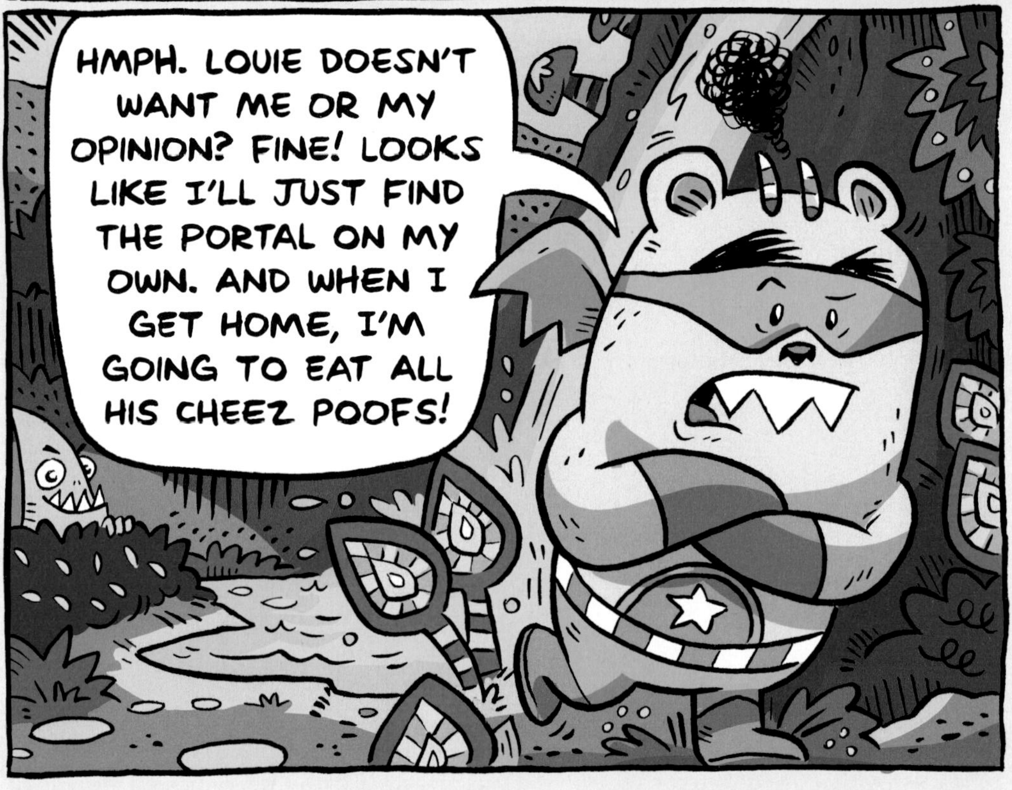
HMPH. LOUIE DOESN'T WANT ME OR MY OPINION? FINE! LOOKS LIKE I'LL JUST FIND THE PORTAL ON MY OWN. AND WHEN I GET HOME, I'M GOING TO EAT ALL HIS CHEEZ POOFS!

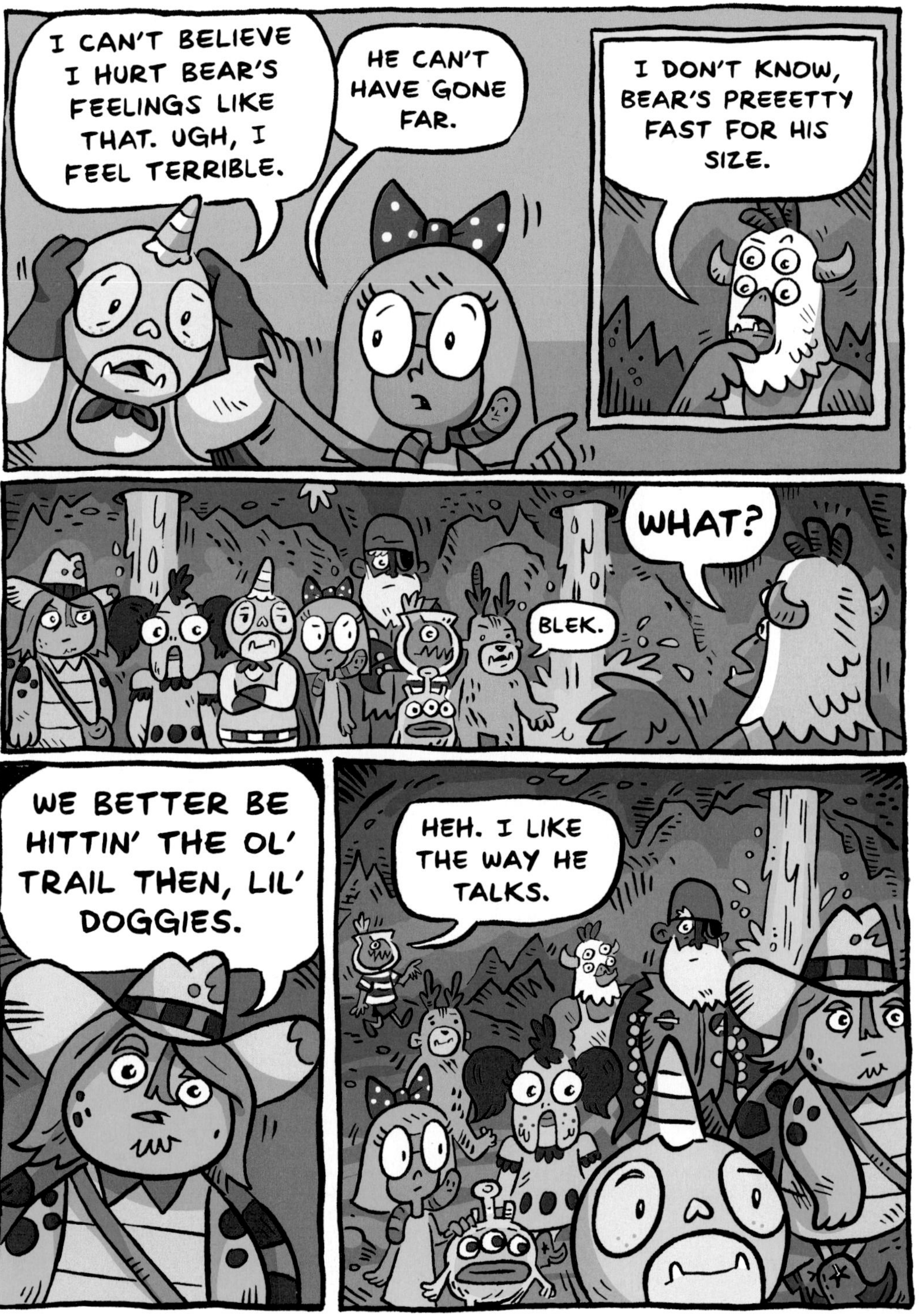
I CAN'T BELIEVE I HURT BEAR'S FEELINGS LIKE THAT. UGH, I FEEL TERRIBLE.
HE CAN'T HAVE GONE FAR.
I DON'T KNOW, BEAR'S PREEETTY FAST FOR HIS SIZE.
WHAT?
BLEK.
WE BETTER BE HITTIN' THE OL' TRAIL THEN, LIL' DOGGIES.
HEH. I LIKE THE WAY HE TALKS.

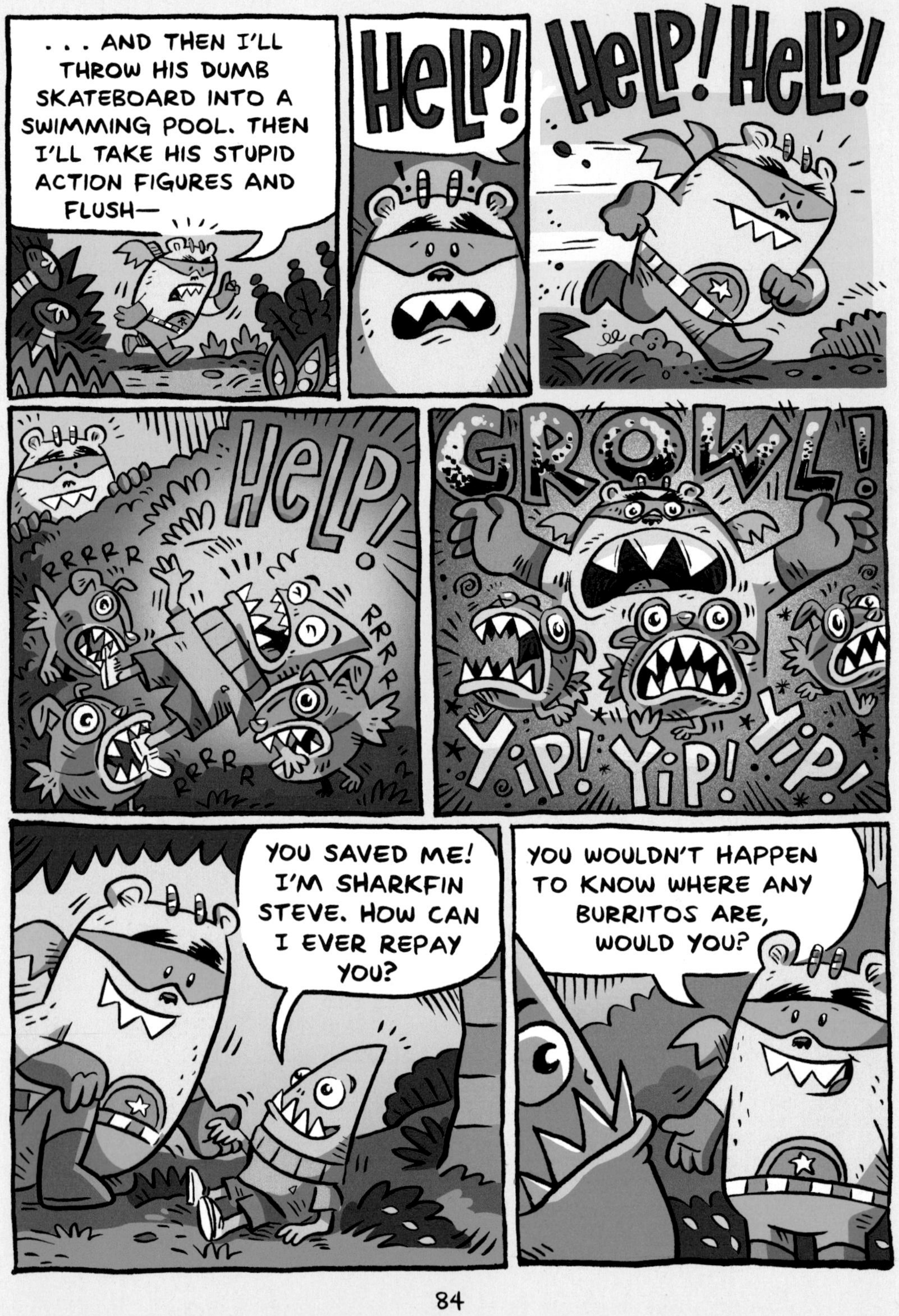

. . . AND THEN I'LL THROW HIS DUMB SKATEBOARD INTO A SWIMMING POOL. THEN I'LL TAKE HIS STUPID ACTION FIGURES AND FLUSH—
HELP!
HELP! HELP!
HELP!
RRRRR
RRRRR
RRRRR
GROWL!
YIP! YIP! YIP!
YOU SAVED ME! I'M SHARKFIN STEVE. HOW CAN I EVER REPAY YOU?
YOU WOULDN'T HAPPEN TO KNOW WHERE ANY BURRITOS ARE, WOULD YOU?

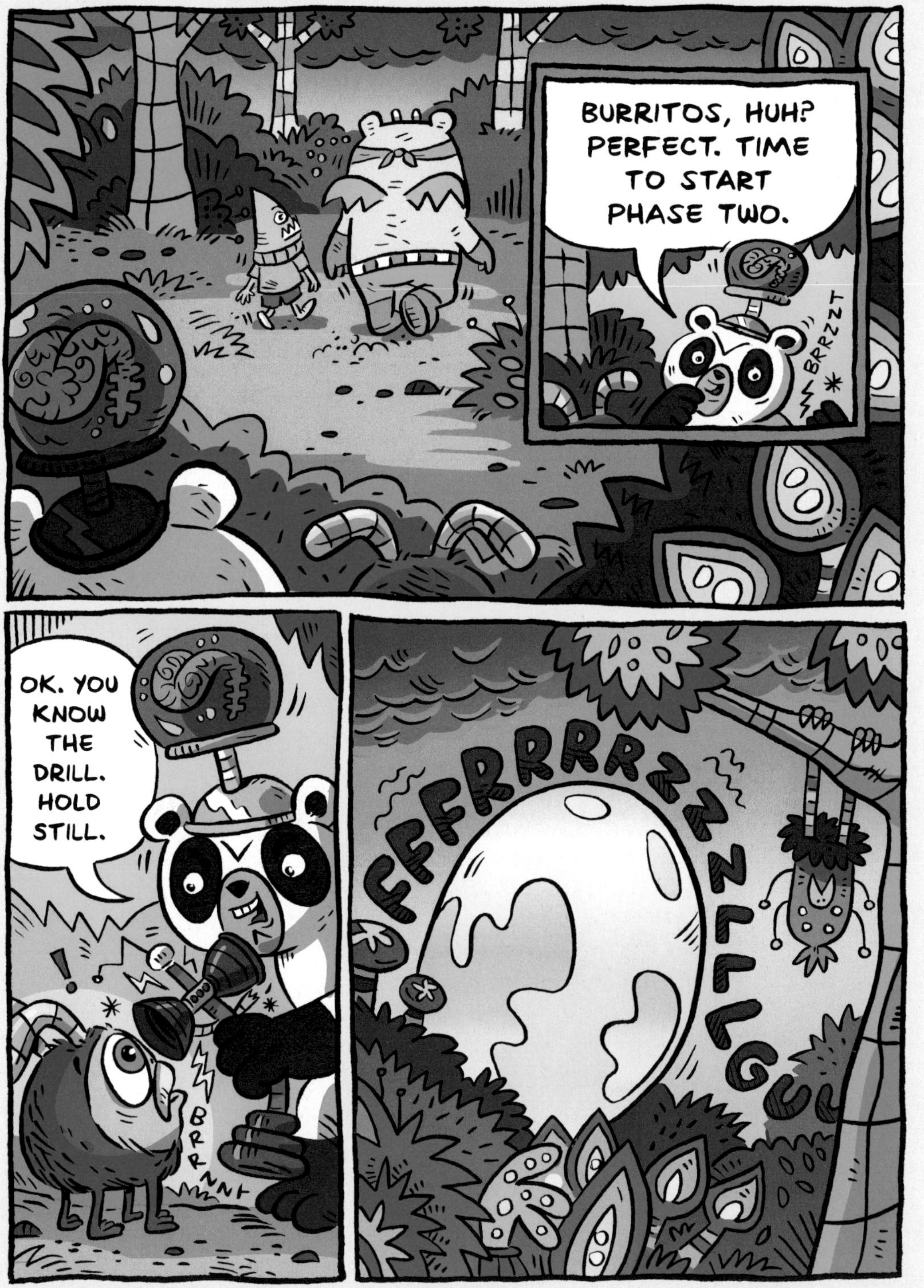
BURRITOS, HUH? PERFECT. TIME TO START PHASE TWO.
BRRZZT
OK. YOU KNOW THE DRILL. HOLD STILL.
!
BRRNNT
FFFRRRRRZZZNNLLLGG

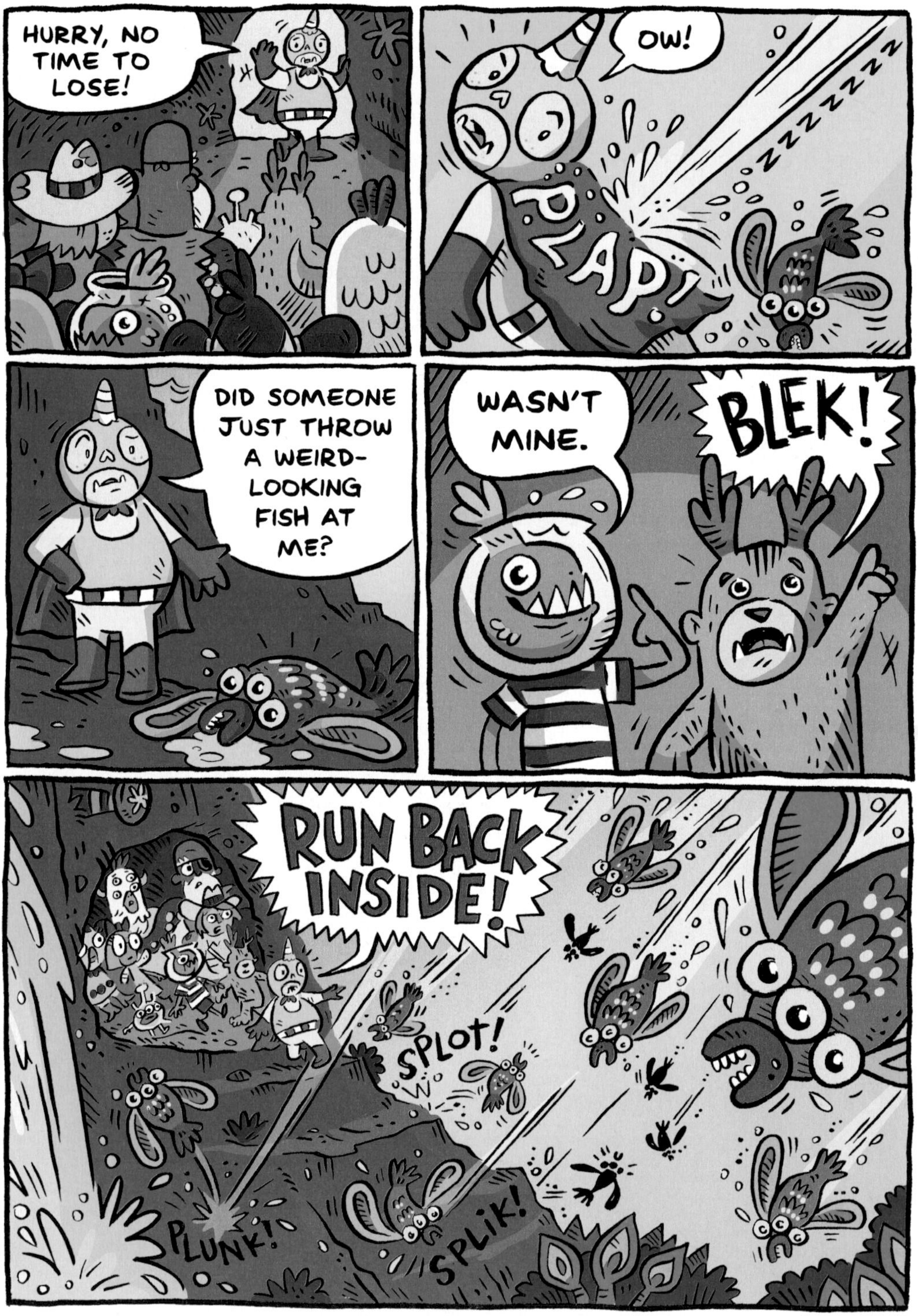
HURRY, NO TIME TO LOSE!
OW!
PLAP!
ZZZZZZZZZ
DID SOMEONE JUST THROW A WEIRD-LOOKING FISH AT ME?
WASN'T MINE.
BLEK!
RUN BACK INSIDE!
SPLOT!
PLUNK!
SPLIK!

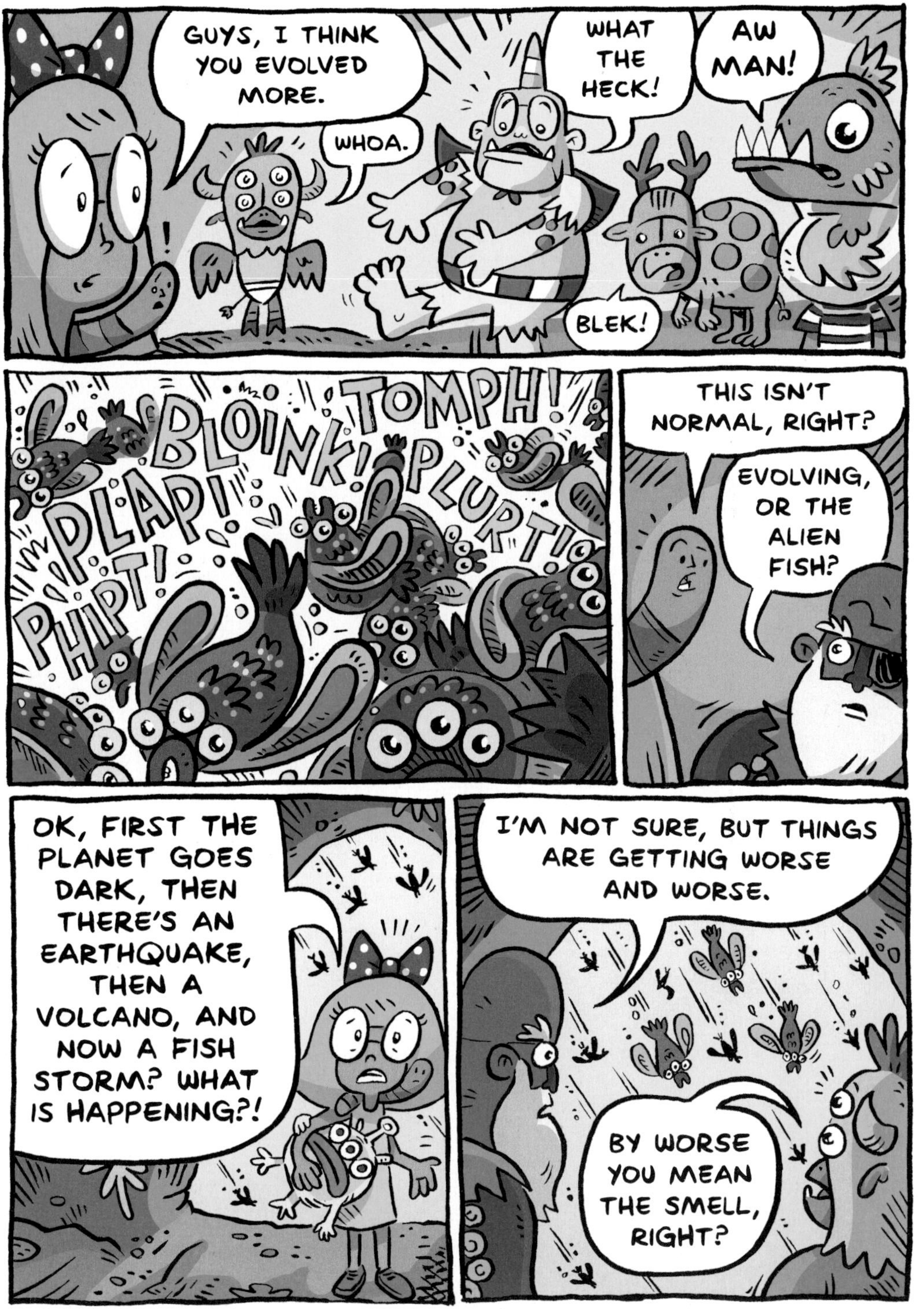
GUYS, I THINK YOU EVOLVED MORE.
WHOA.
WHAT THE HECK!
AW MAN!
BLEK!
PLAP!
BLOINK!
TOMPH!
PLURT!
PHIPT!
THIS ISN'T NORMAL, RIGHT?
EVOLVING, OR THE ALIEN FISH?
OK, FIRST THE PLANET GOES DARK, THEN THERE'S AN EARTHQUAKE, THEN A VOLCANO, AND NOW A FISH STORM? WHAT IS HAPPENING?!
I'M NOT SURE, BUT THINGS ARE GETTING WORSE AND WORSE.
BY WORSE YOU MEAN THE SMELL, RIGHT?

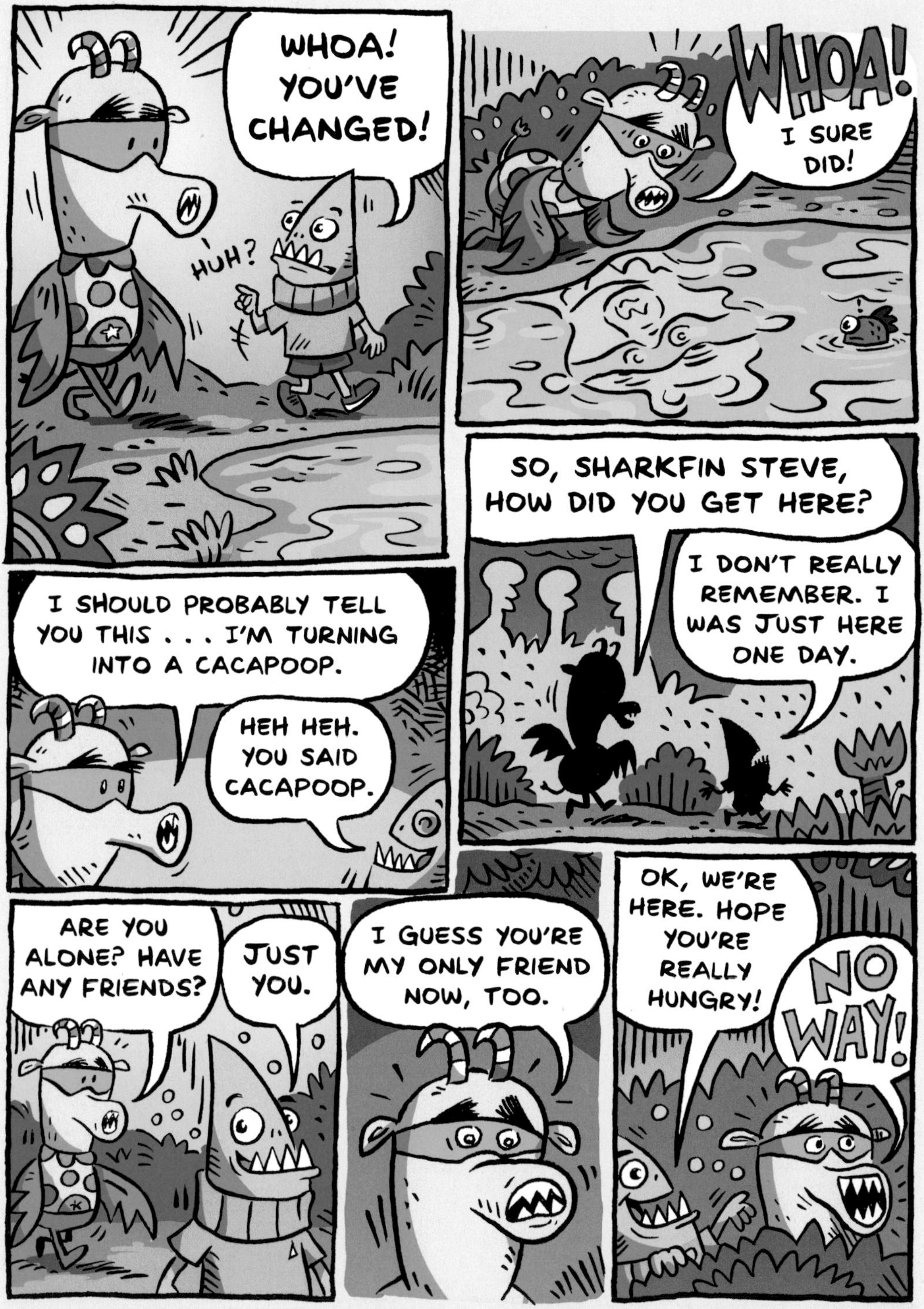
WHOA! YOU'VE CHANGED!
HUH?
WHOA!
I SURE DID!
SO, SHARKFIN STEVE, HOW DID YOU GET HERE?
I DON'T REALLY REMEMBER. I WAS JUST HERE ONE DAY.
I SHOULD PROBABLY TELL YOU THIS . . . I'M TURNING INTO A CACAPOOP.
HEH HEH. YOU SAID CACAPOOP.
ARE YOU ALONE? HAVE ANY FRIENDS?
JUST YOU.
I GUESS YOU'RE MY ONLY FRIEND NOW, TOO.
OK, WE'RE HERE. HOPE YOU'RE REALLY HUNGRY!
NO WAY!

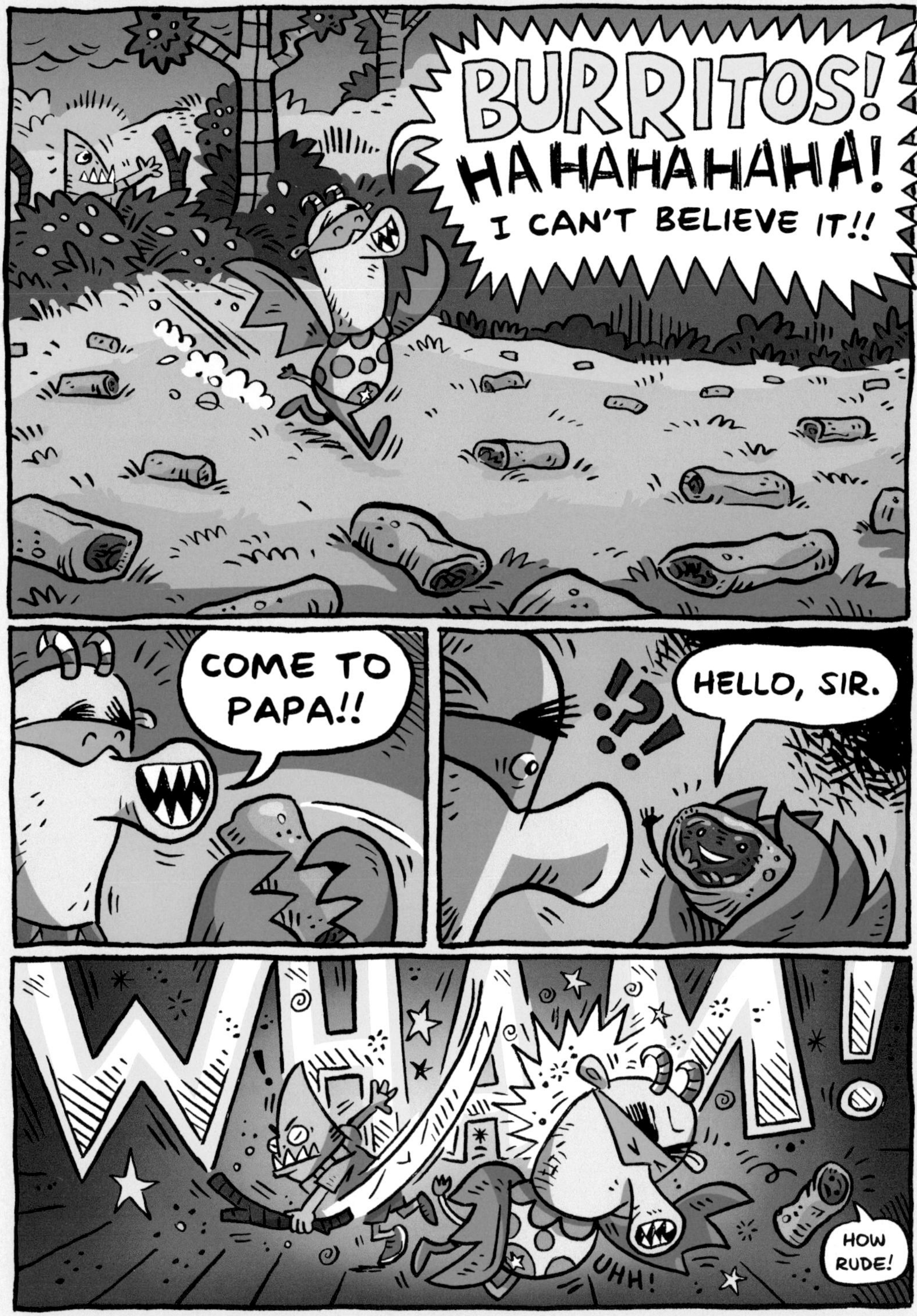
BURRITOS!
HAHAHAHAHA!
I CAN'T BELIEVE IT!!
COME TO PAPA!!
!?!
HELLO, SIR.
WHAM!
UHH!
HOW RUDE!

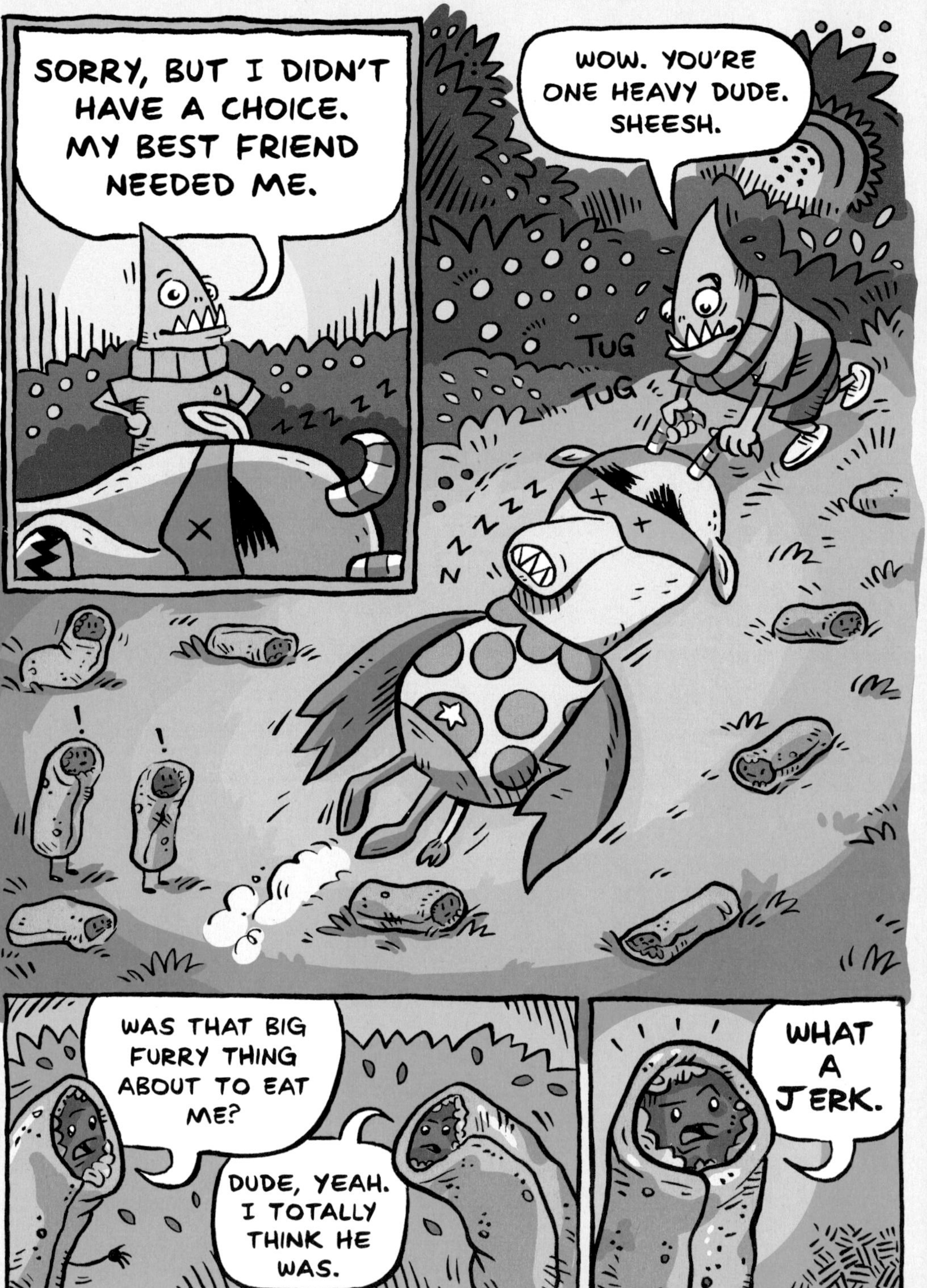
SORRY, BUT I DIDN'T HAVE A CHOICE. MY BEST FRIEND NEEDED ME.
ZZZZZZ
WOW. YOU'RE ONE HEAVY DUDE. SHEESH.
TUG
TUG
ZZZZZZ
!
!
WAS THAT BIG FURRY THING ABOUT TO EAT ME?
DUDE, YEAH. I TOTALLY THINK HE WAS.
WHAT A JERK.

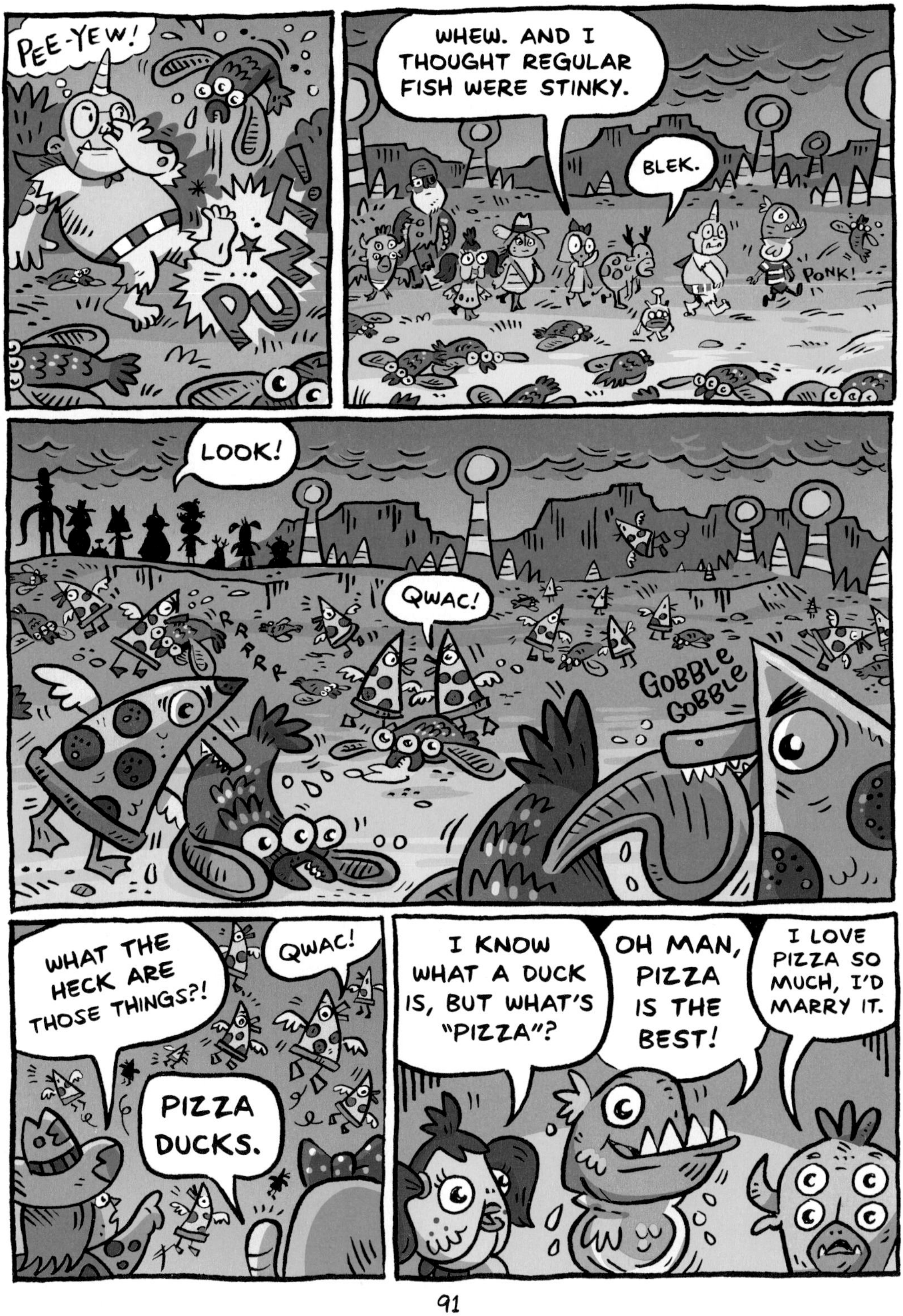
PEE-YEW!
PUTZ!
WHEW. AND I THOUGHT REGULAR FISH WERE STINKY.
BLEK.
PONK!
LOOK!
QWAC!
RRRRR
GOBBLE GOBBLE
WHAT THE HECK ARE THOSE THINGS?!
QWAC!
PIZZA DUCKS.
I KNOW WHAT A DUCK IS, BUT WHAT'S "PIZZA"?
OH MAN, PIZZA IS THE BEST!
I LOVE PIZZA SO MUCH, I'D MARRY IT.

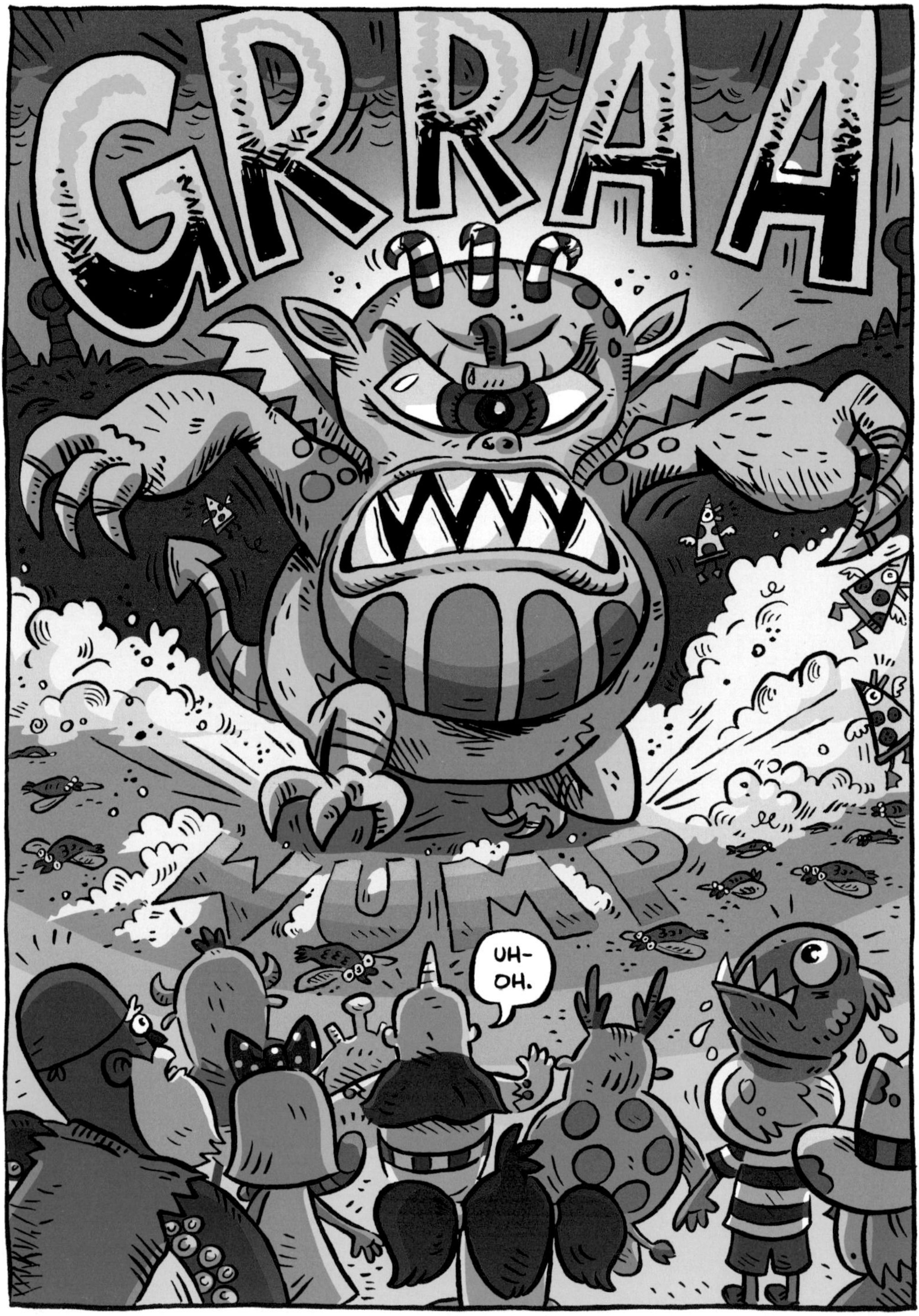
GRRAA
WUMP
UH-OH.

CHAPTER 8

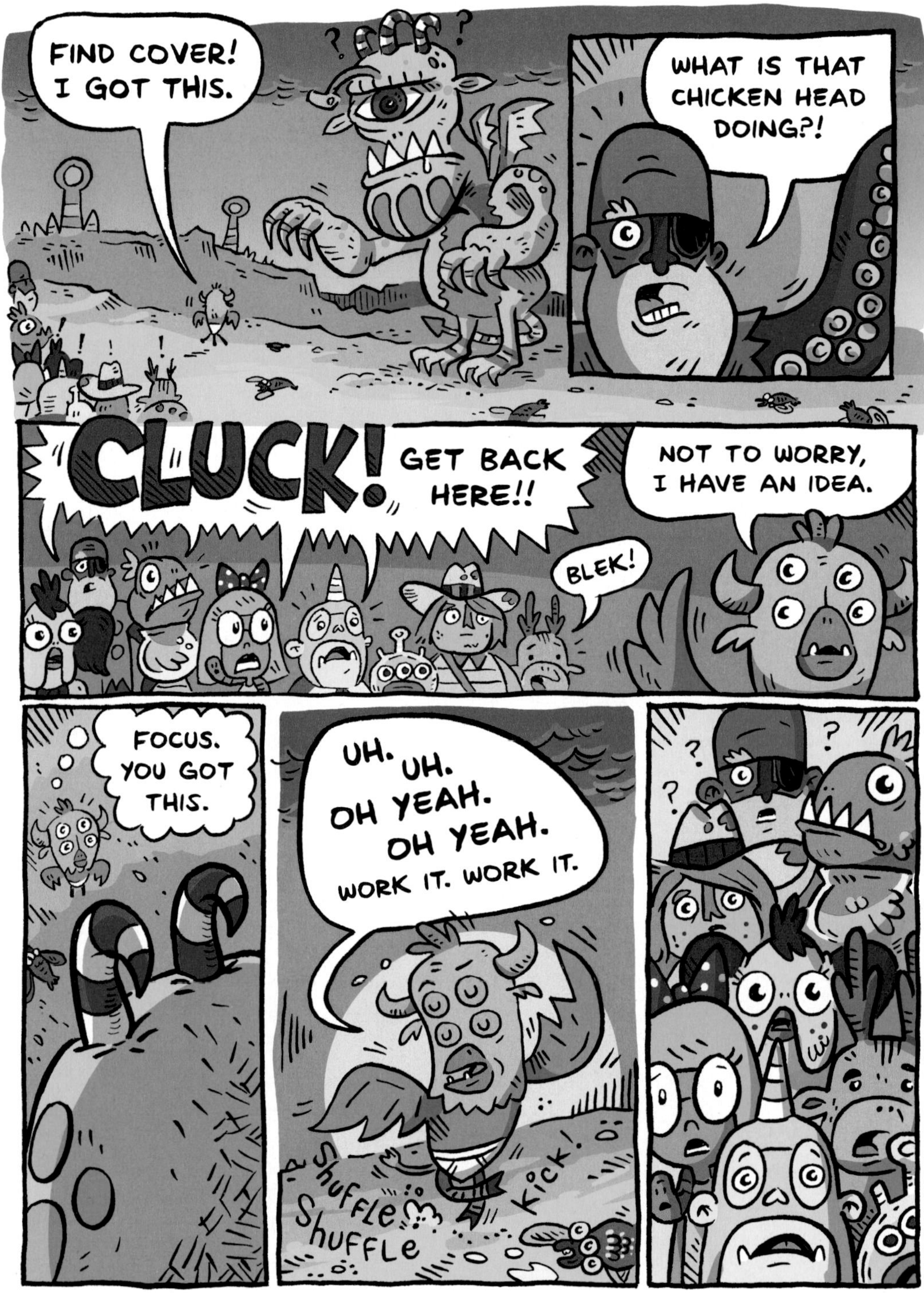
FIND COVER! I GOT THIS.
WHAT IS THAT CHICKEN HEAD DOING?!
CLUCK!
GET BACK HERE!!
NOT TO WORRY, I HAVE AN IDEA.
BLEK!
FOCUS. YOU GOT THIS.
UH. UH. OH YEAH. OH YEAH. WORK IT. WORK IT.
SHUFFLE SHUFFLE
KICK!

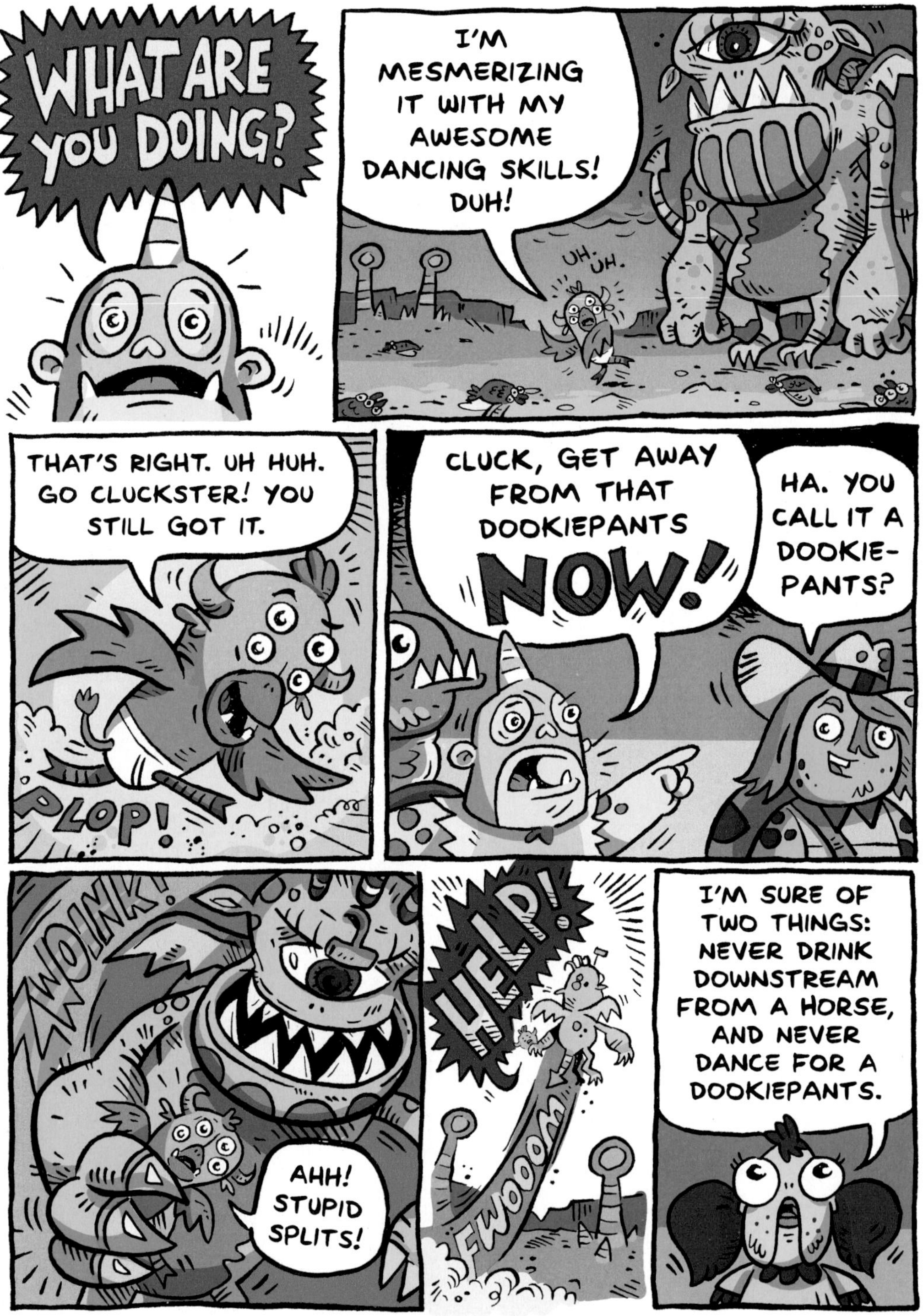
WHAT ARE YOU DOING?
I'M MESMERIZING IT WITH MY AWESOME DANCING SKILLS! DUH!
UH. UH.
THAT'S RIGHT. UH HUH. GO CLUCKSTER! YOU STILL GOT IT.
PLOP!
CLUCK, GET AWAY FROM THAT DOOKIEPANTS NOW!
HA. YOU CALL IT A DOOKIE-PANTS?
WOINK!
AHH! STUPID SPLITS!
HELP!
FWOOOM
I'M SURE OF TWO THINGS: NEVER DRINK DOWNSTREAM FROM A HORSE, AND NEVER DANCE FOR A DOOKIEPANTS.

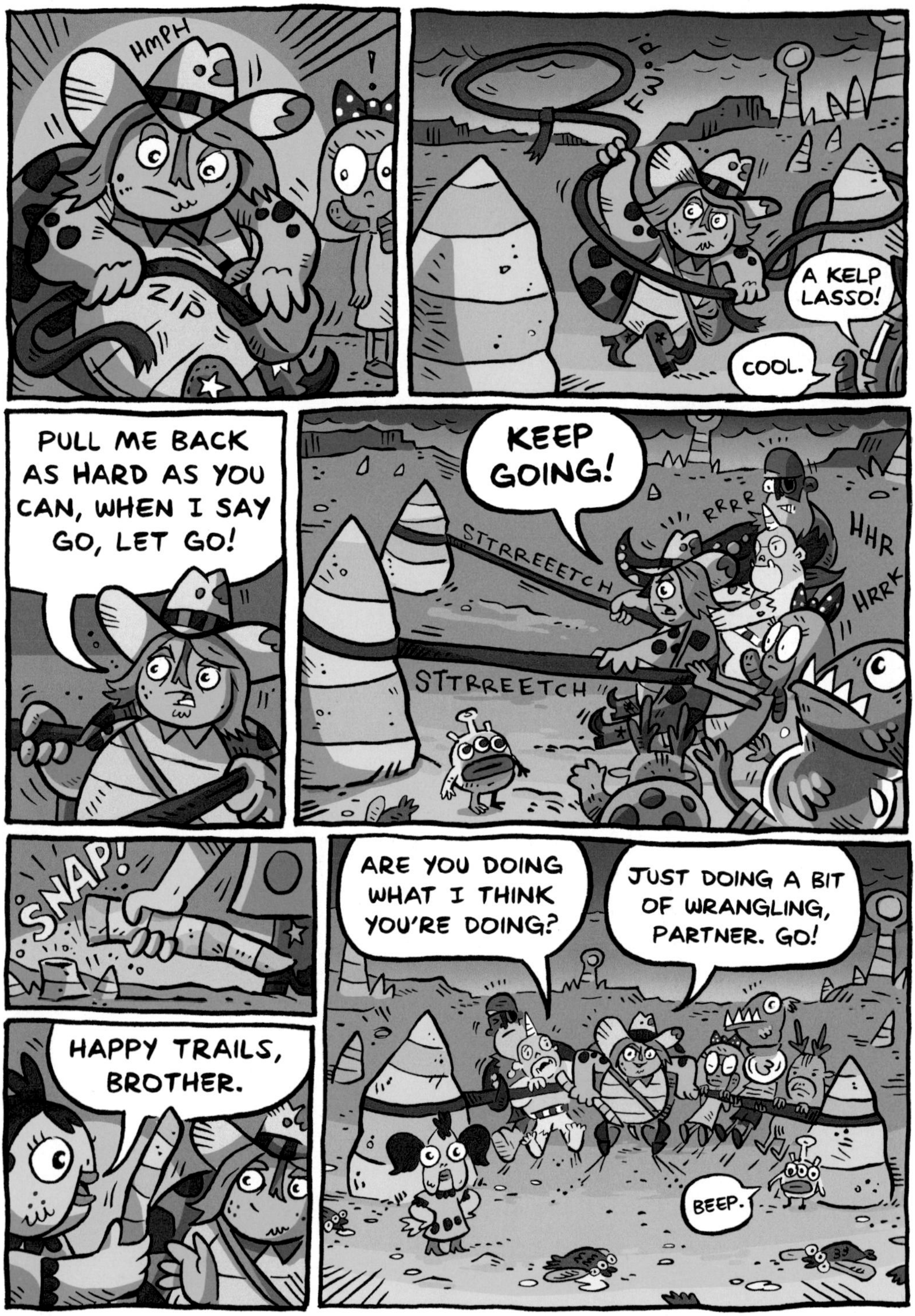
HMPH
!
ZIP
FWIP!
A KELP LASSO!
COOL.
PULL ME BACK AS HARD AS YOU CAN, WHEN I SAY GO, LET GO!
KEEP GOING!
RRRR
STTRREEETCH
HHR
HRRK
STTRREETCH
SNAP!
ARE YOU DOING WHAT I THINK YOU'RE DOING?
JUST DOING A BIT OF WRANGLING, PARTNER. GO!
BEEP.
HAPPY TRAILS, BROTHER.

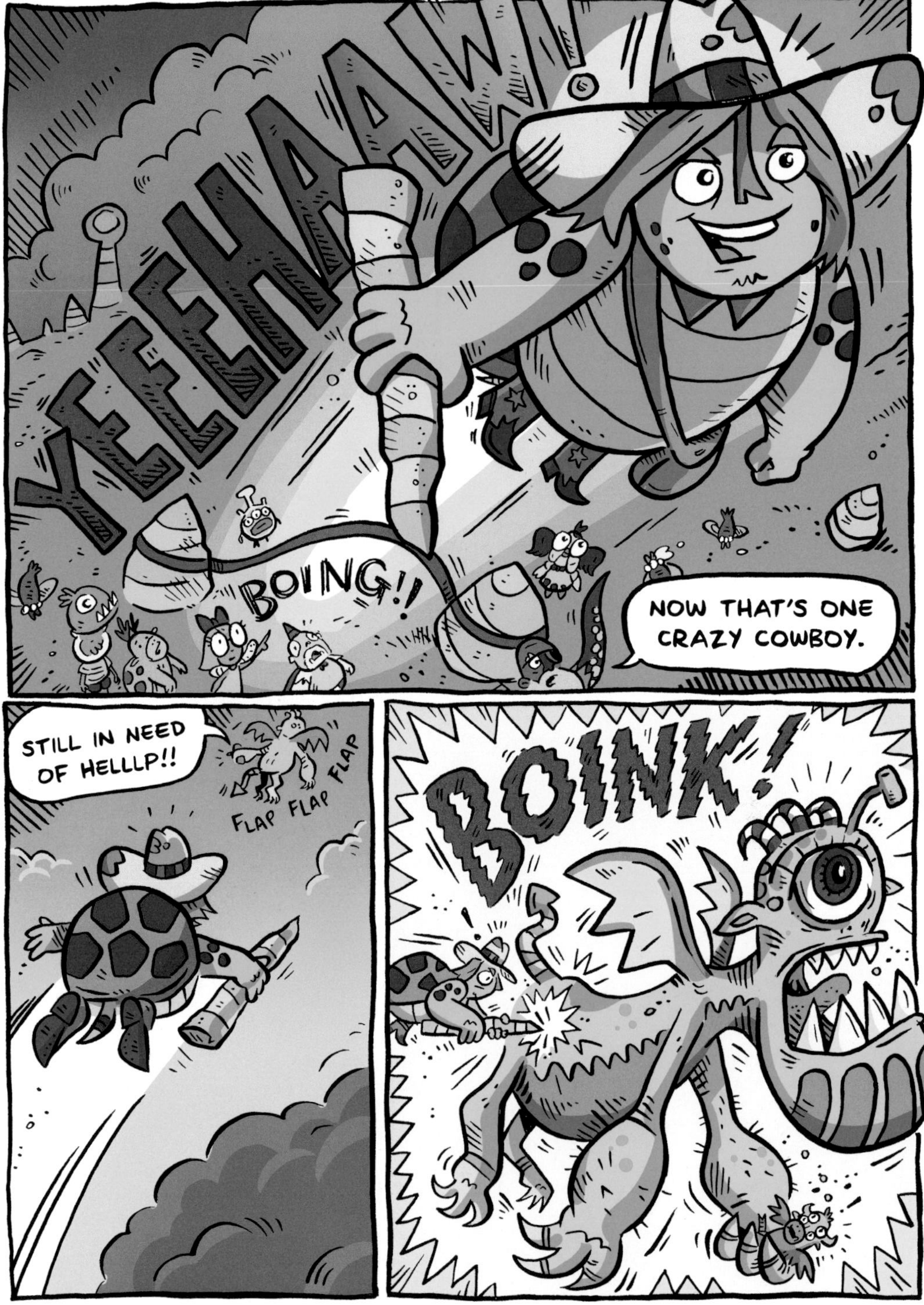
YEEHAAW!!
BOING!!
NOW THAT'S ONE CRAZY COWBOY.
STILL IN NEED OF HELLLP!!
FLAP FLAP FLAP
BOINK!

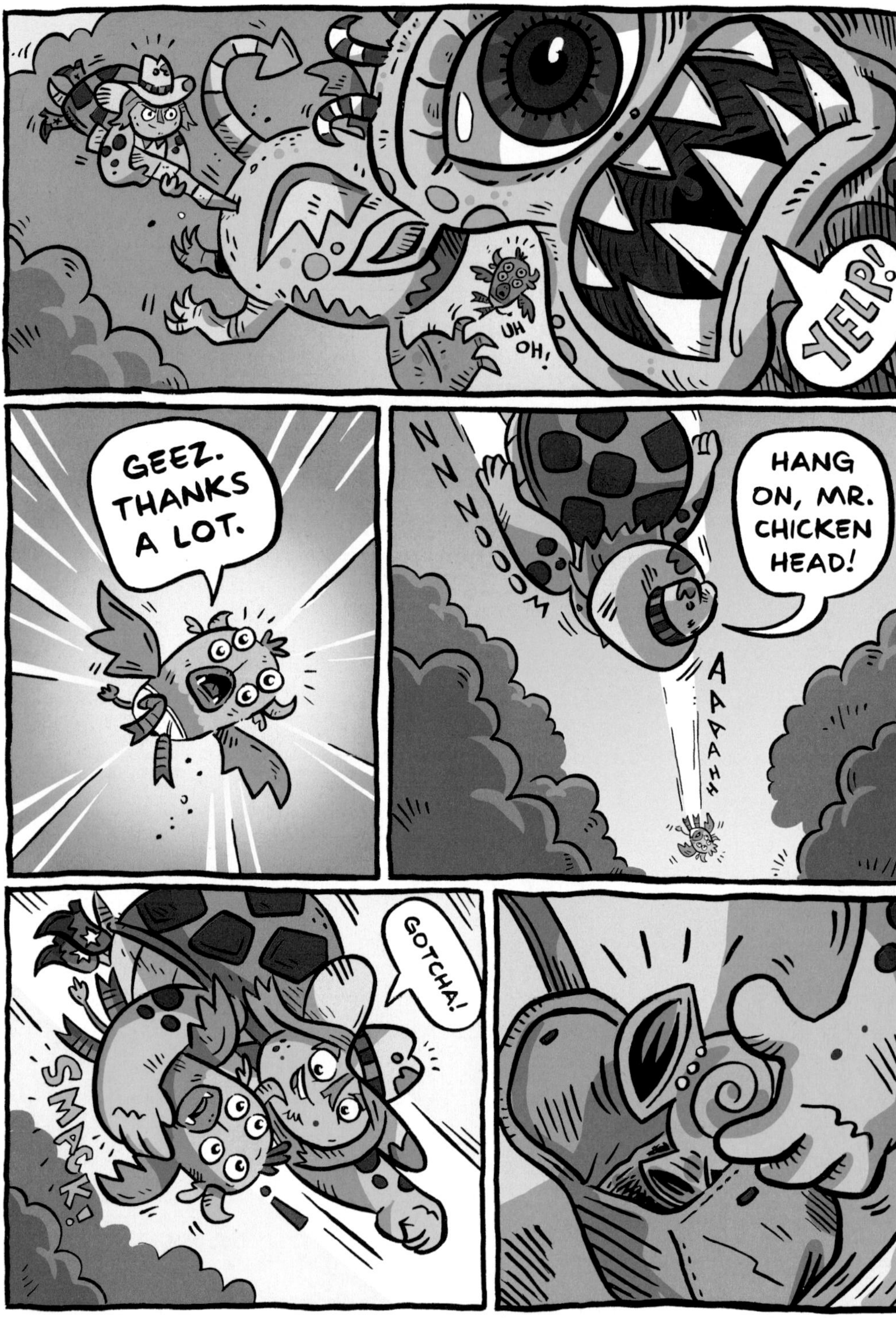
UH OH!
YELP!
GEEZ. THANKS A LOT.
NNNOOOOOW
HANG ON, MR. CHICKEN HEAD!
AAAAAHH
GOTCHA!
SMACK!

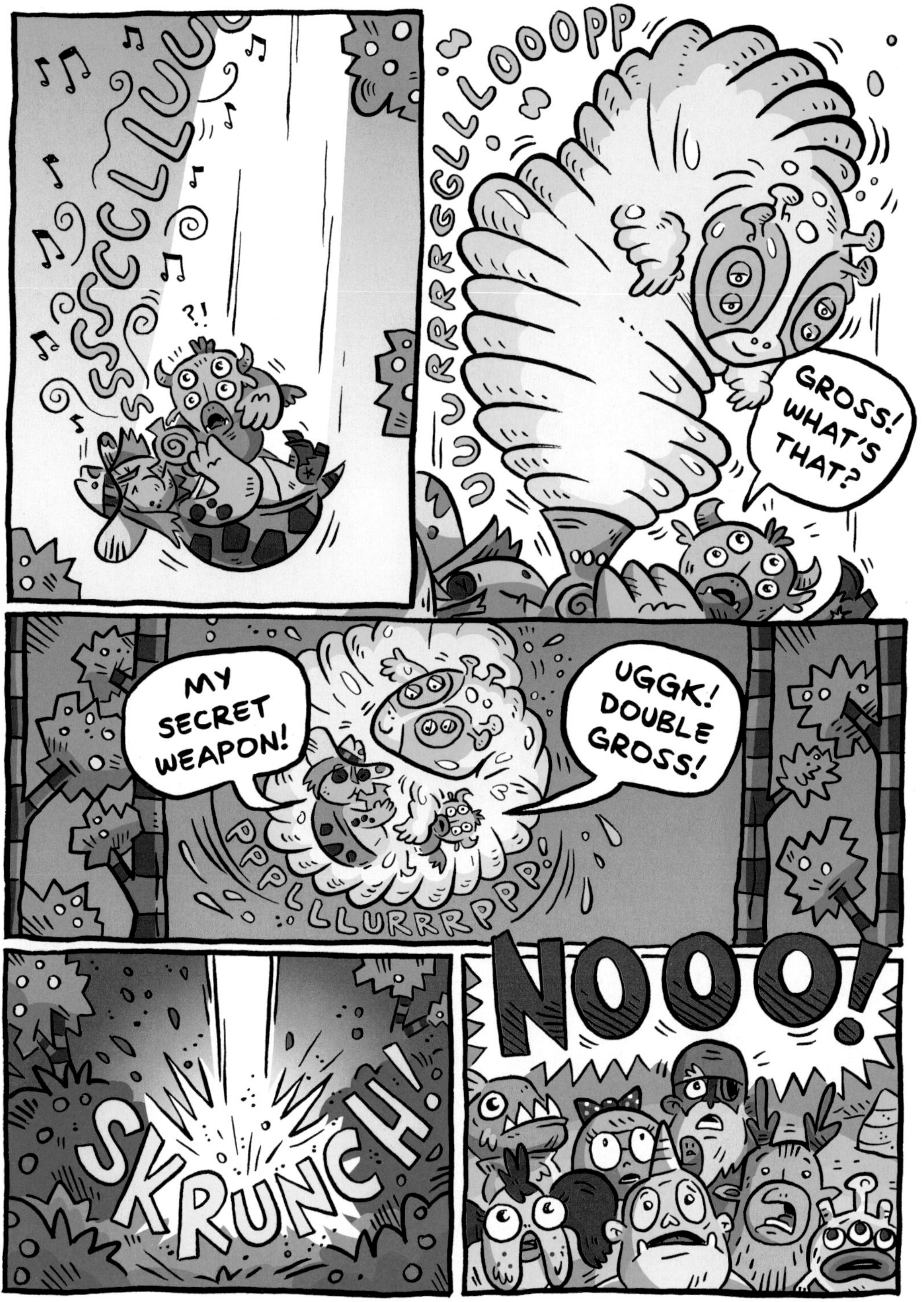
SSCCLLUUU
?!
UURRRGGLLOOOPP
GROSS! WHAT'S THAT?
MY SECRET WEAPON!
UGGK! DOUBLE GROSS!
PPPLLLURRRPPP!
SKRUNCH!
NOOO!

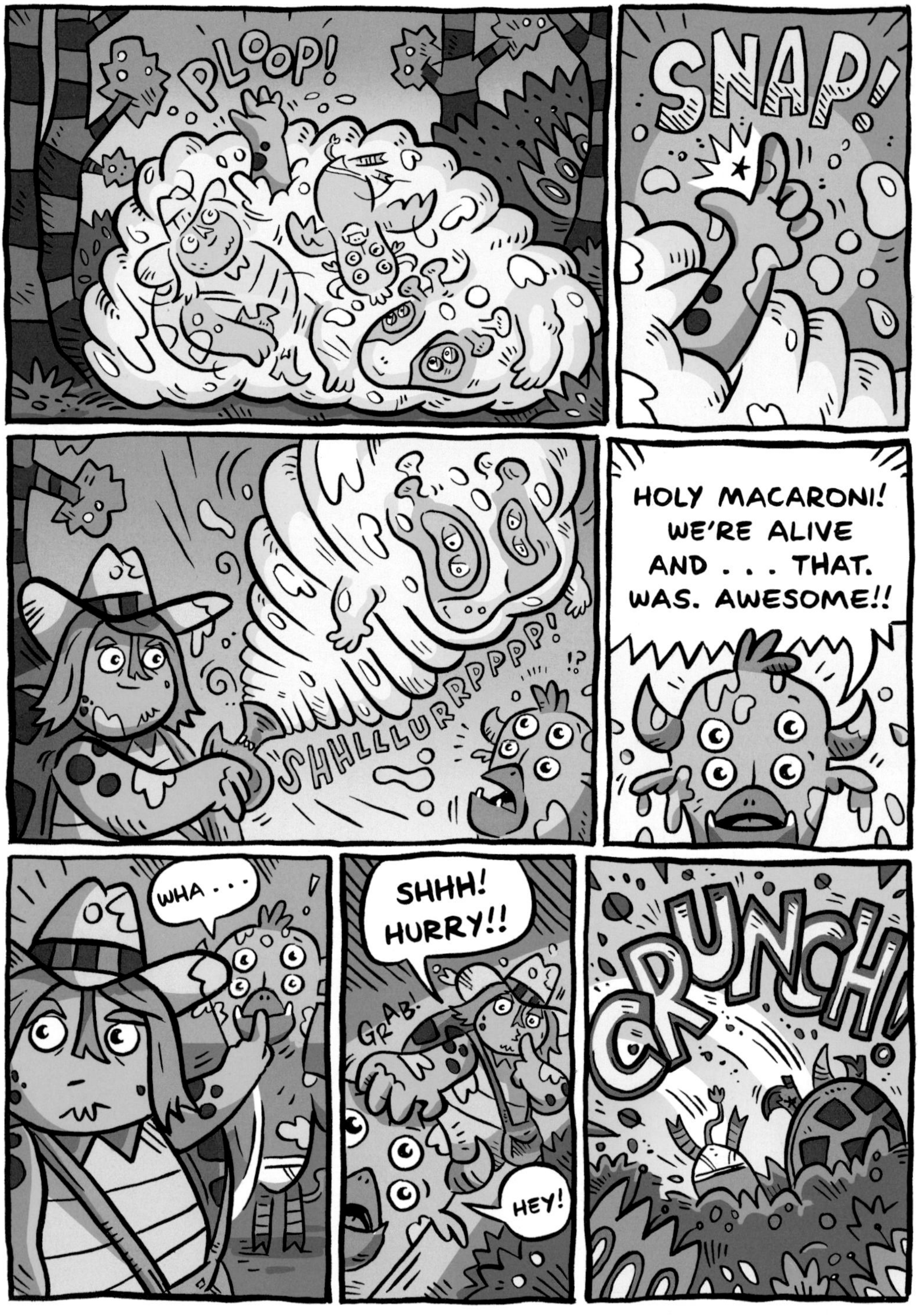
PLOOP!
SNAP!
SHHLLLURRPPPPP!
!?
HOLY MACARONI! WE'RE ALIVE AND . . . THAT. WAS. AWESOME!!
WHA . . .
!
SHHH! HURRY!!
GRAB!
HEY!
CRUNCH!

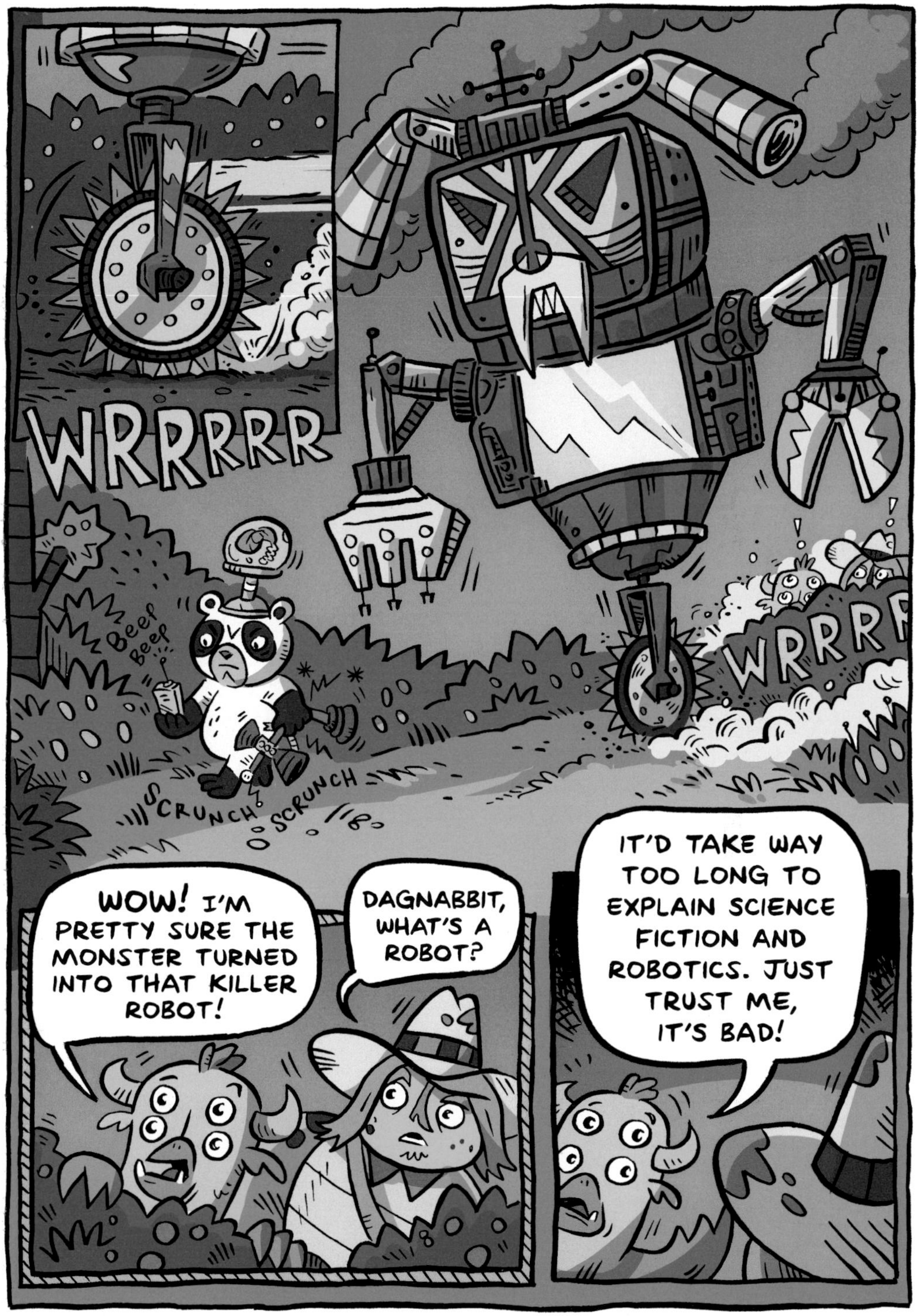
WRRRRR
BEEP
BEEP
SCRUNCH
SCRUNCH
WRRRR
WOW! I'M PRETTY SURE THE MONSTER TURNED INTO THAT KILLER ROBOT!
DAGNABBIT, WHAT'S A ROBOT?
IT'D TAKE WAY TOO LONG TO EXPLAIN SCIENCE FICTION AND ROBOTICS. JUST TRUST ME, IT'S BAD!

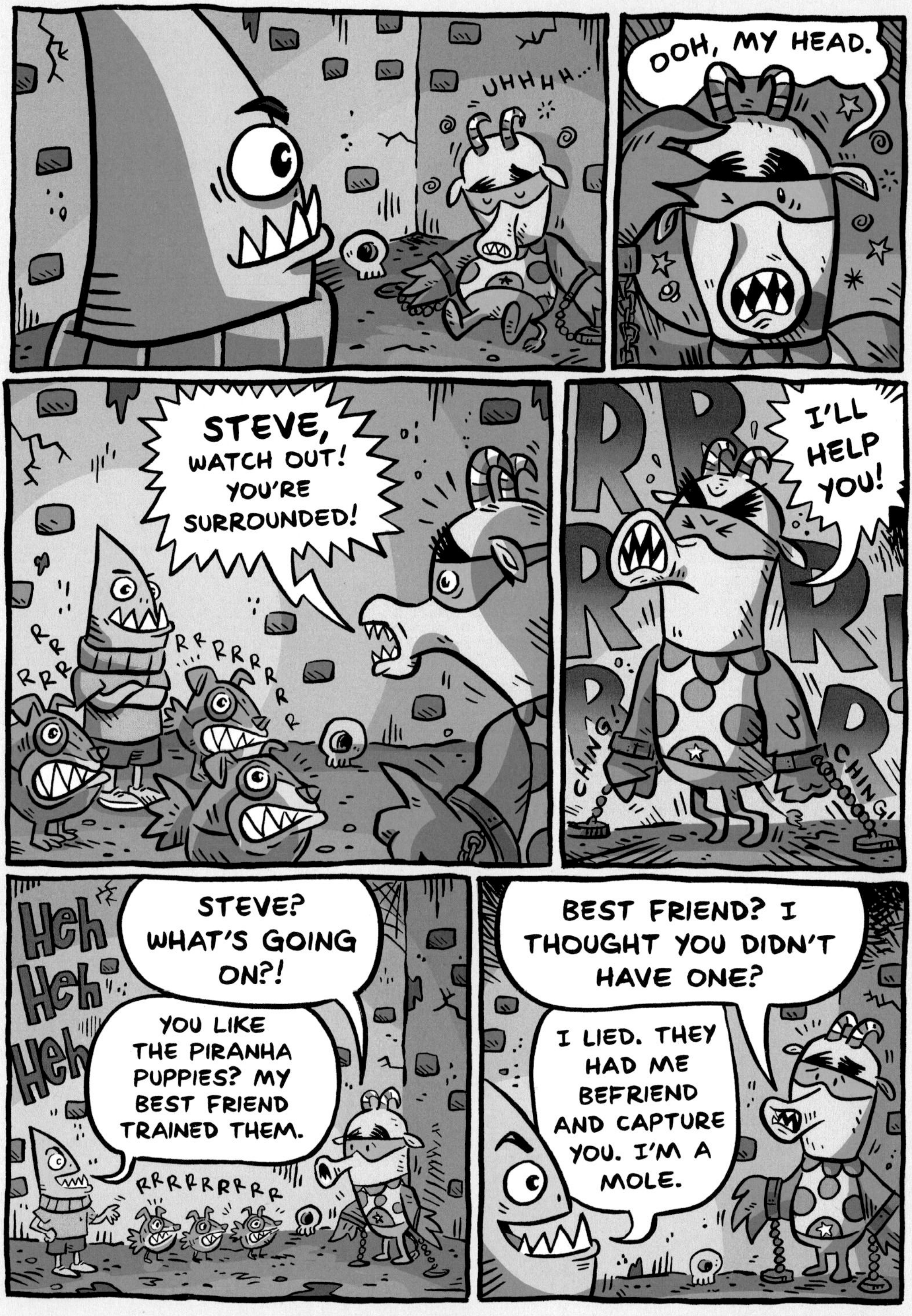
UHHHH...
OOH, MY HEAD.
STEVE, WATCH OUT! YOU'RE SURROUNDED!
RRRRRRRRR
I'LL HELP YOU!
CHING! CHING!
Heh Heh Heh
STEVE? WHAT'S GOING ON?!
YOU LIKE THE PIRANHA PUPPIES? MY BEST FRIEND TRAINED THEM.
RRRRRRRRR
BEST FRIEND? I THOUGHT YOU DIDN'T HAVE ONE?
I LIED. THEY HAD ME BEFRIEND AND CAPTURE YOU. I'M A MOLE.

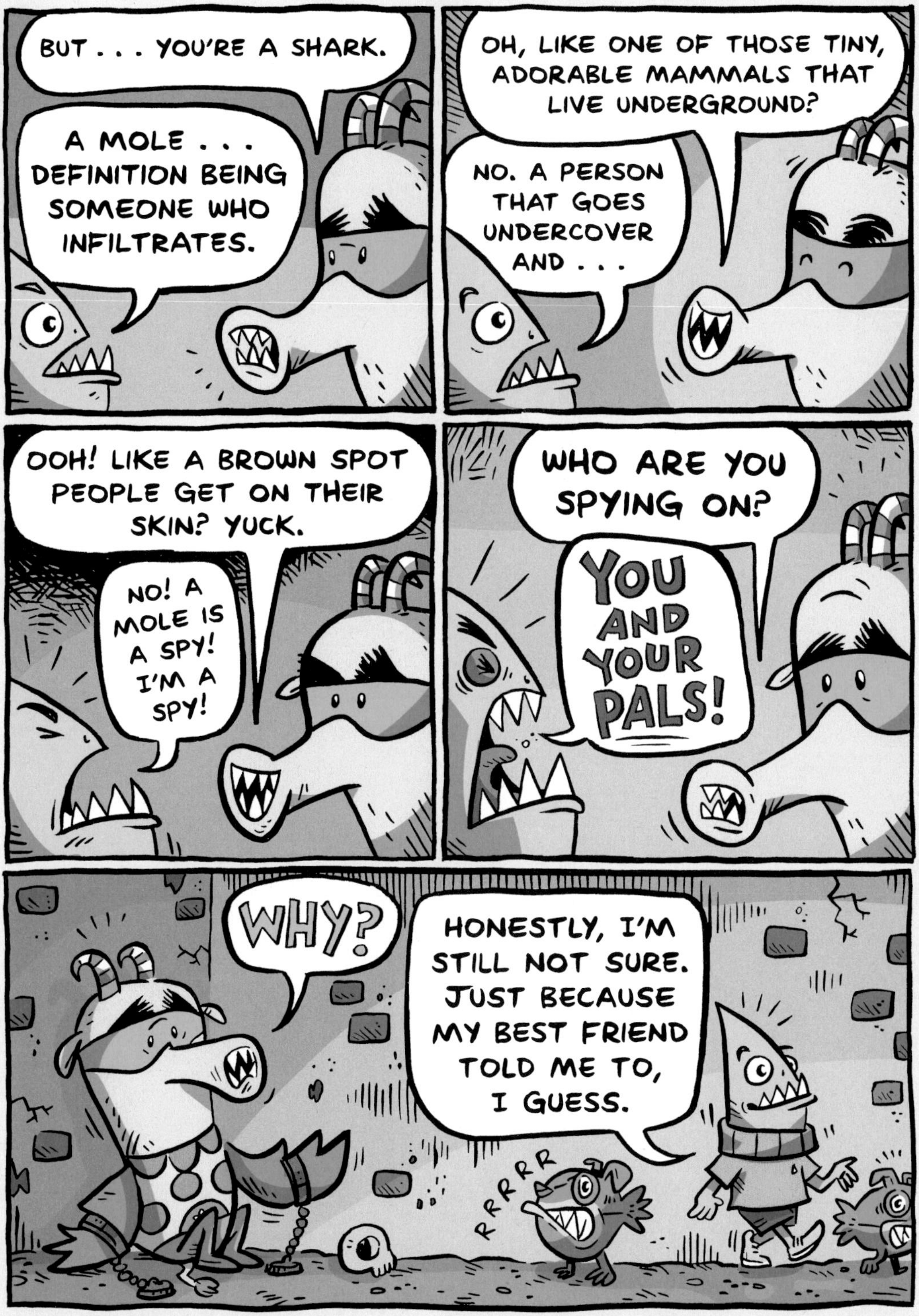
BUT . . . YOU'RE A SHARK.
A MOLE . . . DEFINITION BEING SOMEONE WHO INFILTRATES.
OH, LIKE ONE OF THOSE TINY, ADORABLE MAMMALS THAT LIVE UNDERGROUND?
NO. A PERSON THAT GOES UNDERCOVER AND . . .
OOH! LIKE A BROWN SPOT PEOPLE GET ON THEIR SKIN? YUCK.
NO! A MOLE IS A SPY! I'M A SPY!
WHO ARE YOU SPYING ON?
YOU AND YOUR PALS!
WHY?
HONESTLY, I'M STILL NOT SURE. JUST BECAUSE MY BEST FRIEND TOLD ME TO, I GUESS.
RRRRR

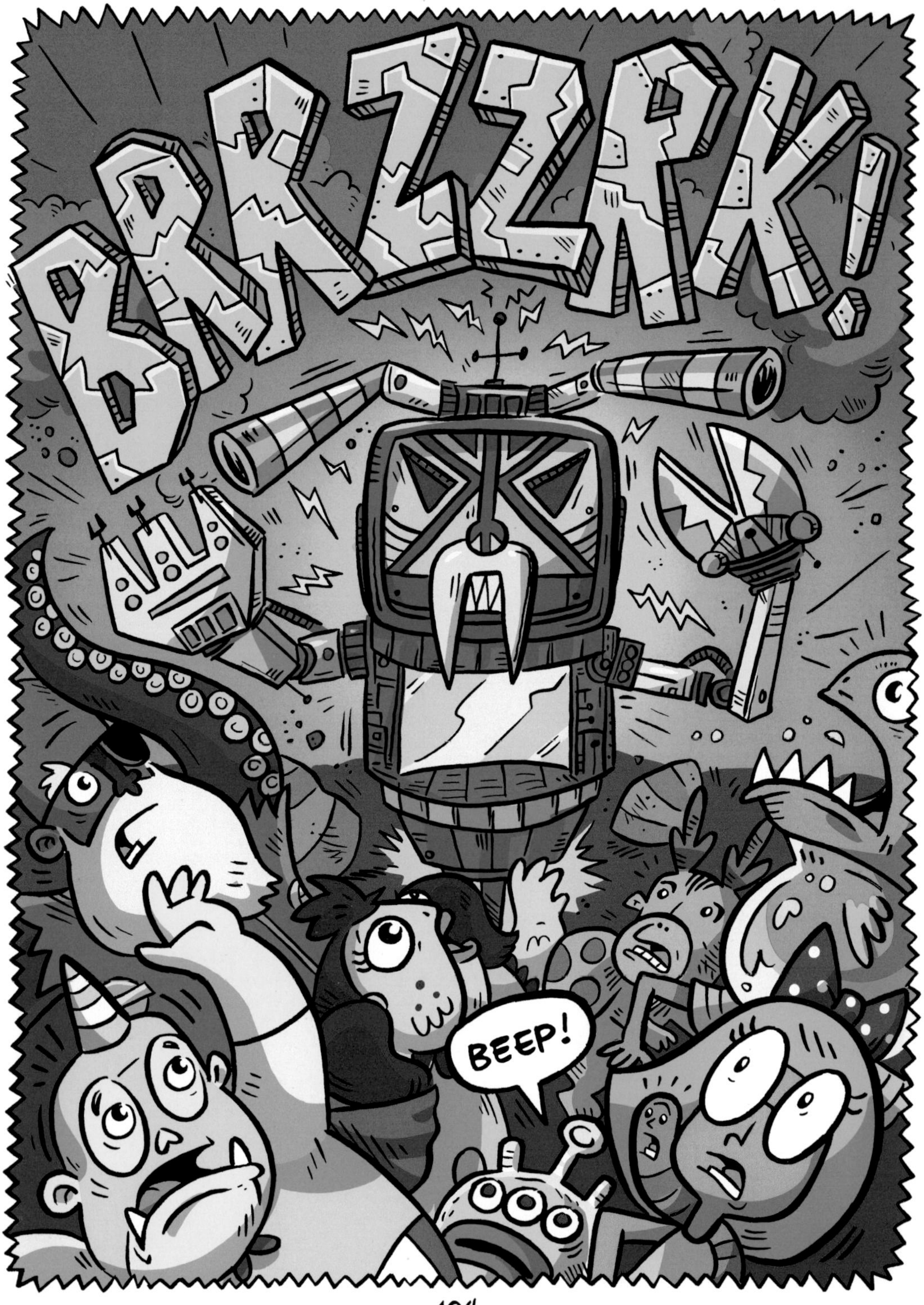
BRZZPK!
BEEP!

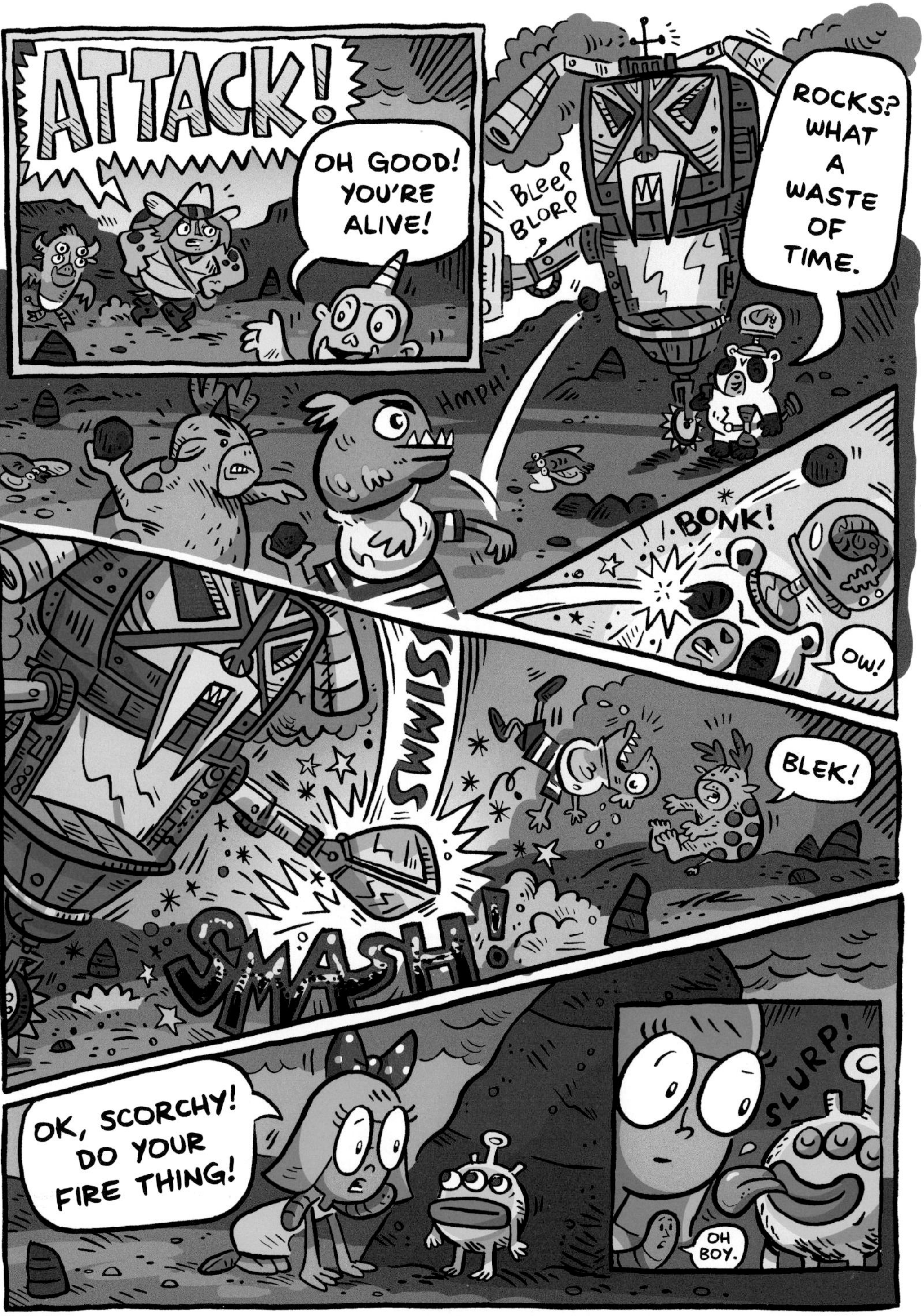

ATTACK!
OH GOOD! YOU'RE ALIVE!
BLEEP BLORP
ROCKS? WHAT A WASTE OF TIME.
HMPH!
BONK!
OW!
SWWISS
BLEK!
SMASH!
OK, SCORCHY! DO YOUR FIRE THING!
SLURP!
OH BOY.

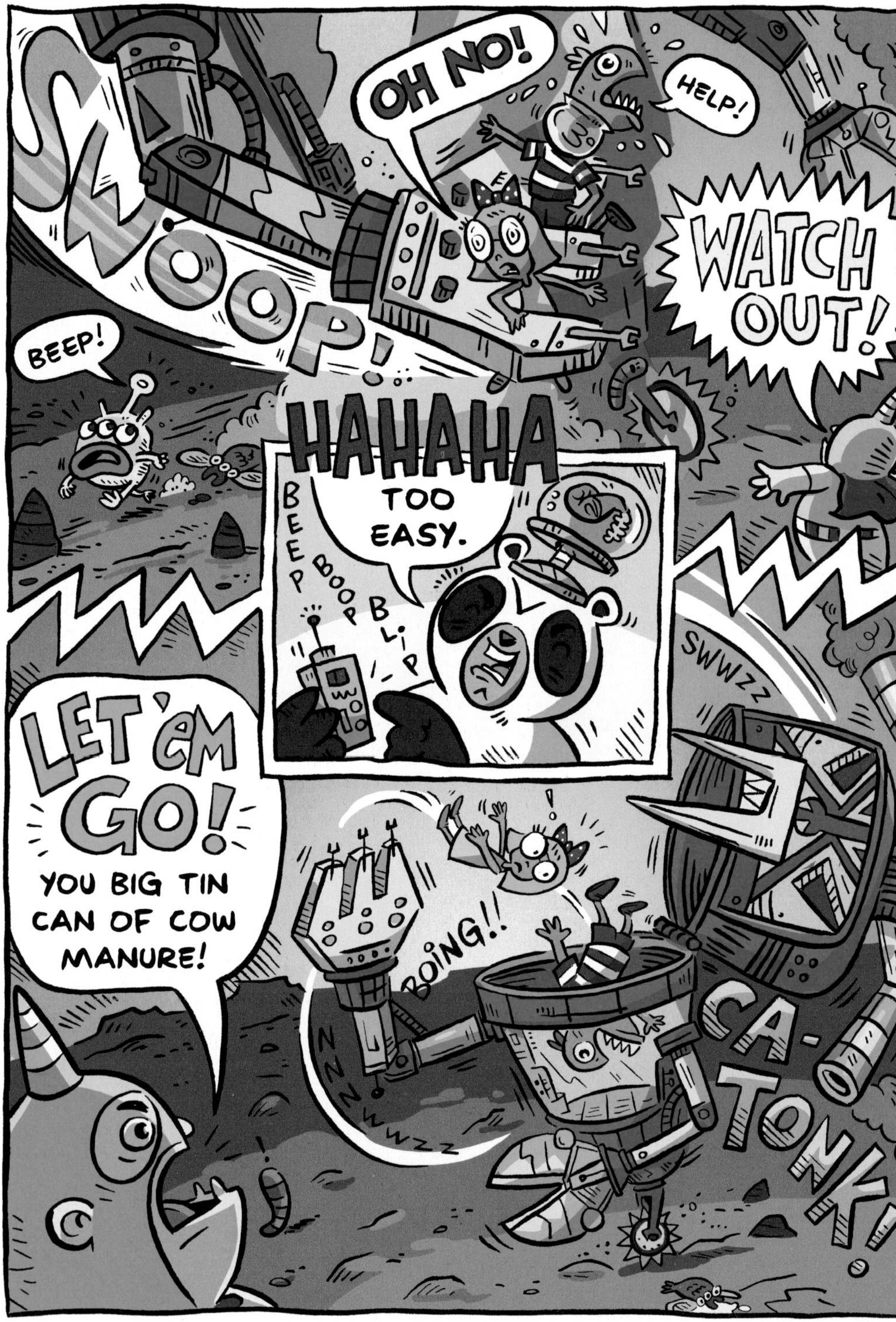
SWOOOP!
OH NO!
HELP!
WATCH OUT!
BEEP!
HAHAHA
TOO EASY.
BEEP
BOOP
BLIP
SWWZZ
LET 'EM GO!
YOU BIG TIN CAN OF COW MANURE!
BOING!!
NNZZWWWZZZ
CA-TONK!

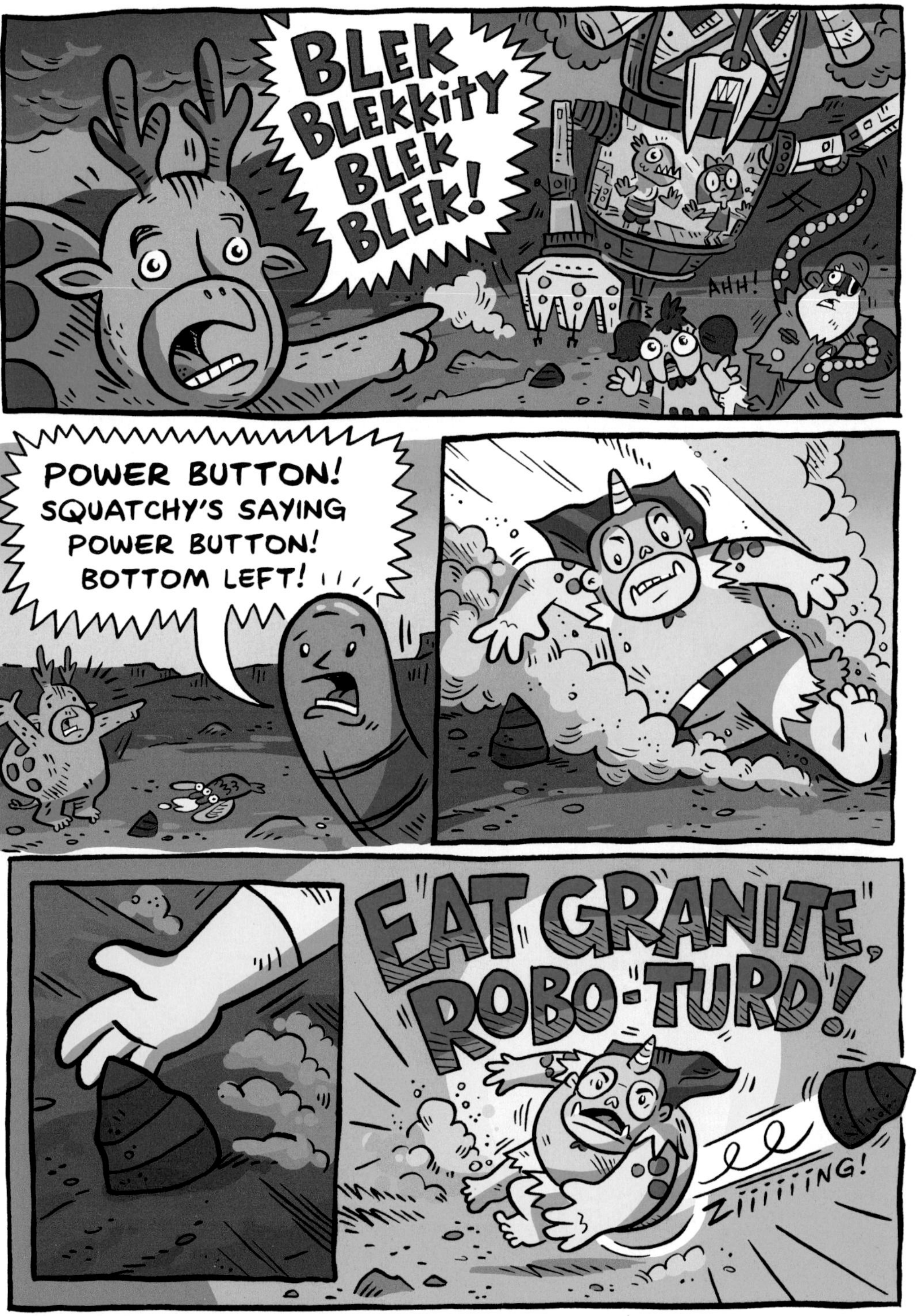

BLEK BLEKKITY BLEK BLEK!
AHH!
POWER BUTTON! SQUATCHY'S SAYING POWER BUTTON! BOTTOM LEFT!
EAT GRANITE, ROBO-TURD!
ZIIIIIING!

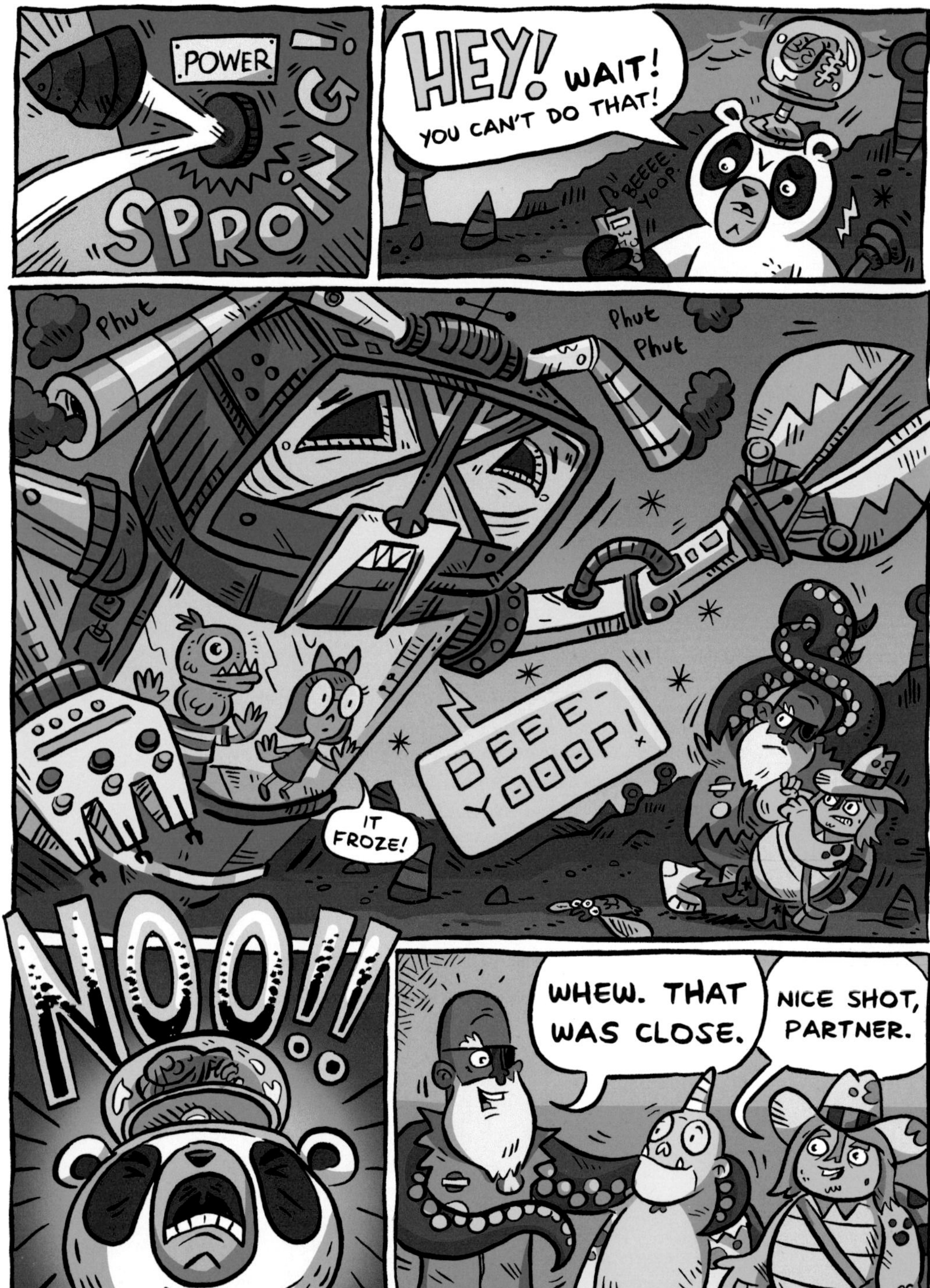
POWER
SPROING
HEY! WAIT! YOU CAN'T DO THAT!
BEEEE YOOP.
Phut
Phut Phut
BEEEE-YOOOOP!
IT FROZE!
NOO!!
WHEW. THAT WAS CLOSE.
NICE SHOT, PARTNER.

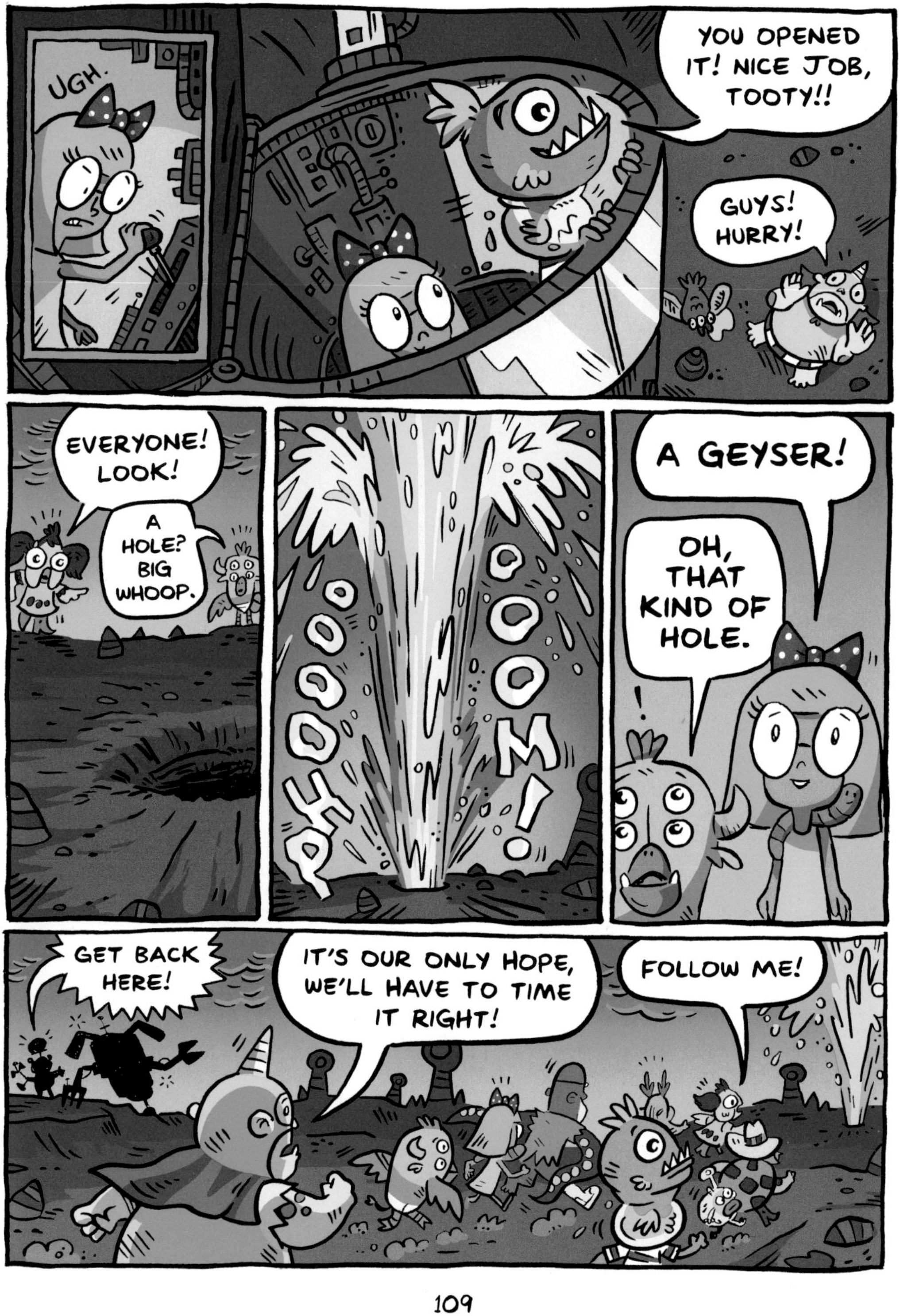
UGH.
YOU OPENED IT! NICE JOB, TOOTY!!
GUYS! HURRY!
EVERYONE! LOOK!
A HOLE? BIG WHOOP.
PHOOOOOOOOM!
A GEYSER!
OH, THAT KIND OF HOLE.
!
GET BACK HERE!
IT'S OUR ONLY HOPE, WE'LL HAVE TO TIME IT RIGHT!
FOLLOW ME!

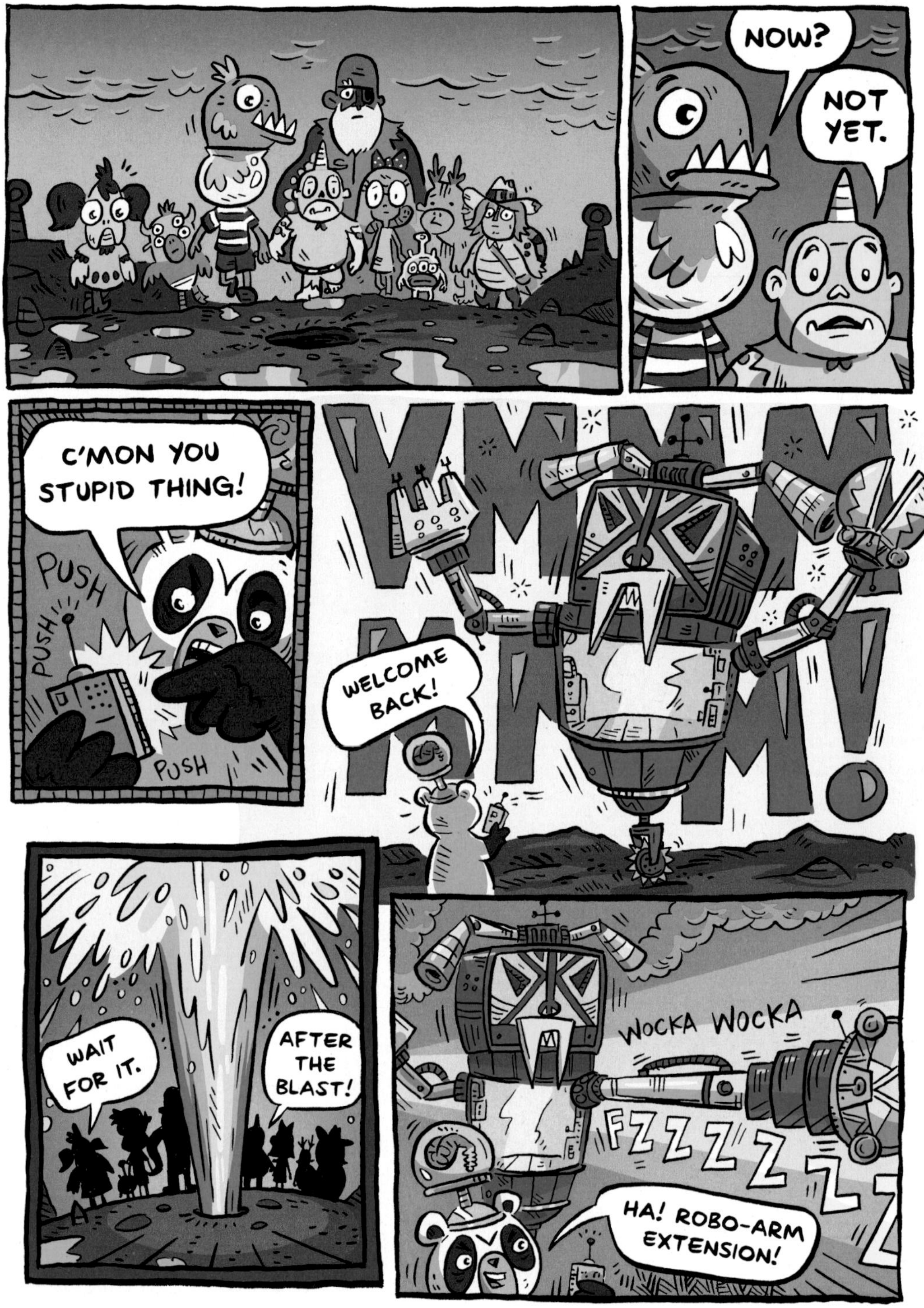
NOW?
NOT YET.
C'MON YOU STUPID THING!
PUSH
PUSH
PUSH
VMMMMMM!
WELCOME BACK!
WAIT FOR IT.
AFTER THE BLAST!
WOCKA WOCKA
FZZZZZZ
HA! ROBO-ARM EXTENSION!

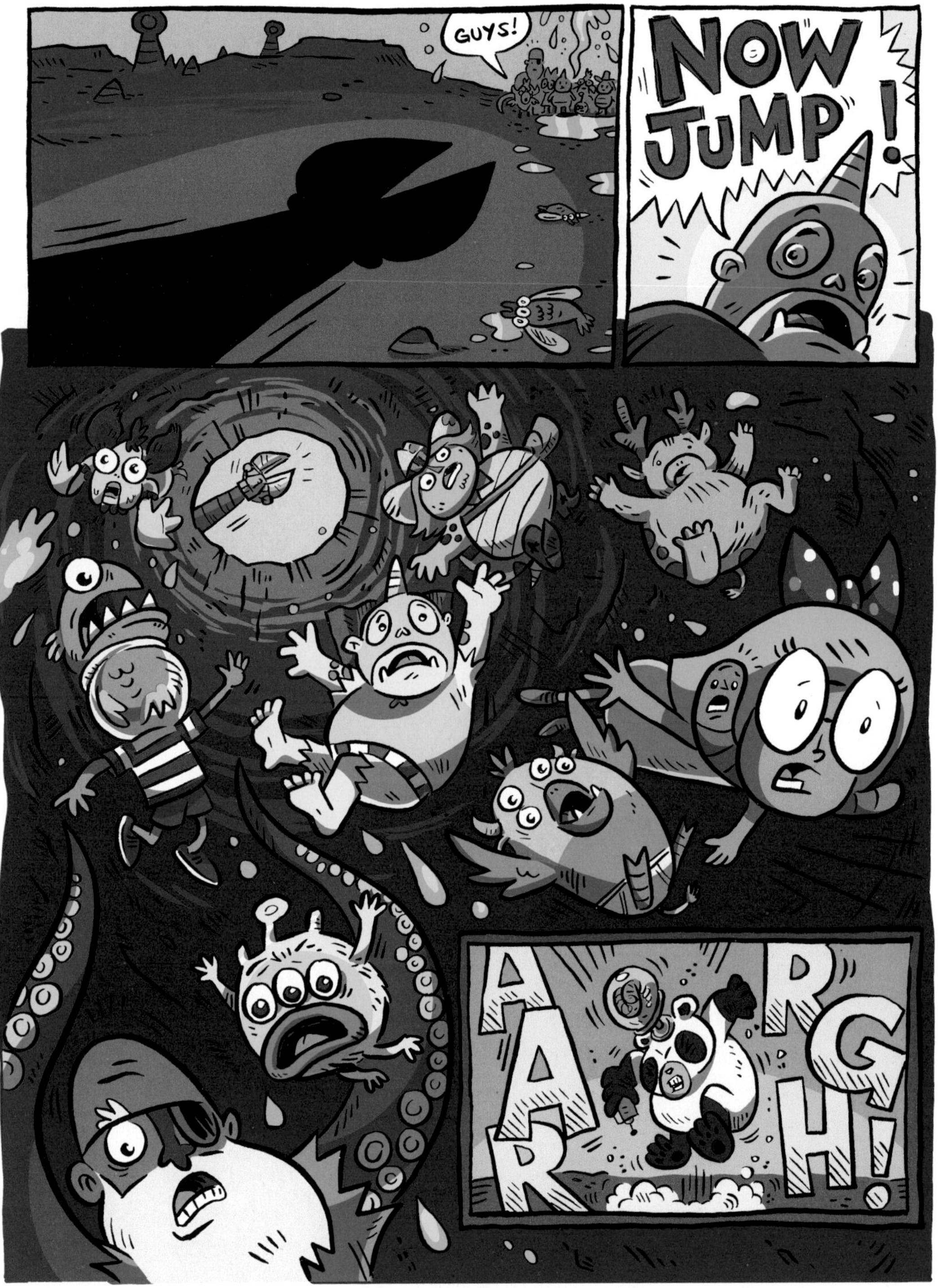
GUYS!
NOW JUMP!
AARRGH!

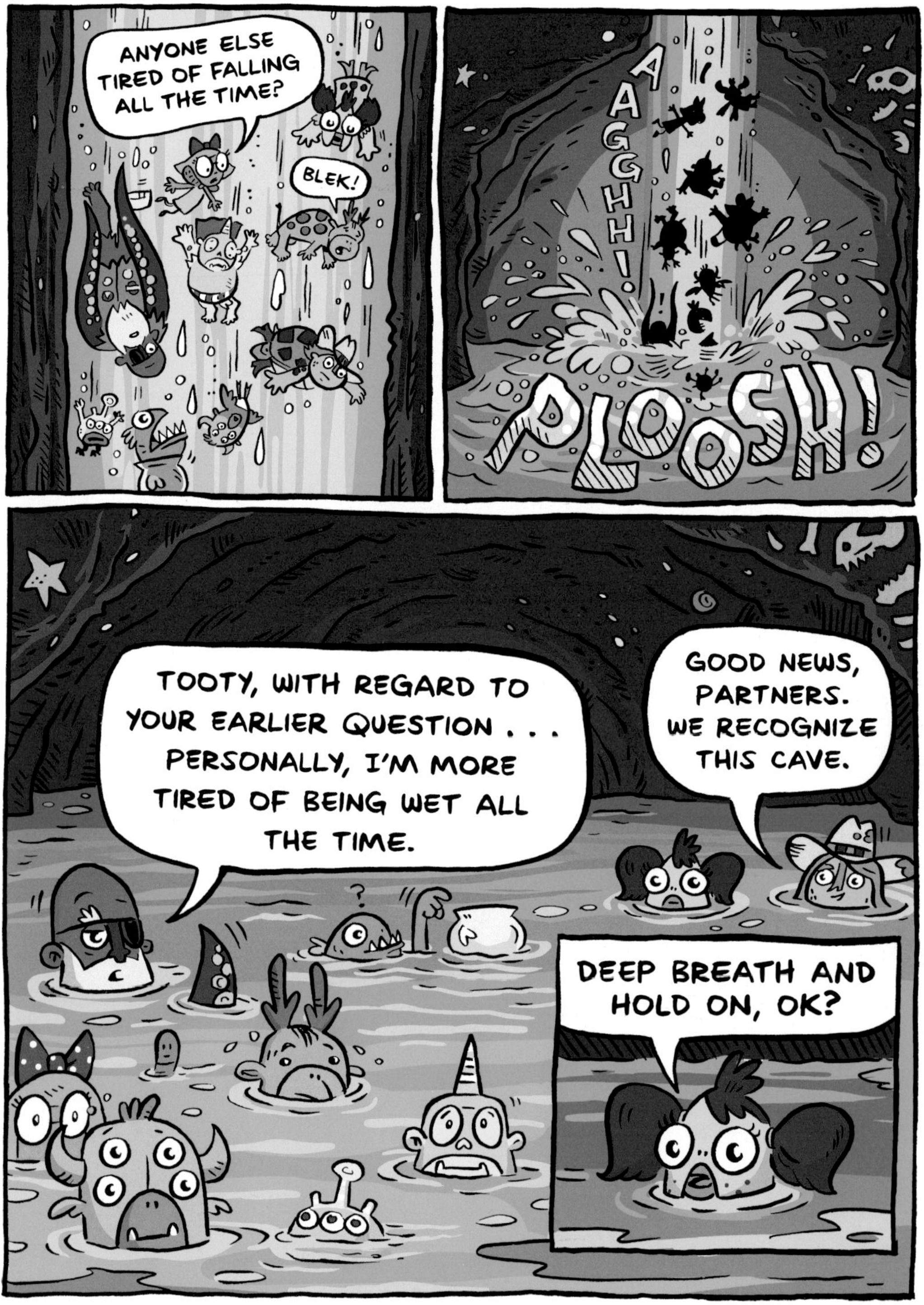
ANYONE ELSE TIRED OF FALLING ALL THE TIME?
BLEK!
AAGGHH!
PLOOSH!
TOOTY, WITH REGARD TO YOUR EARLIER QUESTION . . . PERSONALLY, I'M MORE TIRED OF BEING WET ALL THE TIME.
GOOD NEWS, PARTNERS. WE RECOGNIZE THIS CAVE.
DEEP BREATH AND HOLD ON, OK?

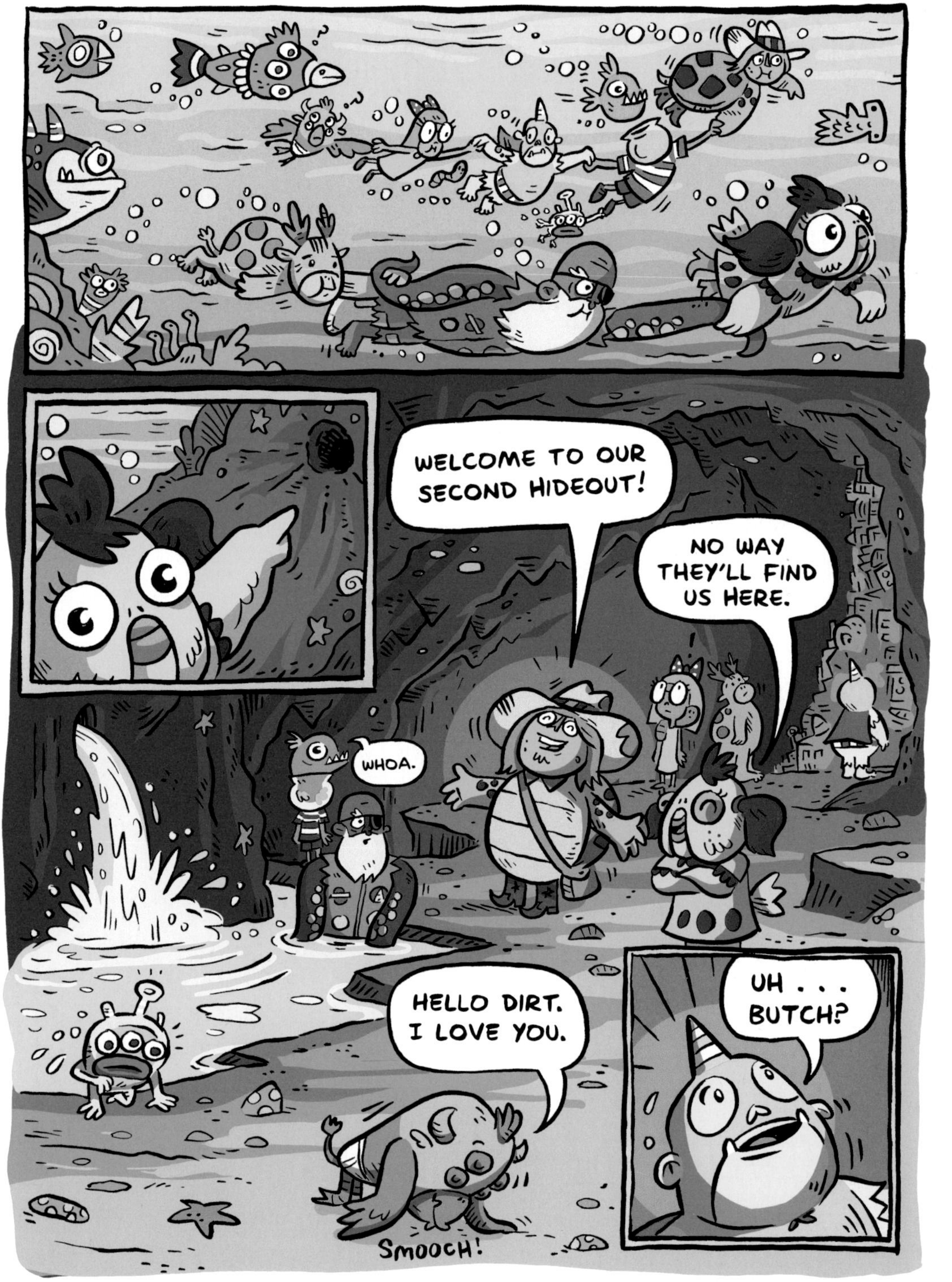
WELCOME TO OUR SECOND HIDEOUT!
NO WAY THEY'LL FIND US HERE.
WHOA.
HELLO DIRT. I LOVE YOU.
SMOOCH!
UH . . . BUTCH?

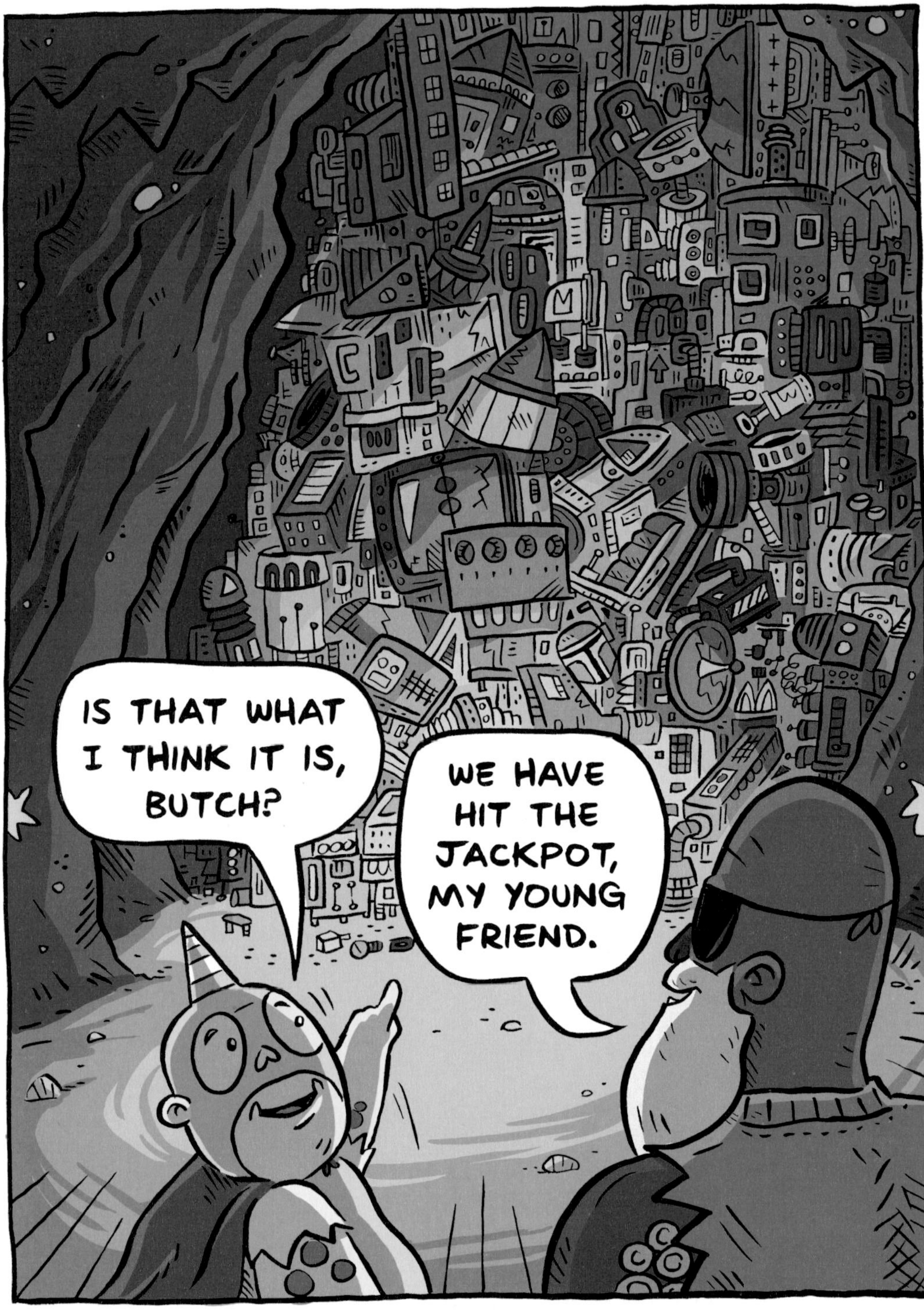
IS THAT WHAT I THINK IT IS, BUTCH?
WE HAVE HIT THE JACKPOT, MY YOUNG FRIEND.

KAW
KAW
KAW

CHAPTER
9

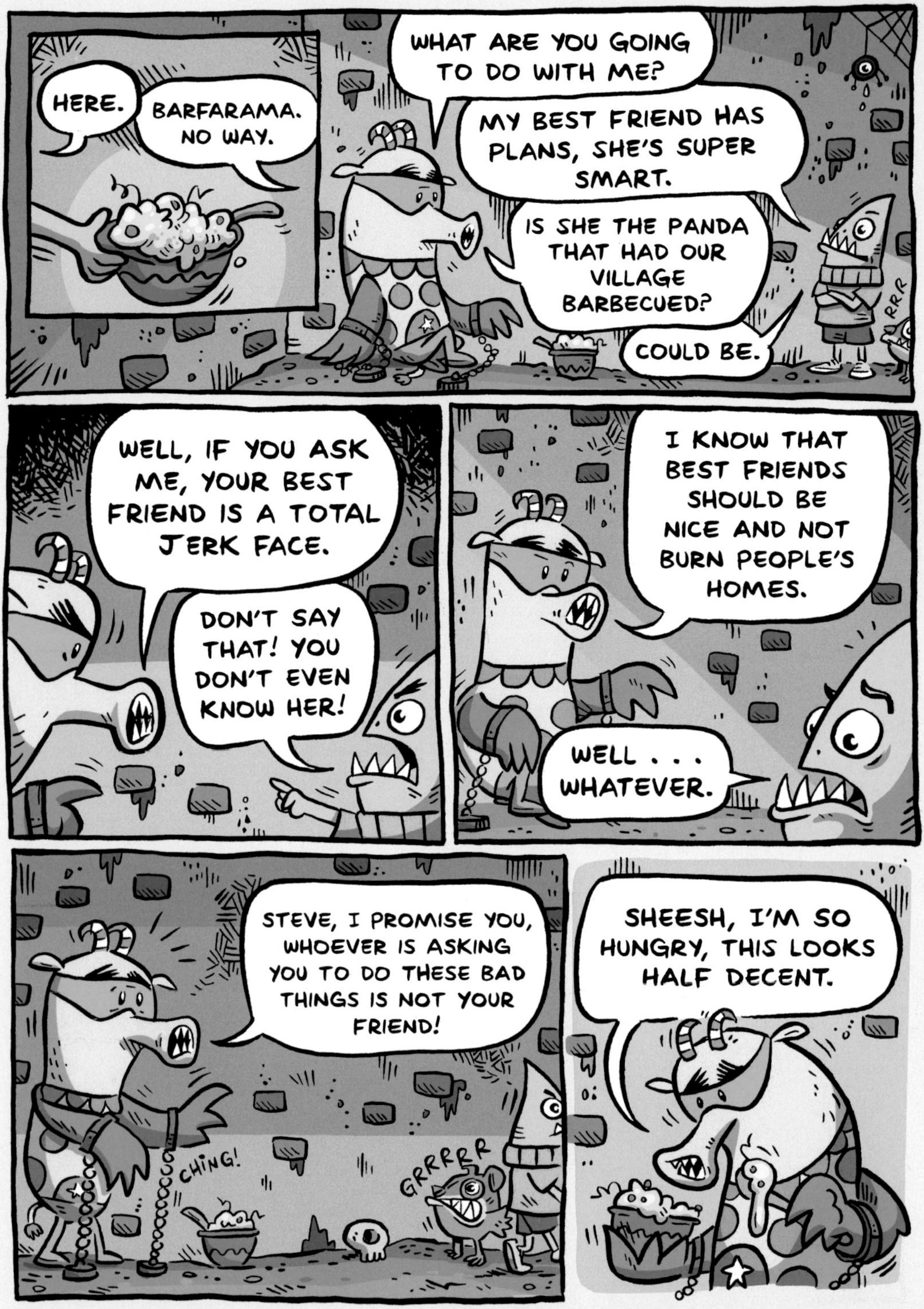
HERE.
BARFARAMA. NO WAY.
WHAT ARE YOU GOING TO DO WITH ME?
MY BEST FRIEND HAS PLANS, SHE'S SUPER SMART.
IS SHE THE PANDA THAT HAD OUR VILLAGE BARBECUED?
COULD BE.
RRR
WELL, IF YOU ASK ME, YOUR BEST FRIEND IS A TOTAL JERK FACE.
DON'T SAY THAT! YOU DON'T EVEN KNOW HER!
I KNOW THAT BEST FRIENDS SHOULD BE NICE AND NOT BURN PEOPLE'S HOMES.
WELL . . . WHATEVER.
STEVE, I PROMISE YOU, WHOEVER IS ASKING YOU TO DO THESE BAD THINGS IS NOT YOUR FRIEND!
CHING!
GRRRRR
SHEESH, I'M SO HUNGRY, THIS LOOKS HALF DECENT.

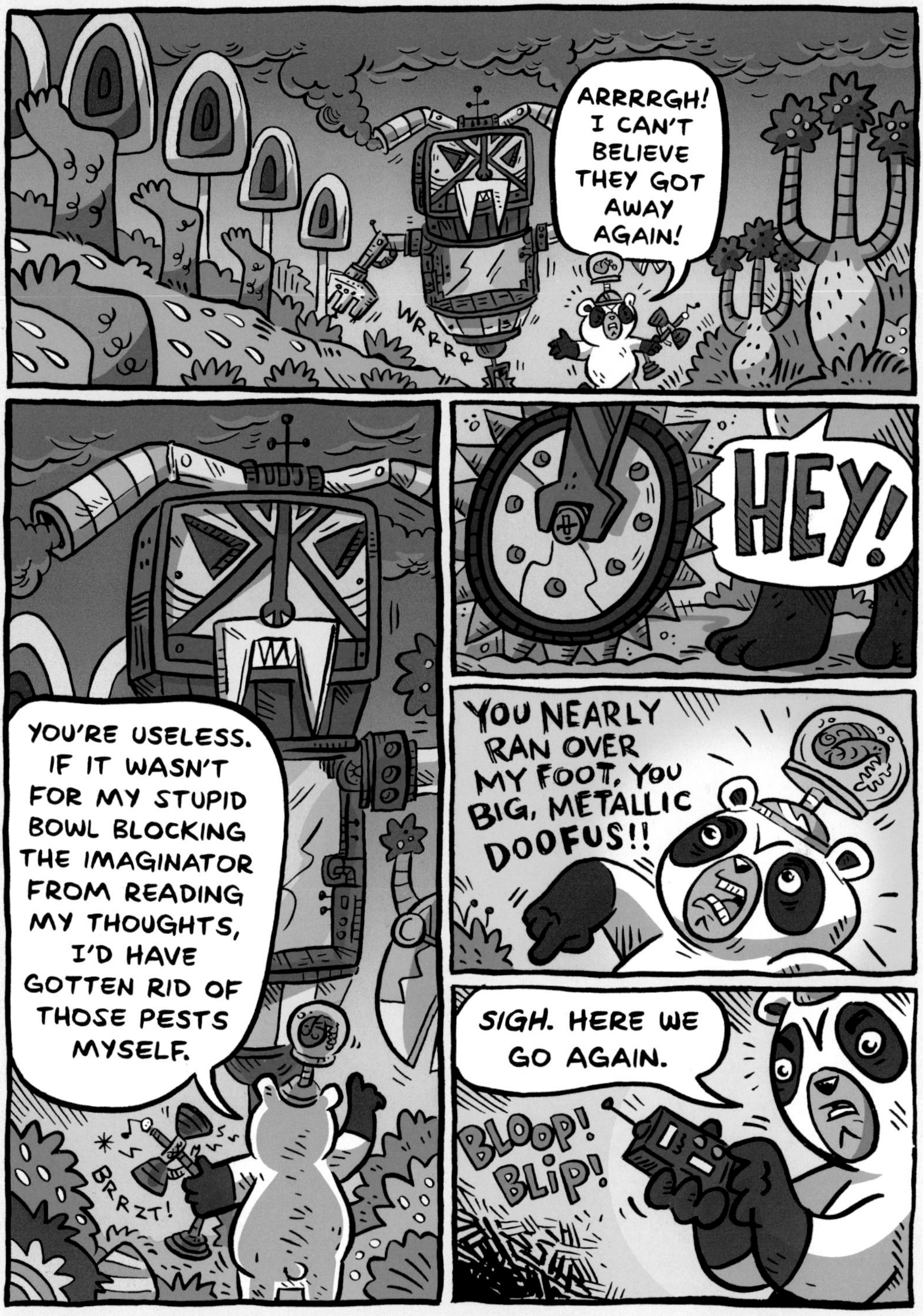
ARRRRGH! I CAN'T BELIEVE THEY GOT AWAY AGAIN!
WRRRRR
HEY!
YOU'RE USELESS. IF IT WASN'T FOR MY STUPID BOWL BLOCKING THE IMAGINATOR FROM READING MY THOUGHTS, I'D HAVE GOTTEN RID OF THOSE PESTS MYSELF.
BRRZT!
YOU NEARLY RAN OVER MY FOOT, YOU BIG, METALLIC DOOFUS!!
SIGH. HERE WE GO AGAIN.
BLOOP! BLIP!

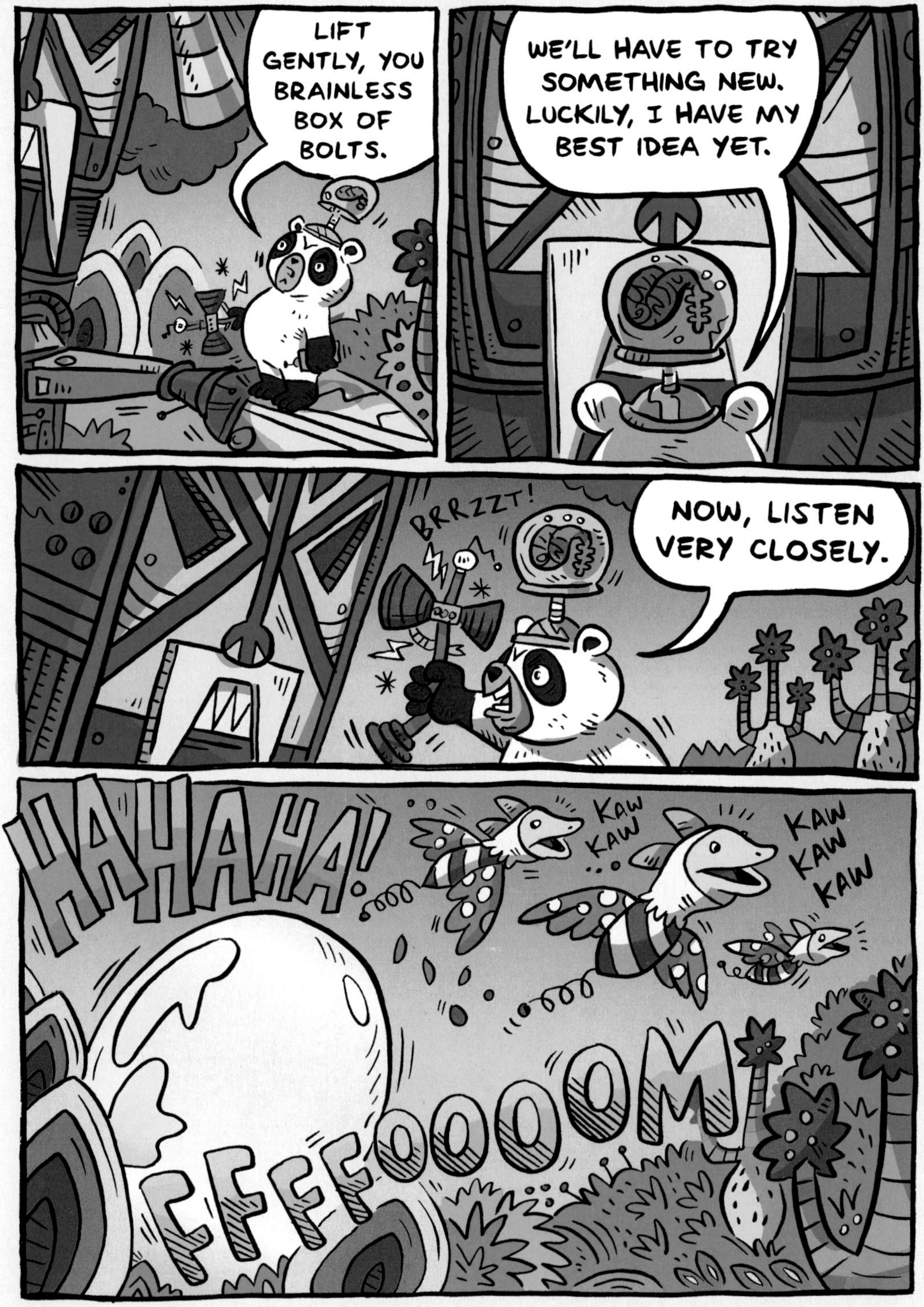
LIFT GENTLY, YOU BRAINLESS BOX OF BOLTS.
WE'LL HAVE TO TRY SOMETHING NEW. LUCKILY, I HAVE MY BEST IDEA YET.
BRRZZT!
NOW, LISTEN VERY CLOSELY.
HAHAHA!
KAW KAW
KAW KAW KAW
FFFFOOOOOM!

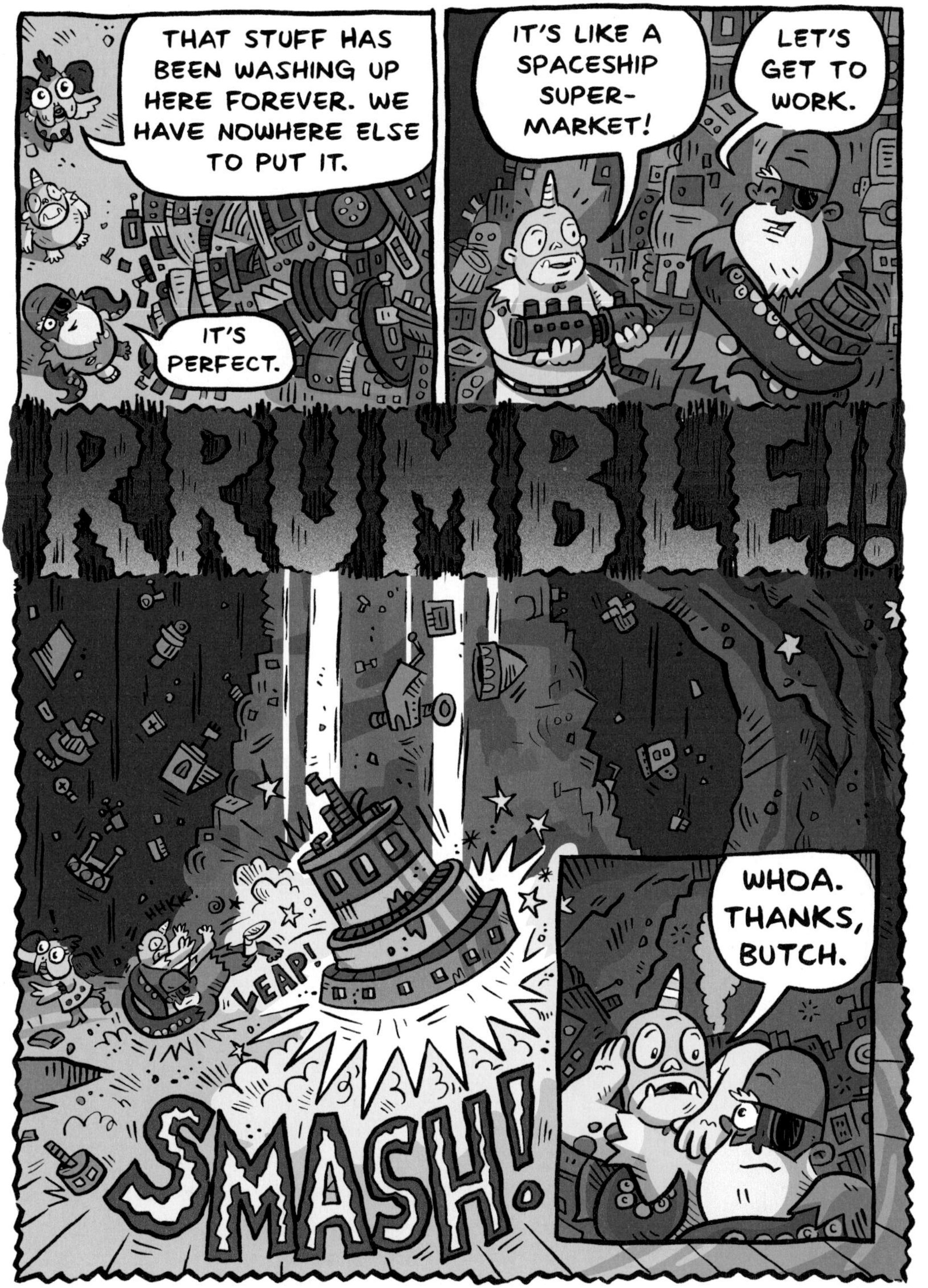
THAT STUFF HAS BEEN WASHING UP HERE FOREVER. WE HAVE NOWHERE ELSE TO PUT IT.
IT'S PERFECT.
IT'S LIKE A SPACESHIP SUPER-MARKET!
LET'S GET TO WORK.
RRUMBLE!!
HHKK
LEAP!
SMASH!
WHOA. THANKS, BUTCH.

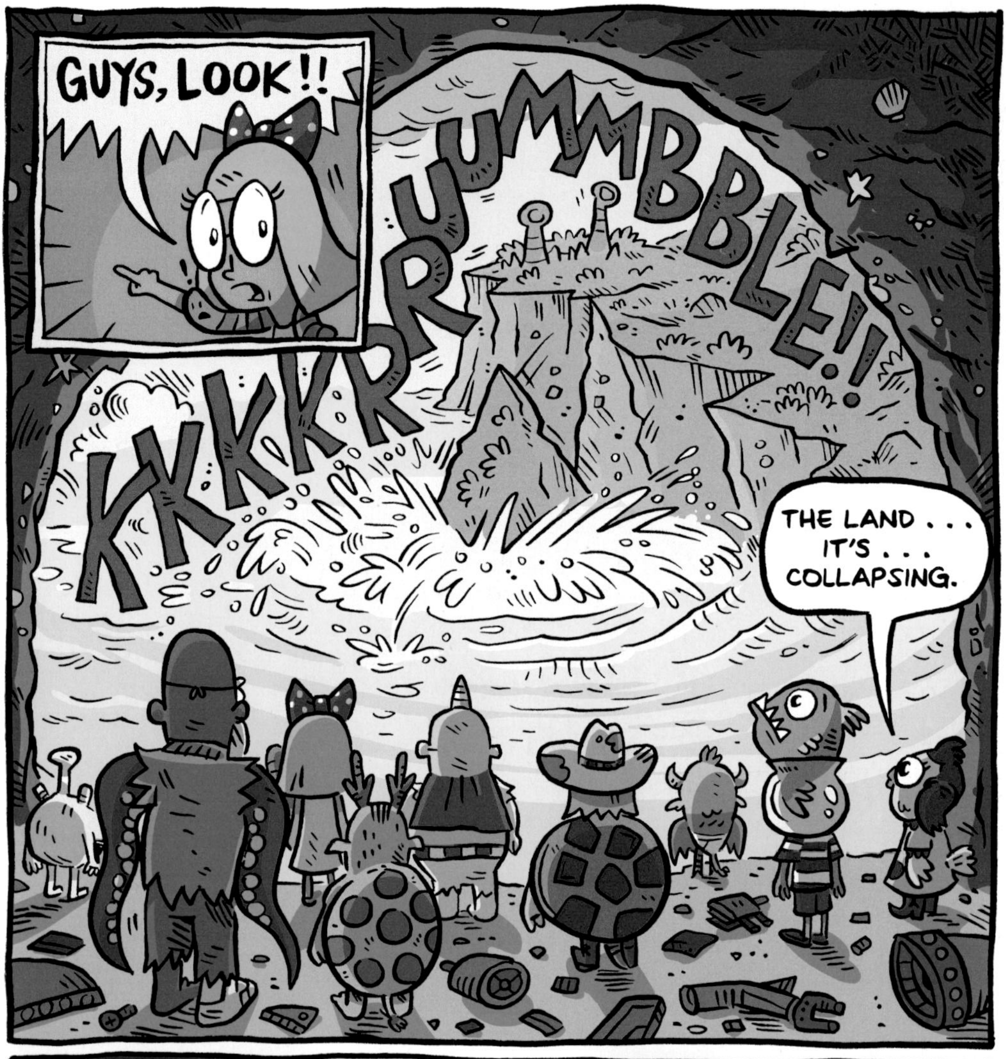
GUYS, LOOK!!
KKKKRRUUMMBBLE!!
THE LAND . . . IT'S . . . COLLAPSING.

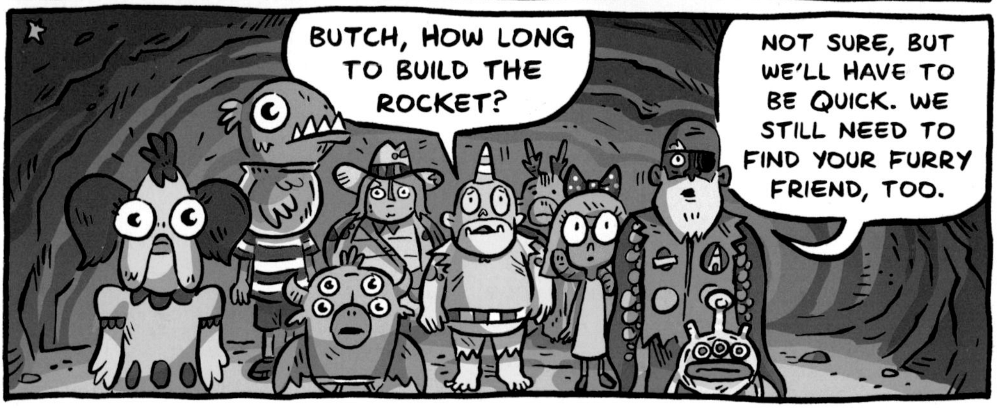
BUTCH, HOW LONG TO BUILD THE ROCKET?
NOT SURE, BUT WE'LL HAVE TO BE QUICK. WE STILL NEED TO FIND YOUR FURRY FRIEND, TOO.

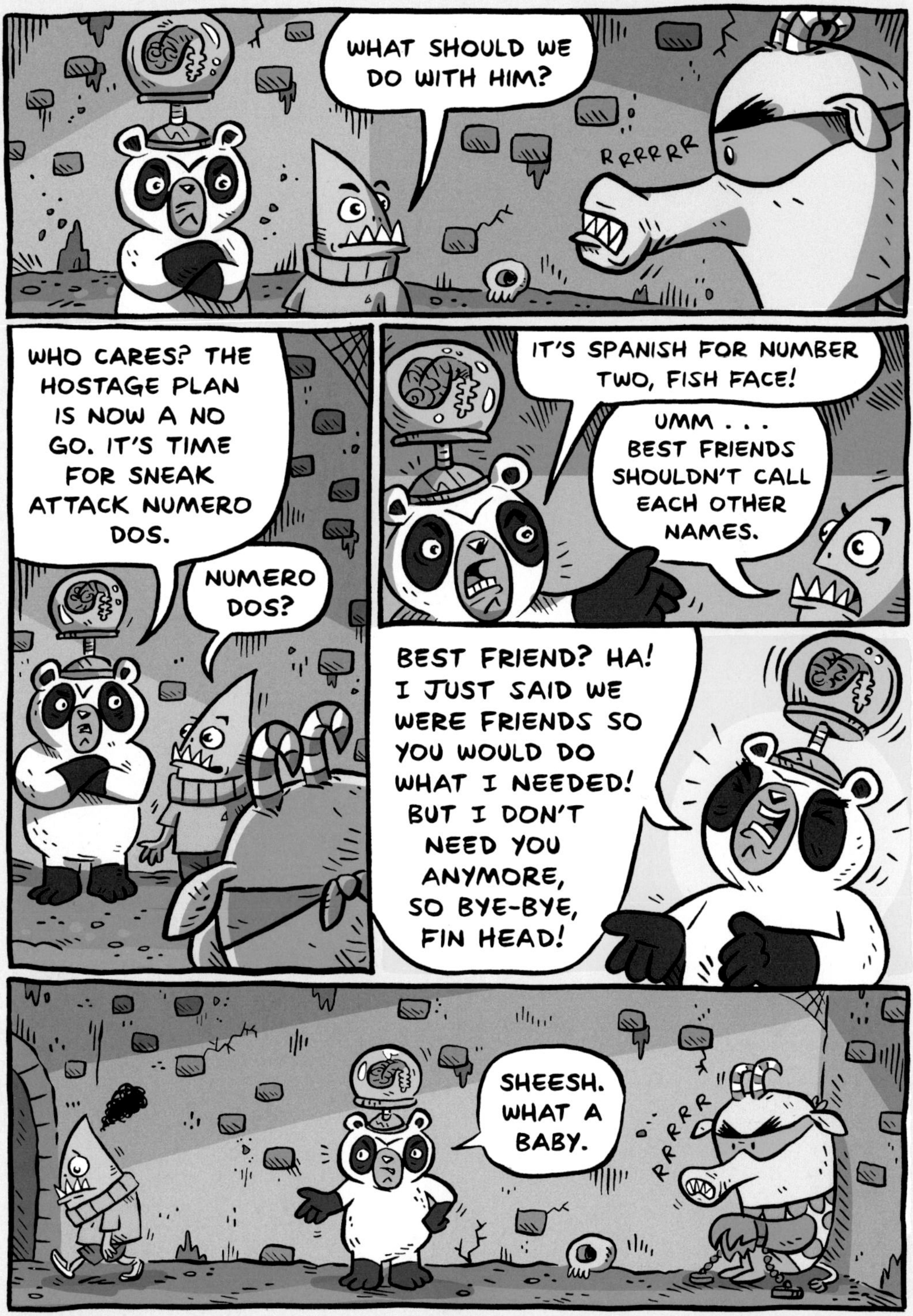
WHAT SHOULD WE DO WITH HIM?
RRRRRR
WHO CARES? THE HOSTAGE PLAN IS NOW A NO GO. IT'S TIME FOR SNEAK ATTACK NUMERO DOS.
NUMERO DOS?
IT'S SPANISH FOR NUMBER TWO, FISH FACE!
UMM . . . BEST FRIENDS SHOULDN'T CALL EACH OTHER NAMES.
BEST FRIEND? HA! I JUST SAID WE WERE FRIENDS SO YOU WOULD DO WHAT I NEEDED! BUT I DON'T NEED YOU ANYMORE, SO BYE-BYE, FIN HEAD!
SHEESH. WHAT A BABY.
RRRRR

Chapter 10

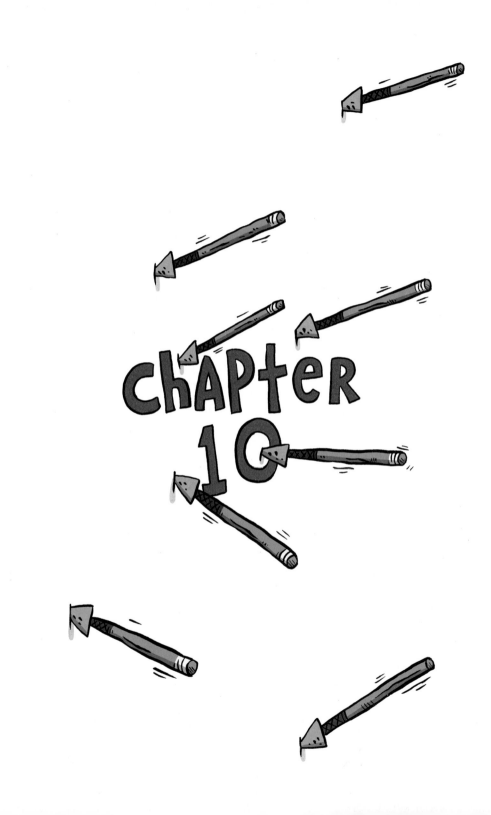

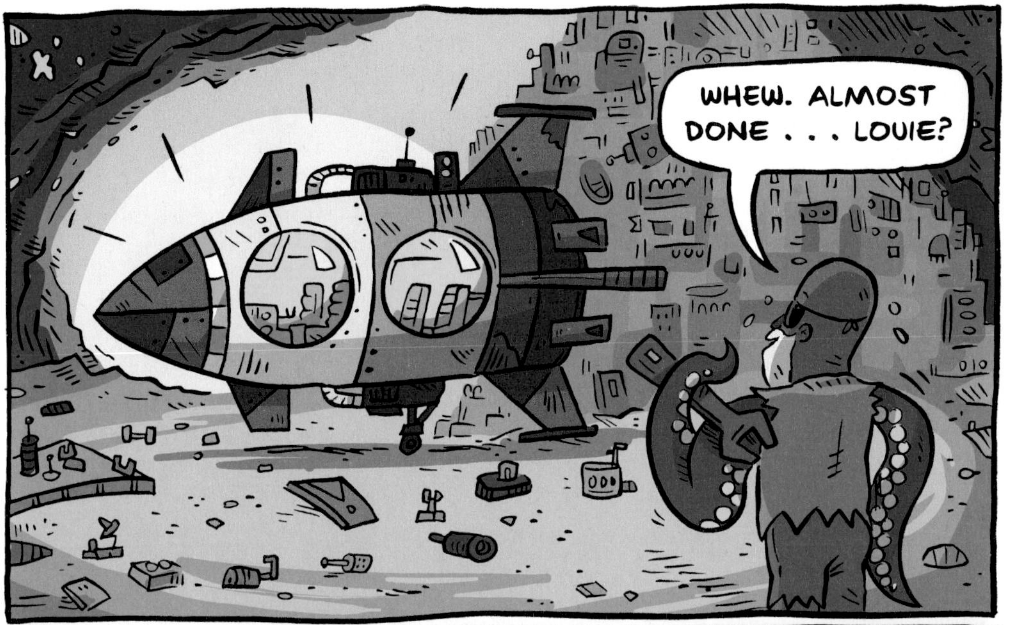
WHEW. ALMOST DONE . . . LOUIE?

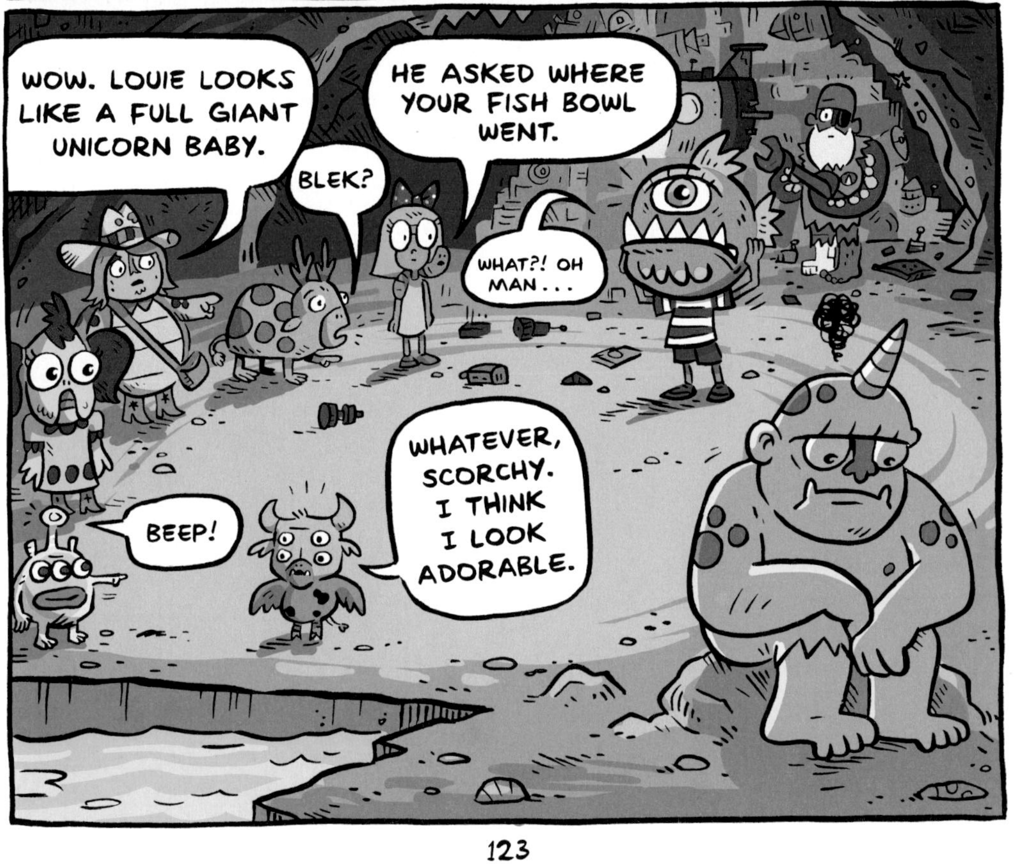
WOW. LOUIE LOOKS LIKE A FULL GIANT UNICORN BABY.
BLEK?
HE ASKED WHERE YOUR FISH BOWL WENT.
WHAT?! OH MAN . . .
BEEP!
WHATEVER, SCORCHY. I THINK I LOOK ADORABLE.

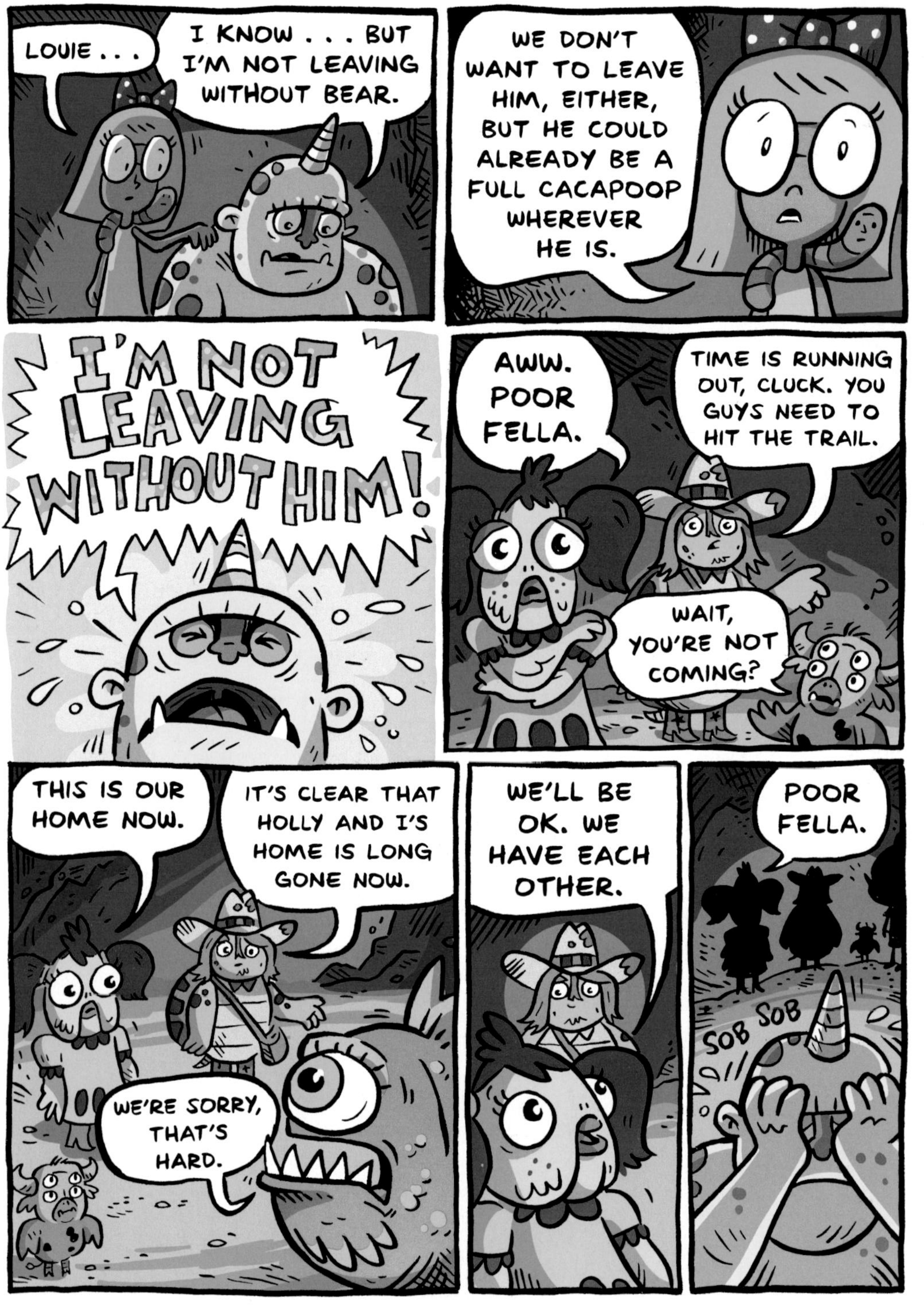
LOUIE . . .
I KNOW . . . BUT I'M NOT LEAVING WITHOUT BEAR.
WE DON'T WANT TO LEAVE HIM, EITHER, BUT HE COULD ALREADY BE A FULL CACAPOOP WHEREVER HE IS.
I'M NOT LEAVING WITHOUT HIM!
AWW. POOR FELLA.
TIME IS RUNNING OUT, CLUCK. YOU GUYS NEED TO HIT THE TRAIL.
WAIT, YOU'RE NOT COMING?
THIS IS OUR HOME NOW.
IT'S CLEAR THAT HOLLY AND I'S HOME IS LONG GONE NOW.
WE'RE SORRY, THAT'S HARD.
WE'LL BE OK. WE HAVE EACH OTHER.
POOR FELLA.
SOB SOB

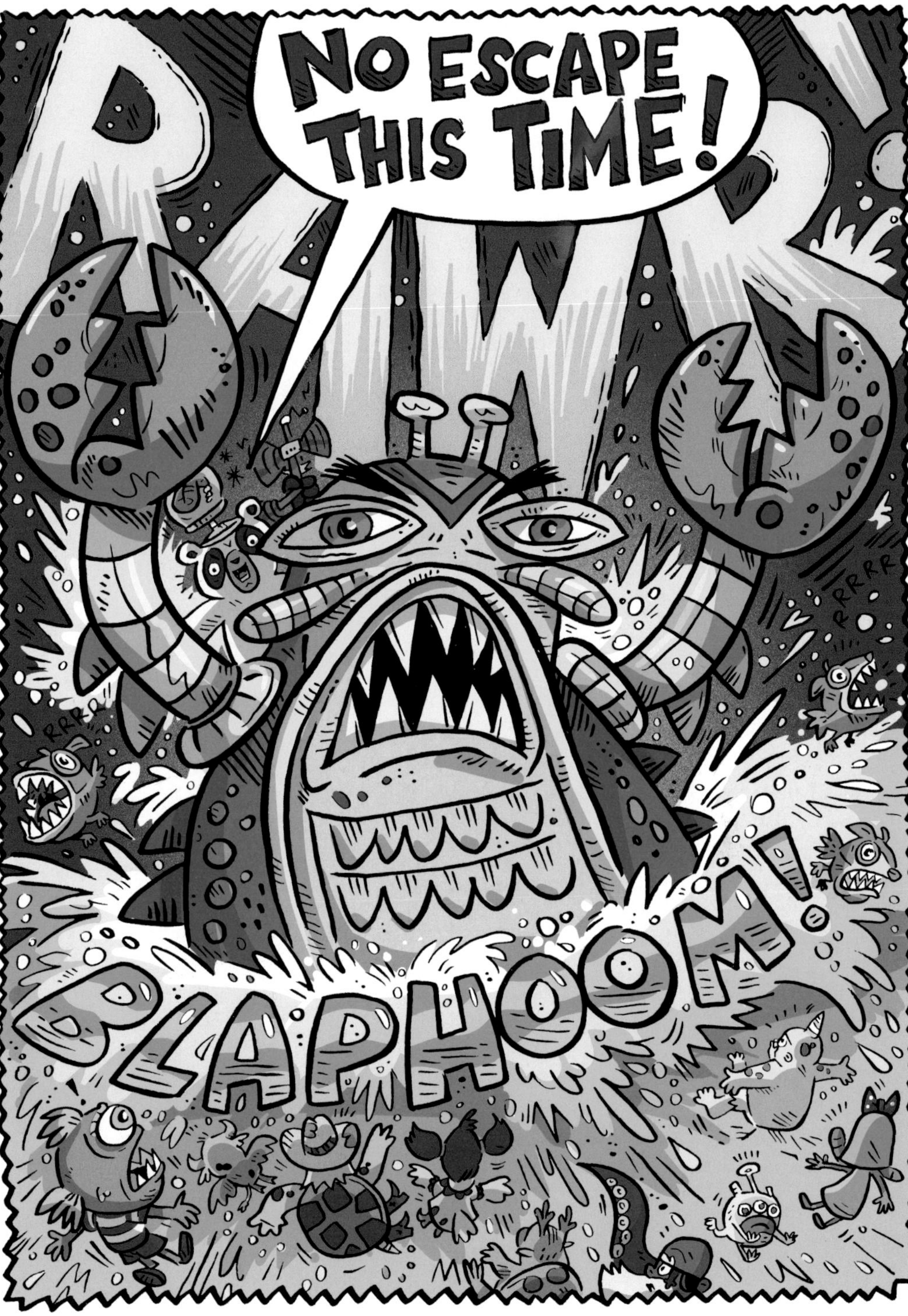
NO ESCAPE THIS TIME!
RRRR
RRRR
BLAPHOOM!

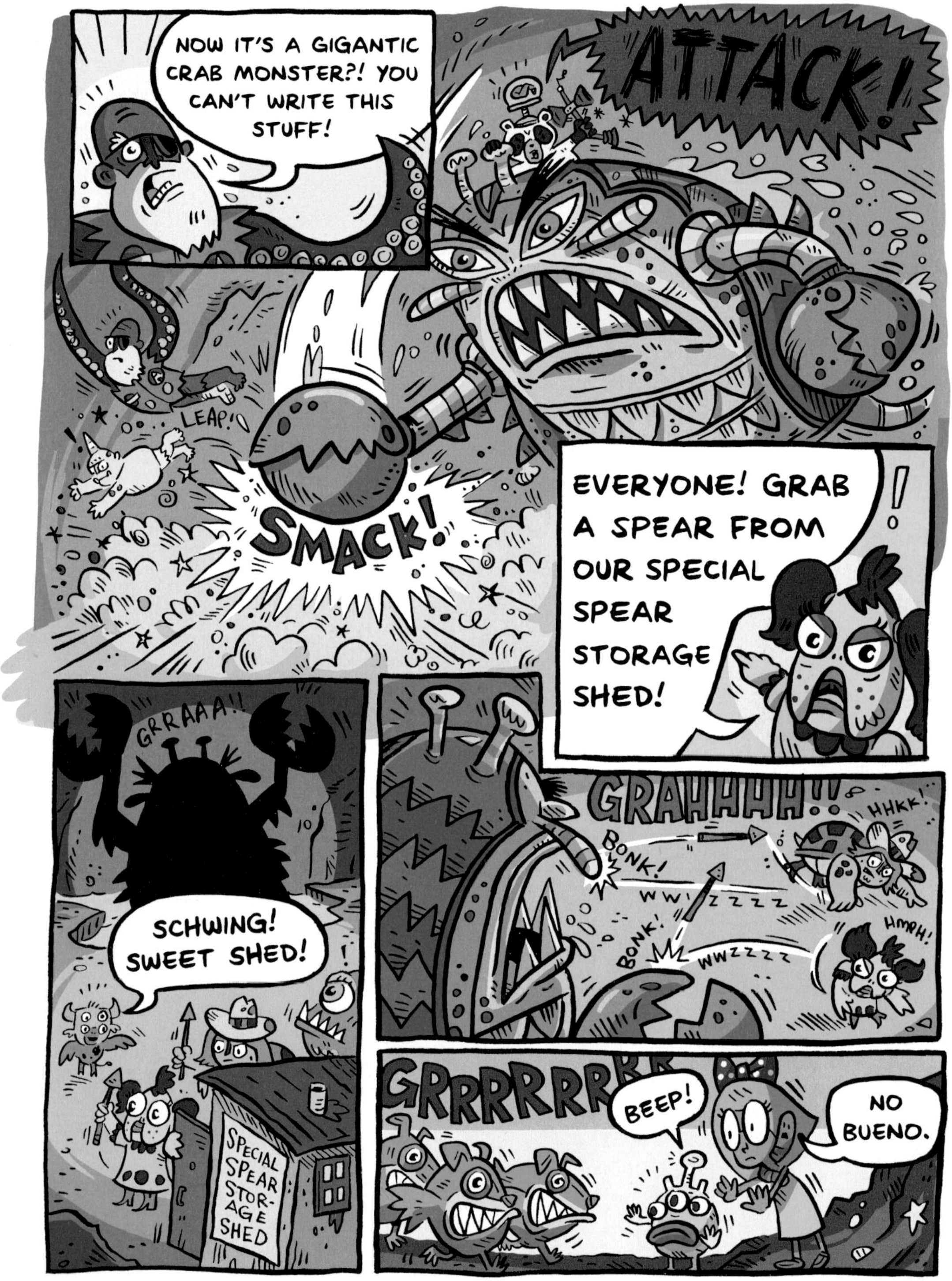
NOW IT'S A GIGANTIC CRAB MONSTER?! YOU CAN'T WRITE THIS STUFF!
ATTACK!
LEAP!
SMACK!
EVERYONE! GRAB A SPEAR FROM OUR SPECIAL SPEAR STORAGE SHED!
GRRAAA!!
SCHWING! SWEET SHED!
SPECIAL SPEAR STORAGE SHED
GRAHHHH!!
HHKK!
BONK!
WWZZZZ
BONK!
WWZZZZ
HMPH!
GRRRRRRRR
BEEP!
NO BUENO.

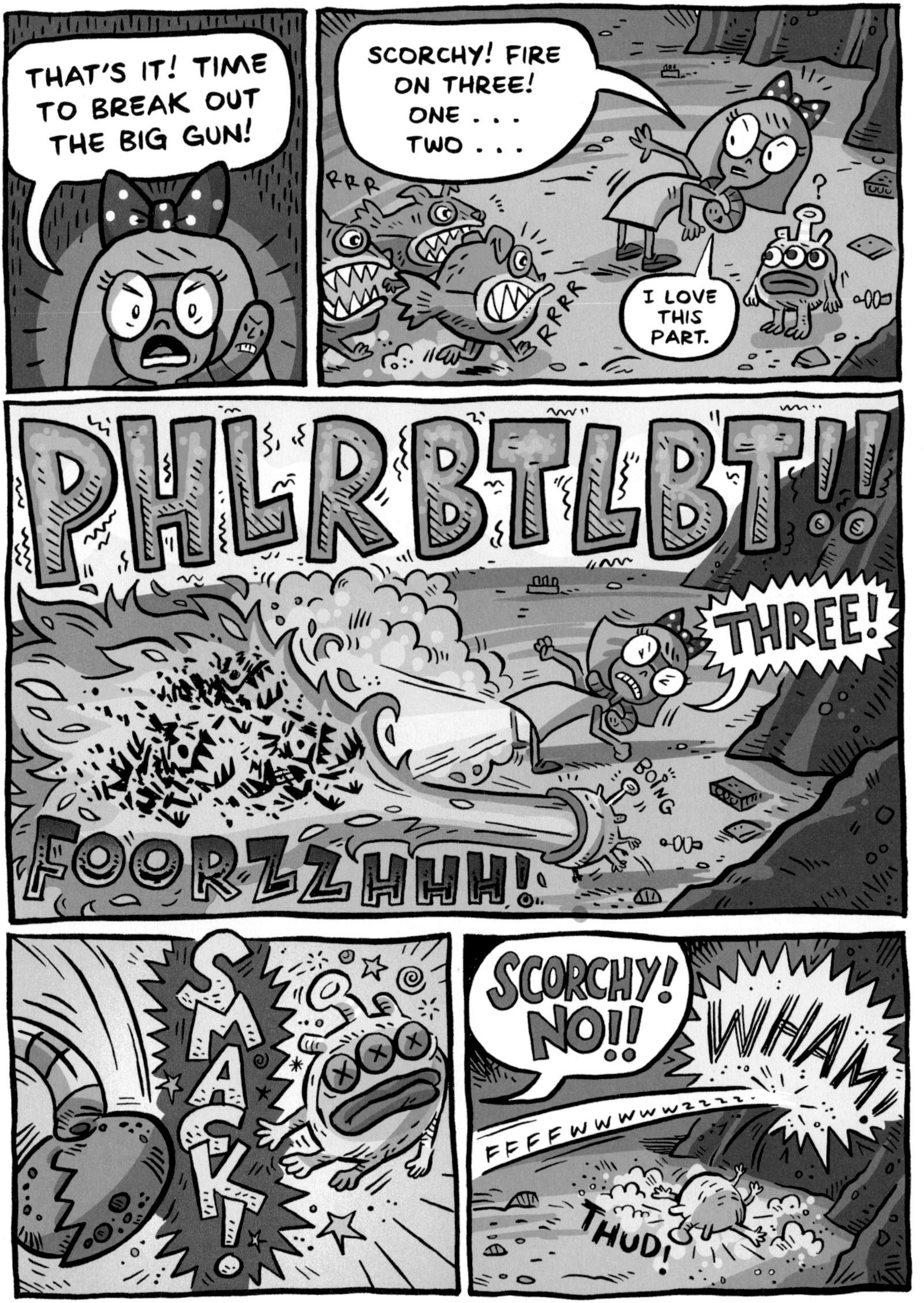
THAT'S IT! TIME TO BREAK OUT THE BIG GUN!
SCORCHY! FIRE ON THREE! ONE . . . TWO . . .
RRR
RRRR
I LOVE THIS PART.
?
PHLRBTLBT!!
THREE!
BOING
FOORZZHHH!
SMACK!
SCORCHY! NO!!
WHAM!
FFFFWWWWWZZZZ
THUD!

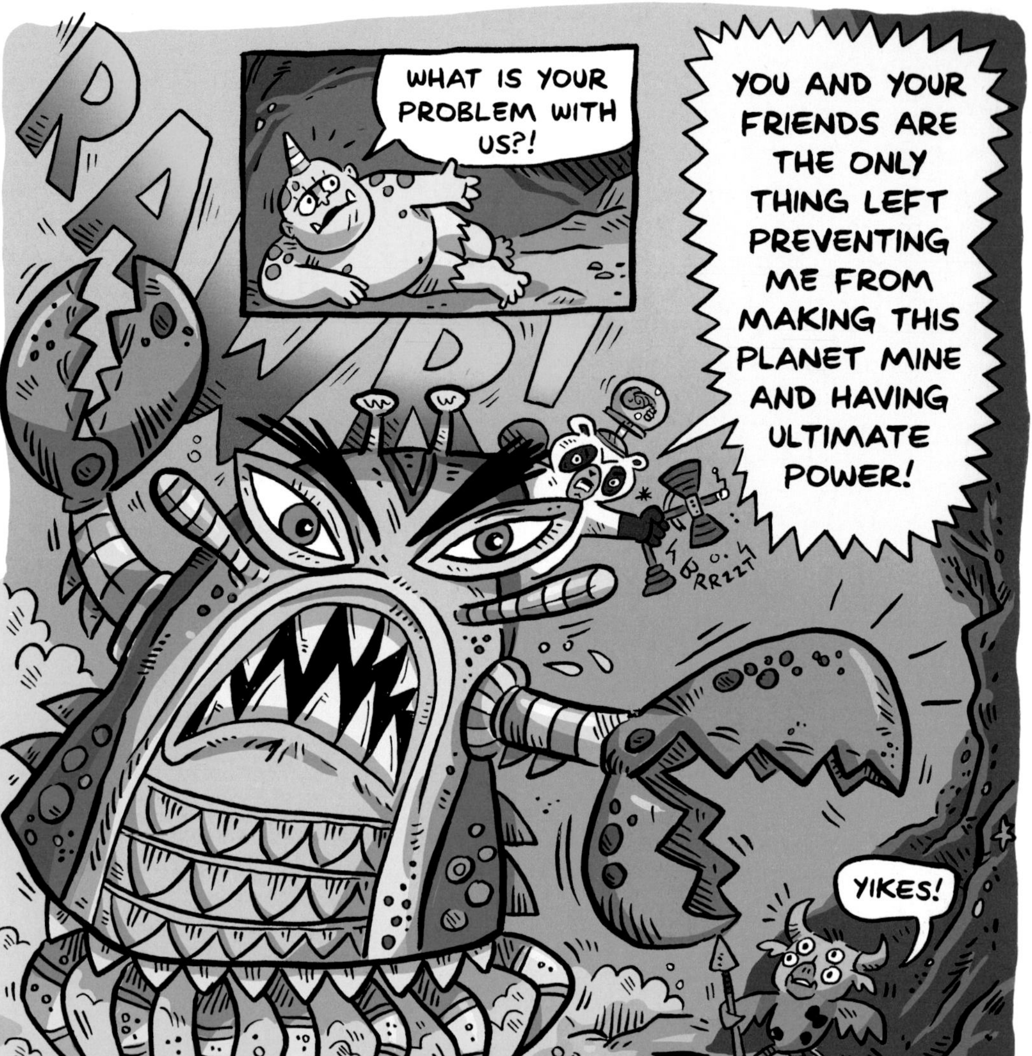
RAWR!
WHAT IS YOUR PROBLEM WITH US?!
YOU AND YOUR FRIENDS ARE THE ONLY THING LEFT PREVENTING ME FROM MAKING THIS PLANET MINE AND HAVING ULTIMATE POWER!
BRRZZT!
YIKES!

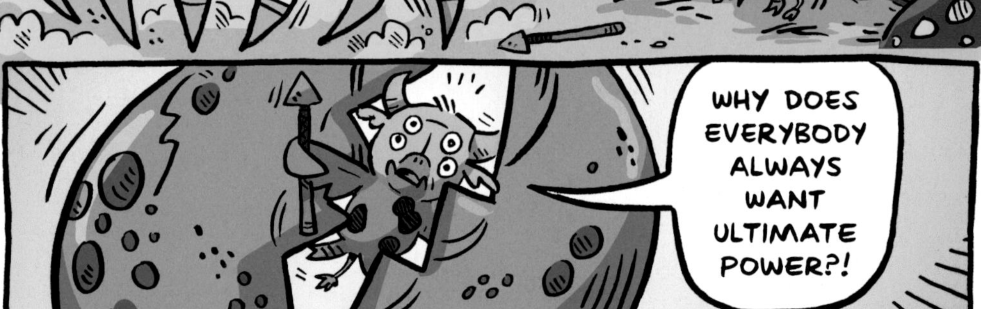
WHY DOES EVERYBODY ALWAYS WANT ULTIMATE POWER?!

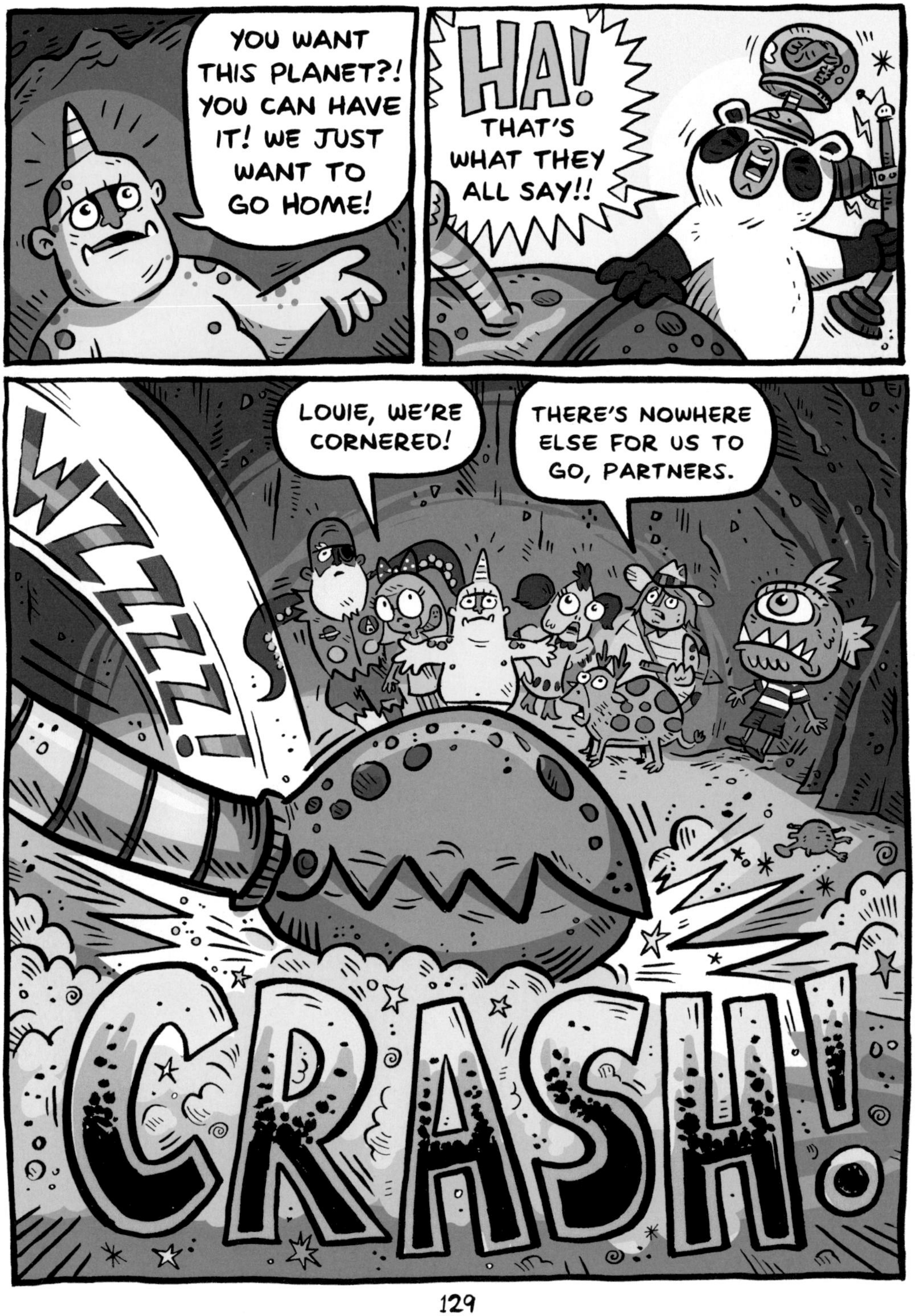
YOU WANT THIS PLANET?! YOU CAN HAVE IT! WE JUST WANT TO GO HOME!
HA! THAT'S WHAT THEY ALL SAY!!
LOUIE, WE'RE CORNERED!
THERE'S NOWHERE ELSE FOR US TO GO, PARTNERS.
WZZZZ!
CRASH!

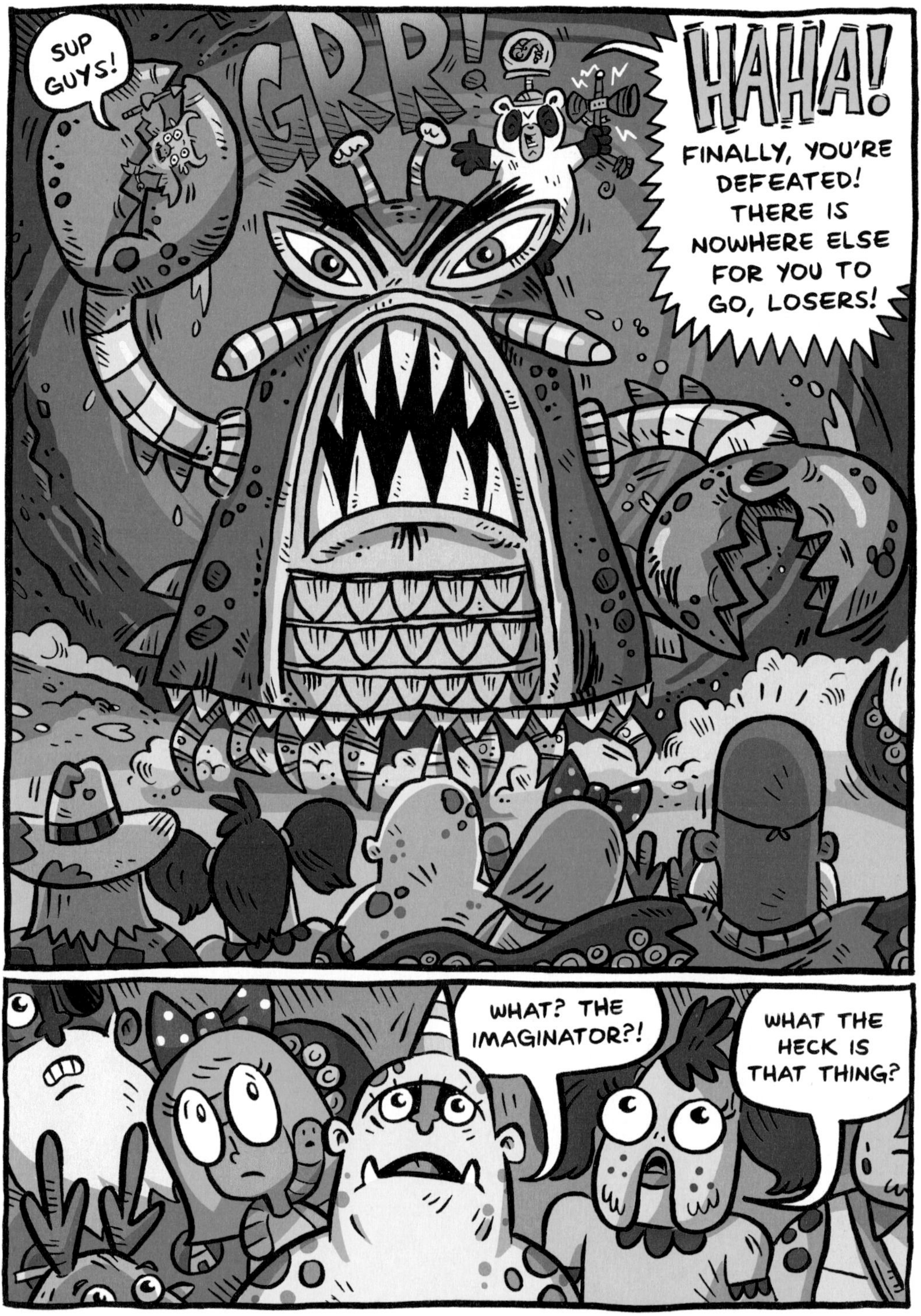
SUP GUYS!
GRR!
HAHA!
FINALLY, YOU'RE DEFEATED! THERE IS NOWHERE ELSE FOR YOU TO GO, LOSERS!
WHAT? THE IMAGINATOR?!
WHAT THE HECK IS THAT THING?

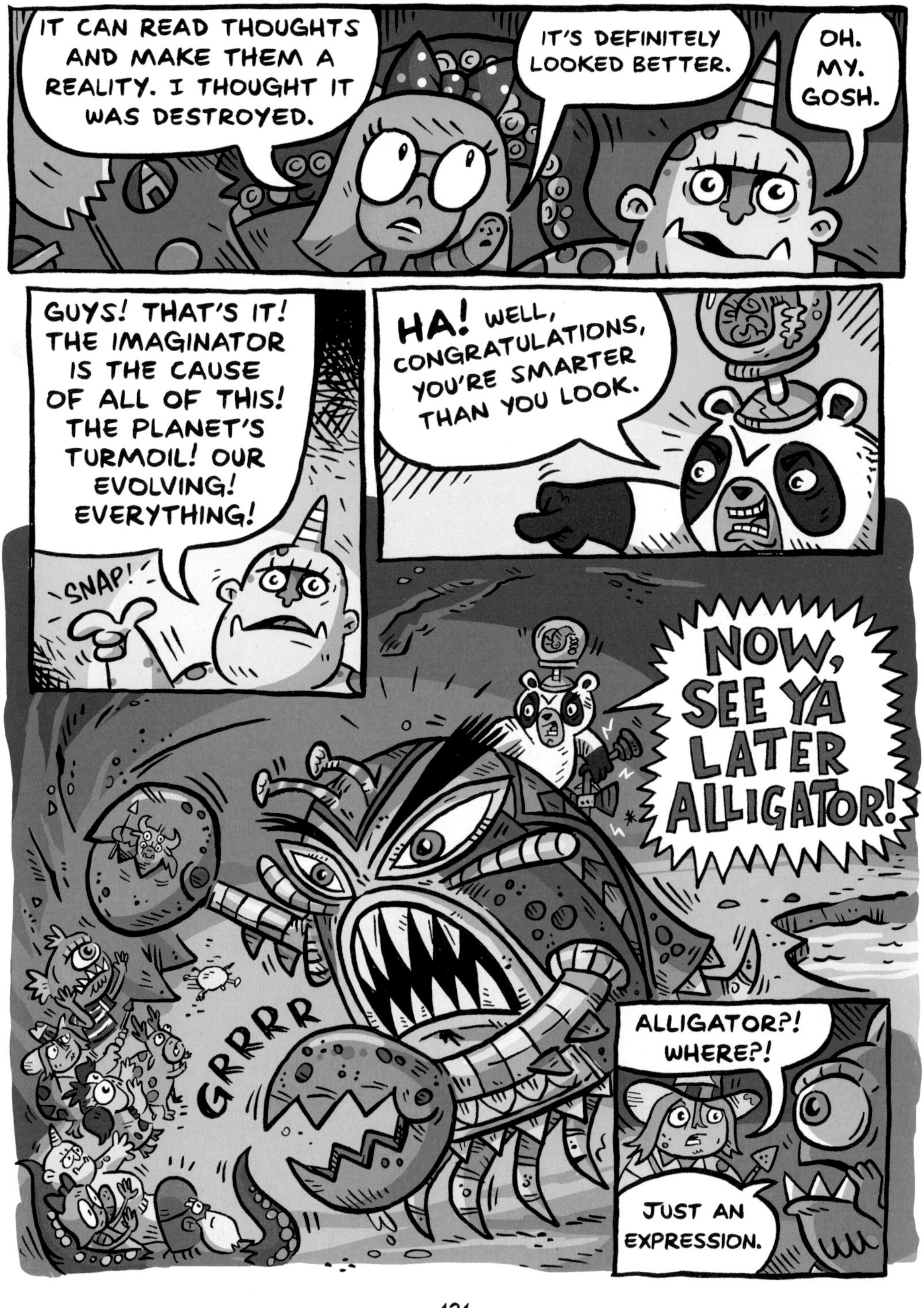
IT CAN READ THOUGHTS AND MAKE THEM A REALITY. I THOUGHT IT WAS DESTROYED.
IT'S DEFINITELY LOOKED BETTER.
OH. MY. GOSH.
GUYS! THAT'S IT! THE IMAGINATOR IS THE CAUSE OF ALL OF THIS! THE PLANET'S TURMOIL! OUR EVOLVING! EVERYTHING!
SNAP!
HA! WELL, CONGRATULATIONS, YOU'RE SMARTER THAN YOU LOOK.
NOW, SEE YA LATER ALLIGATOR!
GRRRR
ALLIGATOR?! WHERE?!
JUST AN EXPRESSION.

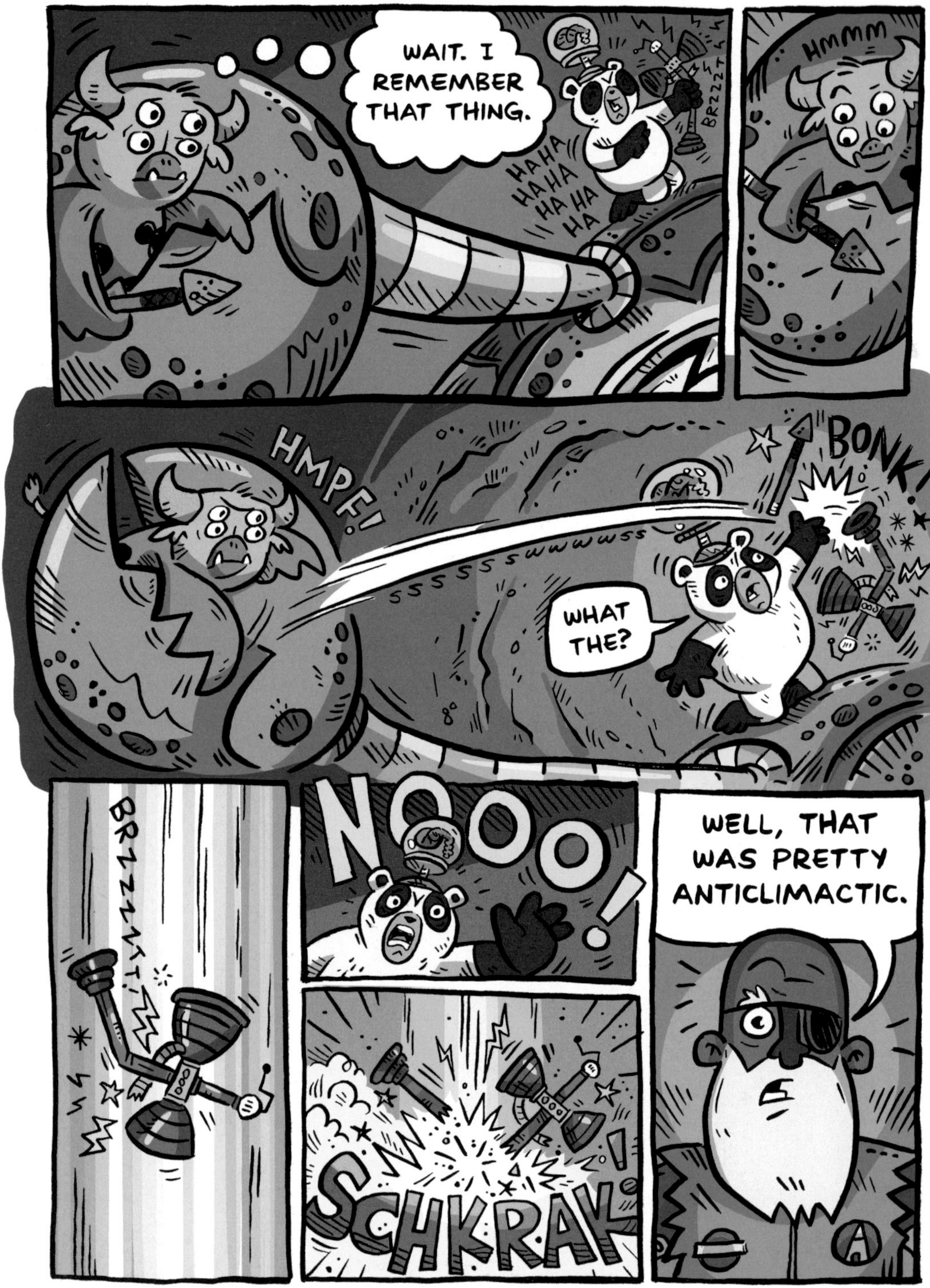
WAIT. I REMEMBER THAT THING.
BRZZZT
HAHA HAHA HAHA HA
HMMM
HMPF!
BONK!
SSSSSSSWWWWSS
WHAT THE?
BRZZZZZT
NOOOO!
SCHKRAK!
WELL, THAT WAS PRETTY ANTICLIMACTIC.

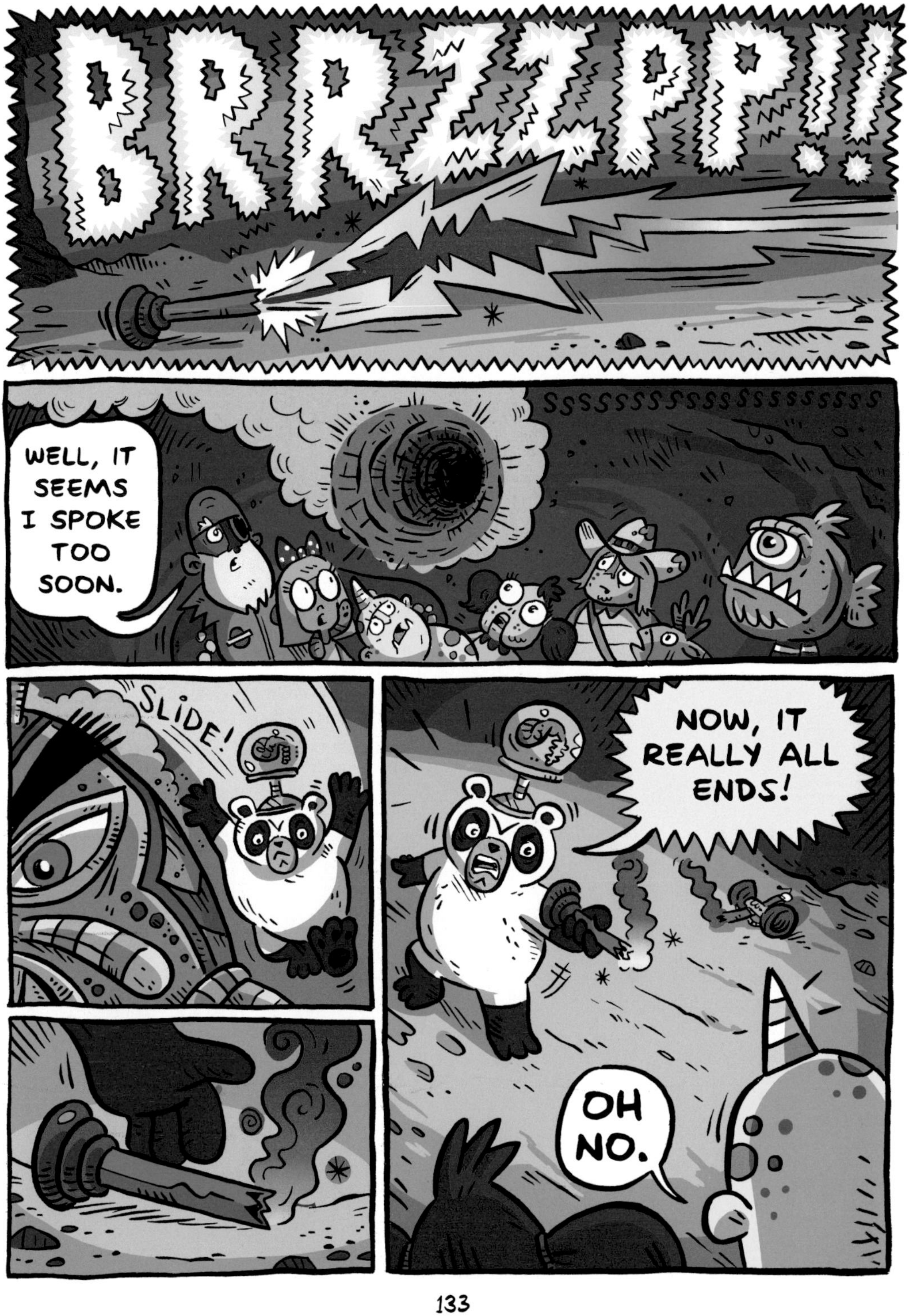
BRRZZPP!!
SSSSSSSSSSSSSSSSSSSSSSS
WELL, IT SEEMS I SPOKE TOO SOON.
SLIDE!
NOW, IT REALLY ALL ENDS!
OH NO.

CHAPTER 11

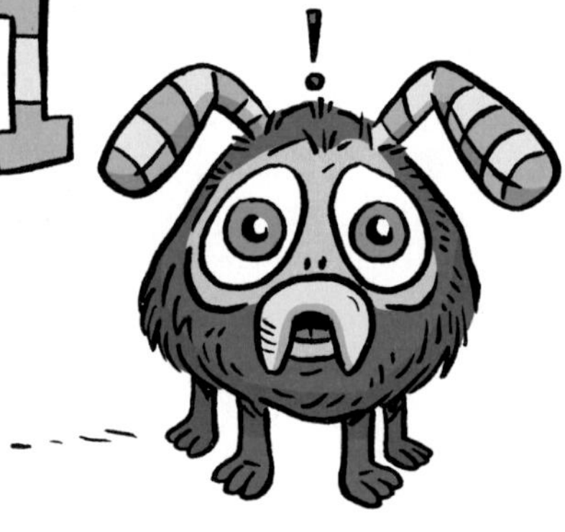

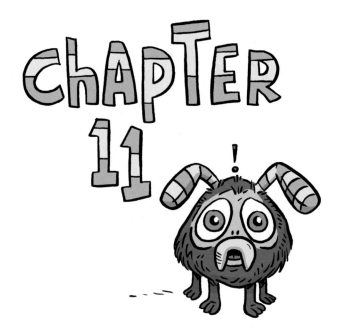

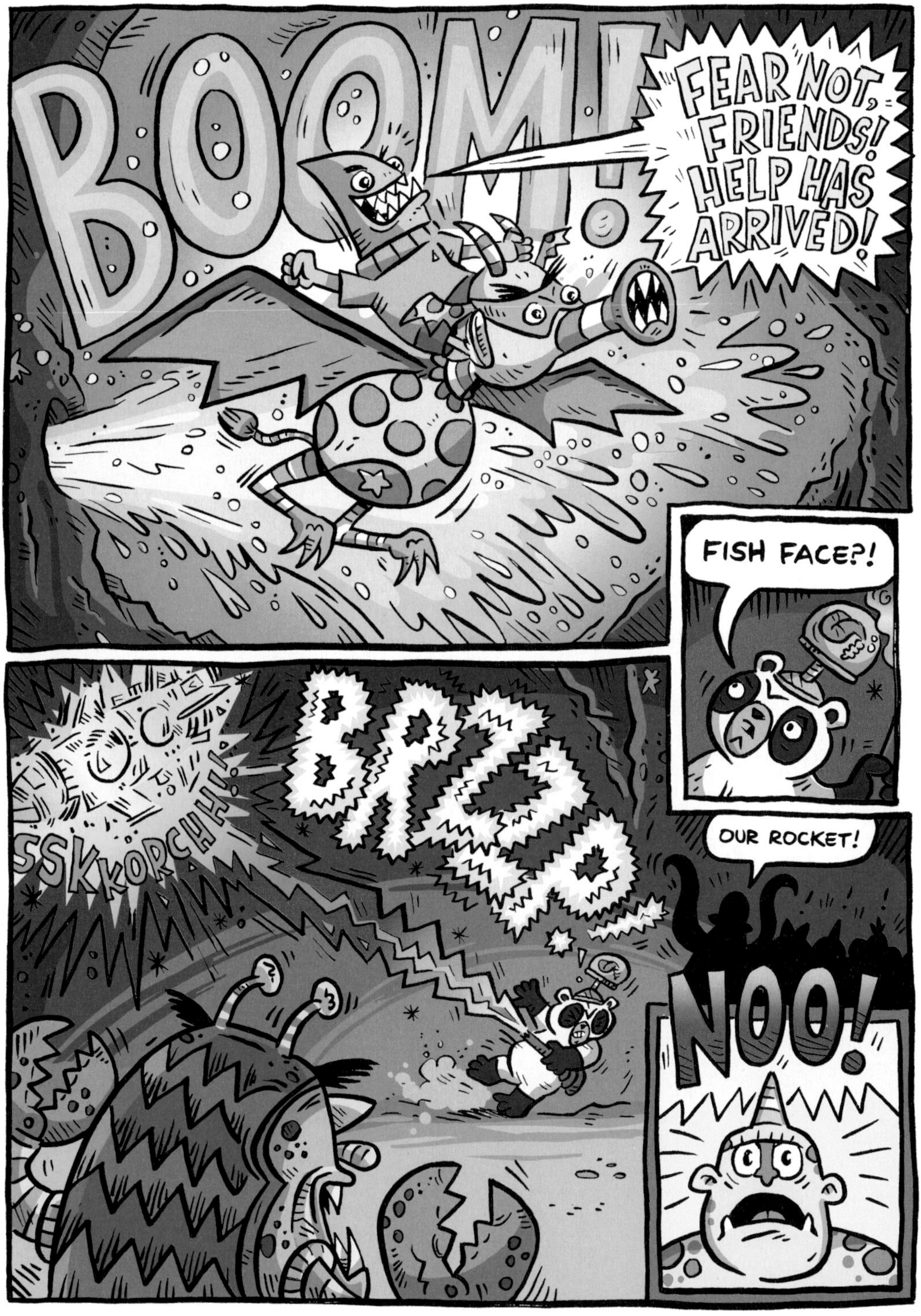
BOOM!
FEAR NOT, FRIENDS! HELP HAS ARRIVED!
FISH FACE?!
SSKKORCHH!!
BRBOOM
OUR ROCKET!
NOO!

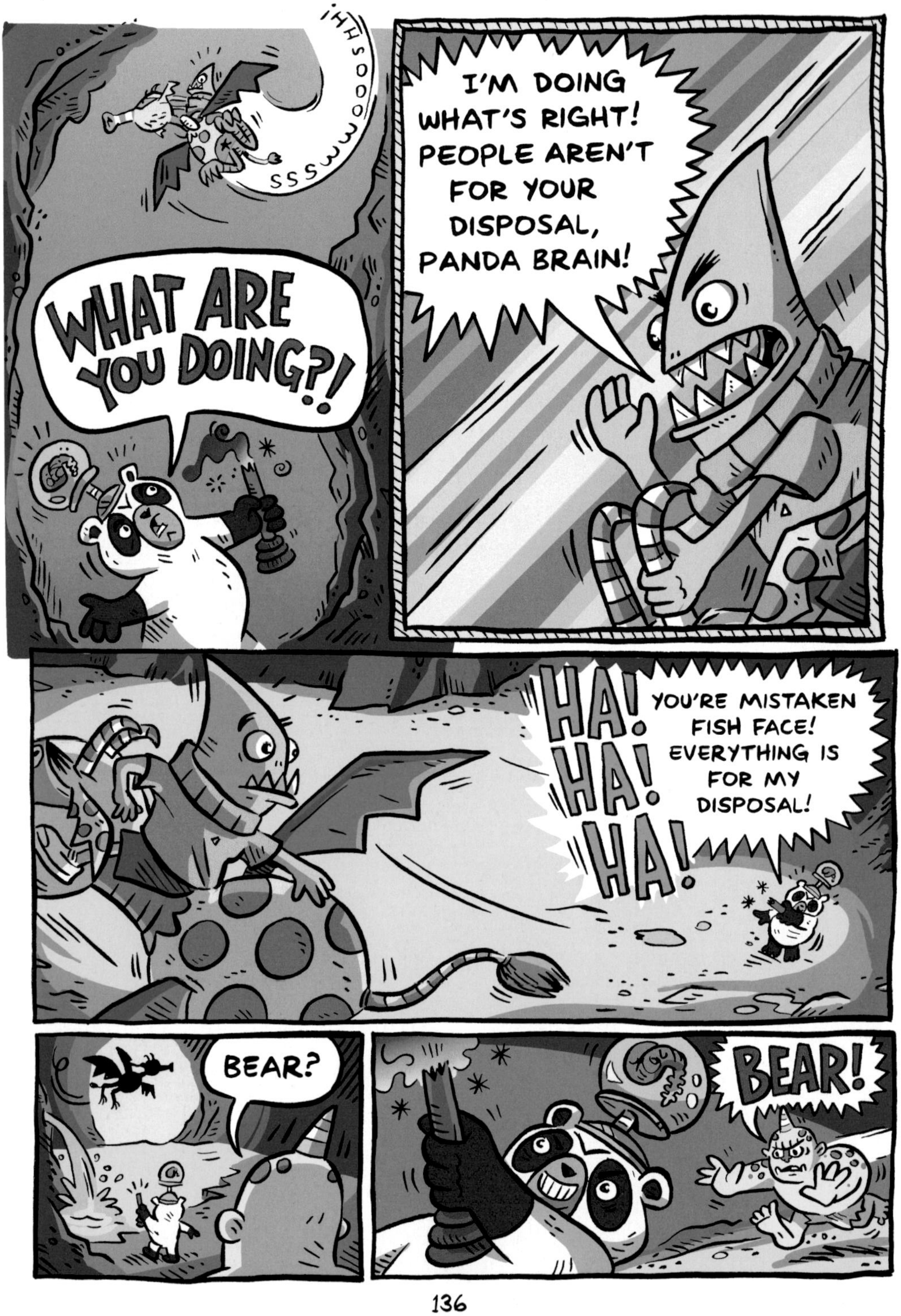
SSSWOOOOSH!
WHAT ARE YOU DOING?!
I'M DOING WHAT'S RIGHT! PEOPLE AREN'T FOR YOUR DISPOSAL, PANDA BRAIN!
HA! HA! HA!
YOU'RE MISTAKEN FISH FACE! EVERYTHING IS FOR MY DISPOSAL!
BEAR?
BEAR!

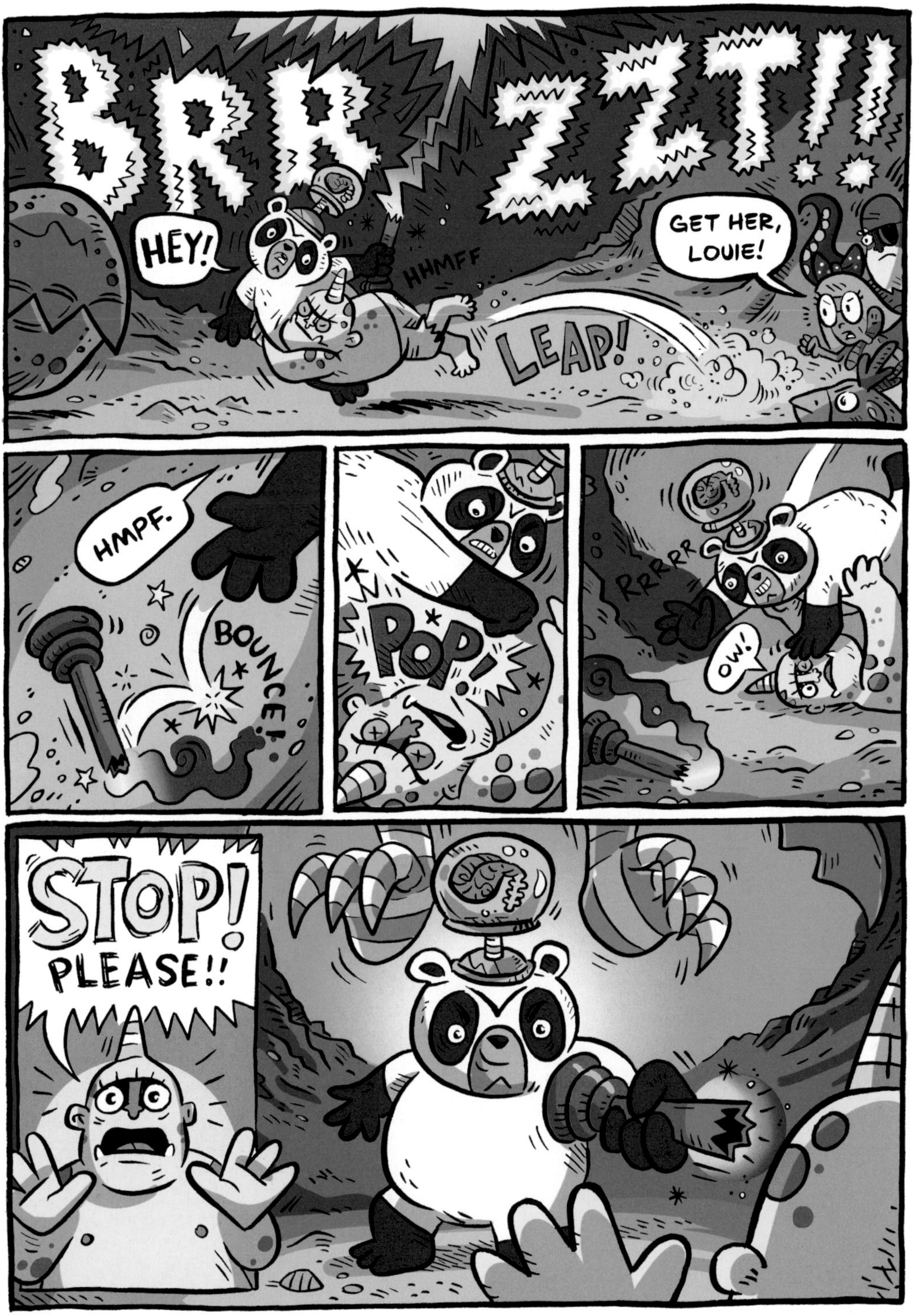
BRRZZT!!
HEY!
HHMFF
GET HER, LOUIE!
LEAP!
HMPF.
BOUNCE!
POP!
RRRRR
OW!
STOP! PLEASE!!

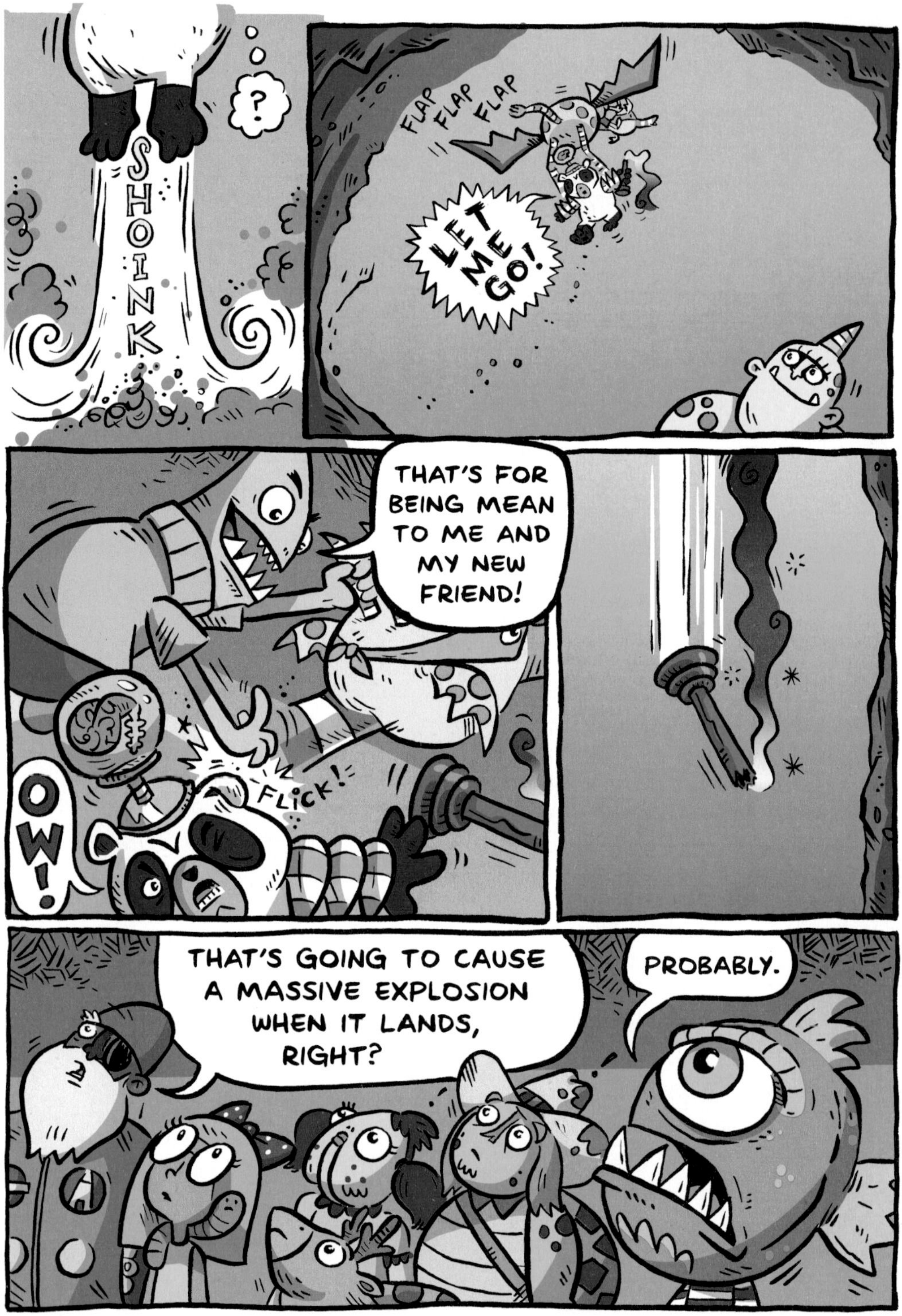
?
SHOINK
FLAP FLAP FLAP
LET ME GO!
THAT'S FOR BEING MEAN TO ME AND MY NEW FRIEND!
FLICK!
OW!
THAT'S GOING TO CAUSE A MASSIVE EXPLOSION WHEN IT LANDS, RIGHT?
PROBABLY.

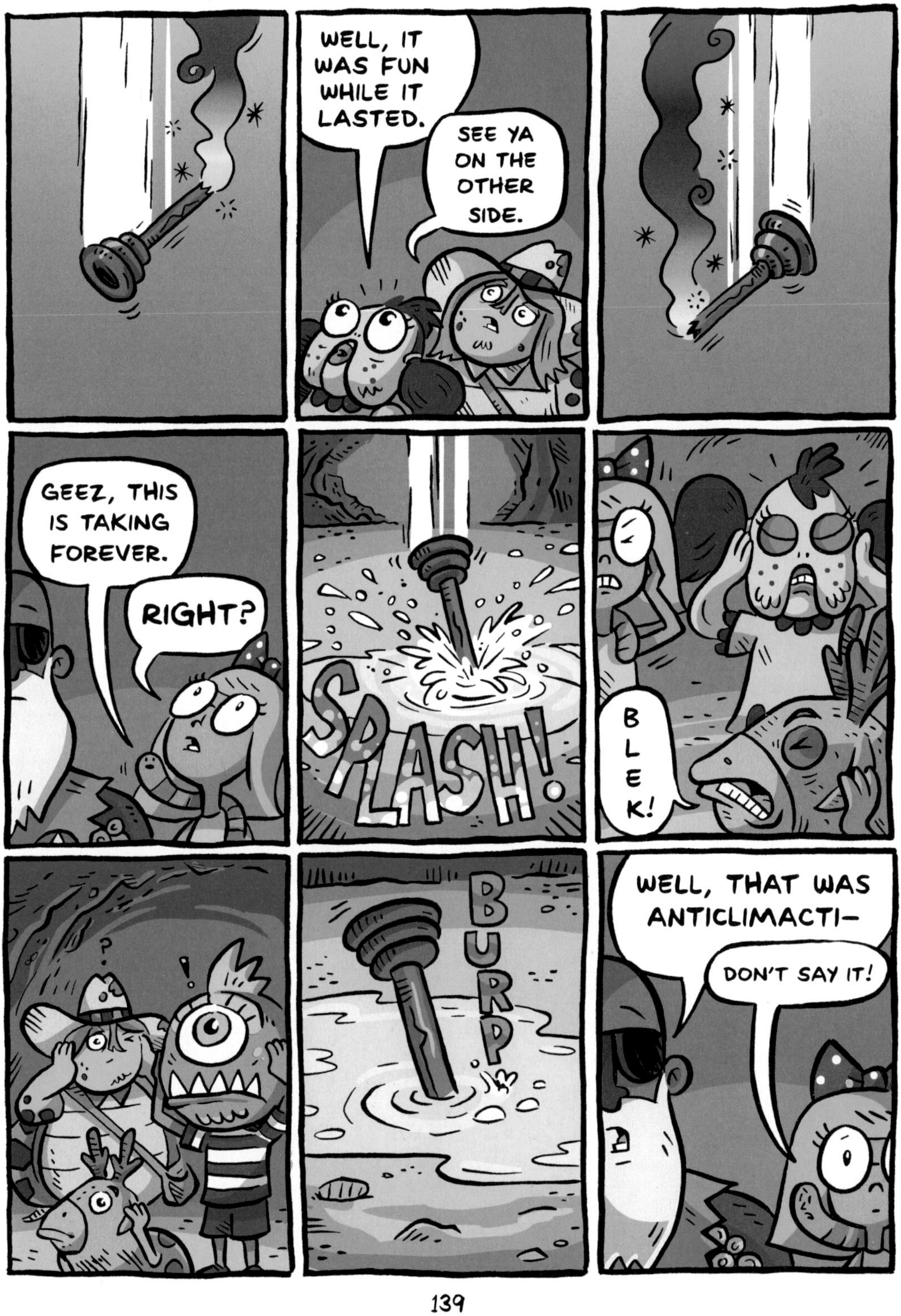
WELL, IT WAS FUN WHILE IT LASTED.
SEE YA ON THE OTHER SIDE.
GEEZ, THIS IS TAKING FOREVER.
RIGHT?
SPLASH!
BLEK!
?
!
BURP
WELL, THAT WAS ANTICLIMACTI—
DON'T SAY IT!

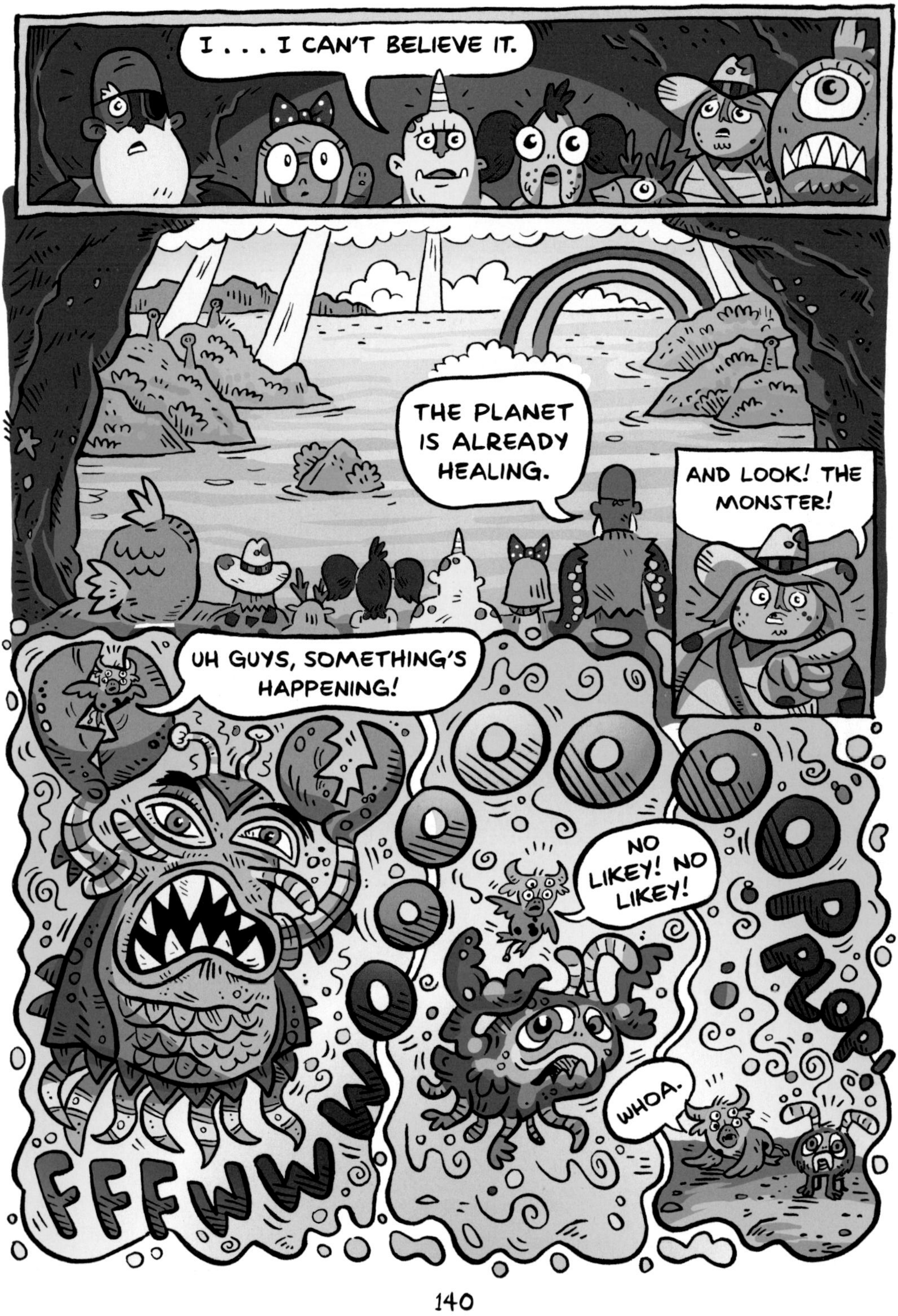
I . . . I CAN'T BELIEVE IT.
THE PLANET IS ALREADY HEALING.
AND LOOK! THE MONSTER!
UH GUYS, SOMETHING'S HAPPENING!
FFFWWWOOOOOOOOOOP
NO LIKEY! NO LIKEY!
PLOP!
WHOA.

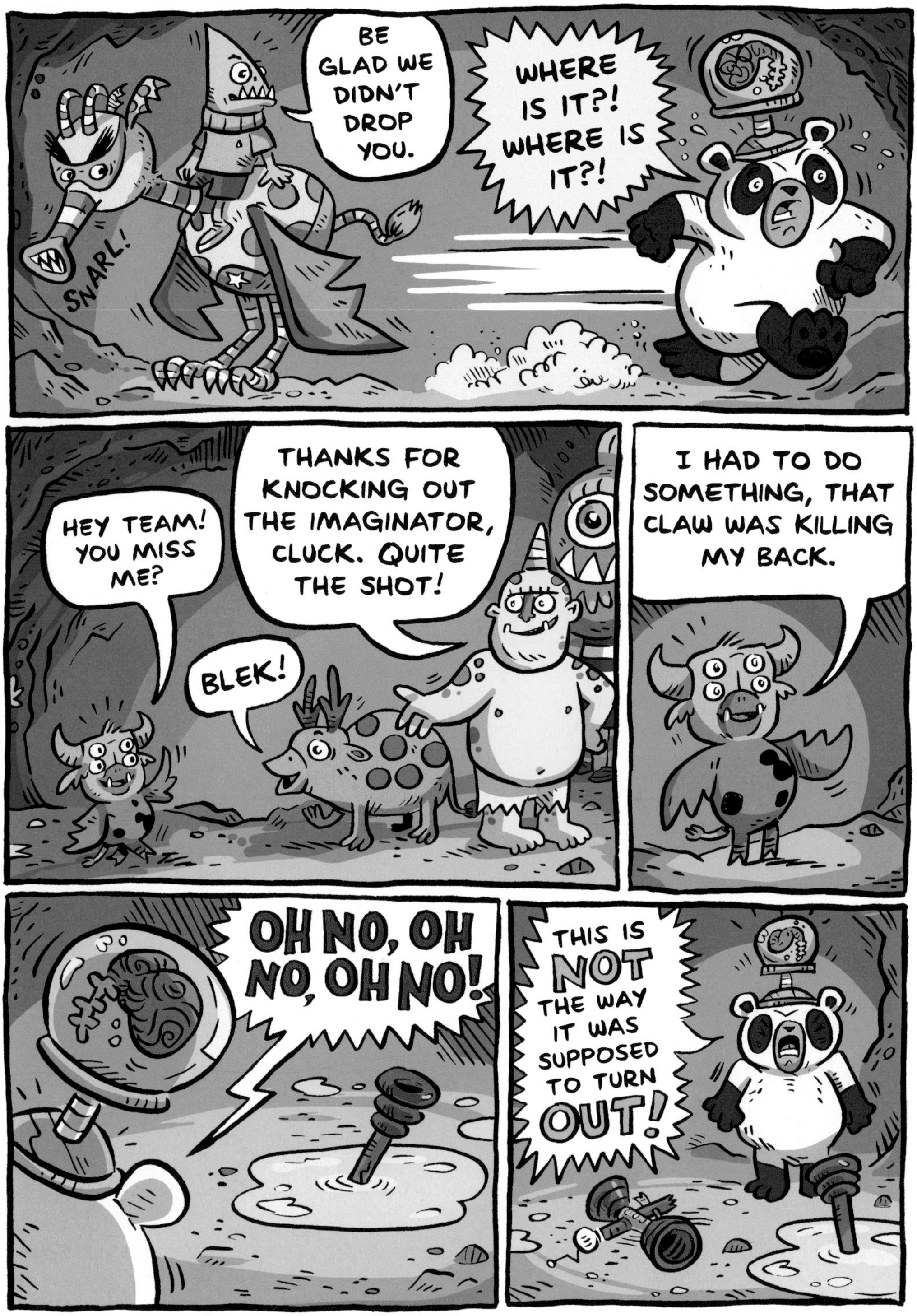
BE GLAD WE DIDN'T DROP YOU.
SNARL!
WHERE IS IT?! WHERE IS IT?!
HEY TEAM! YOU MISS ME?
THANKS FOR KNOCKING OUT THE IMAGINATOR, CLUCK. QUITE THE SHOT!
BLEK!
I HAD TO DO SOMETHING, THAT CLAW WAS KILLING MY BACK.
OH NO, OH NO, OH NO!
THIS IS NOT THE WAY IT WAS SUPPOSED TO TURN OUT!

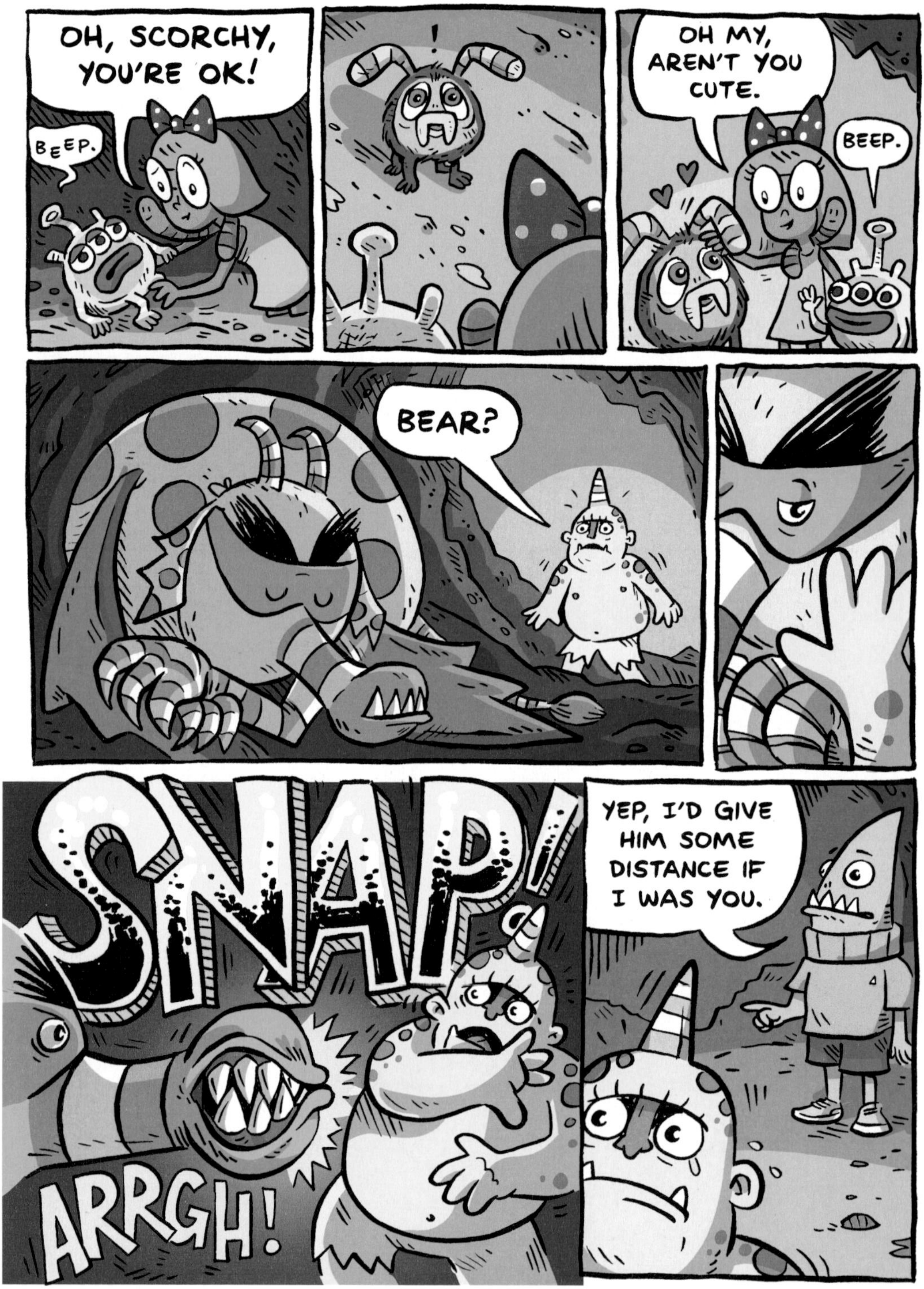
OH, SCORCHY, YOU'RE OK!
BEEP.
!
OH MY, AREN'T YOU CUTE.
BEEP.
BEAR?
SNAP!
ARRGH!
YEP, I'D GIVE HIM SOME DISTANCE IF I WAS YOU.

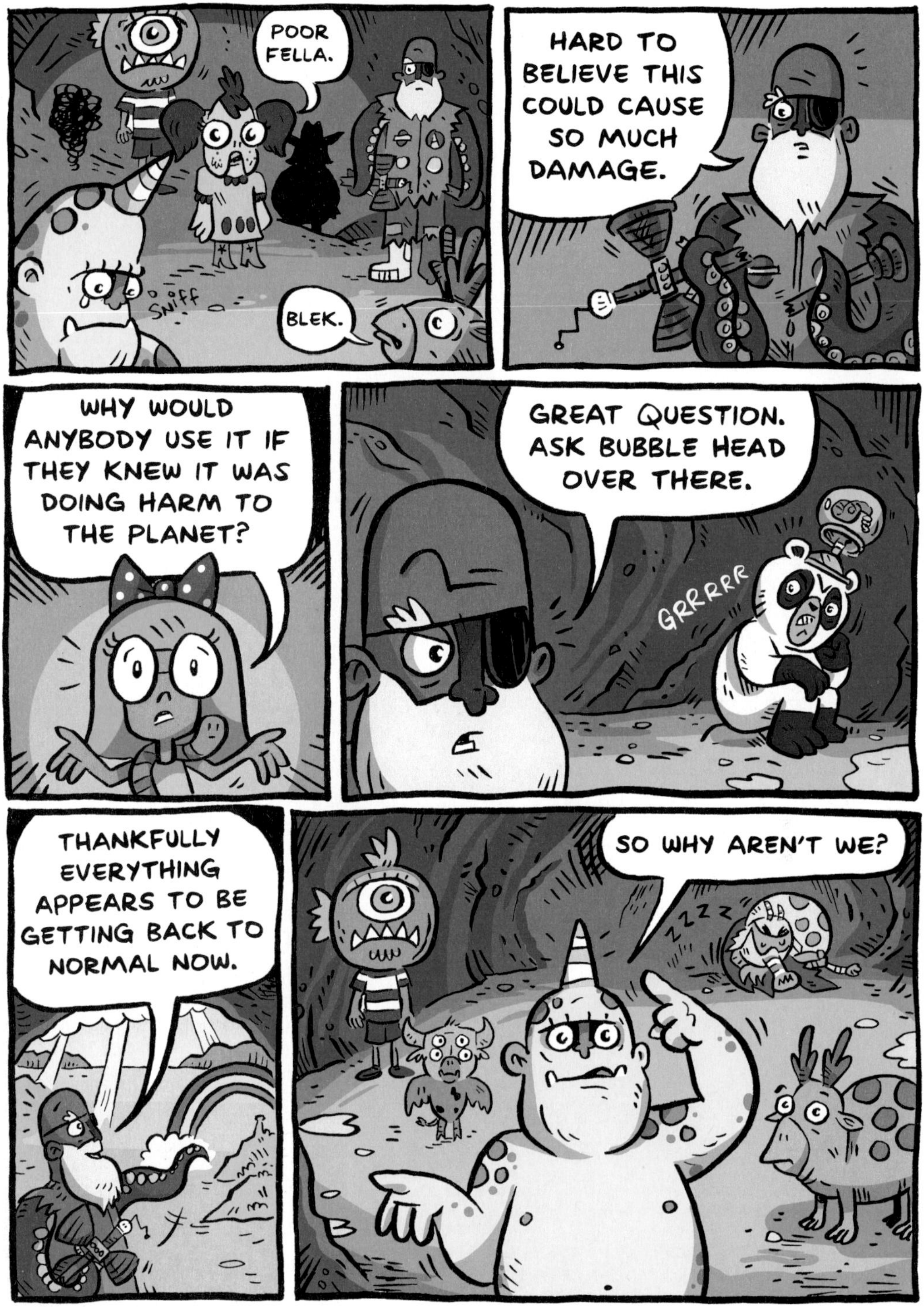
POOR FELLA.
SNIFF
BLEK.
HARD TO BELIEVE THIS COULD CAUSE SO MUCH DAMAGE.
WHY WOULD ANYBODY USE IT IF THEY KNEW IT WAS DOING HARM TO THE PLANET?
GREAT QUESTION. ASK BUBBLE HEAD OVER THERE.
GRRRRR
THANKFULLY EVERYTHING APPEARS TO BE GETTING BACK TO NORMAL NOW.
SO WHY AREN'T WE?
ZZZZ

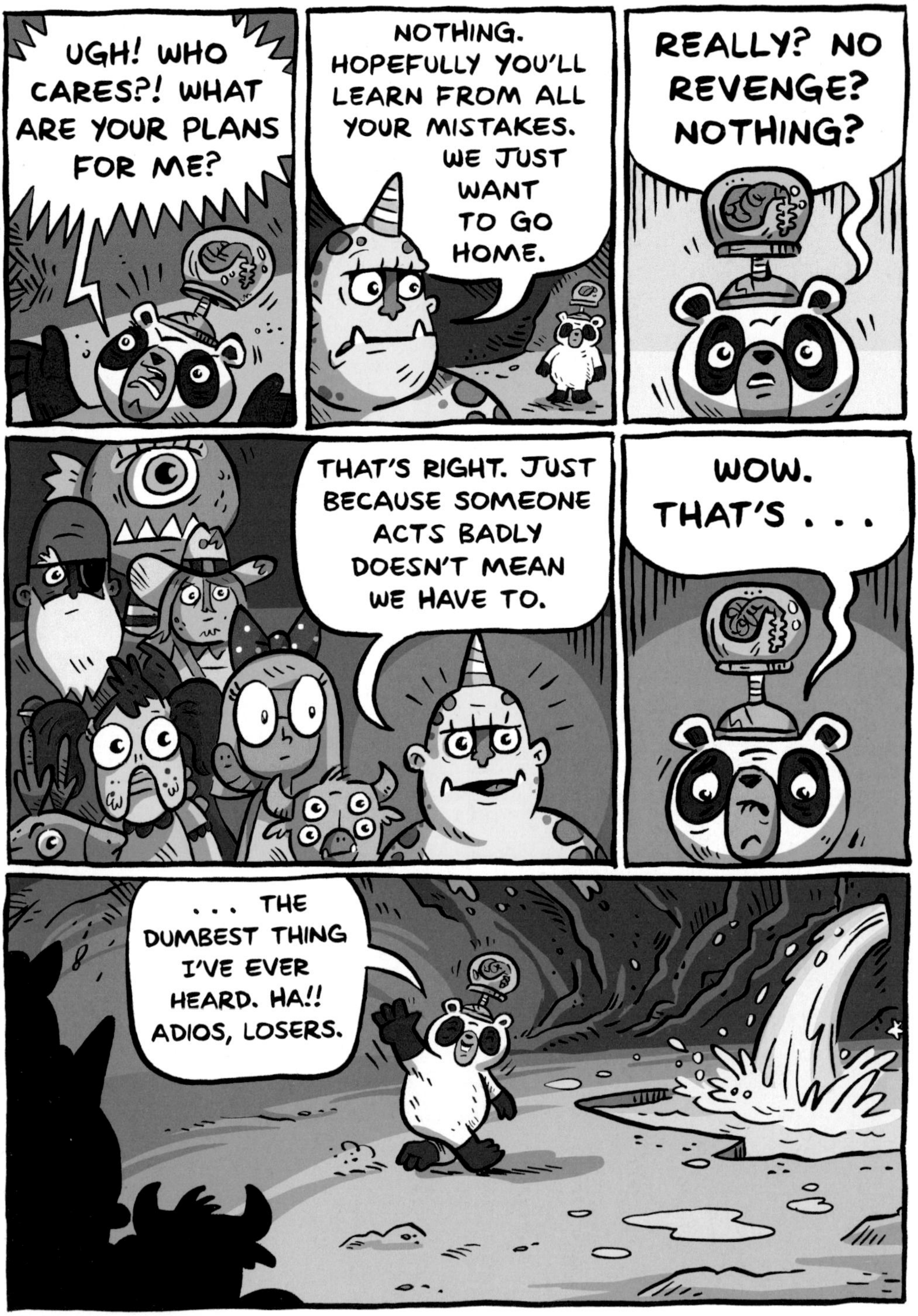
UGH! WHO CARES?! WHAT ARE YOUR PLANS FOR ME?
NOTHING. HOPEFULLY YOU'LL LEARN FROM ALL YOUR MISTAKES.
WE JUST WANT TO GO HOME.
REALLY? NO REVENGE? NOTHING?
THAT'S RIGHT. JUST BECAUSE SOMEONE ACTS BADLY DOESN'T MEAN WE HAVE TO.
WOW. THAT'S . . .
. . . THE DUMBEST THING I'VE EVER HEARD. HA!! ADIOS, LOSERS.

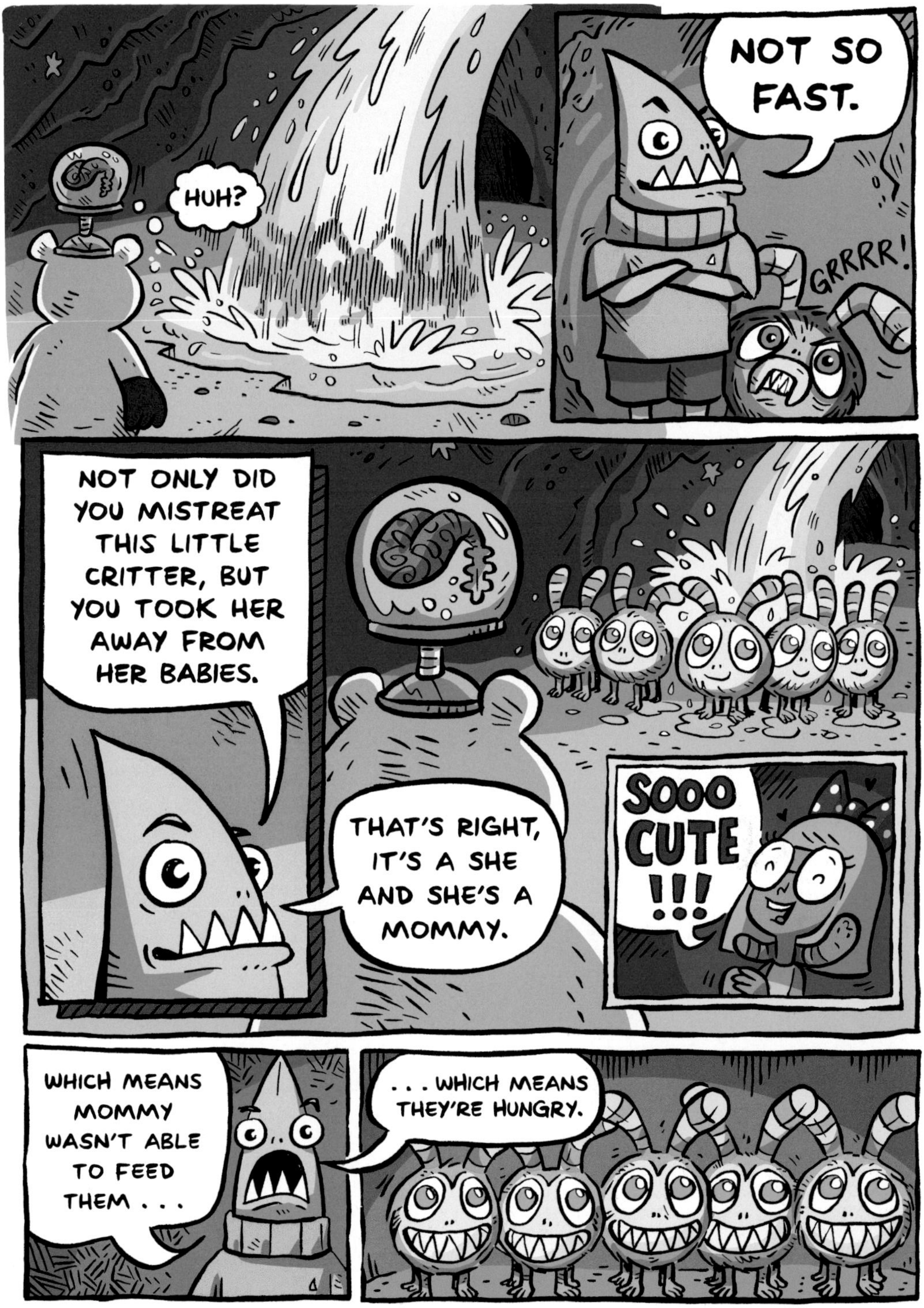
HUH?
NOT SO FAST.
GRRRR!
NOT ONLY DID YOU MISTREAT THIS LITTLE CRITTER, BUT YOU TOOK HER AWAY FROM HER BABIES.
THAT'S RIGHT, IT'S A SHE AND SHE'S A MOMMY.
SOOO CUTE !!!
WHICH MEANS MOMMY WASN'T ABLE TO FEED THEM . . .
. . . WHICH MEANS THEY'RE HUNGRY.

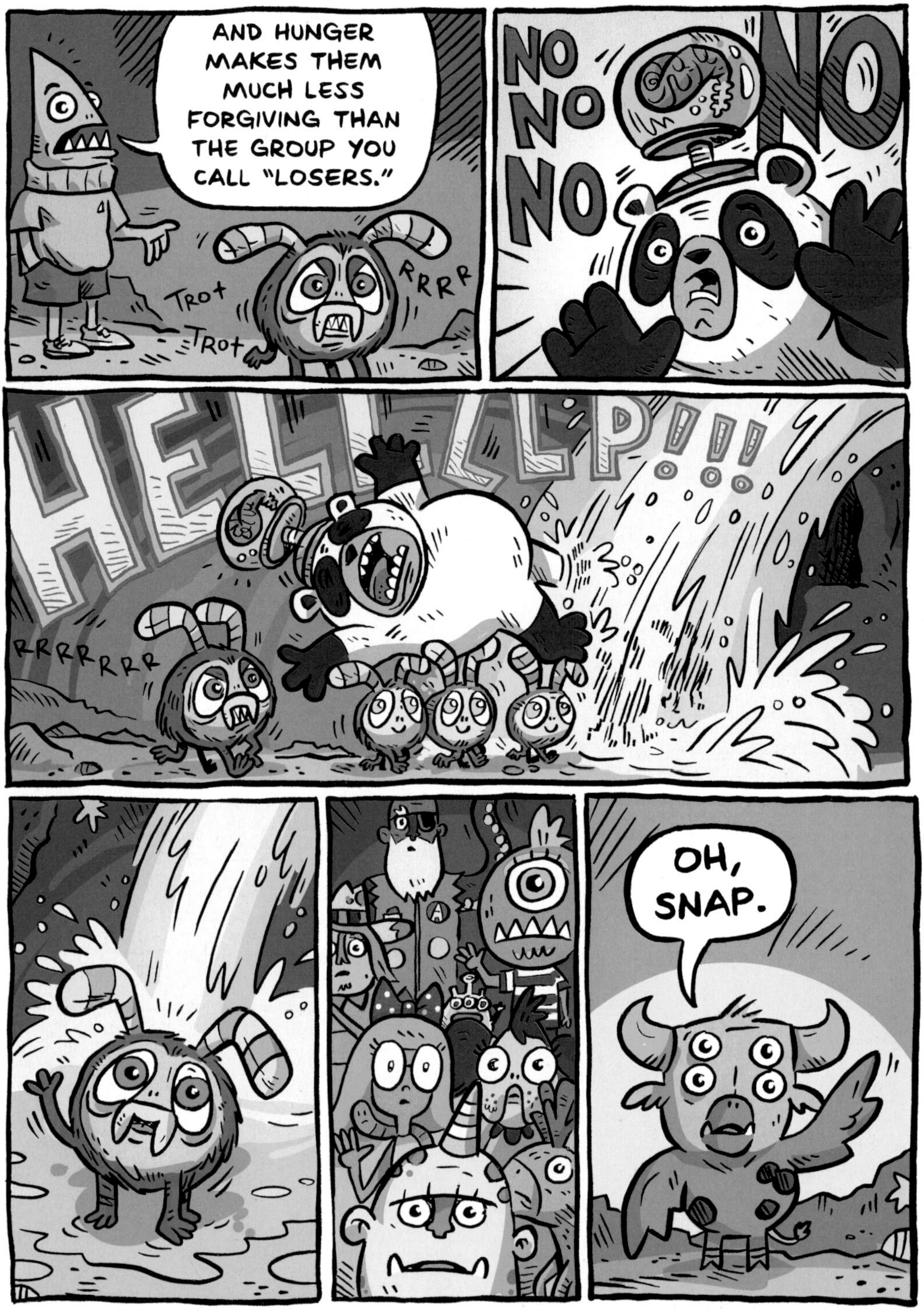
AND HUNGER MAKES THEM MUCH LESS FORGIVING THAN THE GROUP YOU CALL "LOSERS."
TROT
TROT
RRRR
NO
NO
NO
NO
HELLLP!!!
RRRRRRRR
OH, SNAP.

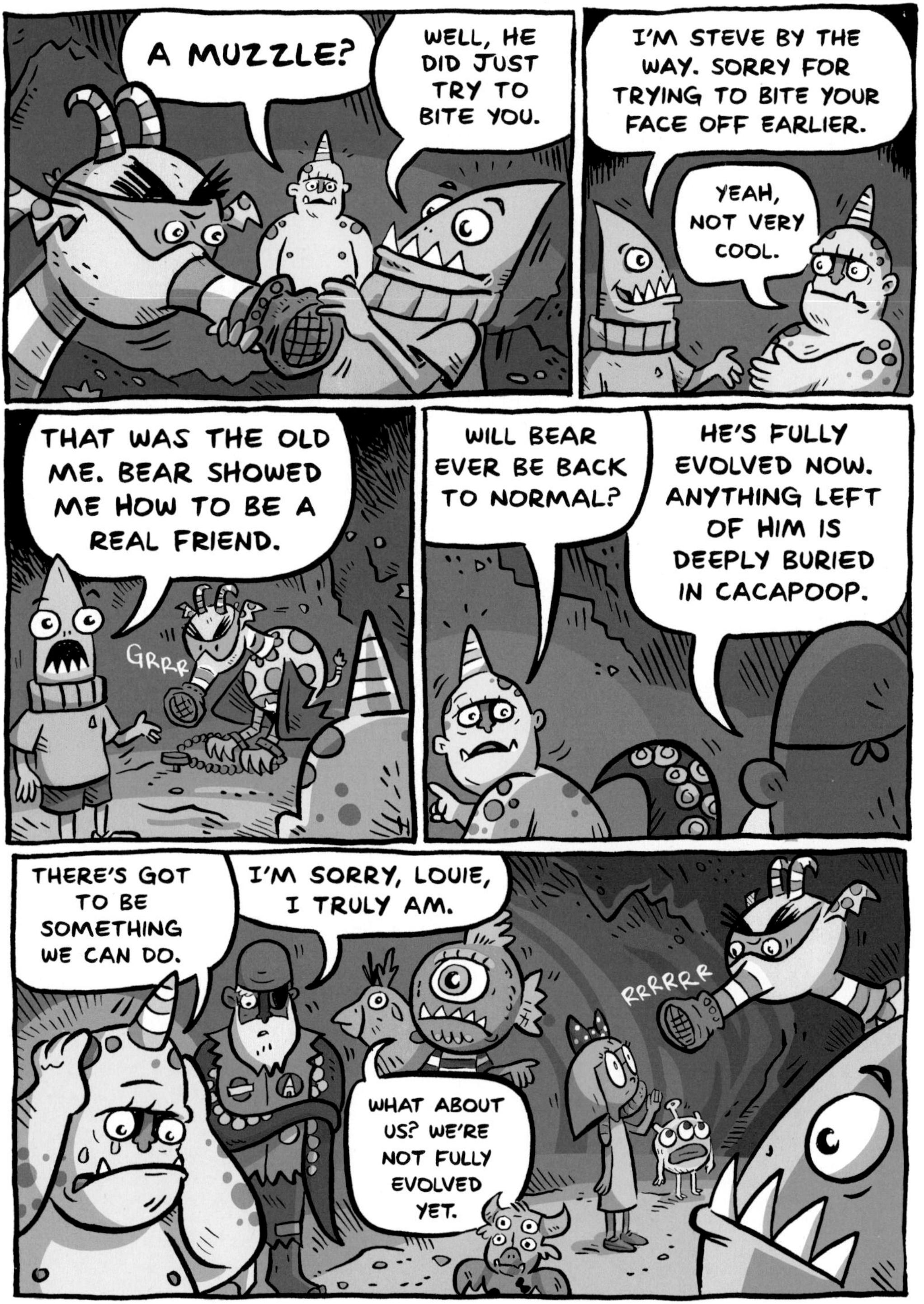
A MUZZLE?
WELL, HE DID JUST TRY TO BITE YOU.
I'M STEVE BY THE WAY. SORRY FOR TRYING TO BITE YOUR FACE OFF EARLIER.
YEAH, NOT VERY COOL.
THAT WAS THE OLD ME. BEAR SHOWED ME HOW TO BE A REAL FRIEND.
GRRR
WILL BEAR EVER BE BACK TO NORMAL?
HE'S FULLY EVOLVED NOW. ANYTHING LEFT OF HIM IS DEEPLY BURIED IN CACAPOOP.
THERE'S GOT TO BE SOMETHING WE CAN DO.
I'M SORRY, LOUIE, I TRULY AM.
RRRRRR
WHAT ABOUT US? WE'RE NOT FULLY EVOLVED YET.

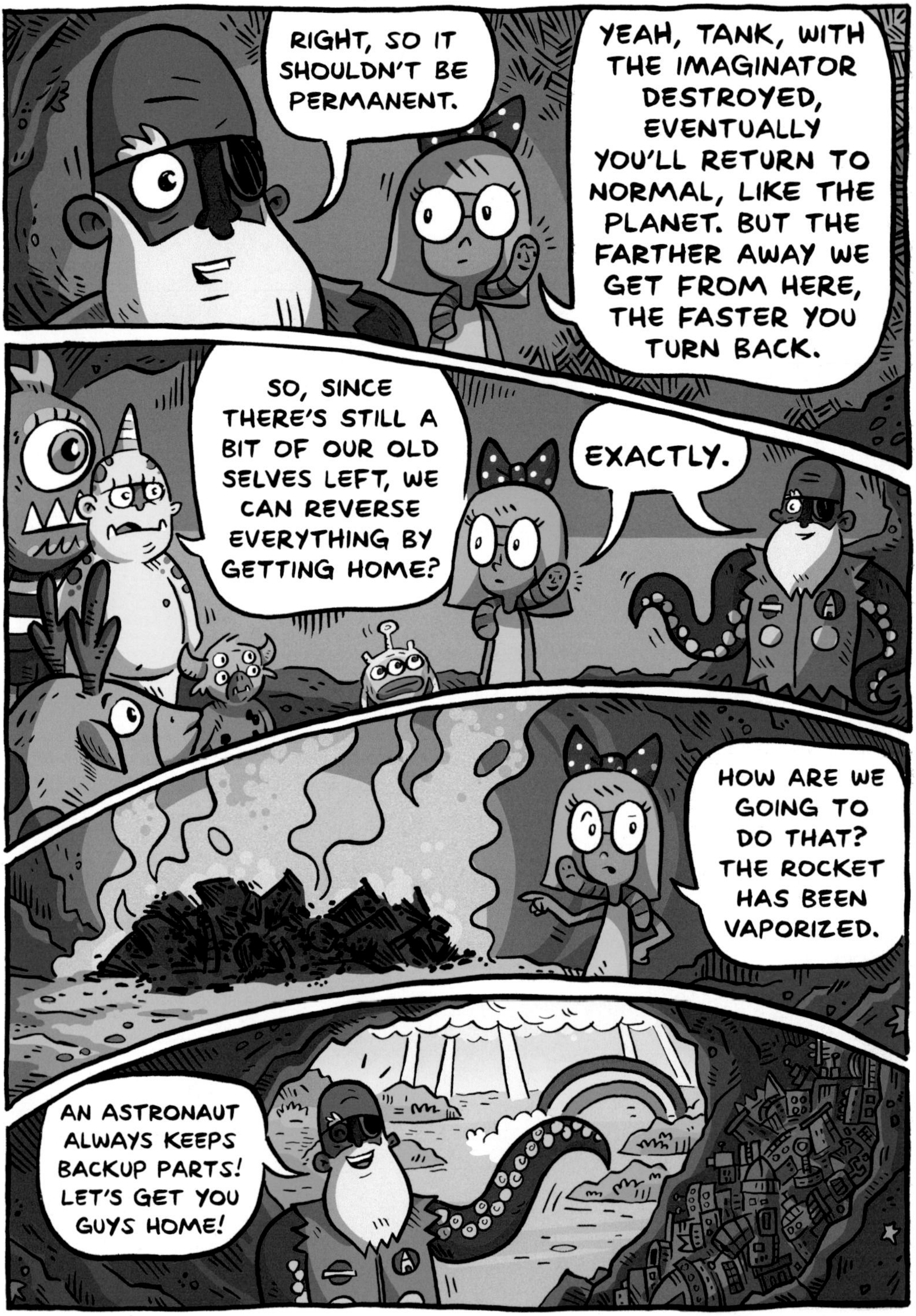
RIGHT, SO IT SHOULDN'T BE PERMANENT.
YEAH, TANK, WITH THE IMAGINATOR DESTROYED, EVENTUALLY YOU'LL RETURN TO NORMAL, LIKE THE PLANET. BUT THE FARTHER AWAY WE GET FROM HERE, THE FASTER YOU TURN BACK.
SO, SINCE THERE'S STILL A BIT OF OUR OLD SELVES LEFT, WE CAN REVERSE EVERYTHING BY GETTING HOME?
EXACTLY.
HOW ARE WE GOING TO DO THAT? THE ROCKET HAS BEEN VAPORIZED.
AN ASTRONAUT ALWAYS KEEPS BACKUP PARTS! LET'S GET YOU GUYS HOME!

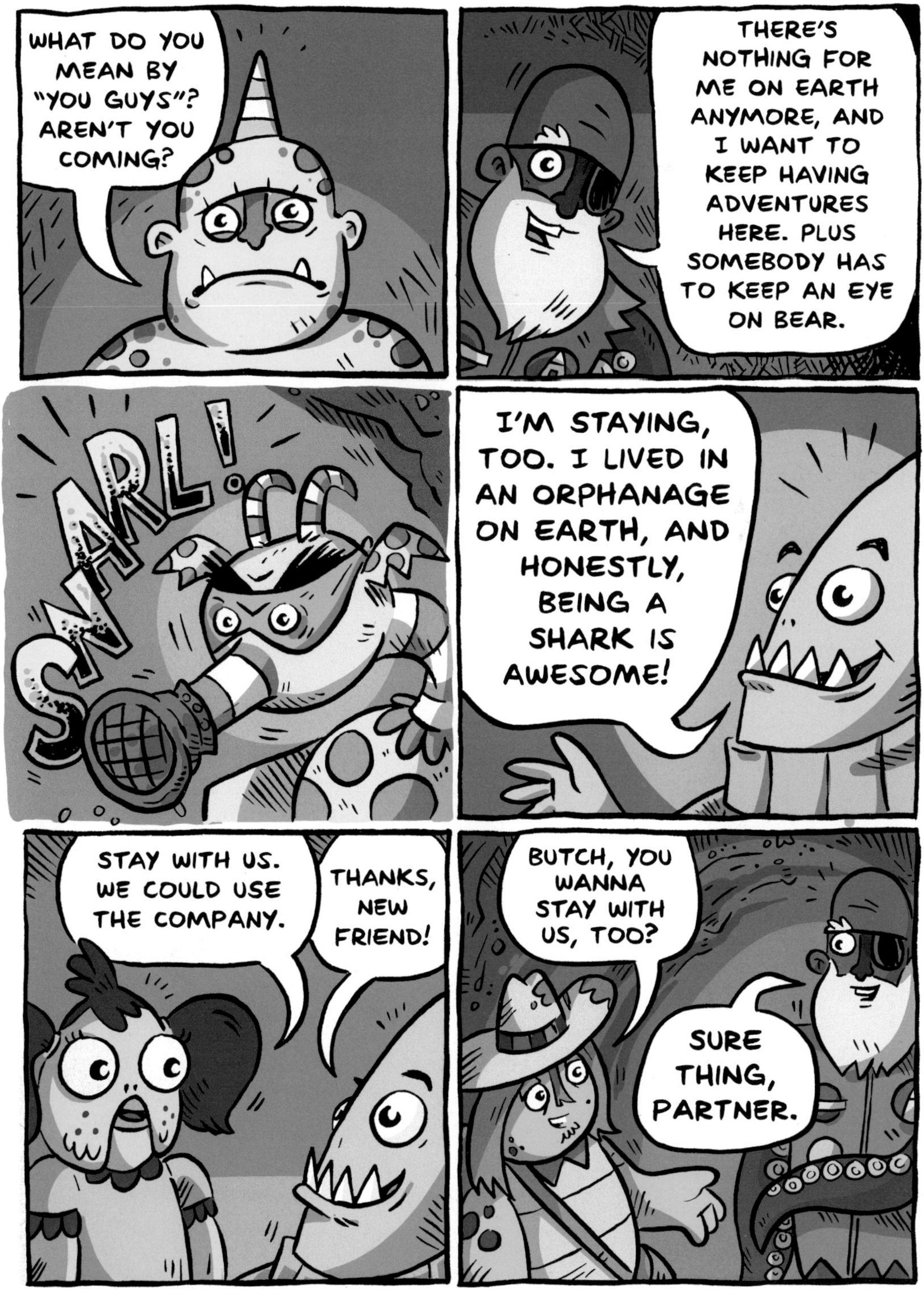

WHAT DO YOU MEAN BY "YOU GUYS"? AREN'T YOU COMING?
THERE'S NOTHING FOR ME ON EARTH ANYMORE, AND I WANT TO KEEP HAVING ADVENTURES HERE. PLUS SOMEBODY HAS TO KEEP AN EYE ON BEAR.
SNARL!
I'M STAYING, TOO. I LIVED IN AN ORPHANAGE ON EARTH, AND HONESTLY, BEING A SHARK IS AWESOME!
STAY WITH US. WE COULD USE THE COMPANY.
THANKS, NEW FRIEND!
BUTCH, YOU WANNA STAY WITH US, TOO?
SURE THING, PARTNER.

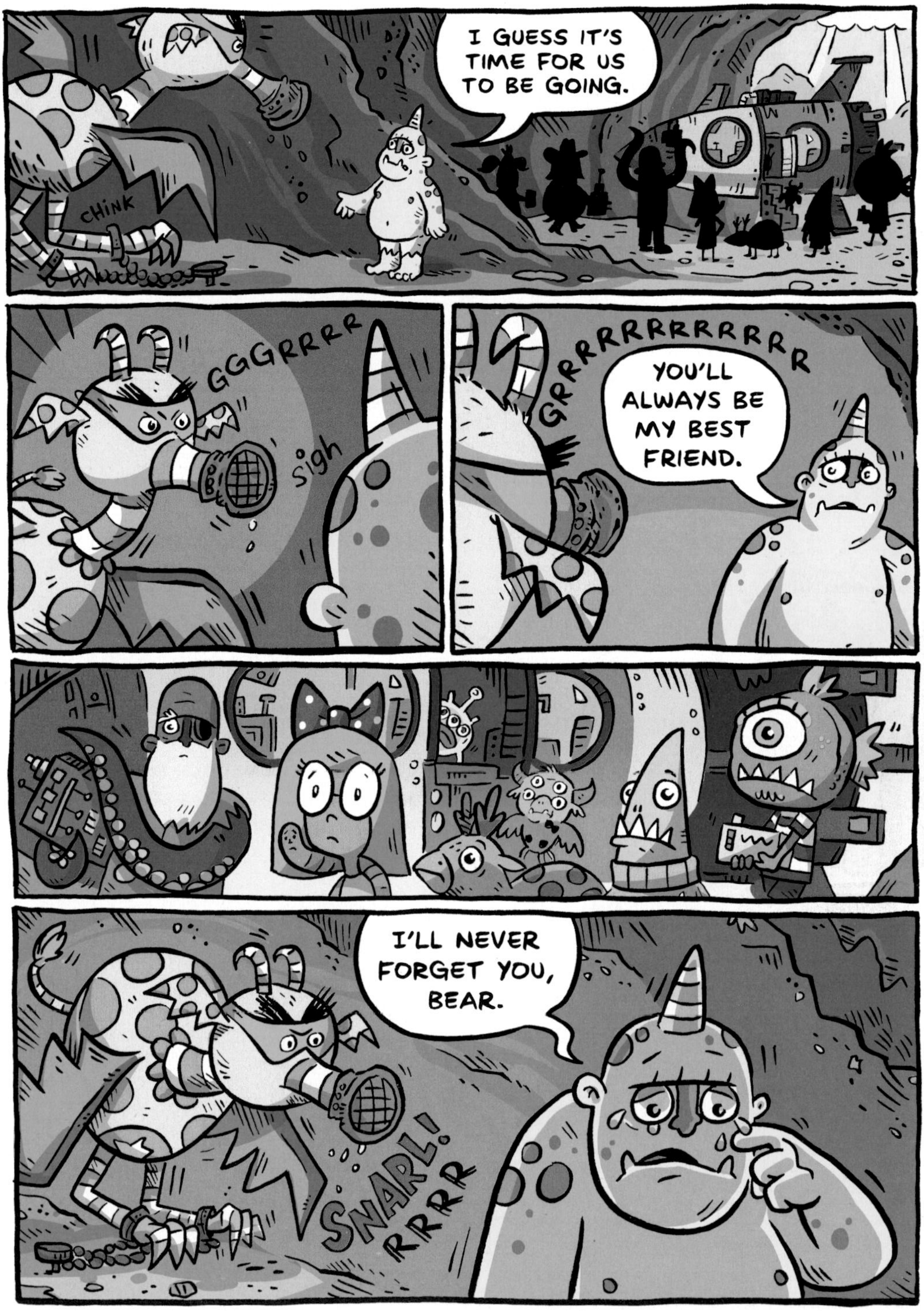
CHINK
I GUESS IT'S TIME FOR US TO BE GOING.
GGGRRRR
sigh
GRRRRRRRRRRRRRRR
YOU'LL ALWAYS BE MY BEST FRIEND.
I'LL NEVER FORGET YOU, BEAR.
SNARL! RRRR

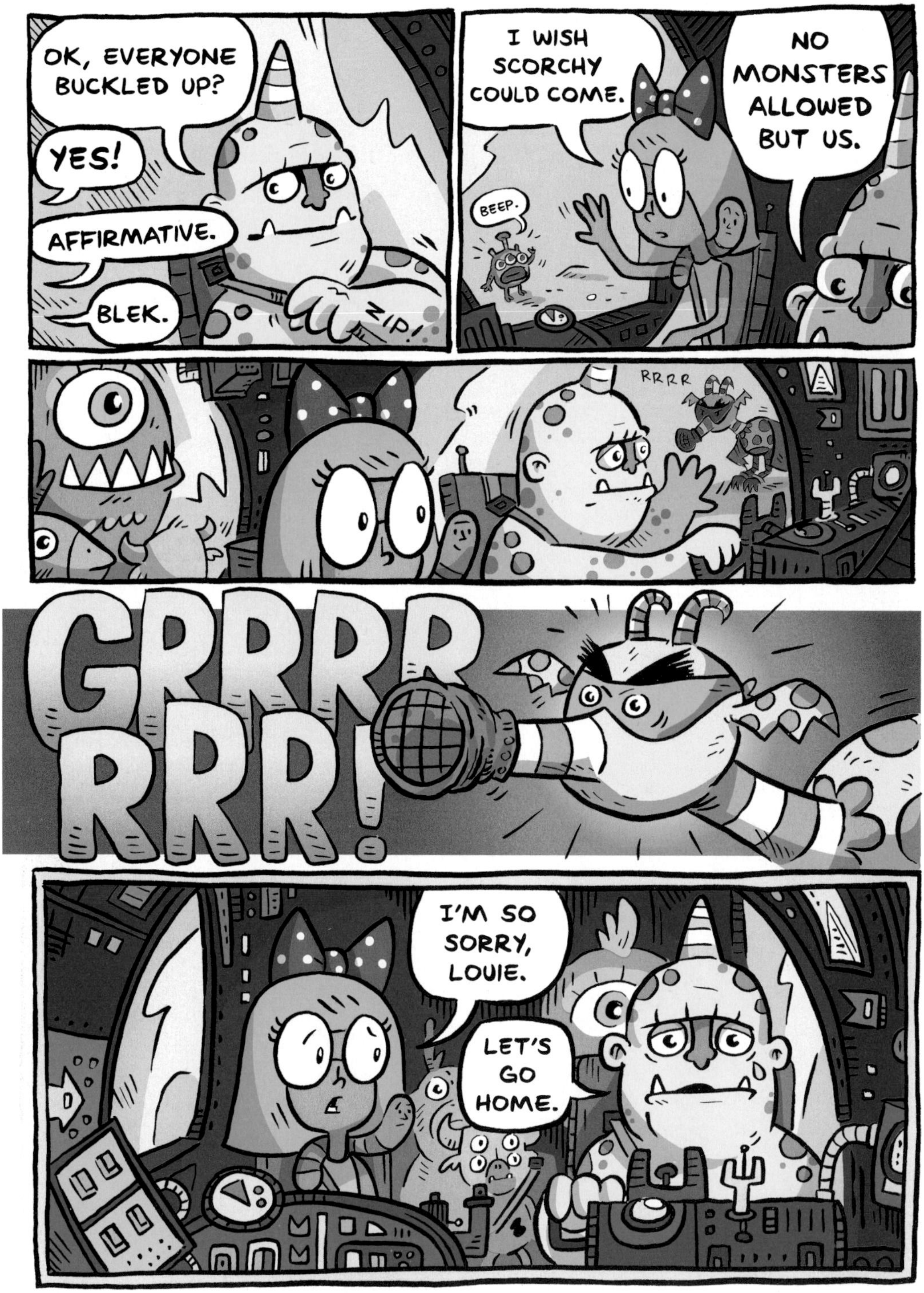
OK, EVERYONE BUCKLED UP?
YES!
AFFIRMATIVE.
BLEK.
ZIP!
I WISH SCORCHY COULD COME.
NO MONSTERS ALLOWED BUT US.
BEEP.
RRRR
GRRRRRR!
I'M SO SORRY, LOUIE.
LET'S GO HOME.

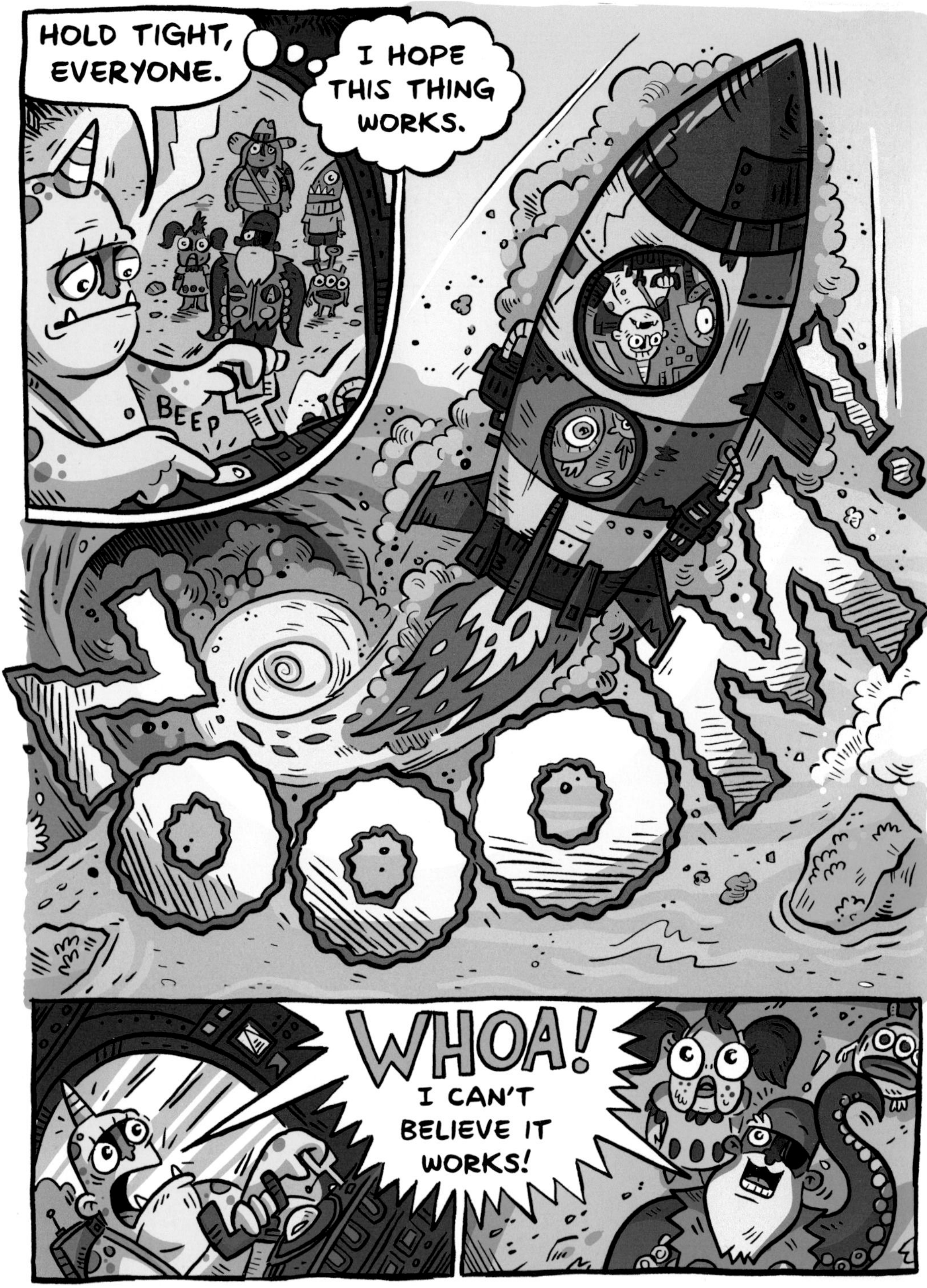
HOLD TIGHT, EVERYONE.
I HOPE THIS THING WORKS.
BEEP
WHOA!
I CAN'T BELIEVE IT WORKS!

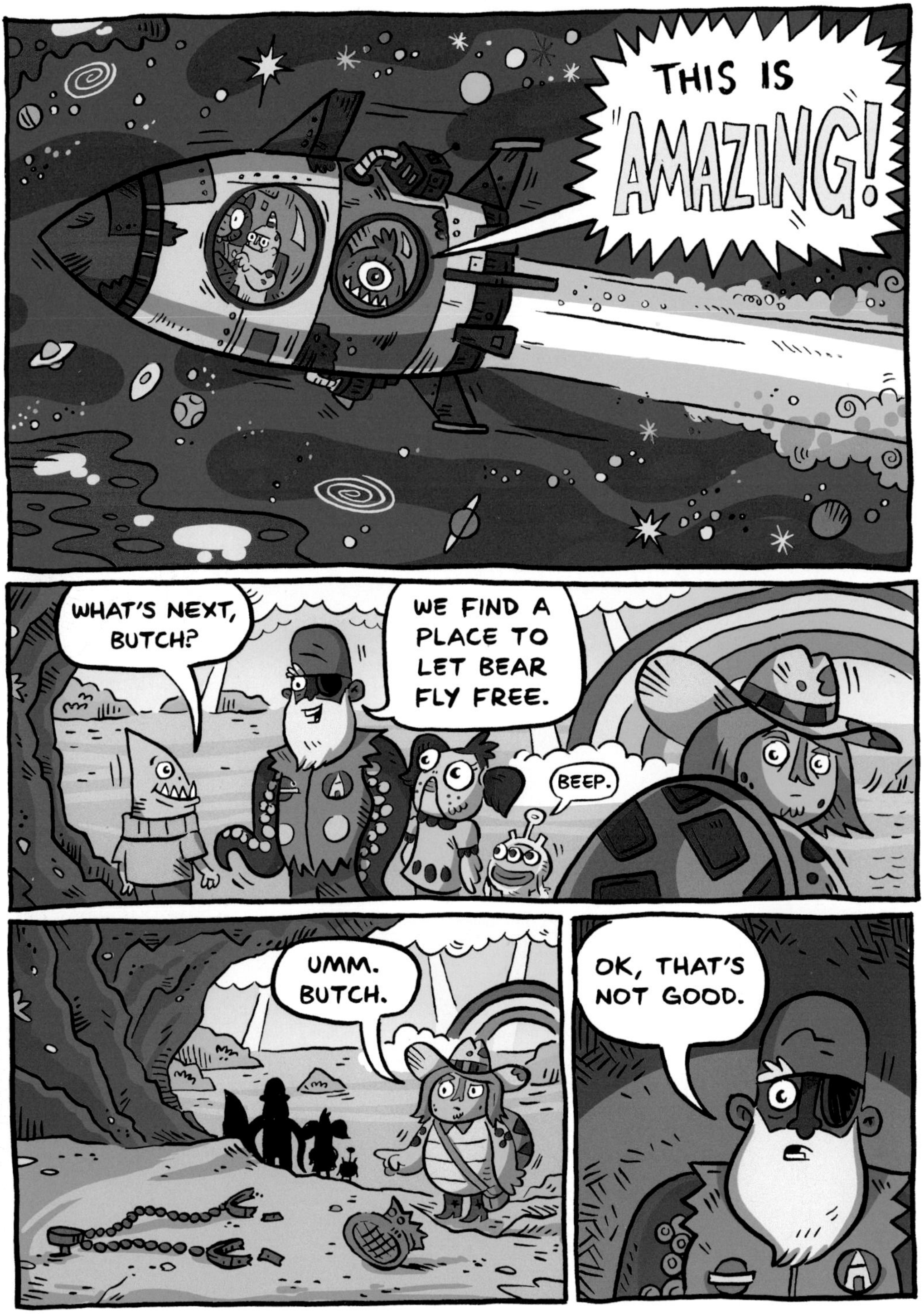
THIS IS AMAZING!
WHAT'S NEXT, BUTCH?
WE FIND A PLACE TO LET BEAR FLY FREE.
BEEP.
UMM. BUTCH.
OK, THAT'S NOT GOOD.

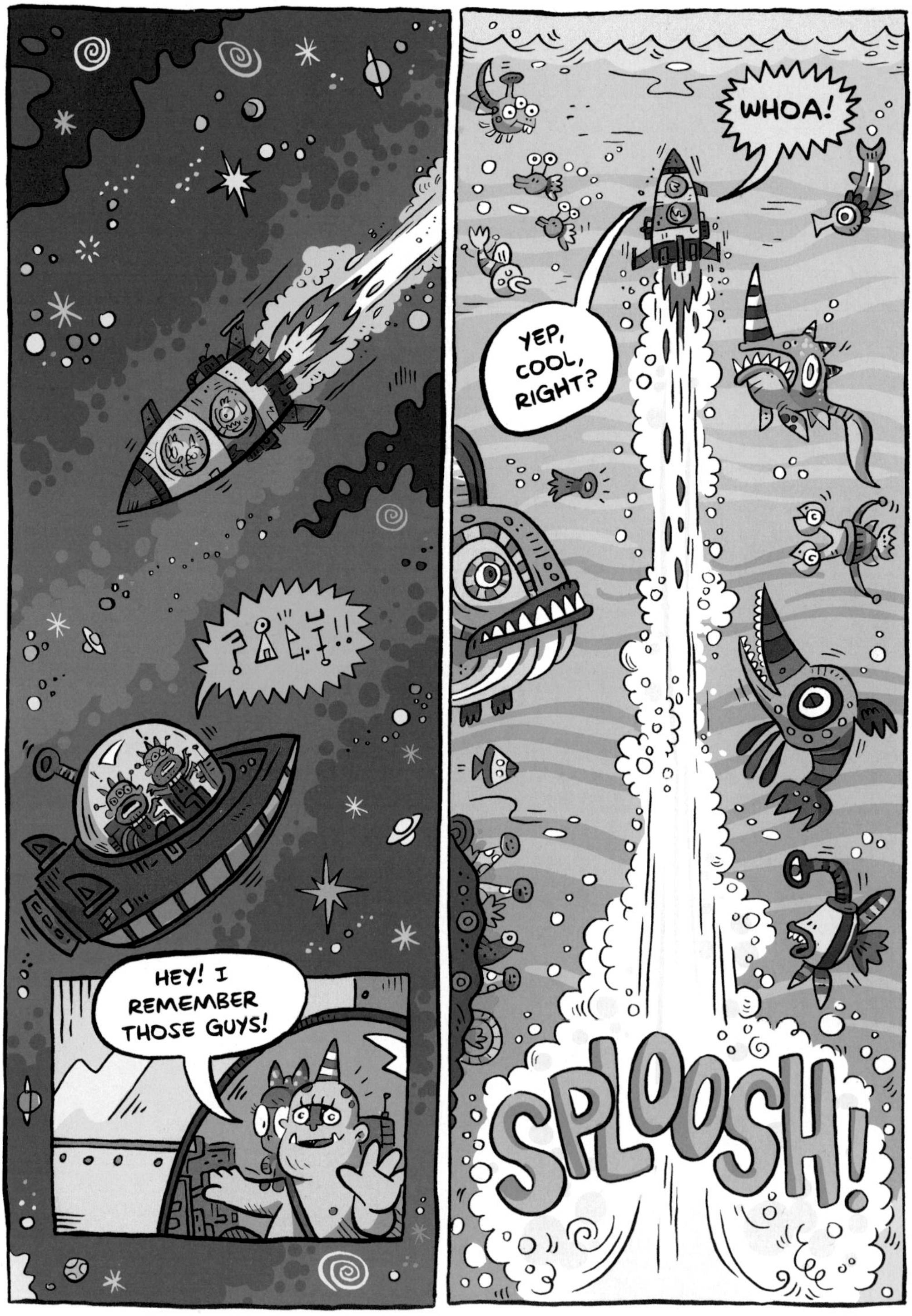

HEY! I REMEMBER THOSE GUYS!
WHOA!
YEP, COOL, RIGHT?
SPLOOSH!

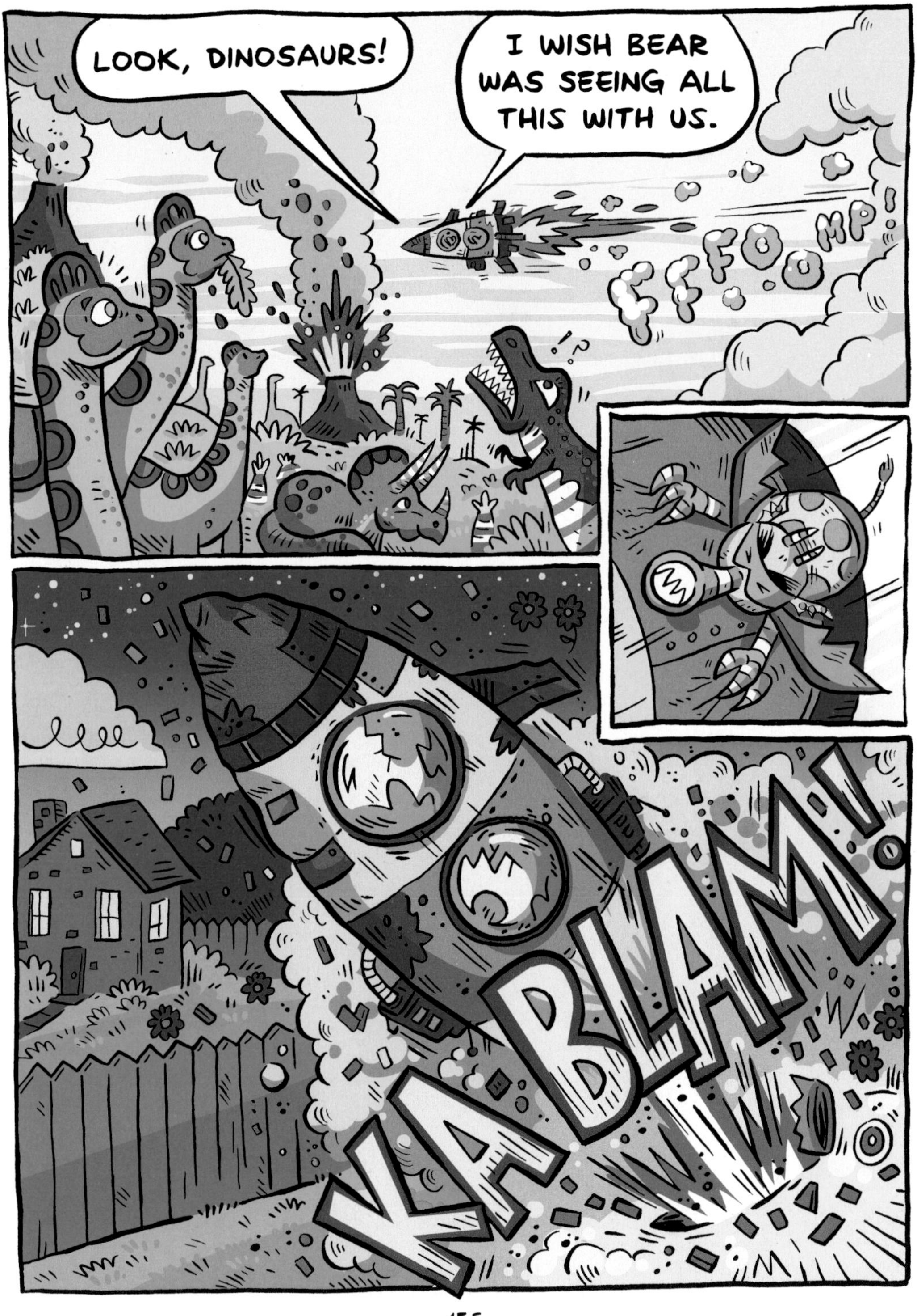
LOOK, DINOSAURS!
I WISH BEAR WAS SEEING ALL THIS WITH US.
FFFOOOMP!
!?
KA-BLAM!

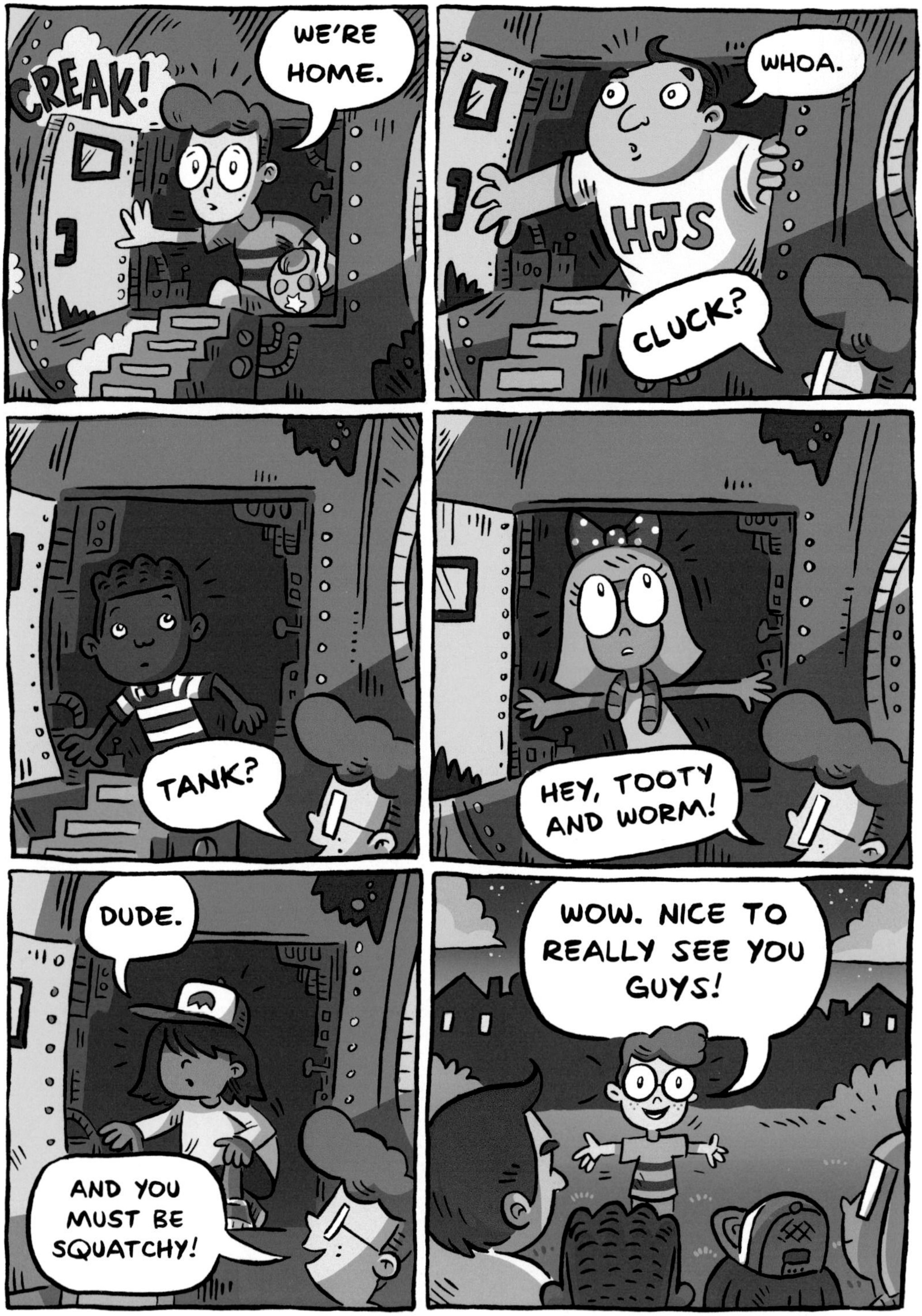
CREAK!
WE'RE HOME.
WHOA.
CLUCK?
TANK?
HEY, TOOTY AND WORM!
DUDE.
AND YOU MUST BE SQUATCHY!
WOW. NICE TO REALLY SEE YOU GUYS!

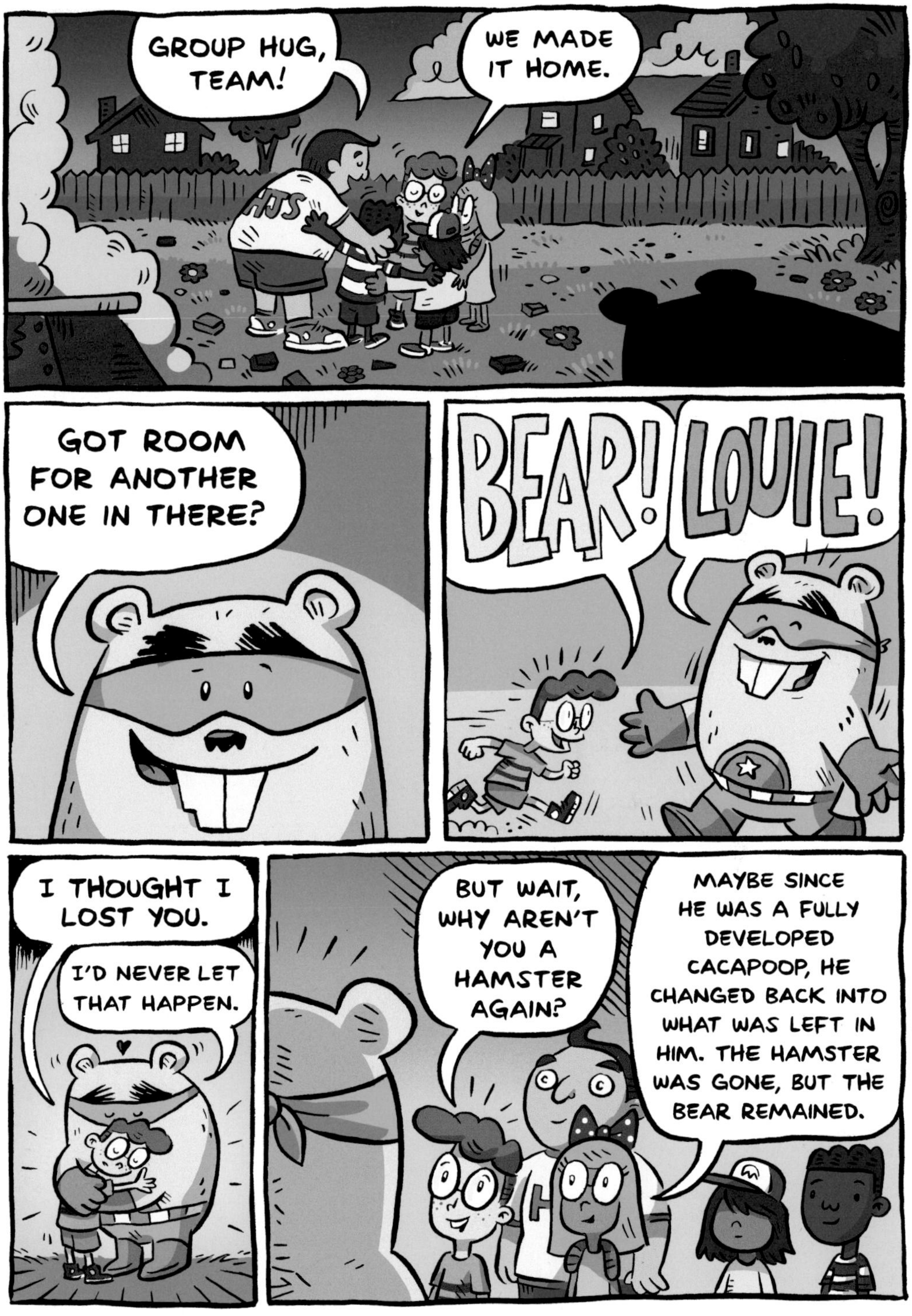

GROUP HUG, TEAM!
WE MADE IT HOME.
GOT ROOM FOR ANOTHER ONE IN THERE?
BEAR!
LOUIE!
I THOUGHT I LOST YOU.
I'D NEVER LET THAT HAPPEN.
BUT WAIT, WHY AREN'T YOU A HAMSTER AGAIN?
MAYBE SINCE HE WAS A FULLY DEVELOPED CACAPOOP, HE CHANGED BACK INTO WHAT WAS LEFT IN HIM. THE HAMSTER WAS GONE, BUT THE BEAR REMAINED.

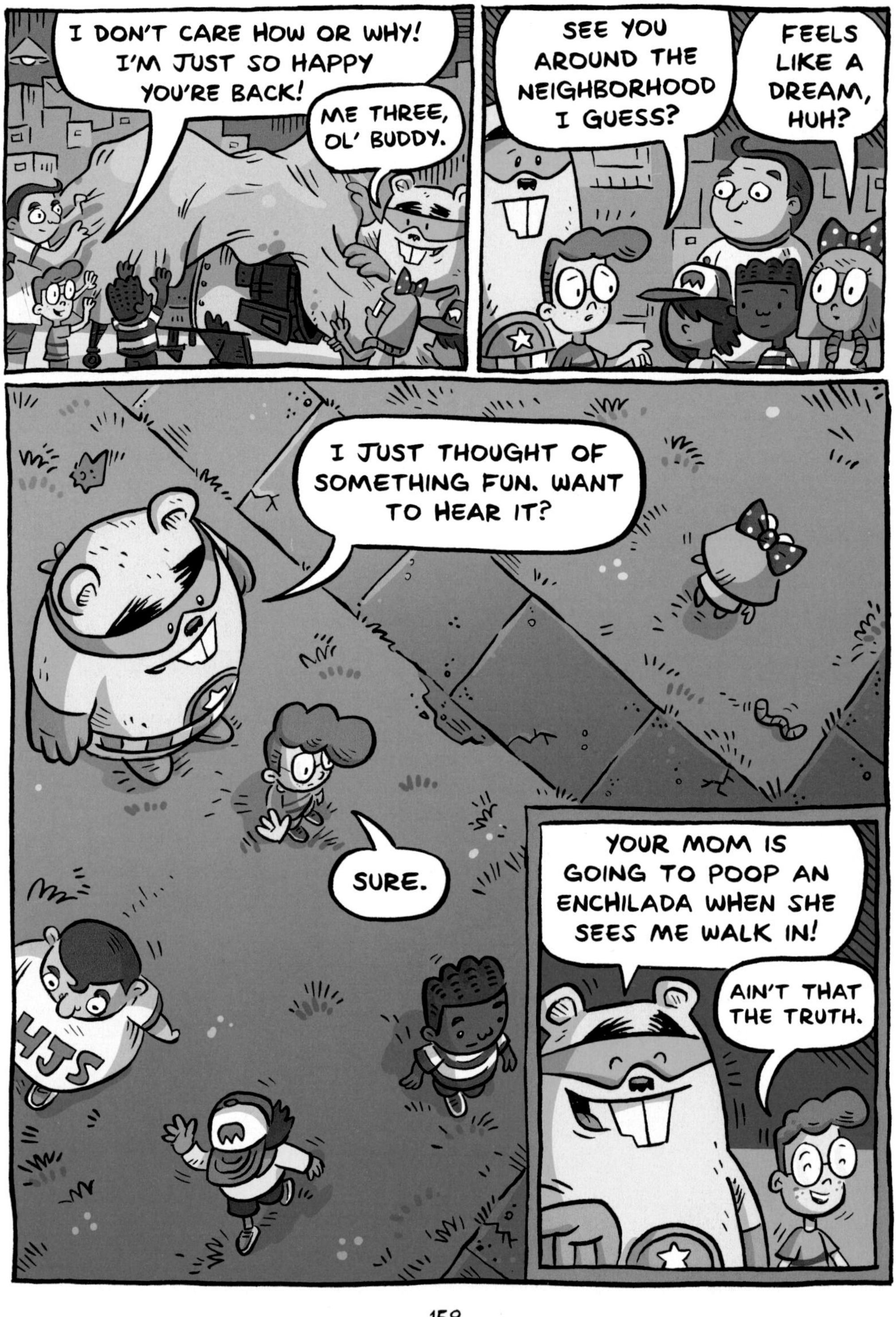
I DON'T CARE HOW OR WHY! I'M JUST SO HAPPY YOU'RE BACK!
ME THREE, OL' BUDDY.
SEE YOU AROUND THE NEIGHBORHOOD I GUESS?
FEELS LIKE A DREAM, HUH?
I JUST THOUGHT OF SOMETHING FUN. WANT TO HEAR IT?
SURE.
HJS
YOUR MOM IS GOING TO POOP AN ENCHILADA WHEN SHE SEES ME WALK IN!
AIN'T THAT THE TRUTH.

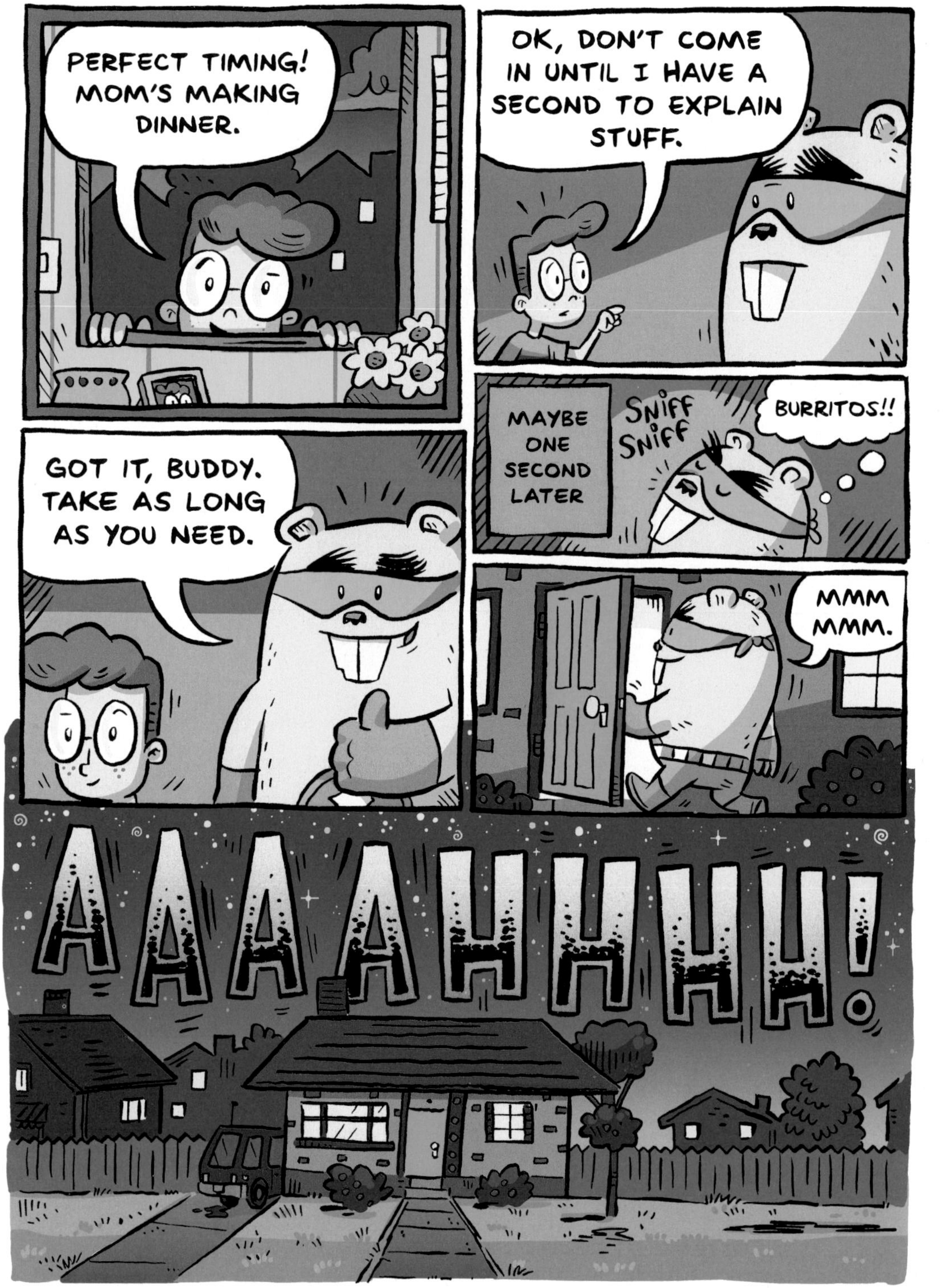
PERFECT TIMING! MOM'S MAKING DINNER.
OK, DON'T COME IN UNTIL I HAVE A SECOND TO EXPLAIN STUFF.
GOT IT, BUDDY. TAKE AS LONG AS YOU NEED.
MAYBE ONE SECOND LATER
SNIFF SNIFF
BURRITOS!!
MMM MMM.
AAAAHHHH!

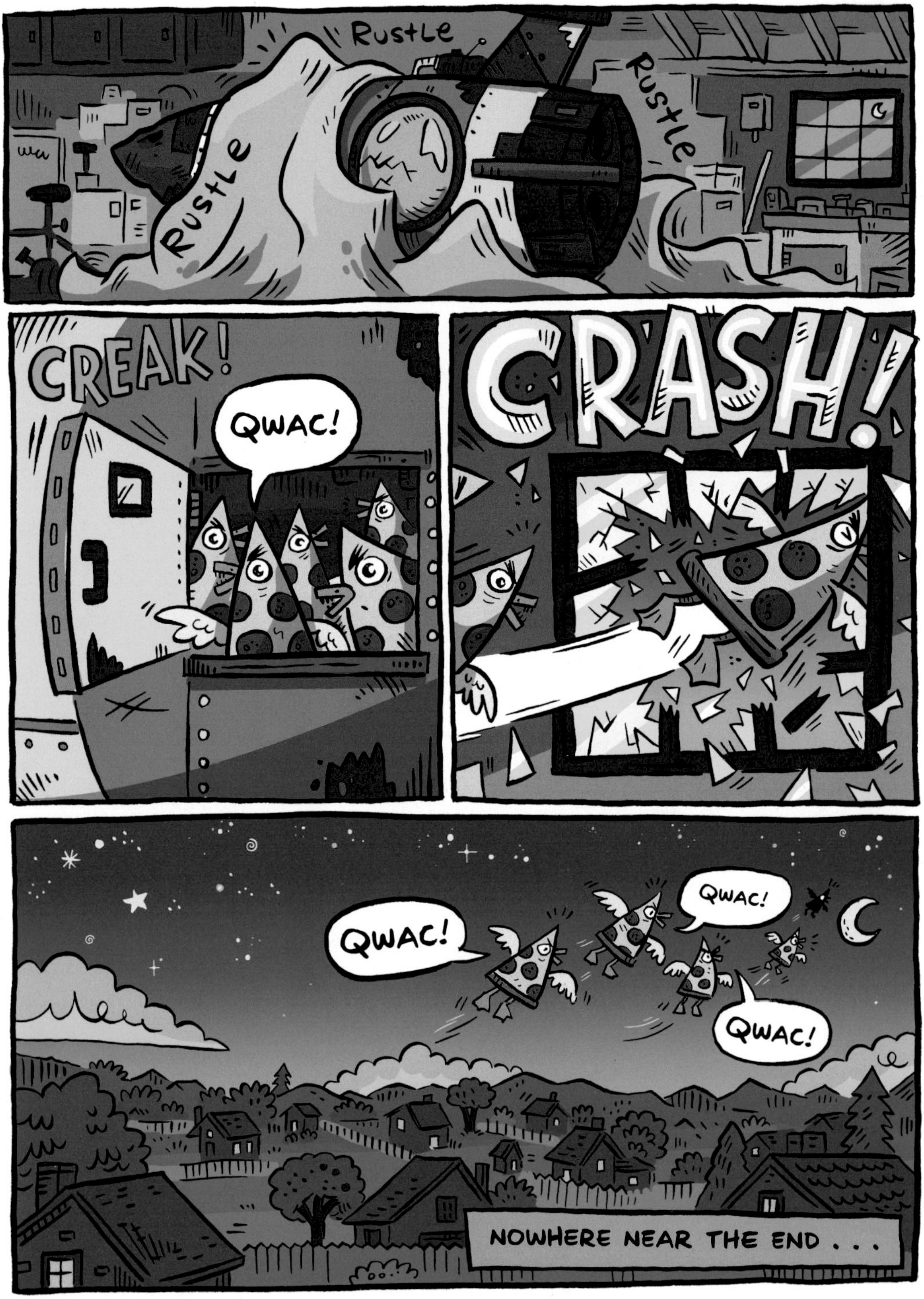
RUSTLE
RUSTLE
RUSTLE
CREAK!
QWAC!
CRASH!
QWAC!
QWAC!
QWAC!
NOWHERE NEAR THE END . . .